THE DEATH OF LYNDON WILDER AND THE CONSEQUENCES THEREOF

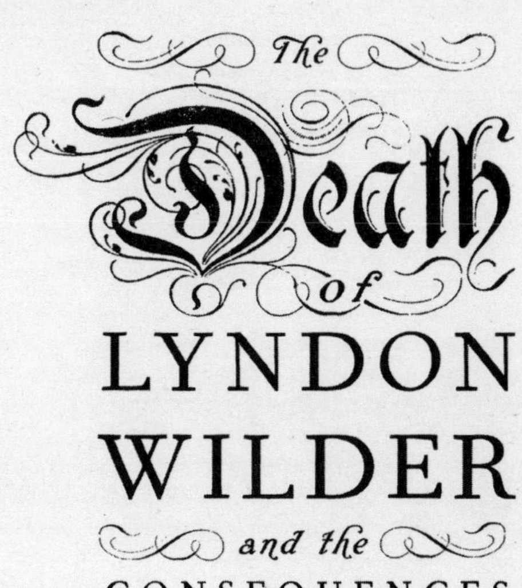

The Death of LYNDON WILDER and the CONSEQUENCES THEREOF

E. A. DINELEY

Constable & Robinson Ltd
55-56 Russell Square
London WC1B 4HP
www.constablerobinson.com

First published in the UK by Corsair,
an imprint of Constable & Robinson Ltd., 2013

This is a work of fiction. Names, characters, places and incidents are either the product of the author's imagination or are used fictitiously, and any resemblance to actual persons, living or dead, or to actual events or locales is entirely coincidental.

A copy of the British Library Cataloguing in Publication Data is available from the British Library

ISBN 978-1-78033-227-7 (hardback)
ISBN 978-1-78033-228-4 (ebook)

Printed and bound in the UK

1 3 5 7 9 10 8 6 4 2

For Pen Milburn, the most patient of friends.

PART I

15 November 1813
Ridley
Wiltshire

My dear Papa,

As I write I hear your voice: 'Circumstances ought not to undermine the general cheerfulness of our spirits.' When the fox took the chickens, when the mice took the peas, when the pony was lame, thus spoke my dear papa, but I do believe we were allowed some initial period of grief at our childish woes. Do you miss me? Of course you do. Does Fanny take her medicine? Is there a letter from Bobby? Are the girls well?

Oh, Papa, this is a sad house, the saddest house I ever was in. My own misfortunes, so dire to me, are truly cast into insignificance. I dare say you will consider that as good a remedy as any. You were concerned they might not send to meet me, but they did. I was ashamed my trunk was so heavy, all those books, but a great, silent footman was in charge of me, it, the vehicle and the horse. I supposed him a groom but now I am here he can be seen to stand in the passage dourly awaiting a bell to ring.

My domain is a small bedroom and a sitting room, nothing in them, one bed, two chairs, a print of the Duchess of Devonshire waving her arm over a baby, and a table, all rather dark, but then the whole house is dark for Lady Charles likes the shutters closed. She says the light intrudes, but really one must have light, though you will be relieved to hear I don't contradict. I keep the schoolroom cheerful with a good bright fire and no shutters. Should we exceed our allotted ration of coal, Miss Wilder and I pick up sticks. My pupil has never before picked up a stick, nor anything else. She is not accustomed to any sort of exercise and is quite a naughty, idle little thing, but I think she has much to try her. One way and another I find I rather like her. A child should not be encouraged to mope and dwell on misfortune. The same rules must, I believe, apply to your daughter,

Anna Arbuthnot

P.S. Now I hear your voice again as from the schoolroom, 'Describe accurately!' The bedroom has a washstand with plain white china; a wardrobe and a chest of drawers. There now, isn't that dull?

The writing was of medium size, with a pronounced slant, even, but the upright strokes, long in comparison to the other, occasioned, from time to time, a certain unsatisfactory entanglement between one line and the next. The letter-writer laid down the pen on the tray beside the inkwell and turned from where she sat at the table to look out of the window. There was the odd angle of the stable roof and much of the red-brick wall of the vegetable garden, and within those walls the neat squares and patches, cordoned apples and pears, glass houses, all to be seen from above through the grey rain. How much to say, to reveal to those at home, of this locked-in bereavement house, this shuttered, melancholy edifice, this unloved garden? Not too much, perhaps. Had she, as it was, said too much?

The letter was folded, sealed, and addressed to the Reverend Arbuthnot, West Staverton, Devonshire.

Lord Charles Wilder had acquired, rather than was born with, his name. His late father-in-law had stipulated the name Wilder should be synonymous with the Ridley property, which was to pass to a distant cousin if the stipulation was not agreed by whoever should marry his only child. Lord Charles was aggrieved at having to comply. He was the ninth and last son of a duke and he thought a duke's name good enough for any property, but being one of such a covey of younger sons, he was not in a position to do more than count his blessings. His wife was a pretty girl, about twelve years younger than himself, and he was thus relieved of the tedium of trading on his illustrious name and the influence of his father. Had he not made this fortunate marriage, he was aware he would have spent his life struggling to retain a series of minor government posts and in making ends meet.

Having sacrificed it, he nearly let the ducal name drop altogether, but it was retained on legal documents pertaining to himself or his children as the useful appendage it was, and as a serviceable name for his eldest son.

Lord Charles was a thin old man now in his seventies who wandered up and down his house wondering, when he could put one sentient thought before another, why he was punished. No misdeed could merit so dire a punishment, and his misdeeds he considered minor and few. His was an uncomprehending sorrow, futile speculation to find logic or reason in tragedy, his Christian faith insufficient for sense to be made of the greater purpose to which the clergy made repeated but useless reference.

So there he was, bent over a stick, little more than a hapless ghost, going from one room to another in his own house, frantic to dispel images of that other ghost who, so loved, would never return. Occasionally he would enter the drawing room where his wife sat with all but one of the shutters closed, a small, tired fire in the grate. In the evening she would light a single candle but she needed no light because she gave herself no occupation. She would say, 'You had better sit down, Charles,' but without warmth or encouragement in her voice so he had little inclination to comply. His rational being would reflect on how the tragedy of their mutual bereavement might have drawn them closer together, but sorrow, contrarily, had driven them apart.

Lady Charles saw him as the old man he had become, his grey, silvery head, his veined hand gripping the head of the stick, for he would stand irresolute, yet fixed, in the single, broad shaft of light from the one unshuttered window.

Thus they went from day to day, equal in their distress, but uncomprehending of each other, his a craving for escape, for his mind to be distracted, for all thought or feeling to be silenced, obliterated; hers to dwell, to linger over and caress every image left. Lady Charles also harboured a destructive notion that her husband was to some extent to blame. Not being in possession of every fact, she made accusations that he was unable to refute. He was not clever at explanations, especially if explanations involved him in a sense of betrayal or in matters of which women need know nothing, especially if those very explanations were to exonerate himself. He wished neither to tell lies nor evade the truth, but his words sounded feeble in his own ears.

That dreary November day, Lord Charles's wanderings bringing him as usual to a halt in front of his wife, and she making the usual suggestion that he should sit, he said, unexpectedly, 'I should like to travel, to go away.'

He was, in the eyes of his wife, too old to travel. It would require retinues of servants and carriages. To Lady Charles travel meant abroad, to Paris, to Rome, but how could one travel when Napoleon Bonaparte was in possession of the continent and the British Isles at war with him? She saw her husband as progressing up and down England like a rat in the confines of a ditch.

As if she were placating a child, she said, 'You must think of the time of year.'

'So I must,' he agreed, 'and then there is the expense.'

'Ah, yes, the expense. I wonder why that is a particular problem at the minute.'

Lord Charles was in the long habit of never discussing monetary matters with his wife so she was unlikely ever to be enlightened. He muttered something incomprehensible about the increase in tax to pay for the war.

'And then,' Lady Charles continued, 'there is the estate.'

This he acknowledged. His agent had been dismissed after he had stepped into the shoes of a long-standing predecessor: he had not been satisfactory. Another must be found, and if there was one thing Lord Charles felt unable to contemplate, it was interviewing and decision-making. Had he not proved himself incompetent on the previous occasion? How was he to undertake such a thing in his new, almost deranged, state of mind?

He said, 'Thomas must return.'

'Thomas.' Lady Charles said the name as if it were new to her. She stood up and went to the window, turning her back on her husband. Her figure was as good as a girl's, her dress, black as befitted her state, swept in a long, elegant line from her bust to her little flat shoes. Her hair, once fair, now white but yet retaining cream, was piled on top of her head and fell back down in curls and ribbons, for her maid continued to prepare and present her mistress as if no catastrophe had occurred. Her face was small and wide, her nose straight, her cheekbones high and rounded, her eyes large and very blue.

She said, 'I doubt Thomas will wish to interrupt his career.'

Lord Charles said, 'It is his duty.'

'Would you have him resign his commission?'

'Why not? What need has he of it?' Having said this he regretted his answer, immediately foreseeing her reply.

'What need had Lyndon?'

'He would go.'

'You let him go.'

'Lyndon wasn't a child.'

This pointless discussion was oft repeated. Lady Charles leant her head on the window and wept. He knew she did so and that he could not comfort her, and by his purchase of Lyndon's commission he was to blame.

Lady Charles was in possession of vague Christian morals acquired through weekly attendance at church but never much studied; the clergyman was there to tell her what to think. She had supposed bereavement should make one a better person rather than a worse, forged, refined by adversity, steeled by the anguish of loss. Now she saw it made one a mass of chaotic and irrational impulses. She knew it was wrong to blame Lord Charles. Was she not his wife, his comfort in sickness and health? She was cheated that no other bereavement – the death, one after the other, of her excellent parents, she their prime concern, the sickening and subsequent death of a small daughter – had prepared her for this death. Now she endeavoured to turn her mind to Thomas, her youngest child and the second of her sons, but her mind barely functioned: Thomas, unseen for several years and then but briefly, had never had much of a place in it. She could think only of Lyndon, grappling with the incomprehensible truth that her charismatic, irresistible son, the most charming and adored, her golden boy, was dead, dead on a mountain pass somewhere in Spain or France, for the details were far from clear.

She said, with difficulty, her voice catching, 'Charles, they will have buried him?'

'Of course,' he replied. 'He will have been wrapped in his cloak and laid to rest at the instigation of his brother officers. Should there have been no clergyman, one will have read the prayers.'

'But you don't really know that.'

Lord Charles, who did not really know any such thing, hoped it was so.

His wife said, 'The letter made no mention of it. It spoke of fog and retreating in the dark, as if we might want to hear such things.'

'We are expected to want to know such things and, indeed, I prefer knowing them. Thomas will tell us the rest, I dare say.'

Lady Charles, distracted, said, 'Ah, so lonely, so bleak.'

Lord Charles could not bear to dwell on such pictures, of his son's wounded, lifeless body, the blood on the scarlet jacket, his sword still clasped in a dead hand. And what after that? Had death disfigured the loved countenance? He had died from a musket shot to the body, but there were questions, should they be asked, that would drive a man to madness.

He was about to turn and leave the room, muffling a pained half-sentence, when his wife spoke again.

'You have been in the Pyrenees, Charles.'

'When I was young. The uppermost parts are barren and rocky but the views . . . very splendid, of course. There were woods.'

What he remembered were the vultures soaring out from the cliff edges, scores of them, cutting great arcs in dazzling skies. Momentarily he put his hands to his head, stick and all, before hobbling to the door.

Lady Charles said, 'He died doing his duty. He died a hero.'

Lord Charles did not hear her. They had both said and thought this but it was more of a comfort to Lady Charles than to her husband. He had no image of heroes, while Lady Charles knew that her pride in Lyndon prevented her spiralling down into some even darker abyss.

Lord Charles ordered his horse for no purpose beyond that of giving himself occupation. As he had not ridden for several months, the demand was received with astonishment and dismay: the master preferred a sprightly thoroughbred over any other more suited to his years. The unsuitable creature was brought to the front door, induced to cavort in the direction of the lower steps and forcibly held still so that the old man could mount.

Once in the saddle, slippery smooth, Lord Charles remembered he was not young but also that should he have an accident it would be of little consequence. At the same time, his affairs being in great disorder, he wondered how he could view so calmly an accidental departure, without his conscience crying out to him as to the difficulties he would leave for his wife, who had never been required to attend practical matters. A groom followed him to open and shut the gates and, he supposed, to bear him home should an accident occur, but the hard, polished leather, unforgiving, was a comfort to him, as was the tangling mass of the double reins, through sheer familiarity.

The drive twisted across the park. The day was overcast, a fine, pale mist, through which he marked where the oaks had stood, felled to pay for Lyndon's commission in a regiment not of Lyndon's choice. There had been no vacancy, or even time, to make him once more an officer in the Guards and it was agreed the extra expense was prohibitive. It need have been but a temporary measure, a stepping stone. Lyndon was an optimist: he assumed cash would become available and vacancies arise. The oaks should have been replaced with saplings for the benefit of another generation, but this Lord Charles had failed to do.

Everything he had done to improve Ridley had been done for Lyndon and Lyndon's sons, but Lyndon had died without sons. An estate – the land, the people who relied on it for their roof, their bread and butter – was worth maintaining for its own sake. It was his duty, his privilege, to maintain Ridley, yet he did not do it. Even prior to Lyndon's death he had allowed his attention to wander, to see the necessity for things to be done, yet not do them, as if the grim future was already directing him. This he viewed as strange now that he had had ample time to reflect on it: a son on active service was just as subject to death and disease as the son of another: a shower of grape or a musket ball, the climate indiscriminately unfit for all. Lady Charles had talked, without cease, of the danger in allowing him to go, but Lyndon had always been lucky, his life charmed.

As Lord Charles left the drive he caught a glimpse of Mrs Kingston's carriage turning in at the lodge. He was glad to think his wife was to have a visitor, though not one likely to distract her to any great degree; one that would, at the least, assist her in passing the afternoon until the hour to dine offered further distraction. After that, the long dark hours of evening and the distant prospect of bed could be disturbed only by the thirty minutes or so in which Lottie's grandmother might read her a story.

The mismanagement of the estate he put down to a combination of his age and to a shortage of income. He was aware of the reasons for that shortage but he did not examine them. He required a regulated plan of retrenchment, but such things took effort and energy. He had expressed a desire to travel but he had meant that they should live abroad because it was cheaper: one could let one's house and live in Rome or some other place like that. His mind was a pre-war mind, it had temporally discounted Napoleon, but now he thought how a young man could still move about, dodge armies, get to places. He, though, was too old for such antics, especially with a wife and a young child to consider; he thought Lady Charles still reluctant to allow Lottie to go to her aunt. He had a momentary vision of foreign inns, travelling carriages, servants, luggage, bandits, mountain passes, postillions with whom he shared no common language, lame horses, detached wheels – why, the list was endless. At his age it was out of the question. Even the considering of it tired him out. In what way could he escape?

He peered at the countryside through the light drizzle, hardly conscious of the horse sidling, rattling its bit, his elderly bones accustomed to the sensations. There were little dark wooded fields; a clear stream; a sweep of downland; some water meadows with willows knotted in exposed winter bareness; farms tucked into hollows: such was the bulk of Ridley's five thousand acres. It was not at all a bad place, but his heart was not in it. Perhaps, he thought, he yearned for the stately expanses that had nurtured his youth: his father's vast estates. He had had the half-formed intention of handing Ridley over to Lyndon, on his expected return from the Peninsula, to manage as best he could. He had believed that campaigning would leave his son a deal more prepared to settle down, remarry and live at home, perhaps with a seat in Parliament, though that would generate considerable further expense. Both Lord and Lady Charles had thought Lyndon quite prepared to marry the pretty, widowed Mrs Kingston, but his sudden precipitation into the army, an inferior regiment and a subordinate rank, had not made that an immediate option.

Lord Charles had had such faith in his son's abilities that he was sure he could have managed a regiment with the minimum of instruction, but the days were gone when regiments could be purchased for the asking, even supposing Lyndon's family had been able to afford such a thing. In his careless, infrequent letters home, full of affection for his parents and Ridley, humour, anecdote and adventure amidst the stark discomforts of life with the army. Lyndon had expressed impatience and humiliation that the officers immediately superior to him were boys. He had died a lieutenant and it was of little compensation that he had been the most senior on the regimental list, and therefore next for promotion. Had not Thomas, four or five years younger, already got a majority in the Royal Horse Artillery? Lyndon had been only too aware of that. As a very young man he had been a subaltern in the Guards, but he had sold out when he became engaged to be married. Had he stayed his rank would, by now, have been quite superior.

The groom, riding behind his master, said tentatively, 'It's very wet, m'lord, and getting fearful dark.'

Lord Charles, who had been about to turn for home, contemplated another three fields, but capitulation seemed the more comfortable option. In the distance he saw a knot of Lyndon's horses, standing with their backs to the rain. Why were they not sold? Why indeed. His own horse bounced forward on finding itself facing home; he slipped in the wet saddle, the wet reins slid through his fingers, but he retained his seat.

He passed in front of the house, rode round to the stables, dismounted and walked stiffly to the back door. His valet met him, dressing-gown to hand, anxious to divest him of his wet coat and boots: even Lyndon had not been allowed to traipse through the house in dirty boots. A chair was placed at the bottom of the back stairs for the convenience of all, but there was now only Lord Charles to use it.

Somewhere upstairs a door opened. He could hear Miss Arbuthnot giving Lottie her singing lesson. Miss Arbuthnot sang, '"Under the greenwood tree, Who loves to lie with me? . . ."' A few lines later she broke off to say, 'You can sing this on your own, but I will sing it the once. "Come hither, come hither, come hither . . ."'

Lottie's thin little voice cheerfully echoed the words.

Miss Arbuthnot said, 'There, did I not say you could do it?'

In the drawing room the candles were lit. Mrs Kingston had departed. Lady Charles had out her workbox. It contained a dull assortment of petticoats and shifts to be distributed among the poor. The work had once given her satisfaction but now it was sluggishly performed, though she supposed her needle hemmed and seamed at much its usual rate.

Mrs Kingston had said to her, picking up a garment to admire the neatness of the handiwork, 'Why not indulge yourself at this difficult time with something more distracting, a pretty thing for Lottie when she is out of mourning?'

Lady Charles had looked at her companion and wondered that a woman whom she had believed almost engaged to her son, whose sense of loss might be considered equal to her own, could make such a remark, but Mrs Kingston had then bowed her head and added, in stifled tones, 'But, my dear Lady Charles, I do understand how it might seem impossible.'

'It is impossible,' Lady Charles had replied. 'It would seem a frivolity. Besides, Lottie must understand her situation.'

Mrs Kingston had departed shortly after, leaving Lady Charles to consider, charitably enough, her guest. With her plump figure, her pretty face, her brown hair, she seemed too young to be a widow, with a little boy barely older than Lottie. It had been assumed Lyndon was on the point of making her an offer, and Mrs Kingston had assumed it herself, as she had frequently hinted, but as far as anyone knew there had been no actual engagement. Lady Charles understood Mrs Kingston would have liked to wear mourning for Lieutenant Lyndon Wilder as his betrothed but she had to make do with silvery greys and pale mauves, which certainly suited her. It was a sort of half-mourning that indicated nothing much, either bereaved or forsaken or neither. Lady Charles thought herself fond of her. She now considered questionable the relationship, had it existed, between her son and the sweet-natured widow, for Lyndon had always liked to be amused, and she was not particularly amusing; but then the poor girl he had married had never seemed amusing either, in the brief period they had known her. Mrs Kingston, though, remained the one person who could remotely enter into the extremes of Lady Charles's grief. As important, perhaps more so, Mrs Kingston appeared to understand the significance of that death as the death of a soldier, one who had died a hero, his image perfect, his death glorious.

Mrs Kingston's brother was on active service in the Peninsula, a further link between them, his letters quoted, his every utterance repeated. At another time Lady Charles might have found this tedious, but now she was hungry to hear of the privations and exigencies that made up the life of a junior officer in a regiment of the line. As Captain Houghton's letters were unfolded and further scrutinized on his sister's pale silken lap, Lady Charles was wondering, Was it thus for Lyndon, the fording of rivers, the night marches, the lack of rations, the baggage trains, the camp followers, the bivouacs, the fleas? Surely he had had the wherewithal to provide himself with sufficient sustenance and a decent bed. Her imagination conjured bands playing, young men clad in scarlet, the regimental colours gaily tugging in the breeze, officers on English thoroughbreds parading up and down. Yes, yes, Mrs Kingston thought this also warfare, but there were, too, fevers, dysentery, mules, and uniforms so gone to rags as to be unrecognizable.

Alone, Lady Charles rose from her chair and made her

way upstairs. It would soon be time to change for dinner but she had a few minutes to enter Lyndon's rooms. They were as he had left them and so they were kept, but she had not allowed the clock to be wound since they had received news of his death.

Miss Wilder was nine years old. She had large blue eyes, a round face, and abundant golden-blonde hair that would have hung to her waist in fat ringlets had not Miss Arbuthnot tied it up with a very ordinary piece of green ribbon.

'I may not wear the ribbon because I am in mourning,' Lottie had said.

'You must ask your grandmother for a length of black,' Miss Arbuthnot had replied. 'The green will answer just for now.' She thought quite so much hair, though pretty, an inconvenience.

'I don't like my hair tied back,' Lottie said, though that was not quite true: she enjoyed the novelty.

Miss Arbuthnot was thinking about the concept of mourning while she put out the lesson books. Did Miss Wilder's little black gown have a profound effect, as a constant reminder of grief, on the child? She thought not. There was no evidence she gave her father a single thought, unless in the presence of her grandmother, but Miss Arbuthnot wished to make no assumption. It was not easy to puzzle out what went on in the head of her pupil. She knew herself what it was to lose a parent, but the circumstances could not be compared. Miss Wilder had not seen her father for at least three years and she had never known her mother. Miss Arbuthnot had cautiously enquired of the housekeeper if there was no picture of the late Mrs Lyndon Wilder that her daughter might have some idea of the woman who had borne her, but it had seemed as though she had passed through Ridley like some pleasing but inconsequential wraith, no one prepared to describe her appearance. She had been pretty, it was certain, for otherwise the late Mr Wilder would not have married her.

Lottie, coldly eyeing her books, played what had been hitherto a trump card in the war with governesses. She said, 'I don't wish to do any lessons just now.'

'How unfortunate,' Miss Arbuthnot replied, 'for it is exactly the hour your grandmother allotted for you to begin.'

'Today I shan't.'

'I shall have to teach Augusta instead.' Miss Arbuthnot waved her hand in the direction of a large china doll propped on innumerable cushions so her china chin might rest on the table. 'I'm sure her spellings aren't learnt. Now, Augusta, be a good girl and open your book. She is rather clumsy, isn't she? I dare say you will have to help her.'

Lottie said, 'I don't believe Augusta can hold her pen.'

'Dear me, isn't she backward? It is just as well you can help her, or I should have to get cross and it rarely does any good. If she works hard until eleven o'clock she shall practise her drawing. I believe Augusta to be fond of drawing.'

Lottie wondered about submitting. Just for now she thought she would and accordingly reached for her spelling book, but then all the horrid squiggles and circles that made up words danced before her eyes: she knew she would never understand them. A tear or two ran down her cheek.

Miss Arbuthnot came round the table and put an arm round her. She said, 'Dearest, it's nothing to cry about. We will start at the very beginning. Here is an A, large and small. We will put a little line under each one so we learn what they look like. You draw the lines. A is for Augusta. I must write her name down so she shall recognize it. She has a large A at the beginning and a small one at the end. What a useful girl she is.'

How was it Miss Wilder had reached the age of nine with only the haziest idea of the alphabet?

'When we have finished, you shall draw a picture of Augusta and we will write her name underneath. You shall do the As and I shall do the other letters.'

Miss Arbuthnot wrote to her father.

My dearest Papa,

Here I am thinking as much as anyone might who has, for the very first time, taken employment. I have been accustomed to running a house, albeit a modest one, let alone the managing of my sisters, though I doubt always with the best results, which may have given me a false sense of my capabilities. Either way I am not accustomed to subservience, except to yourself. Fortunately I am left to my own devices in the schoolroom, for Lady Charles Wilder does not visit us. I say fortunately, but then I think it unfortunate, for interest should be taken. I can sense your growling at me here, both for criticizing my employer and therefore my benefactor and for making insufficient allowance for their sad circumstances.

I call my pupil Miss Wilder when I should much prefer to call her Lottie, for she is just a little girl of nine years old, spoilt and neglected all in the same breath. Perhaps Miss Charlotte would be acceptable. Today she cried a little over her spellings and then all formalities must be dropped.

I cannot puzzle out, Papa, what I have heard you preach from the pulpit, that one should not aspire to better oneself but to be content with making the very best of the situation into which we have been placed. My aspirations, under this philosophy, must be to become the best governess in the world, and hence governess to the little princesses we hope Princess Charlotte will produce, and I am sure I could put some arithmetic into the head of a little prince or two, because it has occurred to me their infant brains might not be different from those of Miss Wilder and my little sisters. It is a pleasure you are rather far off so I cannot hear you growl at me. Another thing, how can all of our great aristocracy have had ancestors as great and grand as themselves? They bettered themselves and got away with it. You will, not for the first time, accuse me of Jacobin leanings, a rebel at heart, but was not my dear mother a rebel, giving up her religion and thereby her family in order to marry you?

A governess is such a betwixt and between thing. The housekeeper occasionally invites me, out of kindness, to take tea in her room. She is a person of such grandeur, we are not sure who is condescending to whom. We discuss the weather. There is a butler who ably manages everyday affairs. His name is Slimmer but I make sure to call him Mr. Slimmer, for reasons of diplomacy. I find his character to be of the slippy-slidy sort. There are two parlour maids, Lady Charles's maid, Lord Charles's valet and an indefinite number of other souls, indoors and out, let alone those attached to the kitchen, which area I am not expected to penetrate. Oh, for the past glories of knowing where one stood. Of Lord and Lady Charles Wilder I see virtually nothing. I send my charge downstairs after dinner, wearing the little black gown with the lace on, in oppose to the ones without, and she is returned to me one hour later. I am the fourth governess to try my hand at her education. I do what you advise: devote my attention to the needs of the child. I graciously accept the position I have been fortunate in obtaining.

I wish it did not separate me from all that I most dearly love. Should you have a letter from Bobby, I need not tell you how much I should appreciate you enclosing it to me, could you bear to part with it,

Ever your affectionate daughter,

Anna Arbuthnot

Mrs Kingston paid a morning visit to Lady Charles. The shutters were put back, for one could not expect a visitor to sit in the dark. The drawing room looked over an expanse of lawn with nothing very much planted. Beyond that was a small hill and a wood. Striped curtains framed the view. The room itself was elegant but bare, furnished with the necessities but nothing else, formal rather than comfortable. Lady Charles disliked the clutter of everyday life.

She said, 'I appreciate your calling again so soon, Mrs Kingston. I am poor company, but you are kind.'

Mrs Kingston sighed. She wished to make a point but was unable to decide how it should be put. Eventually she said, lowering her gaze, 'Could you but know how well I understand, and indeed venture to share, your affliction.'

Lady Charles wondered, for the hundredth time, whether Lyndon had intended to marry Mrs Kingston. She said, obliquely, 'A soldier's life is very exacting.'

'Yes, of course, and what I have to say particularly bears on that. I have told you how my brother, Captain Houghton, has suffered intermittently from the fever ever since he was at Walcheren. Now they are sending him home. I had his letter this morning. I am afraid his health must be a great deal worse than he has ever previously admitted. It makes me very nervous. I almost don't look forward to his coming, to see him so reduced, but I pray rest and care will put him right. His regiment may have been positioned not so very far from that of poor Lieutenant Wilder's. He might be able to tell us more of the circumstances of his death. Of course I have asked him in my letters, but my brother never has been one for actually reading letters and answering what is in them. He fires off a salvo on the horrid place he is in and asks if I can pay his bill at the tailor.'

Lady Charles drew in her breath. She felt a constriction

in her chest. Mrs Kingston seemed to speak of Lyndon's death as if it were any death; the words, although spoken earnestly, seemed to trip off her tongue like any others, even ending on a note of frivolity. She took a long minute to compose herself while Mrs Kingston anxiously proffered her a glass of wine, saying, 'I spoke too hastily, I said too much at once, but I so wish Henry to give you consolation. Lieutenant Wilder died a soldier, he gave his life, but Henry will know the circumstances, the nature of his valour.'

At length Lady Charles stood up and went slowly to her desk, withdrawing, from among many, a letter. She said, 'I'm afraid, Mrs Kingston, you will find me a weak woman. Why can't I display the courage of my darling boy? He would be ashamed of me. "Mother," I hear him say, "I died for England. Be brave, have courage. My death is glorious." This is the letter we received from his colonel. Perhaps you, of all people, have a right to read it . . .' Here she hesitated, distracted from what she had meant to say by so direct a reference to Mrs Kingston's undisclosed relationship to her son. Eventually she continued, 'You may as well read it. I find it curiously unsatisfactory.'

Mrs Kingston smoothed the letter flat on her lilac lap. It was dated 31 July 1813, and had been written from some little village in the Pyrenees whose name she had no idea how to pronounce.

Dear Lord Charles,

It is my melancholy duty to inform you of the death of your son, Lieutenant Wilder, on the 25th of this month. The French, under Marshal Soult, attacked our positions about the pass of Roncesvalles on that day and the fighting, in this mountainous terrain, four thousand feet above the sea, has been more or less continuous. I should like to be have been able to give you an exact account of his heroic death, but I can only say he died gallantly while leading forward the company to which he was attached, Captain Norton having been seriously wounded a short while earlier. I have questioned the men who were with him at the time, but the moment being late in the day, about 6 o'clock, and a fog coming down to add to the smoke from the powder, they were unable to give me any precise account and did not seem to agree among themselves. It is possible Mr Wilder was, in his ardour, a touch further ahead of his men than he might have been, and what with the nature of the ground, rocky and uneven, perhaps no clear picture can ever be drawn. Outnumbered by the enemy, General Cole, anxious for our position, though the pass was held, ordered our immediate retreat, which may have added to their confusion and clouded exact recollection. I can only assure you your son died in the cause of his duty and he will be most sincerely regretted by the regiment.

Mr Wilder left precise instructions, among his effects, that his brother should take charge of his possessions, should he fall in action. I therefore took upon myself the sad task of informing Major Wilder, by letter, of the mournful circumstances, though I believe he had already received such information as there was. Major Wilder has an ever increasing reputation as a very steady and reliable officer, which must be to you a source of gratification amid your affliction. Should the lamented death of his brother necessitate his quitting the Royal Horse Artillery to return home, he will be of considerable loss to the service.

Mrs Kingston stopped short of reading the polite but final salutations of the colonel because she could not decipher his signature. She said, 'Oh dear, it is of course exceedingly distressing, but why unsatisfactory? Is it not a beautiful letter, with so much reference to his duty and his gallantry?'

'The phrases he uses strike me as those he would use every time he is called upon to write such a letter.'

'I pity him for the letters he must write,' Mrs Kingston replied.

'He would prefer to tell me how many feet above sea level he was than the actual circumstances of my son's death.'

'They will, I am sure, have been just as confusing as the colonel says,' Mrs Kingston said, feeling herself on firmer ground. 'The smoke from the muskets and the artillery is so dense you can see only a few yards in each direction. That is how a battle is, Henry has told me. What with the fog coming down, I think it not surprising the men of his company were confused.'

'And then,' Lady Charles continued, as if Mrs Kingston had not spoken, 'why make reference to Thomas? Steady and reliable, damning with faint praise, obviously quite unable to think of anything more interesting to say of him, and so unkindly irrelevant to write in a letter telling us of Lyndon's death.'

'Oh dear, I think, in your distress, you malign the poor colonel, and I can assure you the praise, in military teams, he gives Major Wilder, is of the very highest, and truly ought to be of consolation to you. It is a compliment, even if it appears to us a little mundane. As for what he says of your elder son, he died gallantly, doing his duty. Those of us having the privilege to know his character would have expected nothing less.'

'You are right, you are right. I make too much of the smallest innuendo. The poor colonels must sit in their tents or in some dreadful hovel halfway up a mountain writing these letters half the day. We also had a letter from Thomas, not that it says anything of great moment, but you may as well read that too.'

Lady Charles again went to her desk.

Mrs Kingston said, 'Fancy he's a major now. Isn't he very young?'

'Not so very young, twenty-nine or so,' Lady Charles replied, with a small shrug. 'No, I believe he must be thirty. What is young in the theatre of war? It made it awkward for Lyndon, having a much younger brother so superior in rank, for they were five years apart, but he put the best face on it and was forever joking at Thomas's expense and at the expense of the Artillery.'

'Henry says the Artillery is quite a race apart,' Mrs Kingston said, Major Wilder's letter still folded in her hand.

'We didn't encourage Thomas to make such a choice, but he was clever in that sort of mathematical calculating way and he felt it the natural choice. We took him out of school and sent him to Woolwich as a lad of fourteen, or I believe he was fourteen, and we have seen but little of him since. He was his sister Georgie's pet, so the small amount of leave he takes he tends to spend with her and her family. As for his letters, you may be sure they are taken up with technicalities and troop manoeuvres.'

Mrs Kingston proceeded to unfold the letter, now quite puzzled as to its likely nature. It was written from Pamplona on 27 July. She immediately saw the neat and orderly nature of the hand.

My dear Parents,

I write to you with the saddest heart imaginable for I can only surmise what a terrible blow this news will be to you. I cannot say whether you will hear from me or his colonel first, but Lyndon was killed defending the Roncesvalles pass on the 25th. I at first heard it and prayed it might not be true, that it would turn out he was a prisoner or wounded, under which latter circumstances I could have got leave to go to him.

There seems so little to say, I find it difficult to write. Would I knew more of the circumstances. The blow to you will be inestimable,

Your affectionate and obedient son,

T. Wilder RHA

Mrs Kingston, for a moment contemplating what she considered to be a perfectly feeling letter, said cautiously, 'At such an exacting time, I am sure no one could know how to say the right thing.'

'There is no mention of his loss, only of ours.'

'Ah, yes, his only brother, it is true, but his thoughts are with you.'

'Just so,' Lady Charles replied, 'but think of the difficulty of his position.'

Mrs Kingston wondered what that might be. She said, 'Was he jealous of his brother? It is often so, I believe, but I am sure I loved my poor dear sister, though I thought her prettier than me. What brother could not be jealous of Mr Wilder?'

Lady Charles realized Mrs Kingston had not understood to what she referred, but rather than make further explanation, she merely replied, 'Jealous? I dare say he was, though Lyndon was good to him, having him his fag at school to protect him from the bullies, though he was not in the least use and never did as he was asked. He fought a duel when he was eight years old, he was such a belligerent and warlike little boy, but I don't suppose he wished for Lyndon's death.'

Mrs Kingston was distracted by the idea of such a duel and would have liked to enquire more, but Lady Charles gave her no opportunity, going on to speak of other things. Having further calls to make, Mrs Kingston soon left.

Lady Charles went to the window to watch the barouche going down the drive, wending its way through banks of rank, wet grass. The park was under-grazed, she knew not why, and the grasses bowed their heads in tangled hoops. Had Lyndon married Mrs Kingston before he went away, she might have borne him a son, a beautiful little Lyndon to be the idol of their hearts. Slowly she returned to her desk to replace the letters, those two letters that had killed her, in their correct pigeonhole. She always kept letters. She could have reread all the letters her boy had sent, those from school describing cricket and bathing in the river; the tedium of lessons on sunny days; requests for plum puddings and game pies; requests for his own spaniel and a red tailcoat with fancy buttons to attend the dress ball of the harriers. Lyndon, his mother acknowledged, was always requesting things, suitable or otherwise. His next letters were from Oxford, where he had lived above his income, ignored his father's lectures, was happy, carefree, cheerful, vague, amusing and forever in scrapes from which it was necessary to rescue him; in fact, he was exactly as they had expected. Yes, Lady Charles had kept every one of Lyndon's letters: the pigeonholes, the little drawers of her desk, bulged with them. Among them she had placed, face down, for she feared to see it unprepared, his portrait miniature. At its back was a twist of his yellow-gold hair. Even now she did not turn it up. She knew its every detail, a second lieutenant in the Guards, the scarlet jacket, the blue facings, the gold, and Lyndon's face, not much more than a boy's.

Lady Charles thought of how, at that stage of his life, his career in the military had been so short. She wished he had not sold his uniform, that she had it now to smooth and fold in a cedarwood trunk. Whatever had induced him to join again, and his father only prepared to buy him a commission in an ordinary line regiment? Money was all that was ever considered. Even Thomas had written, though his letter was curious, exclaiming at the necessity of getting Lyndon back into the Guards. She knew the very words of his letter: 'The Guards always get the best billets and the NCOs do all the work, give the orders, the officers not encouraged to speak to, let alone to know or to understand, the men, or that is how I see it.' Why had Thomas said that? Lyndon was as capable as the next man of giving an order. It was as Mrs Kingston had observed: Thomas was jealous of his brother for, though he had done very well for himself, it was inevitable that Lyndon would have overtaken and outshone him.

She returned to the window, the miniature in her hand. The few remaining leaves of the dreary shrubbery had been beaten off by the rain: there was nothing of autumn glory, of bronze or rust. It occurred to her that, had Lyndon remained in the Guards, he might never have been killed. It was not that he would have been exposed to less danger, but he would not have been in that exact spot, defending this unimaginable Roncesvalles Pass, in the fog, at the moment when he was struck. Logic told her he might have been killed in some other battle, for as Thomas, when wounded in the leg, had remarked to Georgie, whose letters from him were always more amusing than theirs, there was a lot of luck in staying alive. Thus Lyndon might still have been alive had they not stinted in the purchase of the commission, and in this she could not fail to blame her husband.

At length she turned the little painting face up. She wished her belief in Christianity, the afterlife, could furnish her with images of Lyndon on some celestial other plane, entered into everlasting bliss, but she could picture only bones, bones with the rags of uniform clinging in decay. She had used to think how boyish and innocent he appeared in his picture, how candid his blue eyes, but now he mocked her from his other world.

With a cry of renewed anguish, she hastened from the window and thrust the miniature back among the letters so carefully preserved in her desk.

Lord Charles was not fond of walking because he had no dog. Why could he not have some warm little spaniel to sit at his feet on a winter evening or to accompany him around the confines of the park? Whenever he set forth he wished he had not because he was cold and there were too many reminders of things left undone. A dog would have cheered him and lent a proper purpose to the exercise. Sometimes he rode instead: he would send for the horse to be brought to the front, consider countermanding the order, and then go off on it just the same with a reluctant groom trailing behind him. The grooms had become idle, having plenty of horses but little to be done with them. On his perambulations he often spotted Lottie and Miss Arbuthnot, their hoods up against the inclement weather. He thought it not much of a life for a woman to be cooped up with only one little girl for company. Governesses were always sad creatures, caught between the drawing room and the servants' hall, unwanted in either. They were driven to accept their posts through financial necessity, and he had been assured this was the case with Miss Arbuthnot. A younger sister was on the point of marrying, the only boy was in the navy and the two younger girls were old enough to do without the assistance of the eldest. Mr Arbuthnot's living was not particularly profitable but he had not wished his daughter to take employment, which Lord Charles understood. Who would wish their daughter to be at the beck and call of others? Was there no hope, he had asked his wife, of the girl getting married herself?

Lady Charles had replied that she was somewhat disfigured. Lord Charles thought Ridley in a sufficiently morbid state without the addition of a haunted fright of a body looming about the place and that Lottie was sure to take a dislike to her. Lady Charles considered it her Christian duty to tolerate what a person could not help. Lord Charles had asked for the disfigurement to be defined. On hearing it was red hair and freckles, he said he could think of worse things and neither of the former was an absolute bar to matrimony. Miss Arbuthnot was also too tall, he was told.

Of course, the subject of a governess for Lottie was a tedious one for they neither stayed nor taught her even the rudiments of what she should know. Georgiana had wanted Lottie to be brought up with her cousins for, she said, Lyndon would not pay her the least attention until she was old enough to be taken to the theatre. Lady Charles had replied that of course Lyndon was unlikely to find interest in a baby, but were there not grandparents to take his place? At the death of her brother Georgie had repeated her offer, but Lady Charles thought Lottie must never be allowed to forget she was the daughter of Lyndon Wilder, and who but her grandmother would keep his memory alive? She had said this to her husband, not to her daughter, to whom she had pointed out the difficulties for a child of being plunged into the hurly-burly of family life when she was accustomed to the dignity and solitude of her own schoolroom and the undivided attention of her governess. Lady Charles had added that it would break a heart already broken if she were to part with her granddaughter.

As the departure of the last governess had coincided with the news of Lyndon's death, the task of finding a new one was undertaken by his sister. Miss Arbuthnot was known to Georgie's closest friend, Mrs Hamilton, the Rev. Arbuthnot being vicar of the parish in which the Hamiltons lived. She had known her since she was a child. Miss Arbuthnot had no experience as a governess but she had taught her three younger sisters, was well read, had been educated to a high standard by her father, played the piano, sang, and spoke perfect French, her mother's native tongue. She was, of course, too young.

Lord Charles, tired of the hysterical departure of governesses, had begun to think it was of little consequence whom they employed, but there was Miss Arbuthnot, with Lottie beside her, picking up sticks in the park, though why they should be doing such a thing he could not imagine. The previous day he had asked Lottie, when she had appeared in the dining room in time for dessert, what it was about Miss Arbuthnot that made her more satisfactory than her predecessors. His wife had frowned at him and Lottie had declined to answer. Lottie and her governesses were extra anxieties to add to a mind already bedevilled with such.

At Michaelmas the farmers had come in with their rents and he had stood at the round table in the office, endeavouring to fathom which of the drawers contained the necessary books and documents pertaining to each, a duty to which his agent had always attended while he had merely stood by and asked after the families. He had thought neither he nor his agent had very onerous tasks, but now he saw there was room for error. Everything had to be written down legibly and correctly, on the spot, in some of which cases he had failed, distracted by the pleasantries that were part of the quarter-day ritual: he found it hard to remember now who was a widower and who had a sickly child after whom he should make enquiry. At least, he thought, they were able to pay their rents, but should the war end, which now seemed likely, the price of corn would drop and they would all be in a pickle, with blockades being lifted and no necessity to supply the army.

Mrs Kingston invited Lottie to spend the morning playing with her son. She had made serious efforts to become acquainted with the child when she had supposed she might become her stepmother, bought her presents and generally courted her, but Lottie, though she received the presents graciously, had resisted. Mrs Kingston was still disposed to be kind to Lottie and her governess, for governesses led such dull lives, and why should not the two solitary children, hers and Lyndon Wilder's, become friends and amuse each other? Mrs Kingston, beyond kindness, had another characteristic: she was inquisitive, and even a governess could interest her.

The walk across the park and through the wood to the village of Ridley was barely two miles. Miss Arbuthnot assured Lady Charles there was no need at all for the carriage to be got out: it was better for herself and Lottie to walk. Lady Charles did not walk: in her heart she did not like the country beyond the flower garden in the summer, and she did not believe Lottie liked walking either. Miss Arbuthnot's brisk stipulations on fresh air and exercise disconcerted her. Had she been reading dubious books on the techniques of rearing a child? Was Lottie to wear loose clothing for fear pressure might lead to the accumulation of stagnant juices in her body, to run about without her bonnet and other such nonsense? Lottie's black little gowns were not in the least tight for the child was thinner than she used to be, a fact that caused her grandmother concern. Miss Arbuthnot had also suggested Lottie should have a garden to work and a dog. Lady Charles did not object to the garden, for gardening was an acceptable hobby for a woman, but only her son Lyndon had ever persuaded her that a dog was a necessary part of a household. To most of Miss Arbuthnot's polite requests, Lady Charles acceded – for was she not still in their employ, even if too young, and was that not a minor miracle?

In the nursery, Lottie wished to ring the bell for Susan to fetch her cloak and assist her with her boots. Miss Arbuthnot, who had never known a child so helpless, asked her if she would like to take part in a revolution.

Lottie said, 'Like the French?'

'Not quite like the French.'

'If I mayn't cut off anyone's head, what am I to do?'

'Much more dull. Fetch your cloak and boots for yourself, as they are only next door, and pop them on without any help from Susan, who is probably three flights downstairs.'

'But Susan always does it.'

'I know.'

'But why shouldn't Susan do it? It is what Susan is here for.'

'I am thinking of all those stairs and Susan's legs, for it seems to me she is getting quite old.'

After some hesitation, Lottie said, 'But I can't do the laces, I can't do the bow.'

'And what when you are a young lady? Now run next door and fetch it all and I will teach you.'

Lottie contemplated rebellion, for surely Miss Arbuthnot had her own way all the time, but then she did as she was bade. After ten minutes she had mastered a double bow, though not without declaring it, at intervals, too difficult. She had noticed her governess never paid the least attention when she said things were difficult, but kept steadily on with them.

'And what should we do,' Miss Arbuthnot asked, 'if our soldiers and sailors said it was too difficult to fight the French?'

'We should tell them they must try harder, and when they catch Napoleon they must chop off his head,' Lottie replied.

Within a short while they were crossing the park. The weather was mild and to begin with Lottie was cheerful, frequently bending to admire the bows on her boots, but after a quarter of an hour she considered herself tired. Had not her grandmother told her she would be and was not Miss Arbuthnot too clever at getting her own way? Seeing a fallen tree that had blown down in a gale, she settled herself on its lowest branch and announced she would go no further.

'Most unfortunate,' Miss Arbuthnot said, 'for Mrs Kingston will be expecting us.'

'I don't care,' Lottie replied. 'I don't want to play with Horatio.'

'Children are always expected to like other children because they live near by. I can't imagine why,' Miss Arbuthnot said.

Lottie, disconcerted, was not sure how to reply, for she had no idea whether she liked Horatio or not.

'Have you often been to play with him?' Miss Arbuthnot asked.

'Not very often. Once; he won at Spillikins all the time.'

'I expect he was very clever at it.'

'I didn't want to play.'

'But what if you had won? You would have liked it better.'

'Much better,' Lottie consented.

Miss Arbuthnot had brought her work bag. She had never met Mrs Kingston and had no idea what role, as governess, she was expected to take. Was she to supervise the children while her hostess did something else, or were the children to be left to their own devices while the adults took a cup of tea? Some form of extra occupation had seemed a good idea, but she had not foreseen needing it so early in the day. Settling down on another branch, she took out some red silk twist and her needles.

'What are you making?' Lottie asked, craning to see.

'I am netting a purse for my brother. Here it is, like a sausage.'

'What is his name?'

'Robert, but we call him Bobby.'

'Is he grown-up?'

'He is twenty years old and is now a lieutenant in the navy, where he has been four years.'

'Don't you mind his being away?'

'Oh, I did, but my uncle got him a place on a ship and paid for his uniforms and all sorts of things. Such an opportunity couldn't go by. Besides, Bobby was extremely anxious to go.'

Lottie's mind moved somewhat sluggishly round the notion of a brother. It was a little alarming. Her memory was good, and though it seemed long ago, when surely she had been very small, Mrs Kingston had asked her if she would not like Horatio as a brother, although it must have been evident she would like no such thing.

Miss Arbuthnot said, 'We are going to be very late for Mrs Kingston.'

Lottie was now ready to continue but she did not like to be the one to give way. She said, 'What will you tell her?'

'I shall tell her you would not walk.'

'I shall tell her you sat on a log and netted a red silk purse for your brother in the navy.'

Miss Arbuthnot laughed. 'Who shall poor Mrs Kingston believe, for we shall both be right?'

'Me, because all my governesses have told me young ladies don't tell lies.'

'A governess certainly shouldn't tell them either, but there is a difference between "ought not" and "don't". Now let's think . . . Perhaps we will never arrive . . . Time will be in suspense, the servants bringing in the biscuits, the kettle boiling on the stove, if there's tea . . . the dog bouncing to the door . . . the cat licking its fur . . . all turned to marble.'

'Like the Sleeping Beauty,' Lottie said, pleased. 'Everything will be asleep, just exactly stopped, frozen like snowmen.'

Miss Arbuthnot was putting away her work bag and standing up as they spoke. They continued to walk across the park while they developed the theme, and were soon in the main street of the village and knocking on Mrs Kingston's door. It was opened by a housemaid who, disappointingly, showed no sign of having been turned to marble.

Mrs Kingston awaited them in the drawing room but cordially rose to greet them, her glossy brown hair, beautifully curled and arranged, and her big brown eyes in a round face. She was pretty in her lilac gown. Miss Arbuthnot explained that they were late because walking with Lottie across the park had taken longer than she had supposed. Lottie, reluctantly holding up her face for the inevitable kiss, saw that no lying had been involved.

'I am sure it is kind of you to bring this dear child to see me,' Mrs Kingston began, 'for I am certain you never get time to yourself. Miss Finchley was governess to my sister and myself and we never gave the dear soul a moment's peace, always wanting to be entertained. Here I live alone with my little boy and he never wants a story read him, he prefers to read for himself. He goes to the rector for his lessons, which is very convenient. Horatio will enter the navy, like his poor father before him, and what shall I do then? My poor dear late husband, Lieutenant Kingston as he was, wrote me from his ship specifying the names for his heir, Horatio William Pitt Kingston, but he did not himself live to see the child. We must go upstairs to the old schoolroom in order to seek him out. Would he wait in the drawing room with his mother? No he would not. He said it was dull.'

Horatio had his mother's brown eyes but none of her comfortable plumpness. He was a white-faced, bony little boy with straight black hair. He and Lottie studiously declined to look at one another.

'The navy,' Mrs Kingston continued, 'is what Lieutenant Kingston would have preferred for his son, so I cannot think otherwise. Horatio looks forward to a life at sea.'

As her son showed every sign of sidling towards the door to make an escape, his mother, having spotted his intention, concluded with the injunction to remember Charlotte was his guest and to show her his battleships.

Horatio swung a skinny arm in the direction of the table where he had drawn up an array of toy ships. 'Here,' he announced, 'are the French and the Spanish drawn up in a line. The British are approaching them in two columns and will turn and give them a broadside. It is, you see, the battle of Trafalgar. This one is *Dreadnought*, this *Prince*, this *Defiance* and so on, *Thunderer*, *Ajax*, *Orion*, *Bellerophon*, *Africa*, *Victory*, *Royal Sovereign*. I can do all their names without looking at my crib, but I expect you would rather I didn't.'

Lottie said, 'I shall go to sea.'

'Girls don't,' Horatio replied.

'I shall cut my hair off and wear boys' clothes.'

'You can go instead of me, if you like.'

'No nonsense, dearest,' his mother said. 'Show Lottie something else.'

'I'll show her my globe,' he said, skidding across the floor with Lottie behind him. 'You find Spain and I will show you where the battle was.'

Lottie was a long time finding Spain or any other place.

Mrs Kingston said, 'Miss Arbuthnot and I are going downstairs to take a dish of tea. Play nicely, Horatio.'

Over the tea Mrs Kingston, settled in her comfortable drawing room, continued to outline her son's career. 'You can see how he loves those ships, Miss Arbuthnot. In two years' time he may go to the naval college at Portsmouth or he may go straight on board the *Prince Adolphus*, seventy-four guns, you know. My brother-in-law is a post captain in the navy. He has had Horatio's name down on the ship's list for three years, since he was seven. It is not a pleasant prospect for a mother, but her natural affection should not stand between her son and his chosen path.'

'Perhaps,' Miss Arbuthnot replied cautiously, 'if his father were alive today, he might not think his son suited to the navy. After all, sons and fathers are not necessarily alike.'

'That is so, and I do wonder whether Horatio is like his father or no. The truth is, when you are married to an officer in the navy, unless they have no ship, which makes them disagreeable, you see them very little, and when they die so young you are left with few memories. You might say my husband and I were comparative strangers.' Mrs Kingston looked wistfully into her teacup, which was distractingly ornamented with blue chrysanthemums and Chinese figures in large hats. 'He did write, of course, but what can a man on a ship write about beyond porpoises and how much salt pork or live chickens they have left on board?'

'My own brother is a lieutenant in the navy. He has only just got his promotion. He doesn't resemble his father in the least but he has a cheerful disposition, which I think very useful.'

'A cheerful disposition gets one over all sorts of obstacles. Mine is quite cheerful, though I should have preferred not to be a widow, but I have this pleasant house, everything convenient; a large garden, for I am fond of gardening, a courtyard with stabling for the pony and a pair of carriage horses, an orchard . . . What more could I need? I feel it the very hub of activities in the village for I am always ready to assist in a worthy cause. I have great independence.' Here Mrs Kingston paused for she was not actually taken with her independence and would willingly have sacrificed it for the married state. 'However, we must count our blessings, as I say to poor, dear Lady Charles. To lose a son like hers . . . Of course, you never knew Mr Wilder, but I don't exaggerate when I say he was perfect. His manner, his address . . . I see him now when he came to bid me goodbye . . . I am not ashamed to say I wept. "Don't I look the brave soldier, Mrs Kingston?" He spoke just so, with the little bit of humour that gets over anything awkward. He was wearing his uniform, all that scarlet, and nothing becomes a man more. Do you not think so, Miss Arbuthnot?'

Miss Arbuthnot hesitated before making a reply. She then said, 'When I was a little girl, I was walking with my mother. We had, I think, been visiting my grandfather. My mother had a basket on her arm. It was spring. I remember the hawthorn bursting green in the hedge for we children used to nibble the buds. We had to pass the public house, a quiet enough place that rarely caused concern. Suddenly the narrow lane was filled with soldiers, or so it seemed to me, though I believe there were no more than five or six. I have since understood it was a recruiting party, for they had all sorts of raggle-taggle young men with them and a drum beating.'

Miss Arbuthnot stopped, as if she thought she had said too much.

Mrs Kingston said, 'That is surely not the end of the story.'

'I didn't wish to tire you with it.'

'But you don't in the least. You describe everything so exactly. How disconcerting for your mother.'

'They were all so very drunk, you see. My mother spoke to me, to tell me to hurry. She never could modify her French accent, and what with that and the fact of her being considered very pretty, the soldiers would come up and push and shove and say they would see her home and carry her basket. One seized her basket, which contained our seed potatoes, and they flew all over the road. I started to cry and hid in my mother's skirts, alarmed by their tall hats, red coats and rough manners. Years later, my mother would laugh about her predicament that day, and wish the basket had contained something less humdrum.'

'But how did you escape?'

'Their officer appeared. I thought him even more alarming, with his white breeches and all the shiny gold on his chest. He gave the men the sharp side of his tongue as well as the flat of his sword – what were they doing, molesting a lady? Though I didn't like them, I thought he was going to kill them when he got out his sword, so I howled some more from behind my mother. Having restored order, he was all bows and apologies, getting the potatoes picked up and insisting on seeing us home. I think he would have carried me, had I screamed less. Fortunately we had not far to go, for Mother said he was just as drunk as his men. Though I find it ridiculous, I still have that feeling of discomfort, I suppose something more, at the sight of soldiers.'

'But most understandable, Miss Arbuthnot. What a very unpleasant experience. I wonder your mother was ever able to laugh about it. I suppose one should never walk out without a manservant . . . but I dare say your mother didn't find that convenient.' Mrs Kingston made this addition in case a manservant had been beyond the means of the Arbuthnot household. 'Had you known Mr Wilder, he would have trounced this unfortunate recollection, for a more perfect gentleman there never was.'

The thought of Mr Wilder cast Mrs Kingston into a melancholy reverie. Had he not intended to marry her the moment he had completed his personal mission of putting Bonaparte to flight? He had shifted anxiously on the heel of his left boot as he spoke about the burden of being on active service while having the responsibility of a wife and child. He said he had left the Guards on marrying Lottie's mother and launched into a dissertation on the war between duty and inclination. England needed him, though his part could be but a small one as a humble infantry officer. He hoped he could say, without undue immodesty, that if he had any natural talent it was for soldiering, and he never should have married so young and given it up. He saw, only too clearly, he must make amends and offer his services in any menial capacity it was seen fit to place him.

Mrs Kingston had teased him a little, for she could not imagine him doing anything in the least menial, at which he had laughed and agreed it had been more a figure of speech than anything else, but he was determined to do his duty. She asked if he had no duty to his parents and his child, to which he had replied his child was in better hands than his and it was not as if he was the only son, though he said he had no intention of allowing the warlike young Thomas to fill his shoes. His brother's only interests could lie in trunnions and capsquares. Mrs Kingston, having no idea what these could be, was about to say something more, when he made her laugh by suggesting that the emotions of artillery men were stifled by their having to do too many calculations.

Again becoming serious, he had given his opinion of the war as it stood. The French soldier could not function without Bonaparte at his head; the Russians had tied the emperor into a disastrous knot. He, Lyndon Wilder, must hasten to assist in the decisive blows that would drive the French back over the Pyrenees and into kingdom come. Mrs Kingston, recalling the whole conversation as though it had been yesterday, thought now that the French might indeed be driven back over the Pyrenees, it was Lyndon Wilder who had gone to kingdom come.

Seeing that Miss Arbuthnot had discreetly taken herself to the window while her hostess was preoccupied, she said, 'I'm sorry, but the mention of Mr Wilder made me pensive. He would take himself off so much against his dear mother's wishes, but of course she understood his gallantry, his determination to do his duty, though I doubt she will ever recover from the shock of his death. He died a hero, and that is the only compensation a mother can have. I shall feel it sorely when Horatio goes away to join the navy.'

Miss Arbuthnot paused before replying. Eventually she said, 'And must he?'

'Why, yes. All the Kingstons have served in the navy.'

'Is it not unfortunate the decision must be made when a child is so young? It suits my brother very well, but then he is extremely robust.'

'Horatio shows quite an enthusiasm. You must judge for yourself how well he has learnt the names of all the ships that were engaged at Trafalgar. I make a sacrifice, of that there is no secret, but it is not for a woman to dispute these things.' Mrs Kingston felt she had made herself clear on the subject already but she added, 'I keep it all at the forefront of my mind that I may be always accustomed to it. I hope in this way that the moment of separation will be less painful.'

Miss Arbuthnot's expression was of one composing a suitable reply, but she was spared the trouble by the door bursting open and Mrs Kingston's little boy shooting through it as from a ship's cannon with a scarlet-faced Lottie in pursuit of him, the latter screaming, 'I'm not a little donkey, I'm not, I'm not, I'm not!'

'She doesn't know anything,' Horatio said. 'Not anything. She can't read.'

'But I'm not a little donkey,' Lottie continued to shriek. 'I can read some things.'

'Well, maybe you are not a donkey,' he replied, as if to placate her, but then he added, 'You're a lion with a big curly yellow mane and a terrible, fierce temper.'

'I'm not, I'm not,' Lottie continued to shout, but then realizing that a lion was a better alternative to a donkey, she ran to Miss Arbuthnot to ask if she could scratch and bite.

Mrs Kingston was transfixed by the outrageous behaviour of the visiting child, albeit encouraged by her own son, but seemed able to do nothing. Instead Miss Arbuthnot spoke, in a manner so vivid that both children forgot themselves and burst out laughing: 'If you were a lion, you could swallow Master Horatio whole and spit out his bones as indigestible.' She then said, more seriously, 'But as you are the guest of his mother, I don't think it would be very polite to do so, any more than entering the drawing room and screaming at the top of your voice is polite.'

'But he told me I was a little donkey,' Lottie said.

'I dare say to Master Kingston, who is clever at his books, you are, but that is because he won't have understood that some people take longer over these things than others.'

Mrs Kingston, galvanized by Miss Arbuthnot's rational tone, said, 'Horatio, I am astonished at your being so unkind and rude. Fancy shaming your mother in this way.'

Horatio said, 'I'm sorry, Mother, but honestly, Lottie can't spell "England".'

Lottie turned sad, questioning eyes on her governess. 'You said "ing" was I-N-G. You said it just this morning and I was pleased to have remembered it.'

'You are right and I did, and I am sorry to have misled you. It is the I-N-G at the end of the word that says "ing". As for England, it is a naughty English word that sounds one thing and is spelt another. Tomorrow we will write it out and if Mrs Kingston should be kind enough to invite you again, for she may well hesitate, you will be able to show Master Kingston just where it is on the globe.'

Mrs Kingston, relieved that Lottie's tantrum had subsided and making a mental note never to entertain the child without her governess, said, 'You will make yourself ill, Lottie, getting into such a state, though I think it very naughty of Horatio to tease you.'

Miss Arbuthnot thought Lottie's constitution up to any amount of tantrums but, rather than comment, she suggested there might be a shuttlecock and some battledores, in which case they could go outdoors together. Mrs Kingston rang for a servant to look in all the cupboards for the necessary articles, which she was sure she possessed but had never made use of. She thought it too much for Lottie to play such an energetic game and then to walk home: she would send them back in her carriage. Miss Arbuthnot thanked her but said she had faith in Miss Wilder having the energy to walk across the park.

Out on the lawn they played with the battledores. Lottie, so long as the shuttlecock came reasonably within her reach, for she did not deign to run, stood with her stout legs braced, the battledore clasped in both hands, her eye fixed on the missile, which she hit with a satisfactory thwack. Mrs Kingston was no natural athlete but she did her best with dainty strokes and little squeals of vexation when she missed, while her son ran about good-humouredly, his spindly form and flailing limbs in any place but the right one.

Later in the day Miss Arbuthnot and Lottie were to be seen marching back across the park, singing loudly and cheerfully all the songs that came to Miss Arbuthnot's mind that might keep her pupil in motion.

> 'When Britain fi-i-irst, at heaven's command,
> Aro-o-ose from the a-a-a-zure main,

Arose, arose, arose from out the a-azure main,
This was the charter, the charter of the land,
And guardian a-a-angels sang this strain . . .'

Lottie stopped to say, 'I'm not a little donkey, am I?'

'No, indeed, but you will have to work hard if you don't want people to think it. Myself, I think you are a little lion, especially when it comes to hitting a shuttlecock.'

At dinner Lord and Lady Charles sat at opposite ends of their dining-table, the extensive space between them peopled by ghosts: their daughters, all metamorphosed from pretty, cheerful girls to married women with children of their own; and their sons, Lyndon just younger than his sisters, and Thomas, much younger still, the unexpected Thomas, the joker at the end of the pack. Lord and Lady Charles could see them all in the mind's eye, from Georgiana down to Thomas, either here at Ridley or in the dining room of their town house, but it was Lyndon's slender form, the one true ghost, from which they could not flee. Lady Charles wondered at what age he had been permitted to escape the nursery in order to take his dinner with the rest of the family. She thought perhaps eight or nine. Was it winter or summer? What had he worn? She could see his little suits in wool or cotton, dark red, dark blue, dark green, short in the leg, his slippers dangling from his toes or kicked off altogether; his lawn shirt, the soft white collar brushed by the buttercup curls, the delicate face, the pink and white of sweet peas. He would not have cared for such musings: he was not an effeminate child.

Lord Charles said, 'Could we but start life over again when all our babes were happy children. We could live that bit again and again, dispensing with the rest.'

Lady Charles thought her husband had not been responsible for nursing the young through whooping cough and scarlatina. Neither had he appeared to suffer quite as she did the agony of Lyndon's departures for school. Lyndon himself had seemed untroubled by the separations, but was that not the buoyant nature of the child? Of course it was necessary to become accustomed to children leaving. The girls had stayed at home until they married, when their departures were abrupt, not altogether pleasant, but certainly mitigated by reflection on the suitability of the match and of a task completed. Their absence did nothing for the dining-table, but Lyndon's marriage had brought his bride to Ridley: a separate establishment for the young couple had never been considered. Not that Lyndon stayed at home, even as a married man, but they all migrated to the house in Stratton Street at the start of the London season. Thomas was the one who had gone away and showed no inclination to return. It occurred to Lady Charles as an anomaly that the child least attached to Ridley should be the one destined to inherit the estate. Their youngest they could picture least! Had he been there at all, or was he a figment of the mind?

In silence, Lord Charles picked up the silver soup ladle with the fine fluted bowl and carefully spooned chicken soup from the tureen into their plates. They ate little: they had not the heart for eating.

Lady Charles's mind now returned to Lyndon, but her husband's had strayed to Lottie. He said, 'Should Lottie sing so much? I am forever hearing singing and music from the schoolroom, and today, all across the park, so loud and cheerful, not very ladylike, and when one considers her situation . . .' There was a pause in which his words trailed into nothing. He thought he was being ridiculous. Should not an orphaned child be cheerful if it could?

'One wonders how she can,' Lady Charles replied, 'but then she is just a child. Should I ask Miss Arbuthnot to remind Lottie that she is bereaved? I wonder Miss Arbuthnot does not think of it for herself. It is a little insensitive. I understand from Georgie she lost her own mother at fourteen. Such an awkward age.'

'Perhaps it is unhealthy for a child to grieve long.'

'But what I impress upon her now is all she will have of her father. Lottie must not forget what she has lost. In her he lives.'

'In that case, we should allow the child to sing and make a noise. Nothing much kept Lyndon down.'

'Lyndon was never raucous or uncouth,' Lady Charles replied, offended.

'But he was a boisterous child.'

Lady Charles decided against demeaning herself or Lyndon's memory with bickering, besides which she thought it irrelevant. Lottie was female, and therefore not expected slavishly to copy her father. Instead she said, 'Miss Arbuthnot wishes Lottie to have a dog and a garden to dig and plant.'

'And does Lottie want to dig and plant?'

'I haven't asked her.'

'She can have a little spade to try it. As for a dog, we always had dogs. You know I like a dog myself. It is you who doesn't.'

'They are dirty,' Lady Charles said, repeating old issues.

'Lottie could have one upstairs.'

'But then it must be trailed all through the house when it wants to go out.'

'It could go out through the back door.' Lord Charles thought of a little dog with pleasure, of its nose on his knee and its comfortable body pressing against his leg under the table.

Lady Charles said, 'The dog would be everywhere and Lottie will lose interest in it.' So it had been when they had given Lyndon his spaniel.

Lord Charles thought of dogs everywhere, asleep by the fire in the library or in the office where he sat for hours and wrestled with his affairs. He said, 'Do you remember that huge dog we had to keep away thieves?'

'It was to roam about.'

'We had two good horses stolen from the park . . . Tally, a favourite . . . I don't remember the dog did any good, but I remember Thomas, as a child, getting into the kennel and spending the night there.'

'And I thought he would have caught a chill and the dog would have savaged him.'

'It would have known Thomas and it was not so very fierce.'

This incident, sufficiently distant to be almost forgotten, was now awoken and considered, while Lord and Lady

Charles picked at modest portions of chicken and fish. Why had this small boy, clad only in a nightshirt, been fast asleep with the dog and not found to be missing until the morning? Why was the dog not doing its duty by roaming the park and keeping the tinkers at bay? Thomas had been severely chastised for spending the night out of doors and for his silence when asked to provide an explanation. Lady Charles remarked that it was no clearer now than it had been then, but he had ever been a wilful child.

A servant came in with a bowl of nuts and a dish of apples and pears. At the same time the door was opened for Lottie.

'I wish they wouldn't open doors for me when it is very easy to open them myself,' she said. Susan had brushed out her hair to absurd dimensions. Her gown was her best but it was now too short. Her grandmother thought her yet thinner and, immediately alarmed, wondered if she sickened for something.

Lottie, rather than rush into the arms of Lady Charles, seated herself at the table precisely halfway between her grandparents, upon whom she bestowed a benevolent smile.

'Well, dearest,' Lady Charles said, 'you walked all across the park and back again. You must be very tired.'

Lottie contemplated the usefulness of being tired: it often meant being sent early to bed. She said, 'And I played at battledore with Horatio.'

'As well? My dearest, you must be quite, quite exhausted. Charles, do you think she looks pale?'

'No,' Lord Charles replied, for he thought just the opposite. 'And did you win?'

'I was much better than Horatio. He is a mere twig of a boy,' Lottie replied, helping herself to a pear.

'Lottie, allow me to peel it,' her grandmother said.

'Give me the knife. I shall do it.'

'You are too young for a knife, dearest.'

'No. Miss Arbuthnot showed me. I peeled an apple as well as anyone, Miss Arbuthnot said.' She held out an imperious hand for the knife, which Lady Charles reluctantly surrendered.

'Do be careful, dear.'

'A knife is not a toy. It won't cut you so long as you give it your attention. You had better not speak to me until it's done.'

Lottie peeled the pear. Pleased with herself, she cut it into segments. They overlapped, cream and green, on the china plate with its sprigs of forget-me-nots and roses.

'You should hold the knife in your right hand,' Lord Charles said.

'No.'

'I do wonder at that,' Lady Charles remarked.

'Miss Arbuthnot says it's better to learn with the left hand than not learn at all.'

'Oh dear,' Lady Charles said. 'Miss Arbuthnot has such firm and contrary notions for a young person.'

Her husband, whom nature had intended to be left-handed, a leaning firmly eradicated, thought of all the peculiar terms associated with the left, from the cap-handed to the bend sinister.

Lottie said, 'I write quite neatly with my left hand, but I have to mind I don't smudge. That, Miss Arbuthnot says, is the real trick. Now, if I were to write backwards, it wouldn't be a problem, but my friends and relations would have to hold my writing up to the glass in order to read it.' Here she stopped to laugh. 'Miss Arbuthnot thinks this too great an inconvenience. Writing is, we must understand, a means of communication.'

Lord and Lady Charles exchanged startled looks over their granddaughter's head. Miss Arbuthnot would surely prove too out of the ordinary, and they never should have left the matter to Georgie – but none other than Miss Arbuthnot had persuaded Lottie to write.

'Communication,' Lady Charles said feebly, 'is a long word for a little girl.'

Lottie was affronted.

'Finish your pear, dear,' her grandmother continued, 'and I will read you a story.'

'Grandpapa shall tell me one,' Lottie said, getting down from the table and laying her hand on Lord Charles's arm.

'Well, well, my pet, Grandpapa doesn't have any stories.'

'Of course you do. You must think of one. I'll get on your lap.'

Lady Charles, rejected, gazed on her husband as he laboriously gathered Lottie, who was solid, on to his knee. She thought, with anguish, of the lissom Lyndon at the same age, yet Lottie reminded her of Lyndon, who had been another child expecting to have his own way.

Lord Charles started, 'Once upon a time . . .' And there paused for inspiration.

'Go on, go on,' Lottie urged.

'Not if you are rude.'

'Please.'

'Once upon a time there was a little boy who went out of

doors in the middle of the night. Think of that. It was dark and the rain came down in torrents, but he would creep out in his little nightshirt and his little nightcap. The door wasn't locked. That was strange.'

'Was he as old as me?'

'I'm not quite sure. Perhaps he was eight years old.'

'Old enough to go to sea,' Lottie said. 'And did he catch his death, as Susan says I will if I lean out of the window in my shift?'

'No, that was not the case. Don't talk about your shift, darling. There was a great big dog kennel for a great big dog, and into that he crept.'

'With the dog?'

'Yes.'

'And was the dog fierce? Did it eat him up and spit out the bones as indigestible?' Lottie asked, delighted.

'Certainly not,' Lord Charles replied, shocked. 'The dog kept him warm and there he was in the morning, perfectly snug, though the doctor came to see if it had done him a mischief.'

'And,' Lottie said triumphantly, knowing the conclusion to most such stories, 'that boy was my papa.'

'Ah, but he wasn't. It was your Uncle Thomas and he never would say why he did it.'

Lady Charles thought her husband's mind ran too much on their remaining son. Was it conceivable he saw him as a substitute for Lyndon? She concluded it could not be so, that he was merely concerned for the future of the estate. If it should pass to a stranger, he had told her, there was little provision for herself, but she thought anxiety had confused him: their London house in Stratton Street was not in the entail. If the worst should come to the worst, she supposed it could be let. To sell it would be wrong, for it had been in the family for several generations, was large and imposing, and from where else could her granddaughter enter society and make an appropriate marriage?

Miss Arbuthnot was surprised by how little could happen in the course of a few weeks. Lottie was allowed her own plot among the vegetables and, to everyone's astonishment, she dug it over industriously. It was a melancholy time of year for a child to receive the gift of a garden, a few bulbs and some broad beans, which were all that could be planted before spring, but Miss Arbuthnot, who missed the cottage-garden borders of her father's vicarage, knew the pleasures of drawing up plans. She and Lottie measured the ground, drew it to scale, made calculations, wrote on wooden pegs and purloined a ball of string from the potting-sheds. The garden became Lottie's chief subject of conversation: she drew pictures of different vegetables and flowers, but the vegetables were to be paramount. She included the flowers to please her grandmother, who thought her taste in vegetables mannish. Lady Charles's activities had never extended beyond deadheading the roses, should the correct implement be placed in her hand, or possibly picking the sweet peas, so she was bewildered by Lottie's sturdy attacks on the dull earth. There was no moderating the child; in her grandmother's eyes, she exceeded gentility, and the blame lay with Miss Arbuthnot to whom she dropped a hint. Miss Arbuthnot replied, calmly, that Lottie now knew how to find a square yard. She would have liked to say more but her father had warned her of the dangers in self-congratulation. Lottie understood things that had previously meant nothing to her – a line of ten beans, planted six inches apart, would take up a yard and a half – and was now prepared to tackle the written word so long as it had some practical application. It was a dilemma to know how much of this could be impressed on Lady Charles, whose priorities, though she wished her granddaughter to be literate, lay elsewhere.

Horatio Kingston was inspired by Lottie to have a garden of his own. He could not turn the earth neatly but Lottie would arrive in a pair of stout boots, a capacious linen pinny over her black frock, ribbons for tying her hair in any available colour, for they were soon lost, and straighten the edges for him. This she did with an air of patronage, counselling him the while on taking care while he ran with a can of water, slopping it all the way. The children's preoccupation with their gardens meant that when Lady Charles visited Mrs Kingston, bringing Lottie with her, they could leave the pair to play unsupervised.

Sitting very upright in Mrs Kingston's drawing room, Lady Charles pondered complexities and contradictions. She said, 'Horatio was, I suppose, too little a boy to have known his father.'

'He was barely six months old when Lieutenant Kingston died. He suffered no grief, for which I am glad, but not to have known his father is deprivation indeed.'

'Quite so. Lottie must remember Lyndon and *understand* her loss.' Lady Charles leant forward in her stiff-backed chair as she spoke.

'Dear little Lottie, she will revere his name, I'm sure.'

'But in a trice she forgets.'

'She is not very old.'

'One must be glad that children are happy,' Lady Charles said, but without conviction.

'Oh, yes,' Mrs Kingston replied, slightly confused, but then adding, 'Miss Arbuthnot is very clever at keeping the dear children cheerful and busy.'

'You don't think she keeps Lottie *too* cheerful?'

'How could she? Lottie does her lessons.'

Lady Charles saw that she was not understood, but felt unable to say more than she had. Surely Mrs Kingston, of all people, should understand the necessary depth of grief for such a one as Lyndon Wilder.

Mrs Kingston then said, 'Of course, I don't believe Miss Arbuthnot to be exactly as she seems.'

'How so?' Lady Charles asked, a trifle disturbed.

'Oh, I didn't mean to alarm you. Miss Arbuthnot is so calm, so moderate, and she laughs and smiles exactly when it is required of her.'

'Estimable,' Lady Charles replied. 'I imagine those are the very qualities for which Georgie chose her.'

'But behind it all there is something else.'

'Don't I tell you not to read so many novels?' Lady Charles answered with a smile.

'Miss Arbuthnot has an air of sadness about her.'

'What can she know of sadness at her age?'

'The loss of her mother.'

'Very unfortunate, but not at all recent.' Others could grieve, but not for ever.

'What about affairs of the heart?'

'Neither lasting nor significant in youth.'

'But are such things less painful at eighteen than twenty-eight?'

'Yes.'

Mrs Kingston was not at all sure she agreed, but it was not in her nature to offer a contrary opinion to such a one as Lady Charles.

Lady Charles, who did not find the love affairs of governesses interesting, continued, 'Some foolish fancy her clergyman papa didn't approve,' thus dismissing the subject entirely.

Mrs Kingston, anxious, hoped her companion would find a new subject of her own choosing and was gratified by Lady Charles leaning forward and saying, in tones almost conspiratorial, 'Lord Charles continually writes to our son Thomas.'

Mrs Kingston, who could not see why he should not, replied, 'I hope this is some little consolation to him.'

'Oh, he always has written now and again and Thomas answered, but Thomas writes a dreary letter. He is interested only in the welfare of his troop and other such stuff, which is no doubt laudable but makes dull reading. No, I believe Lord Charles to be asking him to come home.'

'But that can only be a pleasure,' Mrs Kingston said.

'He will be reluctant to come,' Lady Charles continued, as if Mrs Kingston had not spoken. 'He is married to the Horse Artillery. Lord Charles has only hinted at wanting him home. He is afraid we will disagree.'

'But it will be such a relief to have Major Wilder away from the front.'

'That is true. It would be a great disaster should anything happen to him. Yes, for that I shall be delighted to see him.

Lord Charles and I cannot live for ever and he is our heir. I hope I may live to discharge my duty to my granddaughter, but beyond that, what is there? For the sake of Lottie and Lord Charles it is my duty to go on as best I can but it is with difficulty I retain a measure of sanity, but Thomas has none of the sensitivity, the delicacy, of my dearest lost boy. I am sure he will be good and dutiful in his way, but the house is given over to grief. How can one grieve for a brother whose death makes one the heir to a property such as Ridley? What had Thomas previously? His army pay, six months in arrears, if we are to believe what we are told, and the blue jacket, the overalls and the pelisse of an officer in the Royal Horse Artillery. I doubt Lord Charles has paid his allowance of late. How can I have him here, he who must in his heart be always rejoicing at his good fortune?'

Lady Charles broke down in a paroxysm of weeping. Such was her distress that Mrs Kingston could not contain her own, but she succeeded in ringing the bell for a servant. Lady Charles made an effort to control the violence of her feelings and looked a little coldly on her friend. Suddenly she wished she had confided less.

Mrs Kingston was aware that she had erred, but did not know in what manner, beyond her endeavour to suppress a sense of shock. Surely grief had distorted what should have been Lady Charles's proper assessment of her younger son. Inheriting Ridley would indeed be a great advancement for Major Wilder but it was no bar to his mourning the loss of such an elder brother, no doubt his mentor, probably his idol.

She said, 'I am sure you will find Major Wilder deeply perplexed by the impossible task of having to fill his brother's shoes. I dare say he had no notion of ever doing so.'

Lady Charles was confused. Could Mrs Kingston be right? Even suppose she were, that did not mean Thomas would be mourning Lyndon. He had never seemed to want to have anything to do with his brother. She said, 'Perhaps the disparity in their ages made for a difficulty.'

Mrs Kingston did not understand to what Lady Charles referred. She replied, vaguely, 'I dare say that might have been so.'

'A last child really was a rude shock,' Lady Charles said, unexpectedly smiling, 'but my father was delighted when it turned out another boy. I did have a pang of conscience I didn't nurse him, for I nursed all the others.'

'You were exhausted.'

'So I was, though he entered the world with the minimum inconvenience, but the nursing of an eighth child after I had put such to one side . . . A wet nurse seemed the answer. I remember Georgie begging to take a peep at him. I let her hold him on her lap, for she was quite old enough, and I said, "There's a little brother for you," and she said, taking me literally, "Oh, is he really mine?" Such a sweet-natured child, dear Georgie, I let her think it. She was pleased he was a boy, for she knew the value of boys and remembered how the church bells rang for Lyndon. She wanted them rung for Thomas, but he wasn't the heir.'

'I should so like more children,' Mrs Kingston said. 'What is one but inadequate?'

With the two children occupying one another so

satisfactorily, Mrs Kingston was also obliged to spend time with Miss Arbuthnot, but she did not mind this in the least for she liked company.

Miss Arbuthnot reviewed the matter in her weekly letter to the vicarage in Devonshire.

> *Now, Papa, you have always urged me not to gossip, but what is gossip? Dr Johnson says, among other things, 'mere tattle; trifling talk'. You mean not to speak lightly, or perhaps not to speak at all, of other people, especially of those employing me, so of course I should prefer not to, but Mrs Kingston talks of them all the time. Much of it is a vague suggestion she might have been engaged to be married to the late Lieutenant Wilder, but how could I ever comment on such a thing? Of what, may I ask, are we to talk? Mrs Kingston's little boy, whom I like, is quite a fine subject. On wet days, or when they are satisfied with the state of their gardens, he is happy to help Lottie with reading and writing. His rather frantic brain tumbles out all sorts of plays and stories for which Lottie must draw the pictures and write the captions. However, half an hour is adequate to round him off nicely as a point of conversation with his mother. We may not speak of others, of politics, of religion. I think philosophy no part of Mrs Kingston; she is reading a novel of Mrs Radcliffe's, which will take her a month, so perhaps literature will not do. We are limited to the wonders of nature, and though few find them as wondrous as I, or so I tease myself into believing, they are soon exhausted, especially in winter. It will*

be easier in spring, for Mrs Kingston loves her garden and I shall be very happy to admire it and talk of it every day. At the moment she is preoccupied with the imminent return of her brother from his regiment in the Peninsula. While she says how delighted she is at his coming home, it seems she is uneasy about it, but this she puts down to the precarious state of his health. Sometimes I think she is altogether uncomfortable about him, so perhaps they do not really get on: I hear you growling at me for making such suppositions. Mrs Kingston is kind to me and I like her, but our worlds are disparate, our education and upbringing, but when her brother returns I dare say I shall not go there so much.

I am racking my brains for ways to keep Miss Wilder active and occupied over the long winter months. She is disappointed at the notion of having to put her garden to bed. It is a pity her grandmother is so adamantly against a little dog. It would suit Miss Wilder very well to feed, groom, walk and teach it to behave itself.

The letter was completed with the usual anxious enquiries for the health of her sisters and the request to forward letters from Bobby. It was then sealed and immediately taken downstairs to be laid on the chest in the hall ready for its removal to the post. Miss Arbuthnot needed to take her candle to complete this task as there showed only tiny trails of light beneath the occasional closed door as she traversed the lonely corridors of a house already dark of a winter evening. As she went, the letter in her hand, she thought of her family gathered round the fire at home. Was it the picture every exile, voluntary or otherwise, kept in the mind's eye? She thought it must be so, but it was better not to dwell on such, to allow something more original and less affecting to occupy the mind.

The chest in the hall was covered with leather, worn and scratched, brass studs at the corners. Miss Arbuthnot knew Lady Charles did not like it, old-fashioned and utilitarian as it was, for she had once remarked she did not care to have to keep apologizing for it. A simple light within a lantern relieved the gloom and palely illuminated the little pair of candlesticks the family would take up to bed. Two or three other letters lay near by, the uppermost of which was written in a hand that must once have been bold but now seemed to hesitate and wander; she knew it was that of Lord Charles. Even in the feeble light Miss Arbuthnot could not fail to read the direction, though she did so almost unconsciously: 'Maj. the Hon T. O. L. Wilder, RHA.'

She read no more than that; they all knew Major Wilder was in Spain. The letter would go care of the Royal Horse Artillery. What an uncertain journey such a missive would make, first to a port and then on, bundled up with other anxious letters for sons, husbands and brothers with their various regiments in foreign places, each one, Miss Arbuthnot supposed, 'seeking the bubble reputation even in the cannon's mouth.' Major Wilder might be alive when the letter was written and dead before he received it. The thought disturbed her. Bobby, her only brother, was cruising where? In the Atlantic, seeking alien ships, prize money, any engagement or adventure. And where was Maj.

the Hon. T. O. L.Wilder? Was he blockading San Sebastian or Pamplona? Was he in the Pyrenees, or could not the Horse Artillery climb mountains? She was ignorant of such things. Would he come home if his father requested it? The servants said his father should have him fetched home, though he was a relative stranger to the place, left as a boy and hardly seen since. She knew that might be Dr Johnson's 'mere tittle-tattle', but she could not be deaf to every utterance.

Miss Arbuthnot proceeded in the direction of the back stairs. She only used the front flight when accompanying her pupil. It had never been made clear to her which stairs she should use, so this was a compromise. As she went she wondered at the oddity of allowing sons to go to war when there was no apparent financial necessity, though she supposed younger sons must make their way. Now the younger son was the heir and it seemed there was no immediate other, only women who, in the scale of things, were of no account. Climbing the stairs, she considered the initials of the distant major. The T was for Thomas and the L for Lyndon, that being the family name, for even Lottie had it after a string of others. The O surely stood for Octavius, for was he not the eighth child of Lord and Lady Charles Wilder? By the time Miss Arbuthnot reached her room she also thought he might have his birthday in the month of August.

Lady Charles decided it was an appropriate time for Lottie to work a sampler. Not only would it aid her skill in needlework, rather lacking at the minute, but it could include some useful homily of an improving nature. After casting about for something suitable, she wrote, 'Diligence, industry and proper improvements of time are material duties of the young; to no purpose have they the best abilities, if they want activity for ever.'

Lottie showed little appreciation of her grandmother's efforts, even after she had been shown the piece of linen on which it was to be worked and all the pretty coloured silks from which she might choose two or three. Lady Charles was careful to read out any of the words that might be seen as difficult, but Lottie looked mulish. The task of marking the letters on to the fabric was assigned to Miss Arbuthnot, who might also draw a border of flowers, then Lottie could commence with the stitches, perhaps, if she was good, under the supervision of her grandmother.

As it was nearly the child's bedtime and she had on her face a look of peculiar intractability, Lady Charles thought to avoid a contretemps by a change of subject. She said, 'I hope you remember to say your prayers.'

'Yes, Grandmama, I say them every night. Our Fatherwhichart . . .' Lottie proceeded with the Lord's Prayer as if it were all one word.

Lady Charles interrupted her: 'Dearest, no, that is too dreadful. Say it after me, slowly. Try to understand it.'

Lottie wondered about trespasses. Her grandfather talked of trespassers, which was surely the same word, in a most unforgiving way but she did not think she could have any of her own to forgive. She knew trespassing was going where you were not allowed to go. She was not allowed in the kitchens or the pantries and had never been in either. Well, she thought, in a more compromising mood since there had been no further mention of the sampler, she must say these things if her grandmother thought it did her good.

Lady Charles then said, 'And who do you ask God to bless?'

'You and Grandpapa and Susan and Miss 'Buthnot and Miss 'Buthnot's brother who's gone to sea because Miss 'Buthnot loves him and the sea is rather dangerous. I wish Horatio didn't have to go, for I'm sure he won't like it.'

'Who, most important, have you forgotten?' Lady Charles asked, trying to keep the mortification out of her voice.

'My papa?' Lottie ventured, knowing it was the answer to much.

'Of course. How can you rattle on about Miss Arbuthnot's brother and forget your own papa?'

'I don't really forget,' Lottie replied, a little too quickly.

'I am most relieved to hear you say so.'

'But why does he need prayers?' Lottie asked.

'You must pray for all who are dear to you and for those less fortunate than yourself.'

'But as my papa is already gone to heaven, like you told me, he can't need any prayers at all.'

Her grandmother sighed. She said, 'Go to bed, Lottie. Susan will be waiting for you.'

Until the arrival of Captain Houghton, Mrs Kingston's brother, it was hard to say what did or did not change over that winter. Lord Charles attended to his affairs less and less frequently. He agreed to various things but failed to implement them. Appointments were made that he did not keep and people wearied of finding him in when told he was out.

There was a delicate increase in the air of neglect of which Lady Charles was aware but which did not sufficiently penetrate her cold little cabin of grief. Even before the news of Lyndon's death had reached them, things had not been right. Now it seemed not to matter; neither did she consider it her business to interfere with the masculine world of money and management. Her task was the house, which went on much as usual, the only significant change being Lottie's acceptance of her governess and serious signs of literacy in the schoolroom.

Captain Houghton was a subject much discussed both before and after his arrival. When he was at last ensconced in his sister's neat house overlooking the green, he was, disappointingly, far too ill to be seen. Miss Arbuthnot, bringing Lottie to play with Horatio, for Mrs Kingston said there was no reason for the children to be denied amusement, caught a glimpse of him through Mrs Kingston's drawing-room door, which was a little ajar, a thin, lanky officer, unshaven, laid out on the chaise-longue in his shirt sleeves, a rug thrown over him and a pair of boots askew on the carpet.

Lady Charles was nervous and abstracted at the thought of this officer, straight from the war, who might explain things or talk of the campaign. She knew he was most unlikely to have known her son, yet she hoped. Her imagination, hitherto sluggish, would swoop between his saying how sad he had been to learn of the death of such a dashing and heroic officer as Lieutenant Wilder, of whom all had heard, to his describing some dinner at which they had met. He would speak of Lyndon's wit and conviviality, and thus, for a moment or two, Lyndon would be alive again. Lady Charles knew that none of this would be said, yet she hoped. When Mrs Kingston's barouche rolled up to the Ridley front door after at least a week's absence, it contained, customarily, Mrs Kingston and no other. Lady Charles had received a note that her brother was too poorly to visit, but had felt that if he was not to be confined to his bed, able to lounge about downstairs, as Lottie had reported, he should make the effort to visit her.

Mrs Kingston entered the room with fifty apologies. She knew Lady Charles would be disheartened for she must have set store by learning something, if but little. Her dear Henry was so far from well: his appearance had shocked her more than she could say; she had burst into tears at the sight of him, so emaciated and weak, and that very evening he had run such a fever she thought he had returned merely to die. He had declined to see the apothecary or allow her to send for the doctor, telling her it would pass: given two or three days he would be better. His servant knew how to take care of him, administering the bark, a brown sticky mess, of which he had a supply.

'And is Captain Houghton a little better? Are the two or three days up?' Lady Charles asked, condescending to offer Mrs Kingston a clean handkerchief when the tears ran down her cheeks and her reticule proved empty.

'He is better, but not sufficiently so to risk the cold and the damp. Of course I have talked to him.' Mrs Kingston was glad of the delay while a servant brought in a glass of wine and some plum cake.

Lady Charles said, seeing Mrs Kingston's agitation, 'I am sure I cannot expect your poor brother to remember one officer out of so many thousands, even should they have met.' She said this but she still hoped.

'It is not that he cannot remember him but that he was never anywhere near him,' Mrs Kingston replied, trying to expunge from her mind her brother's actual words, which had been more to the tune of, 'For goodness' sake, Lucy, you silly goose, am I to recall every damned officer of no account who gets his head blown off?' She continued: 'We don't realize how large is the theatre of war.'

Captain Houghton had said, 'Why, our respective regiments are not even in the same division. I believe I was blockading San Sebastian while this fellow Wilder was dying in the Pyrenees, and many others with him. I have heard of Major Wilder of the Horse Artillery because we know of the artillery troops one way or another, not that I care for them. The officers are a bit too clever, or so they think. What do you suppose war is? Some sort of soldiers' picnic?'

'The different divisions,' Mrs Kingston proceeded, 'are often many miles apart. Mr Wilder was in the Sixth Division under General Picton, and of course my brother was not. I was borne up by childish hope.'

Lady Charles painfully relinquished hope: her boy was gone for ever. She turned away and stared, without purpose, out of the window.

Mrs Kingston then said, 'Henry confessed to knowing an officer in the same regiment as Mr Wilder.' She recalled, but did not repeat, her brother's actual words: 'Lucy, if you are going to blub, I'm sure I wish I had come anywhere but here to get my health back, if I ever do, which seems unlikely. I begin to think you took a shine to this Wilder fellow, and it's not just for the sake of his mother you pester me so. I'll confess to one thing: I was at Rugby with Captain Greenway whom I believe to have been in that regiment, though I have not clapped eyes on him since we both went out in the same leaky old tub of a transport ship, four years ago last March.'

'Of course,' Mrs Kingston said, 'I asked him why he had not responded to my letters, why he had not written to this Captain Greenway, since I had so especially requested it.' She sighed. 'What is the point of being cross and disappointed with a man as sick as my brother?'

Lady Charles said, 'Perhaps, when he is stronger, I will ask him, as a personal favour, if he would write to Captain Greenway.'

'Yes, yes, it would come better from you. I am sure he never has taken me seriously, always the little sister stuck in the schoolroom with the governess. It is an odd thing for my brother and I with our parents long gone and my poor, dear sister too. It is only he and I left, bar my little boy who is a perfect stranger to him and they show no sign of liking one another. We are not very familiar. I think Henry must sell his commission and settle down. He is cross at not getting his majority but, though he is nearly forty, he hasn't been a captain for so very long, nothing ever quite seeming to work out as it should, so I am puzzled as to how he thought the next step was to be achieved in a moment.'

Lady Charles was left to reflect on her folly of expecting too much from the presence of Captain Houghton. When she eventually met him a few days later, the incident was as fruitless as she had expected.

Lord Charles thought his wife should spend less time indoors. He knew he himself would have gone mad had he not the freedom of the estate in which to walk and ride, to wear himself out, which, at his age, was soon accomplished and done at the pace of a snail. Though the weather was indifferent, a little exercise, as she was not accustomed to it, might do her good. Lady Charles did not wish good to be done her, for surely to feel better, to be distracted from her loss, was a betrayal: a minute should not pass without a reference, in her mind, to Lyndon Wilder. Lord Charles, who did not understand her, requested she take his arm and walk on the terrace, for though overcast, it was not cold.

Ridley was a plain-looking house, perhaps a couple of hundred years old, red brick. The terrace, with dandelions poking from the cracks, overlooked two rectangular ponds, one of which was empty but for a combination of green slime and desiccated vegetation, while the water in the other was stirred only by the fish, which drifted up and down almost invisible under their canopy of weeds.

Lady Charles, who saw she had a duty to walk with her husband, said, 'What is the matter with the gardeners? They don't seem to do the work.'

'When old Robbins retired, we didn't take on anyone else.'

'But don't we need another, a younger man?'

'It is a small saving.'

'Saving, saving, saving. Why are we always saving?'

'We are short of funds.'

'But why?'

'Times change, unexpected expenses. It will pass. Don't trouble your head with it.'

Lady Charles made no further enquiries. Was she whimsical in thinking even the house and gardens seemed to mourn the bright and beautiful boy, the handsome youth, nurtured within their walls? The air of neglect was appropriate.

'But,' Lord Charles said, 'I must write again to Thomas. It seems there are difficulties attached to his returning.' He thought of the last letter he had received from his son.

Lady Charles was able to think of many reasons why their son should not come home that were easier to pronounce than the paramount one she now regretted confiding in Mrs Kingston. 'How can Thomas be of the slightest use? He will be an extra expense, wanting to entertain his friends. Besides, he won't wish to come. He has never been fond of Ridley.'

Lord Charles said, 'He had no need to be fond of it. Now he is heir to it.'

'Lyndon was your heir. You never demanded he should be at home.'

Lord Charles thought this ground too well covered, but he said, the same as ever, 'He would go. Now I have but the one heir. If we lose him, Ridley goes to a stranger, a man who knows no better than to abide in America, as far as one can tell. For all we know he may be occupied in some very menial capacity. Well, perhaps not a shoemaker or a shopkeeper, that may be going too far, but he can hardly be a gentleman, cousin or no. I am an old man. What becomes of you when I die?'

'What indeed?' Lady Charles had never imagined her manner of living could alter.

'Lottie, as you know, has something from her mother's estate. Your father, when entailing Ridley, allowed for your pin money but not much else. He was delighted when Lyndon was born and just as delighted, perhaps more so, by Thomas.'

Lady Charles paused to consider the undue delight on the part of her father at the birth of a second son. She thought it a pity he had been obsessed with the name of Wilder, for the estate was entailed on male heirs bearing that name. Had it not been so, Ridley could have passed to Lottie, and Thomas left to indulge his passion for the Horse Artillery. She said, 'I don't care for these entails. A man of your age should be allowed to leave his property as he sees fit.'

Lord Charles grunted. 'Entails have saved many an estate from annihilation, the heirs deprived of their natural inheritance, ruined. It is a very proper restriction.'

'But it prevents Lottie inheriting her father's estate, or what should have been his.'

Lord Charles came to an abrupt halt. 'Really, you must say these things especially to tease me.'

'No, I do not. Lottie could inherit Ridley and whoever she may marry could take the name Wilder, as you did yourself, presumably to your satisfaction.'

'It was not at all to my satisfaction: it was a condition imposed on me by your father. If it were possible, I would not consider leaving a single acre of Ridley to any but my remaining son. As he is also your son, how can you suggest such a thing? What has the boy done to offend you so, beyond not being his brother?'

At this Lady Charles broke down into tears and could make no rational reply: she knew there was no rational reply to make. She turned to her husband and said, 'You never loved Lyndon as I did.'

He dropped her arm abruptly and walked away from her, his once tall figure aged and weary. Abandoned, Lady Charles stood helpless on the weed-strewn terrace, under the grey sky, the tears cascading down her cheeks.

Lord Charles retreated to the library. He mused on his own miserable state, on that of his wife, on the discord between them. For himself, he wanted his surviving son at home, however awkward or tiresome Eleanor considered that might be. Of course she did not comprehend the confused state of their affairs, or of Ridley's, and neither did he consider it her business to do so, but Thomas, sooner or later, must understand everything, though when and in what manner any sort of explanation could take place, he could not imagine. He clung to the idea of Thomas's return as a solution to every difficulty. The last letter he had received from him, which he had not shown to his wife, was unsatisfactory. He took it from his desk and unfolded it for the tenth time. Was what Thomas said the exact truth or was he making excuses because he had no wish to take leave either now or later? He then thought, as he read the letter afresh, Thomas would not lie. How I malign him, my own son. At this minute he can take no leave, but neither does he want it . . . yet every day he is in increased danger of being killed.

My dear sir,

I received your last here, St Jean de Luz, this day. I dare say you are aware by now of the various actions that have taken place, in which I have been, with my troop, engaged. I can but write you a line or two for they are at this minute making up the post for England. I appreciate your desire for my return but I cannot abandon my position, even should I feel inclined to do so, until this army is in Paris. To do so would be a dereliction of my duty and I cannot contemplate it. You must also understand that should I ask for leave just now I would not be granted it. I dare say you may think my duty as a son is at odds with my duty as a serving soldier, which is no doubt the case, so I am relieved, at this minute, not to be my own master,

I remain your dutiful son,

T. O. L. Wilder

PART II

The horse was a grey Andalusian with a long, rippling tail and a mane that cascaded down neck and shoulder. It wore the paraphernalia of the military, a black sheepskin, a blue shabraque, while it high-stepped through the village, disdaining the muddy causeway beneath its neat little feet with genteel arrogance. Its rider, for it was a cold, damp day in mid-March, with a light, chill wind blowing, was shrugged inside a dark pelisse, the fur lining visible at collar and cuff, and grey pepper-and-salt overalls, with a broad red stripe running down over his boots. Where he might have worn some tall helmet and plume, his head was covered with a lower, less formidable forage cap with a short, gold tassel. His sword and sabretache dangled against the pale flank of the Andalusian. A mounted servant trailed some yards behind, leading a baggage horse, a piebald pony and a pair of greyhounds, the latter of which he had just caught up, for they had been running loose, as they had entered the village. The servant had more of a swagger than the master as he skilfully managed the assorted strings and ropes of his various charges.

The village street was otherwise almost empty. A boy driving a cow was distracted by the alien sight of a soldier, a stranger, with his long-tailed horse. Could he be a foreigner? With Bonaparte nearly trounced, they could expect to see foreigners, if not yet Frenchmen. The cow wandered on to a cabbage patch, a young woman with a baby on her hip ran from a cottage door waving a broomstick, and several dogs started a frenzy of barking.

The officer and his servant took not the least notice of this commotion. Only the greyhounds, a brindle and a white, twitched their ears and strained at their collars. At the top of the street the road divided to the left and the right, the right the main route and the left to the church. Here they hesitated, the Andalusian brought lightly to a halt. After a moment's indecision, the soldier dismounted stiffly, almost awkwardly, laying the reins on the horse's neck and saying, '*No te mueves.*' It seemed to be addressed to both servant and mount, with a little smile of confidence in their mutual willingness to oblige him.

The boy, having extracted the cow from the cabbage patch, had further abandoned it and run as hard as he could after the soldier. He stood in the mud where the road forked and, on hearing this foreign pronouncement, concluded the gentleman soldier really was a foreigner. He watched him walk away from the horse, taking off his hat to reveal short-cropped brown hair, shorter than was seen on any gentleman, but very soldierly, the boy thought. The man said another word, 'Procrastination,' as incomprehensible as the foreign tongue. Seeing the casual way in which the horse had been left to stand, and sensing an opportunity to gain a penny, the lad steeled himself to call out, ''Old yer 'orse, sir, if y' like.'

The soldier turned to look at him. The boy considered retreat. He thought he was looked at too long, that the officer, for he knew him to be an officer, might be of savage disposition, for was it not so in the army they tied you up and beat you until your bones came through your skin, but then the answer came. 'As you can see, he stands perfectly well for himself. Look to your duty. You have a cow to mind.'

The boy pulled off a ragged cap and touched his forehead. He knew authority when he met it, but the stranger had already passed through the lych-gate and gone on his way.

The path was paved with huge, uneven slabs of stone, each one familiar to the officer, and on either side a row of lime trees, pollarded. There was even a sharp familiarity in the metal ring that operated the latch of the door, smooth under his hand but heavy, he remembered, for a child to twist and lift.

English churches were, he observed dismissively, all the same inside, a similar amount of light filtering through dim, tall windows, at which the odd tortoiseshell butterfly could be found to beat its wings; an airless smell without the odour of incense or other doubtful things, gaudy ornamentation, to which he had become accustomed when contemplating how much of a troop could be sheltered in an ecclesiastical establishment. He was aware of the old cold flags underfoot exacerbating the clatter of his spurs.

Why turn in at the church? Resolution, he knew, must be summoned from within. Spirits, usually buoyant, must be re-sighted and aimed in their more customary direction. One had to set oneself in order, apply the pipe-clay and blacking, the brushes and combs, of one's own internal resources. Had he anything to say to God that it was not as well to say to himself? He thought himself contrary: vexed, amused, bereaved and disturbed, but whatever intention he might have had in making a direct appeal to God was terminated on finding he was not alone.

Two men were measuring a large section of wall. One, wizened and elderly, he recognized as the sexton. The other he could not place; he supposed him a church warden, a member of the vestry. They looked up at the sight of him, surprised. The sexton said, 'Good-day to you, sir.'

The warden, nonplussed, said, 'Cold for the time of year.'

The sexton, naturally garrulous, explained their activity: 'There's to be a girt monument here, and we be measuring up for it. We can't alter the space, that's what I say, short of shifting the pew, and where's they to sit what normally takes it?'

'No, it's to be made to the space,' the warden said patiently.

'This 'ere monument'll be the grandest thing what there is,' the sexton continued. 'Church won't know itself. No church round 'ere 'as the like. Angels and archangels covered all fancy and as much writing as would fill a book.'

The soldier made no rejoinder, beyond a slight inclination of his head and then half turning away. Now the sexton took his appearance amiss. Why should the fellow be clanking about the church with his sword on? An officer ought to know there was no place for swords in church, or boots and spurs, but neither warden nor sexton was bold enough to voice their disapproval while they puzzled over his presence. He began to pace about slowly, stopping here and there, apparently reading worn cursive script on the stones of the chancel floor, looking up at the windows, the odd fragment of coloured glass that had escaped the attention of Cromwell's soldiers long ago. Like other soldiers, they had understood destruction best. The church in which the officer had sought temporary solace merely reminded him of other churches, other places, of meagre villages, dusty plains, high mountains, gum cystus, cork trees, boulders and arcaded towns, then of soldiers and more soldiers and the rattle of the artillery as it crossed some massive bridge the Romans built. These images preoccupied him, but not entirely: he was of a practical nature and there was more to fill his mind than mere nostalgia. Suddenly he ceased his aimless wandering and turned back to the tall, blank wall where the sexton was folding up the measure and the warden was jotting in his pocket book.

Speaking for the first time, he said, 'In whose memory is the monument? May he be worthy of it.'

Miss Arbuthnot and Lottie froze on the stairs, halfway up, as the front door swung wide, the light splitting the gloom of the shuttered hall, which they viewed from their elevation through an open double door, as if it were a theatre set. It was odd that a stranger should enter thus, for none but Lord Charles came or went unannounced. Miss Arbuthnot could not quite put aside her feelings of unease at the sight of a uniform, though she knew there was no need for it and was indeed ashamed of her weakness. What was uniform after all? A sort of fancy dress to frighten enemies, a tall hat to make a man formidable. The soldier thrust open the door and stood in the shaft of light, a silhouette, bare-headed, the short black fur-lined pelisse and the red stripe on the overalls signifying his profession. He stood there for only a second or two, before striding purposefully to the window and folding back the shutter, illuminating the room in one sweeping gesture.

Lottie, mesmerized, indifferent to Miss Arbuthnot tugging at her hand, whispered, 'Is that my Uncle Thomas?'

Alert to being observed, the soldier turned abruptly and Lottie bolted up the remainder of the stairs, Miss Arbuthnot scampering after her.

'Hey,' he called, though softly, 'don't run away,' but they were gone.

He smiled at their precipitous retreat. It was time the little girl was out of mourning. He returned to the window, though the view disturbed him. Why take the oaks from the park and not replace them? He had seen where last year's cow parsley had billowed at the lodge gates and the nettles crowded the drive. Was this the effect that Lyndon's death had had on his father? The house was shrouded like a mausoleum and it would soon be necessary to beat one's way to the door through undergrowth and brambles. Where were the servants? The stableyard had been deserted and the house seemed the same, beyond the escaping black-clad child and her attendant.

He turned again to the hall, placing his forage cap on the side table. He espied the butler making towards him from a distant corridor. When the man, an obsequious fellow, came up to him, he said, 'I hope you're well, Slimmer.'

'Oh, sir, most kind of you to ask. You didn't ring. I'm as well as can be expected, seeing the sad state we're in, her ladyship so distressed and the master not much better. They never will get over it, of that I'm sure. I hope I may presume on my long acquaintance with the family to congratulate you on your majority.'

Major Wilder thought his majority would be of little use to him, but did not say so, or that he thought Slimmer presumptuous. In Slimmer's eyes his elevation would be of a different sort, but not one upon which he could be congratulated.

Slimmer said, 'You are expected, though earlier than anticipated . . . Oh dear, the shutters are open. Her ladyship doesn't like them so.' He glanced at Major Wilder to see if he might close them again.

Major Wilder said, 'Never mind the shutters.' He crossed the hall, passed through the double doors and approached the stairs. He was thinking of various previous homecomings, his return from school with Lyndon, his father on the steps, saying, 'Well, well, Thomas, you have grown,' after he had embraced Lyndon. He always said that for want of anything else. They would go upstairs, wash, change, go down to the drawing room and find their mother seated there in dignified but trembling anticipation of her elder son's arrival. It was an unvarying ritual she must have enjoyed, he thought: the careful registering of the carriage going out to meet the coach, the crunch of its return on the gravel, the noise and bustle in the hall, the light footstep of her beloved on the stair and, at last, Lyndon in her arms. As the younger son, he was neither jealous nor resentful. Lyndon was the heir to Ridley and Thomas had no particular interest in gaining the attention of his mother. In a day or two he would be back on the coach wending his way to his sister. Such had been his return to Ridley, until Lyndon had left school and he had returned alone.

At the top of the stairs he hesitated. Where were his quarters? He should have asked Slimmer. Was it intended he should still occupy the room looking out over the stableyard that had been his as a boy? It was adequate for a boy but not for a man taking up permanent residence, if it was to be permanent. It was whither his feet took him, but when he opened the door he saw it had not been prepared for him. The bed was not made and a dust sheet was thrown over the only chair. It seemed unfamiliar, too small, though the books he had had as a boy were lined up on the shelf. He crossed to the window and looked out. His servant, York, was dismantling the packs from his baggage horse; the piebald pony still had its panniers. The greyhounds had been tied together and left to their own devices. The Andalusian was impatiently swinging his long tail. How many times had he witnessed just such a scene, York and his Portuguese servant, whom reluctantly he had been compelled to leave behind, making the best of whatever billet they had been assigned, all be it no more than the shade of a cork oak. He had never thought to see it replicated in the stable yard at Ridley.

Major Wilder closed the door and returned to the landing. Where was his father? He could not wander about indefinitely. Besides, York had not yet brought up his bags. Opposite him were Lyndon's rooms. He was most unlikely to be sleeping there. Impatiently he ran down the stairs and made his way along a variety of passages to the library. He entered impatiently, without knocking, wondering why he had not gone there in the first place.

Lord Charles sat crouched at his desk, his back to the door. Major Wilder said, 'Sir,' tentatively, afraid of startling him.

His father stood up and turned round. 'Why, Thomas, Slimmer didn't tell me . . .'

They approached each other down the length of the room. Lord Charles thought, My younger son is a soldier, thirty years old, with a cropped head and a fur-lined black pelisse, little circles of braid on the sleeve to denote the cannon balls of his profession. He is no longer a schoolboy with a pointed chin and a mop of curls.

Why he should have expected him to be so, he could not have explained. Within a few feet of this sturdy officer of the Royal Horse Artillery he burst into uncontrollable tears.

Major Wilder, perturbed, for he had never seen his father cry and was uncertain whether the tears were for himself or Lyndon, anxious lest this collapse of morale should lead to a physical one, said, 'You had better sit down, sir.' His father had turned into a frail old man.

Slimmer was at the door but before he could enter Major Wilder blocked his way.

'I was just coming to tell his lordship you were here, sir.'

'Why not before?'

'I've been with her ladyship.'

Major Wilder accepted this. 'My servant, York, will be in with my baggage. Tell him where he is to go and that he is to unpack my portmanteau but nothing else. Show him his room.'

'Is Mr York indoor or outdoor staff?'

'He fulfils all functions. I shall expect him to be housed

in the greatest comfort, for he has certainly earned it.'

Slimmer backed away to delegate these duties to the footman. Had MajorWilder forgotten the dignity of his position as butler at Ridley? And a man was either indoor or outdoor staff, not something of both.

'And, Slimmer, tell him to bring in the dogs.'

'The dogs!' Slimmer said, aghast.

'The dogs,' Major Wilder repeated.

Slimmer went. Lord Charles looked up from his position on a hard-backed library chair, halfway down the room. He could not help a smile. 'Did you say dogs, Thomas?'

'Why, yes, I did. Now you look better.'

'It was relief, Thomas, relief that you are here.'

Lady Charles had initially thought the return of her younger son would be more than she could bear, and that he had shown no sign of taking leave, or even attempting to, had pleased her. Lord Charles had written to Thomas's commanding officer, first asking him to use his influence, then beseeching him to give up their son. Thomas had made it plain he would not return until the end of the war. Unexpectedly he had changed his mind.

Lady Charles, too, had had a change of heart. She had been cruelly disappointed in Captain Houghton, who had given her not the smallest item of information worth receiving on the awful subject of Lyndon's death. When Thomas came home, he must reveal all. Had he not Lyndon's things, his sword, his watch and seals, probably his uniforms, though he had not mentioned them in his letter to his father? She longed for all these things and, most of all, for the small brass-bound mahogany writing box she had herself supplied with sealing wax, pens and paper; and had filled the little, square inkwells, with their ingenious lids to prevent spillage. She had included a pocketbook for 1811 and had sent another for 1812, though he had given her no reason to suppose he wrote in them. Had he but penned a few lines, he would speak to her once more, if from the grave. Would those pocketbooks be tucked inside the lid or slid within the secret drawer? She could see this box in her mind's eye, the green baize lining and the inscription on the brass plate, J. L. Wilder: John Lyndon Wilder.

Without Thomas, there was nothing and, perhaps of greater significance, Thomas had visited Lyndon's regiment to take charge of his kit. Though he had not said so, he would have spoken to the very officers who must have been present at his brother's death. It would have been most strange had they not been anxious to talk to him. Why had she fretted so at the failures of Captain Houghton if Thomas was returning? It was customary when an officer died, even one of some seniority, to auction his effects, but Lyndon had requested that his brother take all his belongings. Had he his mother in mind when he opened his writing box and got out the pen and paper to write these final instructions? Had he foreseen his death? It seemed out of character, for part of his charm had been a cheerful optimism. She tried to picture him bent over the writing box, his fair hair, the red coat, perhaps with the button at the throat undone, the cravat loosed or the lapels turned back to show the colour of the facings. But at what had he sat? Had he been in some little Spanish or Portuguese hovel, with a rickety table, or in a tent with nothing? He was not a general with a whole set of campaign furniture. For a second or two she felt she had conjured his image but it faded at her attempt to make it more realistic. She had said, half out loud, 'Ah, Lyndon, how could you leave me?'

She had pressed her fingers to her eyes to try to prevent the tears. Was she not waiting for Thomas? Would she not this very day lay her hand on the objects last touched by her beloved boy? The very clothes he wore must retain some lingering sense of him.

And then Slimmer had come in. He said, 'Major Wilder is here, my lady.'

She had given a little start, as if, after all, she had forgotten Thomas, but she had said calmly, 'Thank you, Slimmer. He will come down when he is ready. I take it you told him which rooms were prepared for him?'

'No, my lady. He pushed off double quick up the stairs.'

'You should have gone with him.'

'I didn't like to, my lady, with him being so brisk. He opened the shutters in the hall, my lady.'

'Very good, Slimmer. Open the shutters here.'

It had been an instinctive rejoinder. Slimmer, in a sly way, was capable of making mischief. A united front must always be maintained before servants, even those, such as Slimmer, of long standing. He had proceeded to make a great labour of the shutters. She had not been able to see how he could be so long about it. Little by little daylight had flooded the room but there was no sun, of which she was glad.

'Will the Major be wanting refreshment?' Slimmer had asked.

Lady Charles had had no idea what the Major might want. It was curiosity that kept Slimmer so long in the room: he wished to be there when she and Thomas greeted one another.

'I will ring,' she had said. 'You may leave me.'

She had again settled to waiting. Why was Thomas so long changing? Where was her husband? Locked in the library seeing to his papers, or not seeing to them.

The schoolroom at Ridley also looked out over the stables. Miss Arbuthnot had given up her attempt to persuade Lottie to sit at her books and was leaning out of the open window as enthusiastically as her pupil. So little occurred to interrupt their daily lives that advantage must be taken of the odd distraction.

They looked down on the backs of the four horses, the two bays, the piebald pony with the bulging panniers and the grey Andalusian, with the beautiful flowing tail, the black sheepskin and the shabraque.

'Isn't it gorgeous?' Lottie whispered, rolling the word round her tongue: she had never had cause to use it before. She was transfixed by the Andalusian, afraid the scene might vanish.

'Absolutely gorgeous,' Miss Arbuthnot agreed, herself whispering.

'But it's wearing so many clothes.'

'The long piece under the saddle is the shabraque. That is what the cavalry horses wear, or so I believe, for I have never had call to mention it before.'

'The poor man hasn't enough hands for so many

creatures. Where is Hall that he doesn't come out to help him? Oh, Buth, look! Dogs!' Lottie turned an even more ecstatic face to her governess, then craned yet further out of the window.

'Be careful, dearest.' Formality was forgotten at such moments.

'Beautiful dogs. Perhaps my uncle Thomas will give one to me. The white one is pretty. Look, the man is tying them up to the pony and he's letting them loose. What if they run off?'

'I expect he knows what it's safe to do.'

'Now he has put Gorgeous in the stable and we can't see it, which is a pity. He has taken all the bags off the other one, which is just an ordinary horse. Now here is Hall at last.'

The voice of Lord Charles's head groom travelled up to the window. 'Hey, you there, you can't use that box. That's kept special. What's your name then?'

For a while there was no reply. The man did not so much as turn round from his task of dismantling the packs. He then ran his hand along the horse's back with exploratory fingers. Apparently satisfied, he said, 'York.'

'Well, Mr York, that stable is kept special, so you best shift that foreign nag out of it.'

York now turned with infinite slowness. Lottie and Miss Arbuthnot exchanged half-anxious, half-amused glances. 'Kept special for who?' he asked.

'Kept special for one of the late Mr Wilder's hunters what's a bit delicate.'

Miss Arbuthnot could see rather than hear York's deep, incredulous sigh. 'I said for who, not for what. York's my name, and my master is Major the Honourable Thomas Wilder of the Royal Horse Artillery. When I sees a good billet for the Andalusian I tucks him in, and the same for the others, even the pony, what's a good sort. I moves out for generals and I moves out for colonels, though not gracefully, like. Course, I knows our place and I've got no choice, and I don't move out for the cussed infantry, nor I never will.'

Hall, clearly out of his depth, said, 'I'm sure I don't know what Lord Charles will say.'

'Don't care what anyone says 'cept for the Major. Now, if you ain't got nothing better to do than gawp, lend a hand and get those beds down, for I see there's plenty of straw, alongside of the Andalusian. I keeps 'em close up at night so I can watch the lot of them. Can't have some rascal pinch one, can I?'

'You going to sleep beside them?' Hall asked, with an incredulous smirk.

'Often have, but seeing we've landed on our feet here, I dare say there won't be the need. Now either give a hand or cut and run. Can't you see I've work to do?'

Miss Arbuthnot, suddenly remembering her position and Lottie's, said, 'Oh dear, what are we doing, listening to other people's conversation without their knowing it?'

She drew a reluctant Lottie from the window and closed it. Down below the morose footman appeared to impart Slimmer's instructions.

When Major Wilder stood in the open doorway to the drawing room, his mother took immediate note of his appearance. He had not changed from his uniform. She saw he was clean-shaven, which she had not expected because Lyndon used to joke of how the cavalry officers were proud of their whiskers, and this must have included the Horse Artillery. Lyndon had been bullied by his colonel to shave his off, being a mere infantryman. Surely he had never cropped his hair so. That was beyond imagination. It almost made her smile.

Thomas shocked her. He looked older than he should. Of course, it was a hard life he had led. Had Lyndon aged in the same way? Had he that weathered countenance, that look, yes, of having seen too much? Ah, no, Lyndon never changed, and now, God bless him, he never would.

As Thomas Wilder walked towards her, she was glad to see he was not lame, for he had received a serious wound to the thigh at some engagement or other. Perhaps she had maligned him all along. She had not, after all, seen him for five years, when he had appeared at Ridley to say goodbye before embarking with the Artillery. Were the lines about his face etched by his grief for Lyndon? Were she and Thomas to be in perfect accord as he told and retold all he knew of Lyndon, from happy boyhood to fearful death, that she might live his life again? She stood up to receive Thomas's, she thought dutiful, kiss. She had forgotten his eyes, a medium light brown. They had, she thought, a guarded expression. When he was a little boy those light brown eyes had peered out warily from under a forest of curls, which had given him a fawn-like look, though what he had to be wary about, she could not imagine, with a big sister to dote on him and a big brother to watch his every step. How unlike those eyes, that hair, were to Lyndon's, but they had never resembled one another. That was not true. Now, in Thomas's face, she could perceive, like a haunting, a vague distortion of her other son.

Lady Charles retreated to her chair. She said, 'Sit down, Thomas. You look tired.' It was then that she noticed the dogs. Her initial fears were confirmed. He would have no sympathy for her whatsoever. They would never speak the same language. He had been jealous of Lyndon and now he would be relishing his position as heir to Ridley.

Major Wilder seated himself opposite his mother. He was surprised by how little she had altered. She was still pretty. He noted her change of expression as the greyhounds nestled against his knees. He was aware she did not care for dogs, but if he was to live at Ridley it must be on his own terms, or he would return to the Artillery: he had not, after all, resigned. What should he speak of, other than Lyndon? Would she ask about his journey? That was customary. What sort of scrape might he get himself into for being a stranger, for coming home, for having no joy in his heart? He said, 'I am sorry I haven't changed. York has not yet got in the baggage.' He was not sorry to be wearing his pelisse. Ridley was a cold house and it seemed little was done to make it less so.

Lady Charles said, 'Would you care for some refreshments? We are at least an hour from dinner.'

Of course, that was the other thing of which one spoke. He said, 'I can wait.' Would he have to sit and talk to his mother for more than an hour? 'I am glad you have put the shutters back. The house had its eyes closed as I came up the drive. I can see things have got out of hand. Georgie wrote me so but I wasn't quite expecting it. My father doesn't look well. Does he see the doctor?' He found, after all, there were things to be said. 'The shock will have affected him, I realize that.'

Lady Charles thought, why does he not ask if the shock has affected me? 'You will no doubt be able to assist him, though I'm sure I don't know what needs to be done.'

'Is that not why I've come home?'

Lady Charles supposed a little help with the estate would be beneficial.

There was a pause, as if they had said all they could say.

Then Major Wilder said, 'Tell me about Lottie.'

'She is very well. Of course, she grieves for her papa.'

'I would not have thought she could remember much of Lyndon.'

'In that you would be quite wrong. How could one forget him?'

'I meant that she was only little when he left. I have brought a pony for her, one from Portugal. Does she have one?'

'No, indeed. It was kind of you but it would have been more sensible to ask. I doubt she would like it.'

'Why not? Can't the child learn to ride?'

'Had she been a boy it would have been different.'

Thomas Wilder thought, had Lottie been a boy he would himself be hovering somewhere in the vicinity of Toulouse or Bayonne, not sitting in the Ridley drawing room opposite his mother. 'I believe riding to enrich the life of a child. I don't want her namby-pamby.'

Lady Charles could not see of what concern Lottie could be to her uncle, beyond the fact she was Lyndon's child, or why he should express views on her upbringing.

He now said, with a sudden quick smile, which she thought out of place, 'I hear she eats governesses for breakfast. How is she with Georgie's Miss Arbuthnot?'

'Miss Arbuthnot is, of course, too young. Your father and I would have chosen an older woman.'

'Never mind her age. Does Lottie like her?'

'It seems so.'

'And can she read now?'

Lady Charles was affronted. Georgie confided too much in her brother. That Lottie was a little slow should not be a subject for frivolous discussion – or discussion of any sort.

Major Wilder then said, disconcertingly, 'But I understand Lottie to be quite clever.'

'Lottie has made advances under the management of Miss Arbuthnot. We think Miss Arbuthnot to have opinions perhaps not suited to her position.'

'Do you consider her a democrat or, perhaps worse, a radical?'

'How should I know such a thing?' Lady Charles said crossly, because he seemed amused.

Thomas Wilder thought it her duty to know but he did not say so. He was aware that he was not saying any of the things his mother wanted him to say. She wished him to talk about Lyndon.

Lady Charles now brought her mind to bear on the dogs. She had initially resolved not to mention them but now she changed her mind. It then occurred to her she might alienate this stranger son and that he might withhold the things she wished to know, upon which she felt her life depended. She said, cautiously, 'Thomas, I think it must have slipped your mind, for you have been away so long, that I don't allow dogs in the house.'

He said, 'I hadn't forgotten.'

She waited for an explanation but he made none. He was preoccupied, gently pulling an ear of each dog, both of which gazed at him with devotion. At last he said, 'The brindle is called Fuente. He is not accustomed to be separated from me, though I never have allowed him on the battlefield. He is a good dog, useful. As for the white one, she is fast, but nervous and highly strung.' He paused for a moment before adding, 'She belonged to Lyndon.'

Was he cruel to tell her this? He watched her face change, stricken, then tearful. She held out her hands as if entreating the dog to come to her. She then said, 'Of course Lyndon would have a dog, but I never thought of it, and he would have a dog like this. Will it come to me? I can see it is a beautiful dog, very refined.'

Thomas Wilder knew the dog would not approach her, that it would press itself ever closer to his knee and look to him for reassurance. He said, 'Give her time.'

'I want to touch her.'

'She will sense your anxiety.'

'What is her name?'

'Lyndon's servant called her Blanca, but she is English bred.'

'You didn't bring the man back? His name was Robinson, I believe.'

'No. He came from the ranks and returned to them when Lyndon was killed. His name was Smith.'

'Could he have changed his man?'

'If they didn't suit one another.'

'He had another servant.'

'Yes, a young Spaniard.'

'And you spoke to them?'

'Only to the Spaniard. Smith was out on picket.' He had asked to speak to Smith, but Smith had not appeared. He decided against explaining this to his mother.

'And the Spaniard? Do you speak Spanish?'

'Yes, of course. He had little to say. I kept him on until I had sold Lyndon's horses. He had a couple of mules as well, both of which I sold.'

'Could you not have kept them?'

'I couldn't have got sufficient fodder.'

With Thomas's simple explanation, the strange world that Lyndon had inexplicably chosen to inhabit came a little closer. That, in her sea of ignorance, she understood. She remembered her husband wanting her to study the map of the Iberian Peninsula but she had declined to do so. She could not bear to think of Lyndon there, so far away, in a place she could not visualize.

Major Wilder stood up. 'Where am I sleeping?'

'Has no one told you? How strange. We thought it best for you to have the rooms last occupied by your grandfather. They are clean and aired.'

He smiled, and she saw he was pleased. 'But you are not going yet? You have told me nothing.'

'No.' He hesitated. 'I am afraid of disappointing you, of being unable to tell you what you wish to know.'

Lady Charles thought, He is tired, he has made a long journey. I must try to make allowances for him. Although he was her son they might as well have been strangers. She must charm and soothe him for it now occurred to her he might find it impossibly painful to recount what she wished him to tell. He had surely loved Lyndon, for everyone had.

The rooms once used by Lady Charles's father had been untenanted since the old gentleman had died. As this had been approximately twenty-five years ago, Major Wilder was prepared to revise his initial reaction of pleasure to one of mild dismay, but he was pleasantly surprised. The rooms, all panelled, ran one into the next and all overlooked the park: a bedroom, a dressing room and a room in which to sit with a desk, a table and two comfortable chairs, one on each side of a fireplace before which his dogs immediately settled. He could not remember having been in them since he was a small child. Here he could be alone. The smell of beeswax reassured him: effort had been put to securing his comfort and, as this was surely a household concern, it would have been under the management of his mother. On the whole he thought it unlikely that he and his mother would ever have the least understanding of each other, but he must keep up the civilities. On the other hand, being of a straightforward nature, he was not prepared to lie to or flatter her to make things comfortable.

He went to the window and looked down on the park. It was a dismal sight, the back road leading to the north lodge through the stumps of oak. There were seven or eight horses in a bunch. He wondered why so many. They could not want more than a pair of carriage horses and a hack for his father, perhaps another for a groom to accompany him: his father did not look fit to go out alone. They would need to put sheep or cows in the park to graze the sour patches left by horses. Perhaps the horses had been his brother's, kept because his parents lacked the heart to sell them. Lyndon, who set store by his hunters, might have said, in that easy way he had, 'I'll be back, keep my horses.'

He set about inspecting the desk, opening the drawers. They were empty. He had rather hoped for something of his grandfather's to give him a sense of continuity. The pictures on the wall were of his grandfather's choosing, several small views of Ridley, a favourite hunter, a portrait of Thomas's great-aunt over the fireplace, and another, smaller, of his grandmother. A sketch of a child, bare-shouldered but for a wisp of drapery, a fawn-like face, curls, lay on the desk. He took it to the window. Was it Georgie, the eldest grandchild, adored by the old gentleman? When he turned it over he found it inscribed on the back 'T. O. L. Wilder aged four, 1788'. That it should be of himself astonished him. He had no recollection of it. He had difficulty in remembering his grandfather: he was not much more than a many-buttoned waistcoat, a wig and an aroma of snuff. He noted that there were no drawings of Lyndon, none of their sisters: had the old gentleman second sight?

In the dressing room York had laid out his dress uniform and civilian evening wear. Did he need an additional servant? York, though sometimes irascible to his fellow man, understood the exact needs of his master and clung tenaciously to orders. He was as capable of looking after the Major's horses as he was, in a rough way, of his clothes, had been in his service for a long time, and together they had weathered all sorts of curious and uncomfortable circumstances. Now York had posed the all-important question: was the Major wearing uniform or was he returning to civilian life? A cursory glance out of the window was enough to inform him things were awry. He supposed it was the premature ageing of his father coupled with Lyndon's death . . . but there had always been sufficient funds to run the estate as it should be run. It was not only his duty to stay but in his own interest, at least for the time being, until he understood the situation and had corrected it.

For the time being he would wear civilian clothes but no one divested themselves of their uniform more reluctantly than he, hampered as he was by the bandage round his left shoulder. As he unwound the crimson sash, theoretically of sufficient length to carry him wounded from the battlefield, he thought of the flaying of Marsyas. He was aware that he might never put it on again: he, a dedicated soldier, for whom life was to offer nothing else, would not casually discard the blue jacket now laid out on the bed with the red facings, collar and cuffs, a startling finery of gold braid and the innumerable buttons with the insignia of the Royal Horse Artillery. York had laid his dress sword on a chair. What was he supposed to do with it? Put it in a cabinet? It had only ever been on parade. His regulation officer's sword he was now unbuckling: though not so fancy, it had led the more interesting life, the nicks in the blade testifying to its active service. The very thought swept him back to scenes he was hard put to know if he wished to remember or not: maintaining the discipline and coordination of his men amid the roaring of the six-pounders, the re-sighting of the guns amid the blood, the heat and the violence.

York had also arranged his razors, his toothbrush and his hairbrushes on the washstand and filled the jug with warm water. The agreeable thing about York, especially while on campaign, was his staunch refusal to be disconcerted. He would view Ridley as a challenge, especially as Major Wilder had dropped him no hint as to what he might expect. Undaunted by the quantity of back rooms and strange corridors, he would have demanded hot water for his master. To be able to wash and put on clean clothes at will was a luxury. York had everything there, underclothes, clean shirt, linen waistcoat, a pair of black trousers and a black coat. These latter Major Wilder had had made up by his tailor before coming down to the country; both were of a distinctly military cut. The silk stock he wound round his neck was black, and he tied it, out of habit, with the regulation one inch of shirt collar emerging above it. He would be obliged to wear mourning for a year from Lyndon's death, and he knew his appearance was sufficiently subdued to satisfy his family.

Returning to the other room, he could not help smiling at the way his dogs were making the most of their new circumstances, laid out before the fire, their eyes closed in delicious repose.

York shoved open the door, his arms full of baggage. At the sight of his master, he gave a sly smile, rather a rarity in York, and said, 'I lit the fire. They need more wood got in. Very good quarters, sir, best we've 'ad.'

As it was not yet time for dinner, Major Wilder stepped across the corridor and pushed open the door that led to the rooms of his late brother. There was a little sitting room or study that he thought had been intended as a boudoir for Lyndon's wife, a figure without substance. Lyndon had removed to these rooms on his marriage: they had been prepared to receive his bride. After her death he had retained them and they had reverted to a bachelor apartment. Now, Thomas Wilder observed with distaste, they were a shrine to Lyndon, even a bunch of fresh violets on the side table. Indeed, Lyndon could have left the room a moment before: to give just such an impression the purpose of it, he supposed. He opened and shut the drawers of the desk, which, unlike those of his grandfather, were full of old letters, packs of cards, snuff boxes, gloves, ledgers that contained Lyndon's wild attempts to keep accounts, and a boxed pair of Mortimer duelling pistols. These last he examined with disapproval.

In the dressing room his brother's clothes, numerous, filled the wardrobes, racks of coats, boots, breeches, pantaloons and hats. It would be better to give it all away before the moth inhabited it as it could only be of interest as a resumé of fashion from Lyndon's youth until 1811, when he had rejoined the army for a purpose unexplained. Somehow these garments smelt of Lyndon, of the snuff he used, even of the way he lived. Major Wilder shut the doors in haste.

There was nothing much in the bedroom apart from the objects to be expected, a nightshirt and cap laid out on the bed, carefully pressed, but his attention was drawn to the bracket clock on the mantelpiece. He saw it was by Richard Baker and at least fifty years old. Its hands had stopped at ten past twelve. He got out his own watch that had, ironically, once belonged to Lyndon, and checked the time before taking the key from a neighbouring Chinese dish, opening the glass cover to the face, and winding it, correctly estimating the thirty turns to each side, before he reset the hands.

The last room he looked at had belonged to Lyndon's wife. The bed curtains were striped pink and white, as was the wallpaper, with the addition of swags and bows. He supposed nothing had been altered here since the simultaneous events of Lottie's birth and her mother's death. As he re-entered the corridor whence he had come he had the satisfaction of hearing the clock strike six. Thomas Wilder liked clocks.

Susan was attempting to untangle Lottie's hair in preparation for her attendance in the dining room at the moment of dessert. 'Hold still, missy,' she said. Lottie was the second generation of Wilder children to whom she had acted as nanny and nursery maid. 'What will young Master Thomas, or the Major I should say, be thinking if he sees you in such a state? Ever since you took up that gardening your hair has got the widdershins in it.'

Lottie, in her shift, twisted about in the chair. 'Susan?'

'Mmm.' Susan had put a piece of ribbon between her lips. After a moment or two she took it out and replaced it with a comb.

'Why has my Uncle Thomas come?'

Susan removed the comb from her teeth and said, 'Goodness, child, why should the likes of you and me know that? Your grandpapa is getting old and that'll be at the root of it.'

'Was my papa like me when he was little?'

'Proper little gentleman, he was, the poor young master, do this, do that and ever so pretty, a real picture, if ever.'

'What does it mean when you are dead? Where have you gone?'

'Why, under the good earth to help make the flowers grow.'

'That isn't what Grandmama says. She says we go to Heaven to be with the angels. I can't see how we can do both.'

'There now, 'tis the great mystery of the Lord,' Susan replied, unmoved by logic or eternal verities.

'Do you think they have flowers in Spain?' Lottie asked.

'Grass, deary, I dare say, but if they have flowers they'll be big and bright, more like what comes from the glass-house. 'Tis hot in Spain, I've heard tell.'

Lottie now said, 'Perhaps I won't go down this evening.'

'Why ever not?'

'I don't want to. My Uncle Thomas won't want to see me. I should like to see the dogs, though. Do you think they have been put in the kennel?'

Susan knew the dogs were not in the kennel. The confidence with which Major Wilder had strode into the house accompanied by his dogs was the talk of the servants' hall.

'Uncle Thomas being here won't make any difference, will it, Susan? He won't want to know about me.'

Susan had succeeded in untangling Lottie's hair, as far as such a task was possible. 'There's no telling, so you go on downstairs at the proper time and make him a nice curtsy, so he knows you're going on as you ought.'

'If the French hadn't killed my papa, Uncle Thomas need

not have come.' Lottie was not sure how she knew this. The thought of a stranger, especially a man, in the house made her anxious. What exactly was her Uncle Thomas? Might he be like Horatio's Captain Houghton, of whom she had seen little? Horatio said he was a nasty soldier, and though he was often too sick to leave his room, Horatio wished he would go away.

Susan slipped the black gown with the lace edging over Lottie's head and then rearranged her hair so it fell in its customary abundance. The daytime ribbons were discarded. Lady Charles had said such beauty should not be confined.

It was Lady Charles's custom to look at the clock in the little parlour attached to her bedroom, where she would be sitting dressed for dinner, and, when the hands reached twenty-five minutes past six, pick up her shawl and go straight down to the dining room. Thus her maid spent much of the day comparing the time on that clock with the regulator in the servants' hall, and altering the former to correspond with the latter. Lady Charles considered her hour for dinner fashionably late. The bell would be rung as she was going downstairs. The perfect timing of the procedure gave her a nice sense of the orderliness and efficiency of her household. She was unaware that her maid, Sally, who was devoted to her but saw no harm in a little deception, occasionally obliged the kitchen by altering her clock because the dinner was not quite ready. As it was she always entered the dining room exactly as the last dish was put on the table. Lord Charles would be waiting, either with his back to the fire or looking out of the windows, those that gave on to the weedy terrace and the sad ponds. When his wife entered he would give her a bow.

Major Wilder appeared after this ritual had been enacted. Lady Charles thought, He still looks like a soldier though he is divested of his uniform. For some reason she did not quite like it that he did: now he was at home he should look like a gentleman, his career, his previous life, of no significance, but she was relieved to see his clothes reflected his state of mourning, the loss of his brother. She noted, with equal distaste, that he was accompanied by his dogs, but she said nothing, for the white dog had belonged to Lyndon.

Lord Charles thought, The boy has long gone and is replaced with a man of consequence.

Major Wilder said, glancing at the table, which was laid for three. 'Doesn't Miss Arbuthnot join us? Perhaps it is just for today as I am so newly arrived.'

Lady Charles said, 'Miss Arbuthnot does not dine with us.'

He considered the table, reduced to its least dimension but still too large for three, especially as his parents took their places at the diverse ends.

He said, 'Why not? There were always at least two governesses when the girls were growing up and they lived as family.' He struggled to repopulate the table with his sisters, their governesses and Lyndon.

Lady Charles said, 'We could not think of having a stranger with us at such a time.' She noticed the butler hanging about at the sideboard, though he had already decanted the wine, so she added firmly, for she knew he loved to eavesdrop, 'That will do, Slimmer. We will help ourselves.'

Slimmer left the room reluctantly.

Lady Charles was surprised to hear Thomas continue with the subject of Miss Arbuthnot, as if it were some business of his. 'But what happens to her in the evenings?'

'Dinner is taken up to her room.'

'But who does she see other than Lottie?'

'Sometimes she sees Mrs Kingston, who has a little boy Lottie likes to play with.'

'No one should be expected to live totally incarcerated with a small child.'

They had taken their places at the table. For a moment there was silence but then Major Wilder looked at his father and said, 'I am surprised she stays.'

Lord Charles said, 'I hadn't given it much thought.'

Lady Charles, angry that Thomas should even contemplate questioning their conduct, said nothing.

'I had imagined,' Major Wilder continued, 'that her presence and Lottie's would help to cheer your evenings, distract you a little.'

Lady Charles said coldly, 'I have no wish to be distracted.'

'Lottie must be nine. It is time she came downstairs when it is just the family, as we did, even if it is only to stop her governess dying of loneliness or boredom or both.'

'Lottie comes down for dessert. We will consider the matter.' Lady Charles saw that she was on the point of quarrelling with Thomas on his first evening, and he her only source of information.

Lord Charles decided he would not be averse to the presence of Lottie and her governess but he considered it the wrong moment to say so and he was pleasantly preoccupied with the dogs. How was it Thomas had marched in with his dogs and nothing had been said? The white one had been Lyndon's. He could not tell whether he found that more or less painful. He tried to imagine Lyndon, rakishly handsome in his scarlet jacket, with the white greyhound at his heel, out on some hot, boulder-strewn Spanish plain.

Lady Charles said, 'Thomas, we need to know more of Lyndon's last days, even his last hours. I see you are reluctant to talk of these things, but for me—' She broke off, having no idea how to say what she wished.

Her son laid down his soup spoon and turned to look at her. Eventually he said, 'I am afraid that I shall not tell you what you want to hear and of your thinking I know things I do not.'

'But you visited his regiment, you collected his possessions.'

'I did.' His mind travelled reluctantly to the miserable village that had been the temporary home of his brother's regiment, somewhere at the base of the Pyrenees. It was on the Spanish side and the date early September. He remembered little of that village but the officers of the regiment lounging about, flirting with the Spanish girls, laughing together. They were barely polite when he asked to be conducted to their colonel but his superior rank told, and one bestirred himself to do as he was bade.

The colonel had got up to shake his hand, very civil, but he received the impression that the older man would have preferred to be spared the interview. He made the proper condolences but when it came to the point, he had told nothing.

Lady Charles said, 'And the officers spoke to you?'

'Not much. I considered them a sulky lot.' Had they been under himself, they would soon not have known themselves.

Lady Charles leant forward. She said, harshly, 'How do we know Lyndon is dead? They talked of fog and of darkness. Why should he not be a prisoner of the French?'

'I had considered that possibility myself but a badly wounded ensign had gone back to him, I'm not sure how or why, and had reported to the colonel that he was, without question, dead. In the end, I could not doubt Lyndon was killed that day.'

'Did you speak to the ensign?'

'I asked if I might, but he had died. Had I been able to get up to Lyndon's regiment sooner, I might have seen him. His name was Parker. He was in the same company as Lyndon. He was wounded in the same engagement, crawled back to where Lyndon lay, and then was gathered up by some men of that company. He lived only a few days but long enough to report Lyndon dead.'

'But if that was the case for this Parker, why was Lyndon not brought in?'

'An engagement is not like a game of chess in which you can see all the pieces on the board together. Perhaps the men were not where they should have been. There may have been time only to bring in the wounded. I doubt we will ever know.'

'I understand you were unable to see Lyndon's soldier servant but what of his Spanish servant? From Lyndon's letters he was called Joseph.'

'He was minding Lyndon's things, waiting for me,

waiting to be paid off. Another officer was ready to employ him.'

Lord Charles said, 'I wish you had brought this Joseph home with you.'

'I had two servants of my own. I didn't need another.'

'But what of Lyndon's things?' Lady Charles asked. 'Where are they? You have everything of his?'

'How could I?' He was glad that Slimmer had come in to remove their soup plates and put another dish on the table. He thought of his brother's mules and horses, his quantities of clothes, pantaloons, shirts, gloves, vests, greatcoat, dress uniform, boots, shoes, stockings, saddles, bridles, a bearskin bed, canteens, various articles, luxuries that most officers of the line could not afford, and about twice the kit that the more Spartan Thomas considered necessary. He had wondered at the time whether Lyndon's request it should be passed to his younger brother was an attempt to cause him maximum inconvenience in its disposal or an act of generosity, almost a peace-offering. This he would never know, but he had made use of what he could, shirts, drawers, vests, any articles that were less worn than his own.

He said, when they again had the room to themselves, 'I have some things of Lyndon's, but not all. How could I get about with it? What use were his uniforms to me?'

'You should have kept them all the same,' Lady Charles said. 'How could you not? A few precious reminders of your only brother. You could have packed it up and sent it to Lisbon, right to the last pocket handkerchief. I can't believe you auctioned it. Isn't that what they do, and laugh at the torn shirt? Captain Houghton told me this. It was not yours to dispose of. Lyndon made the arrangement that you might gather up his goods and return them here to me, to Ridley, where they belong.'

'I can't say what Lyndon thought or intended, but he must have known I was unlikely to undertake something so impractical and expensive. Yes, I asked for them to be auctioned, his uniforms, his horses, his mules, and all the rest of his clothes and kit that I could not accommodate. I kept his dress sword, a few things, his dog. The sword he had at his death, his watch and seals, all these I have.'

Lord Charles said, 'But did that officer, the one who died, did he bring those things from the body?' He wanted to know if Lyndon had been buried but he was afraid of the answer: it was also too much to expect Thomas to reply.

Again Major Wilder shook his head. He said, looking at his mother, 'You need not know all these things. You are not at war. You won't understand it. Why should you? There is no need for you to do so.'

The dead were stripped of their clothes and left naked. It was unlikely to have been different for Lyndon, but he could not say so. He could say the watch and seal had been brought back by Parker, but that would be a lie, and he did not choose to lie. Eventually he said, with reluctance, 'They were looted but, by the vigilance of an officer in the Portuguese service, they were returned to me. He had let it be known he had them.'

He began to think of his singular interview with Captain Allington, who had had a company of Portuguese *caçadores* in Vera, a village on the banks of the Bidasoa. Lyndon's colonel had not offered him dinner, with the excuse of his needing to go straight to Vera in order to catch Captain

Allington, on the grounds he thought they would get orders to march at any minute, and he was sure Major Wilder would want to see Captain Allington in person, to thank him for the trouble he had taken. Major Wilder had agreed this was so but he also thought the colonel could not wait to be rid of him. At Vera, among the wooded slopes, densely green, of the Pyrenees, it was pouring with rain. There had been a recent action there to defend the bridge, so he had been told, and two officers killed.

He had found Captain Allington in a tall house facing on to the street. Thus far, he could think equably, but his recollection of subsequent events disturbed him and he endeavoured to push them away.

Lady Charles was silent, in her own way distraught. It was true she understood nothing and as Thomas spoke she understood less. What, on the other hand, did Thomas understand? He who could auction the clothes of his dead brother, who had nurtured and protected him as a child, understood nothing. He must, after all, be glad of Lyndon's death, if he had disposed of his brother's goods in that most callous, but at the time most convenient, way. He must have hated Lyndon. She noticed that Thomas, as he had spoken, had become pale. He appeared ill. He was concealing things for some purpose of his own.

Lady Charles examined him more closely. She gazed at his cropped brown hair, his strong shoulders, for indeed he looked physically strong, and at his face, in which lurked Lyndon's – although in what way she could not tell: Thomas had that high, broad brow, an indication that, even as a child, he was clever; his eyes were large, like Lyndon's, but light brown, his nose slightly aquiline, his teeth reasonable and his jaw narrow. His mouth she thought unforgiving: wide but thin-lipped.

Lord Charles said to himself, Thomas has pushed his plate aside and he doesn't eat. He wondered, Why did Eleanor want to know so much. Lyndon was dead and his uniforms wouldn't bring him back. Thomas had probably done his best, and hadn't he come home with the dog? It was wiser not to trouble him with the things that made him uncomfortable.

Lady Charles said coldly, 'Perhaps whatever you do have of Lyndon's, you would be so kind as to bring me after dinner. I am sure you can't want anything of his for yourself.'

Major Wilder said, 'Why not? Lyndon chose to leave what he had to me, and I respect that.'

Lady Charles stared at him with horrified but confused astonishment.

Her husband said, 'What makes you say that?'

Major Wilder shrugged. 'It was in his will. Did he not write?'

'Not of a will.'

'It is not unusual for an officer to prepare one. I am sorry Lyndon chose not to tell you of the arrangements he was making.'

'Lyndon,' Lady Charles said at last, 'would never have written a word he thought might cause us distress.'

'Well, I can't say he had a great deal to leave,' Major Wilder said, 'but he took care of the document, leaving one with his colonel and another in his writing box, both witnessed.'

Lady Charles said, 'His writing box . . .' But she could say no more.

'Yes, I kept that, though it was an inconvenience to pack.' He turned to his mother. 'I thought you would like it.'

'But was there nothing in it? Only his will? No journal, no jottings? I sent him pocketbooks. I . . . I hoped he would—' Lady Charles again broke off. 'It had a secret drawer. Was there nothing in that?'

Major Wilder had found time to examine his brother's writing box. It was still September and they were enjoying a patch of warm weather, as yet in the north of Spain, and he was billeted in the house of a priest. He had settled himself in the corner of the courtyard, stripped to his shirt and hoped he would not be required in any official capacity for an hour or so. Blanca was at his feet, waiting for him to pay her some attention, learning not to be nervous of him. The mahogany writing box, bound in brass, lay across his knee. The key, not much more than an inch long, had been in the pocket of Lyndon's uniform jacket, the one in which he had been killed. It was a perfect fit to the lock, which confirmed that the jacket he had been offered as his brother's really was Lyndon's. The facings were the correct colour but it was denuded of buttons, though these had also been returned to him. It was at Vera on the Bidasoa, in the rain, that he had received it, but that was all beyond contemplation.

He turned his mind from the courtyard of the priest, Vera, Captain Allington and his Portuguese *caçadores*, with all that pertained to them, for the more pressing purpose of deciding what he might say to his mother.

Impatient at his hesitation, Lady Charles said, 'The pocketbooks, where are they?'

He recalled turning the little key in the lock, lifting the

lid and opening the box flat. It had looked much as other boxes, the glass inkwells, with their screw-down brass lids, a compartment for pens and pencils, another for sealing wax, candle holders to be fitted into the appropriate holes at the top, and beneath the green baize a further compartment for paper or letters. In Lyndon's case there had been no letters, merely a few blank sheets ready for use, the copy of his will and one of the two pocketbooks.

He said, 'I burnt them.'

'Burnt them? The precious last words of my son? You gave no thought to your grieving mother.' Lady Charles raised her voice in an agony between rage and despair.

Major Wilder thought this comment unjust because it was exactly of his mother he had been thinking when he put the pocketbooks on the fire. One, rather squeezed, was all that had lain in the secret drawer. Most such boxes had a secret drawer and, as he doubted Lyndon's to be the exception, it had been a matter of pressing and pushing until he located the spring. After a minute or two of experimentation he had removed the right-hand inkwell, applied pressure to the base of the compartment and the panel had been released. The first pocketbook he had already examined: it had contained a summary of his brother's financial affairs, including his gaming debts, or that was what Major Wilder assumed them to be. It was hard to tell if the sums were owed or owing, and the other officers involved were alluded to by nothing more than a scratched initial. A Captain Greenway had been owed forty dollars and had left a discourteous note with the colonel, assuming Major Wilder would honour the debt. If they were Spanish dollars, as he supposed, though they might have been Portuguese, this would have amounted to something over eight pounds. Major Wilder was not interested in the settling of such debts, particularly as he had an antipathy for card games.

He said, 'One book contained his accounts, a series of scrawls that I believe to have indicated his current state. I took note of the odd item that needed to be paid. Otherwise there was nothing to keep.'

'And the other?'

'It was of a very personal nature. I was sure Lyndon would not have wished me to do anything but burn it.'

He had thought that if one was so unwise as to record an affair with some Portuguese girl in precise detail, one could only hope to have it burnt – one certainly did not want it read by one's mother – so he had done that for Lyndon, if nothing else. It had not in the least surprised him, for Lyndon liked women as much as any other, and officers were forever getting into such scrapes. He had himself learnt how far to carry a flirtation and when to stop, though there were times when he felt himself too prone to calculation.

Slimmer chose this moment to enter the room, remove the cloth and lay out the dessert. Major Wilder supposed Slimmer had his uses after all. The child was hesitating at the door.

Lady Charles, with an effort controlling herself, said, 'Come along, Lottie, and say how do you do to your uncle. You are causing a draught.'

Lottie did not wish to say how do you do to her uncle. She remained in the doorway. Augusta was under her arm: she had brought her as moral support, but somehow Augusta was not as interesting as she used to be. Lottie ran back and placed her at the foot of the stairs, before returning.

Major Wilder thought, So this is Lyndon's child, poor little monkey. She did not answer Georgie's description of her, which was obviously out of date. Why did she still have to wear that unbecoming black for a father she could barely remember, and suffer such a troublesome quantity of hair? Seeing she was shy he got up to greet her, saying as she struggled with her curtsy, 'Don't look so scared, *niña*.'

'What does that mean?' Lottie asked.

'It's Spanish for "little girl".'

'Spanish,' she said. 'I never heard that before. I must tell Miss 'Buthnot.'

'You certainly should,' he replied.

Lord Charles said, as Lottie went to receive his kiss, 'Well, well, my pet, here is your Uncle Thomas, and do you know what? He thinks it time you came down to dinner.'

Lady Charles, again gathering herself together, said 'Really, what a thing to say to the child when it has not been discussed. It is not decided, Lottie, it is to be discussed.'

'It should be discussed with me if it's me to come down to dinner,' Lottie said, swinging on the arm of her grandfather's chair while trying to decide if coming down to dinner was an advantage or no.

Major Wilder said, 'Aunt Georgie's children come down to dinner and very pleasant it is to have them there, governesses, tutor, the lot.' Though he spoke truthfully he also saw Lottie's presence would save him from many a conversation with his mother that was best avoided.

Lottie said, 'I need not come down without Miss Arbuthnot?'

'You will do as you are told,' Lady Charles replied, but her husband said, 'Ah, yes, Miss Arbuthnot shall come down. Thomas has reminded us of our duty. We shall all be more cheerful.' He did not look at his wife as he spoke: she thought it wrong they should ever be cheerful again, but he was delighted with the arrival of his other son.

Lottie saw the dogs by the fire and, looking at her uncle, asked if she could touch them.

'Speak to the brindle one, Fuente,' he said. 'The other is nervous.'

Lottie stroked the dog's head with two fingers. She said, 'I wish he was mine.'

'Did you want a dog? I never thought to bring you one. I did bring you a pony but your grandmother thought you wouldn't like it. She is very quiet and well behaved. That's why I brought her home, hoping you would like her.'

Lottie looked at him in astonishment. 'A pony for me to ride?'

'Why not? Your cousins all have them, boys and girls alike, to tumble about on.' Major Wilder's ideas on the rearing of children were based entirely on his sister's. Her offspring, quite numerous, led a life untrammelled by supervision when not actually in the schoolroom or at table, and were as likely to be found in the kitchens or the stables as in the drawing room.

Lottie thought, Horatio's uncle never brought Horatio a pony. She said, 'May I see her now, this very minute?'

'No. She's gone to bed. You and I are going to have some dessert.'

'I saw a little black and white one from the window of the schoolroom. Now that one couldn't be mine, could it?'

'Why not?' he said, laughing. 'We must look out a side-saddle.'

Lady Charles interrupted: 'Lottie, you have no habit.'

'Nor I have.' Her face fell.

'Something can be got together,' Major Wilder said. 'Georgie's girls wear some sort of pantaloon under their skirts. You will have to be a little patient.'

Lady Charles stopped to consider the possible indelicacy of her granddaughters' riding wear and the further indelicacy of Thomas knowing anything about their nether garments. Had years of soldiering coarsened him, deprived him of all finer feeling? It seemed it had in all respects.

Lottie said, 'Who will teach me? Will Grandpapa teach me?'

'I expect he's too busy. York will teach you. He's very rude and bad-mannered but he will teach you.'

'Is he your servant?'

'Yes, and a very good one he is.'

'Don't you mind that he's rude?'

'He's far too clever to be rude to me. Just remember not to copy what he says, or you will get into trouble.'

'I'm too excited to eat my dessert. I'm going to run back upstairs and tell Miss Arbuthnot, not just about the pony but about coming down to dinner, and tomorrow, after I've seen the pony, I'm going to run across the park with Miss 'Buthnot to Horatio's house and tell him.'

Lord Charles beckoned Lottie to him and whispered something. She turned back to her uncle and said, 'Grandpapa is reminding me to say thank you, but at my age, I ought to have remembered for myself.'

'There now. I'll count it as said.'

Lottie continued, 'And I was dreadfully afraid you would

be like Captain Houghton who is Horatio's uncle.' She ran round to her grandmother and gave her a goodnight kiss before continuing, 'I didn't know I was going to be so happy today. Now, what am I, Grandmama? I'm a *niña*.'

Lady Charles looked at her beaming face and thought, even in her distress, Children will be children, so insensitive to anything but the immediate, and Thomas was anxious to curry favour with the child in such an extraordinary manner by bringing her a pony. She said, 'There now, dearest, I can see it's all gone to your head, which is rather bad for you so close to bedtime. You may find you don't like the pony as much as you suppose. As for this York, I can't think he's suitable.'

'Oh, I shan't mind him. Miss 'Buthnot and I heard him through the window.' Lottie lowered her voice: '"York's my name and my master is Major the Honourable Thomas Wilder of the Royal Horse Artillery".'

Her grandfather and uncle laughed. She thought she might continue but she had lost track of what else had been said and her grandmother, feigning tolerance, interrupted her: 'Now, Lottie, it really is time for you to go upstairs. In all this hilarity, I hope you won't forget to say your prayers.'

'I shall remember them especially, for I shall add my Uncle Thomas and the pony, which will make them more interesting.'

Lady Charles thought her granddaughter a difficult child to guide. Why could she not have had the subtle compliance of her father, so alive to one's mood? 'You may certainly pray for your uncle but it would not be right to add the pony. If you think about it, dearest, you will see it is not appropriate.'

'Won't the pony go to heaven with the angels if she dies?' Lottie asked. 'Or will she be under the good earth and help make the flowers grow?'

'Oh dear, Lottie, do go upstairs. I can't answer those questions now,' Lady Charles said, putting her head in her hands.

Lottie thought her grandmother the least useful person she knew for answering questions but, not wishing to stay a moment longer in the dining room, she flew to kiss her grandfather, wondered about kissing her Uncle Thomas, rejected the notion, revised it and rejected it again before disappearing.

After she had gone there was a long silence. Major Wilder had given up any idea of eating dessert and was absent-mindedly pulling the ears of Blanca, who had crept up to lay her head on his knee.

Eventually Lady Charles said, 'Thomas, you mustn't suppose I don't appreciate your thinking of Lottie, for she is, after all, your niece and your brother's only child. Of course it was kind of you to bring the pony. However, I would not like you to think it any part of yours to interfere with her upbringing. How do you know we wish her to ride or to be attended by rough servants, let alone to hang about in the stables? I must always be consulted before anything is said to Lottie. Look how she assumes she is to come down to dinner. I admit that was the fault of your father, but I'm sure it was none of your business to suggest it in the first place, though I dare say you meant well.'

Major Wilder replied, irritated, 'Why don't you think the child any of my business? I don't want her growing up namby-pamby. Let her be a child while she can. There is enough trouble in the world later on.'

Lady Charles repeated coldly, 'But she is no business of yours.'

Major Wilder stood up with some abruptness and went to stand before the fire. He said, 'I see Lyndon never wrote or told you any of his intentions. He certainly said nothing to me on the rare occasions when we met, but that was less of a surprise. That he said nothing to you certainly is. Whether he wished to make my life more difficult or yours, who is to say? Did he care one way or another? I have told you he made a will. You may see it. In that will he made me sole guardian of his daughter, Charlotte Wilder, for what purpose I cannot say. I intend to carry out the duty I am assigned, for what else can I do? As he did not consult me, at which point I might have declined the office, as he probably guessed, it is clear to me he meant me to have the management of Lottie. As you are aware, Lyndon and I were not close, but I shall carry out his last will and testament to the very letter.'

As Thomas Wilder contemplated the devastated, shocked, mortified faces of his parents, particularly his mother's, he bit back a whole lot of other things he felt like saying and left the room, muttering about checking his horses. The greyhounds hastened after him, a scuttling of claws on the polished boards.

Ridley
20 March 1814

Dearest Papa,

What a turmoil here. I dare say you will think I should not say it, but our lives are topsy-turvy with the arrival of Major Wilder. We, that is Miss Wilder and I, are to come down to dinner. I believe it has made Lady Charles nervous. You would rather think we were wild beasts, and I must admit that my pupil has a habit of holding her knife and fork with the knife in the left hand, which will not do. It is so long since I ate a meal in company I am a little afraid of making a similar mistake. I have been inspecting my wardrobe, which I believe to be adequate. You had said you suspected I would come down to dinner but until now it was not so. Only Lady Charles will notice what I wear, or I suppose she might.

As I got one thing after another out of the cupboard I was homesick for the little supper parties when it was my duty to preside over the cold meat and apple-pie at my very dear father's table. I am sure Fanny manages beautifully in my place. I thought of Fanny and Minette when I showed Major Wilder Miss Teachwell's Grammar Box, for Miss Wilder likes it just as much as they did. Oh dear, I do miss them so.

Miss Arbuthnot laid down the pen. Her mind had gone to the vicarage schoolroom and her three young sisters round the table, Kate, three years younger than herself, and the two little ones, Fanny and Minette. She thought of summer, with a breeze blowing the curtains and the birds singing in the garden, and of winter, with a fire in the grate and the children's nightgowns airing on the fender. Kate paid no attention and seemed to learn nothing, but the other two were industrious and eager. Was it her struggles with

Kate that had enabled her to succeed with Miss Wilder The thought of the supper parties also made her think o the Manor at West Staverton, where they had been used t dine at least once a week, and of the daughters there, he dearest friends, who had begged her not to take the post o governess to Miss Wilder, certain, if she must take a post a all, they could find something satisfactory much closer t home. They could not grasp, or else did not wish to, that t stay at home or even to be in the vicinity was impossible.

What else could she tell her father? Would he wish t know more of Major Wilder? Well, Major Wilder was man of thirty years old or so, accustomed to giving orders brisk, perhaps not patient, direct in his manner. He wa kind to his niece and had an unaccountable interest in he education, which had taken Miss Arbuthnot by surpris as she had long since given up the idea that anyone migh visit the schoolroom. Ah, but his military bearing neve left him: he was a soldier through and through. She coul remind her father of the incident when she was a little girl of her mother and the recruiting party, but he was no likely to have forgotten it, so indignant was he at the time She could say, 'Therein lies my discomfort,' but it woul not be the exact truth. The exact truth could only be tol by the mention of Mr Langley, and Mr Langley was not person she could bring herself to mention.

Mr Langley had been the first to extol, in her hearing the glories of the French Revolution, both the justice an the logic of it, and to extol Napoleon Bonaparte, whom he idolized. Mr Langley had, she supposed, many absurd ities, but he was a scholar and a poet. In the spring of th previous year he had made a prolonged visit to his uncle who lived in the parish, for the sake of his health. He had been ill, it was thought from overwork at his studies, and it had been decided country air was the best remedy. He had made a lively addition to the restricted world of society in West Staverton, but he had taken no note of herself until she had ventured to disagree with him. She did not disagree with him in every respect, she understood him, but she thought him, much of the time, entirely wrong. She could not initially find the arguments to refute what he said, but later, when less in awe of his intellect, she did.

He had a great dislike of the military. She could see him now, his lank figure, his lean face, his dark hair, worn rather longer than was customary, perhaps owing to his poetical inclinations, and his fiery blue eyes as he expostulated on the notion of keeping a standing army, or any army at all: was it not in order to contravene the liberties of the people? As for soldiers, they fell into two categories: the first hiding behind the dandy red coat and ridiculous hat to play at soldiering and then, at the threat of India, using the influence of a wealthy father to transfer to another regiment with a less exacting posting; the second and more venal, the professional soldier using the complicated ladders of army promotion for his own ends, war his best means, hardened to endless bloodshed while flogging his men into terrified submission. When she contemplated Major Wilder, whom she barely knew, she saw he did not belong to the first category and she certainly was not sufficiently acquainted with him to place him in the second. Mr Langley was particularly against artillerymen for he said they could kill many with a single weapon while the ordinary soldier with his musket could dispatch only one at a time. Miss Arbuthnot had pointed out, with a smile, that she thought it took a combined effort of quite a few men to fire a cannon, so his assumptions must be substantiated with mathematics. Of course she did not believe everything Mr Langley said, yet he influenced her. She discussed it with her father, who agreed with him on the subject of the standing army but considered him too extreme on other matters. Thus she concluded that her father, to a degree, sympathized with much of what Mr Langley said – yet he had had the church bells rung at the news of victories at Vitoria and Salamanca, whereas Mr Langley had been appalled and despondent.

What, she had ventured to ask Mr Langley, was England to do, should Napoleon invade? He had replied that the French should be received with open arms for peace and equality would be established throughout Europe; all would be ruled by one just law and Britain's mad or immoral monarchs could be shipped to Australia along with the convicts. An invasion, he said, should be welcomed rather than resisted. Miss Arbuthnot had pointed out the King was just and it was his misfortune, not his fault, to have lost his senses. As for the Prince Regent, he was not moral but no more was Bonaparte, divorcing his wife of many years to marry an Austrian princess. Mr Langley, who was never without an answer, told her she was but a child: she had failed to see the necessity of the Emperor securing the succession. Miss Arbuthnot considered such talk to be both dangerous and treasonable, but Mr Langley was, all the same, fascinating.

So now, she thought, picking up the pen and dipping it

into the ink, what could she say to her father on the subject of Major Wilder? Could she repeat the gossip of servants, that he had upset Lady Charles in filling the house with dogs, but Lord Charles was delighted with him? No, her father never liked anything that resembled gossip, so it was probably best to make no further mention of him. When she conjured him into her mind the image she had was of the officer, glimpsed so briefly from her position on the stairs, his fur-lined pelisse buttoned to his throat and the long red stripe on his trouser.

She continued her letter:

> *Miss Wilder has a pony to ride that her uncle brought her all the way from Spain. She is rather in love with it and when she has her first ride I am to walk with her, on the instructions of Lady Charles, to prevent Major Wilder's servant saying anything untoward, for he is in charge of the pony.*

It was Lady Charles's habit to visit those rooms once occupied by her son, to sit at his desk, occasionally writing letters there, letters to her daughters in which she might talk freely of her loss, and then strive to make proper comment, to direct, praise or criticize their domestic arrangements and the management of her grandchildren. Sometimes she would bring a little sewing and place herself so she half faced the window, half the room, and lull herself with dreaming of Lyndon's tread on the stair, of his thrusting open the door and standing before her in all his careless splendour. As far as the season could provide, there were fresh flowers on the table, violets now, snowdrops previously, though it was unlucky to bring them indoors and her maid, Sally, scolded her. Sally loved her and scolded her accordingly, as if she were a child, but snowdrops were pretty, bad luck had exhausted itself, and what else was there so early in the year? Only fresh flowers gave the illusion that a room was occupied.

For a few days after the arrival of her younger son, she had not gone to Lyndon's rooms. At first, on hearing of Lyndon's will, she had felt betrayed by him, but then, thinking more rationally, she chastised herself for even supposing Lyndon could betray her: it was impossible. No one had ever adored her as Lyndon had, so how could he have betrayed her and for what purpose? He must have had a particular object in making Thomas heir to his few possessions, and that object had been, as she had pointed out, that his effects would be returned to Ridley, though Thomas had not chosen to see it in that light. What object he had had in making Thomas guardian to Lottie she could not conceive. Had he thought them too old and the child a burden? But what sort of burden was a child in a house full of servants? She thought Lyndon's act extraordinary, but she also thought that, with time and contemplation, she would understand his motive. He had not forewarned them of the arrangements he was making because he would have supposed his will most likely unnecessary and would not have wished to distress his parents with its contents. He might indeed have intended to write on the matter but delayed until it was too late, for Lyndon had always been careless in that way. As for Lottie, the only time she had been a burden was in her refusal to accept her previous governesses. Now that Miss Arbuthnot was established in the schoolroom, Lady Charles was concerned that, the governess having too great an influence on her pupil, Lottie should come to prefer her to her own relatives. She thought it most unlikely, though, that Thomas would oppose her should she decide Miss Arbuthnot was in some way unsuitable.

Lady Charles sat in Lyndon Wilder's rooms occupied by these reflections. She contemplated writing to Georgie on the subject. Her eldest daughter was her natural confidante but she was also the one most likely to disagree and the most likely to tell the truth. Lady Charles did not always like to be told the truth, and she might have asked, Who does? But it gave her an almost unconscious respect for Georgie, who remained the daughter she consulted most frequently. In this particular matter, perhaps too painful to discuss, her mother thought her partiality for Thomas might colour her opinion: it had been ever thus. Lady Charles recalled her saying, 'Why can't you believe Thomas rather than Lyndon, just for once?' There had been a report from school that Thomas was perpetually late, sometimes missing a whole class, despite several birchings intended to act as a deterrent. Thomas had been white-faced and sulky, hanging his head, while questioned. As a child he had had a large head on a small, skinny body, like a tadpole, she had thought at the time, or some other strange little creature: it was quite difficult to equate the child with the man. After a while he had answered that Lyndon made him late.

'Don't tell lies, Thomas. We know that can't be true and, if it were, it would be telling tales.'

Lyndon had laughed when they had applied to him

for the truth and chanted, on catching sight of his young brother,

> 'Tell tale tit,
> Your tongue shall split
> And all the dogs in the town
> Shall have a little bit.'

But he said that it was true, he did make him late: Thomas was a lazy little tyke and he shut him into his room until he had correctly completed the tasks he had set him as his fag. The senior boys all had some little boy as a fag, he had pointed out, for running errands and blacking shoes, and he viewed Thomas as his personal property, though it was of singularly little advantage to himself. He had concluded, 'If I don't get him into trouble, he will be in far worse trouble with someone else.'

Yes, Georgie would champion her favourite, as she had then: she would say Thomas was well suited to the responsibilities Lyndon had imposed on him.

Lady Charles now stood up and walked about the room. She opened and shut the drawers, smiling gently, forgivingly, at Lyndon's clutter, the vague, careless disorder of his life. In the bedroom the clock began to strike. For a moment she did not register the fact: it seemed natural that it should. Lyndon was there to wind it up, the thirty turns each side of the face. When he had left she had wound it herself so it was ever in readiness for his return. Now, of course, it was not to be wound: it had gently ticked itself to a halt. She hurried through to the bedroom but Lyndon's presence had been an illusion of seconds. The tears poured down her cheeks: Thomas had already been in these rooms, this sanctuary, turning over Lyndon's things, winding the clock.

At dinner Lord and Lady Charles sat at each end of the table; Major Wilder sat on one side, Lottie and Miss Arbuthnot on the other: the table was still too long. Major Wilder thought he could now assess Miss Arbuthnot as other than Lottie's governess. In the schoolroom she had explained Lottie's difficulties with the written word, and the devices she used to help her overcome them. Miss Arbuthnot was calm and Lottie cheerful. Was it not, he thought, much the same in the army? He was of the progressive school, seeing flogging as a last resort rather than as an everyday occurrence. In order to avoid desertions, drunkenness and thieving, the good officer must have the confidence of his men, and they the desire to please him. He could see Miss Arbuthnot liked and understood Lottie. He had liked the men in his troop, though some were bad lots, hard nuts to crack. He was ever finding excuses for their lapses in conduct, while at the same time being considered strict. It was a delicate balance, one Miss Arbuthnot had achieved in her relationship with her pupil.

Georgie had said Miss Arbuthnot was rather young for the post, and now he came to consider her, he saw she was not more than eighteen or nineteen. Was that young? Had they not ensigns, cornets of sixteen, sometimes less, and expected to go into battle, mere boys in charge of men not only twice their age but often more? No, he could not consider Miss Arbuthnot too young. She had charge of one little girl, and had that little girl been a boy, he might by now have been in the navy. Experience could not be discounted but he understood Miss Arbuthnot to have had the management of three younger sisters and that must be experience enough for the management of Lottie.

Though she had a look of calm and intelligence, the girl she was still lurked in her eyes and her face. She had that even creaminess of skin and the freckles associated with red hair, rather more than a female was supposed to welcome. He wondered her mother had never succeeded in suppressing them with concoctions of cucumber or lemon juice, but perhaps with red hair they were too indigenous to be eradicated. As for the hair, it was of the proverbial copper, cut short, with a bit of a curl to it. For a woman she was tall, nearly, he hoped not quite, as tall as himself. Lord Charles had told him his mother considered her plain to the point of ugliness, but he fancied his father did not agree Miss Arbuthnot was so very plain as all that. Of course his mother would not like to suppose they considered the appearance of the governess at all, for a governess was hardly expected to have an appearance beyond that of modest self-effacement. It was rather odd his mother did not know, or did not choose to know, that men always looked at women to see if they were pretty, duchesses, governesses or servant girls, and he was himself no exception.

Beyond the fact that Miss Arbuthnot was governess to his niece, who was now, peculiarly, his ward, he had an inclination to take an interest in her, for Georgie had told him of the circumstances, beyond financial, that had induced Miss Arbuthnot to take a post as a governess. She had been courted by a young man of sufficient means to marry her, but before the expected announcement of their engagement, her younger sister, an apparently feather-headed, bonny fifteen-year-old, had returned from a prolonged visit to her godmother. The young man had switched his attentions and was now wed to the younger sister, though he had been obliged to wait, on the insistence of her father, until she had reached the age of sixteen. Georgie had not told Lord and Lady Charles because she thought it unfortunate for Miss Arbuthnot that everyone should know of her history, both sad and humiliating. She had told her brother, partly because she was in the habit of telling him things and partly because she knew him to admire courage, which surely Miss Arbuthnot possessed.

Lord Charles, pleased at seeing more faces round the table, said, 'Well, Lottie, how do you go on with the pony?'

Lottie did not reply because her mouth was full, and that she had known about even before Miss Arbuthnot had reminded her. She had a piece of ribbon round her right wrist to help her to remember that most people wielded the knife in their right hand and that it was best to comply with what was customary if one was not to draw attention to oneself, and also not to exchange the knife for the fork in an absent moment.

'I wish you and Grandmama would come and watch me ride. Though I'm not any good at it yet, I like it better than anything.'

'And York,' Lady Charles said, 'I hope he doesn't use bad language.'

Lottie, forgetting previous advice, could not refrain from lowering her voice and saying, 'What's them legs for? Them legs is for gripping the pommel. Now, missy, don't you ’ang on to the pony’s ’ead or I’ll ’ave yer guts fer garters.’ She burst out laughing.

‘Oh dear, Lottie,’ her grandfather said, ‘I fear you will have to go on the stage,’ but he could not help laughing himself. Why, he thought, I had nearly forgotten how to laugh.

Lottie thought she had an appreciative audience but for her grandmother, who did not understand when things were funny, but perhaps she could not help herself. Lottie was charitable, enjoying her dinner, more varied and nicer than that served up in the schoolroom. She also remembered to say, ‘No, thank you,’ in a polite, disinterested manner when faced with something new: Lottie had not outgrown the notion that anything new could not be considered a comestible.

Lady Charles now said, ‘I’m sure we won’t know what to do with you when you are a grown-up young lady.’

‘I don’t want to be a grown-up young lady,’ Lottie replied. ‘I want to be a boy and go to sea with Horatio, and I shall climb the yardarm once I know what it is.’

‘Don’t be silly, dear.’

Major Wilder said, ‘Perhaps Miss Arbuthnot would tell us how York behaves himself.’ He wondered whether she would be too shy, in her circumstances, to speak with confidence. In the schoolroom she had talked confidently of Lottie’s schooling, but that was her employment, of which he would expect her to speak with confidence.

Miss Arbuthnot said calmly, ‘I think, despite his manner, York is fond of children and he knows how to make himself clear.’

‘You are perfectly correct, though he would not own to

it: York is fond of children.' Major Wilder had once praised York for his rough kindness to the little boys, Spanish and Portuguese, or the children of the camp followers, for little boys seemed the same the world over: they were inclined to hang about the artillery park, fascinated by the guns. York, who gave no impression he liked praise, had muttered that he had had two of his own who had been with him in the winter of 1808, when he was still a serving soldier. Major Wilder had not needed to be told more. In the winter of 1808 the army had retreated to Corunna, and men, women and babies, children, horses, mules and donkeys had died in the snowy passes; starved, exhausted, harried by the French. York had then received his discharge, having served his time as a soldier, but having nothing for which to remain at home, and knowing no other life, he had offered himself as a servant with experience of campaigning. Major Wilder, then a captain, had employed him.

Lord Charles said, 'And he lost both those boys?'

Major Wilder merely repeated that York had lost his children but he did not tell them in what manner.

Miss Arbuthnot looked thoughtful. He said to her, 'You see York's merit?'

She replied, 'When Master Kingston joins us, he takes the trouble to change the side-saddle and to give him a lesson of his own.'

'Horatio is all arms and legs,' Lottie said. 'Miss 'Buthnot says it does me no harm to share but at first I didn't like it. Now I can say, without fibbing, I like Horatio to have his turn. Miss 'Buthnot has to walk and walk because we can go right round the park with the pony.'

'And what are your plans, Thomas,' Lady Charles asked, 'for when Lottie can ride without anyone to lead her?'

Major Wilder thought his mother worried about curious things. 'York can still take her and ride himself.'

'But she cannot go on her own. Is Miss Arbuthnot to run behind them?'

'That would, I believe, be exceeding her duties.'

'Miss 'Buthnot knows how to ride a horse,' Lottie said.

Major Wilder, looking at Miss Arbuthnot, said, 'Is that so?'

She smiled and agreed that it was.

'And how did you come to learn?' Lord Charles asked.

She turned towards him, hesitated and then replied, 'Through disobedience and naughtiness.'

'Why, my dear,' he replied benignly, 'I hope we are to hear about that.'

Major Wilder, seeing she still hesitated, said, half laughing, 'We will bring up the guns in support of you.'

Lady Charles thought Thomas had been too long in the army. She wished he would not lace a conversation with military phrases.

Lord Charles said, 'Yes, certainly you must tell, and we won't condemn you for youthful indiscretion,' though when he looked down the table at Miss Arbuthnot, he thought youth still apparent.

Miss Arbuthnot said, 'When I was a child we had a pony for fetching things from market and suchlike. My brother Robert, from whom I was inseparable, liked to ride it and I would scramble along after him as best I could. Bobby was a fair-minded boy, so after a bit, when we were out on the moor and thought no one could see us, he would get off Jenny Wren, as we called her, and I would get on, like a boy. I learnt to canter and gallop, just like Bobby.' She thought this picture too vividly conjured her brother, her dearest Bobby, and those carefree days so abruptly ended.

Lady Charles said, 'And I suppose your father heard of it?'

Miss Arbuthnot smiled, but it was a sad smile. She said, 'He was angrier than I had ever seen him, my mother too.' While she spoke she thought of her mother who, though shocked, had not been nearly as angry as her father. Her mother had had that happy knack of finding something a little funny in most situations, even in the wrath of her husband. 'My father was equally cross with Bobby and neither of us was to take the pony out ever again, but of course it was never as simple as that. Bobby had always been required to take messages and run errands, and my father found it inconvenient to dispense with his services. The parish is a large one and it was impractical not to use the pony. I started to tag along as usual. It crossed our minds I could learn to sit sideways on Bobby's saddle, that no one could object to that, though I thought it rather tricky when I tried it. When I got bold enough to trot, I fell off and banged my head.'

Major Wilder contemplated the image of this red-headed child in pinny and smock tumbling about the moors. Lord Charles thought his own daughters had lacked such an adventurous spirit, for which he supposed he ought to be grateful.

Lady Charles said, 'That must have been the finish of your riding a horse.'

'Oh, no,' Miss Arbuthnot said. 'It was the beginning.

Through the great kindness of our neighbour, our friend and also our patron, Mr Hamilton, who heard of our exploits, I was able to ride as much as I liked. He told me to take out his daughters' pony, larger then Jenny, for they didn't ride it, being nervous. He had his groom put the side-saddle on it. My father thought we should be punished rather than indulged, but Mr Hamilton said, "Let them enjoy themselves while they can, before young Robert goes to sea." My father couldn't refuse, so Bobby and I had a pony each and we rode nearly every day, until he did go to sea. Since then I have not ridden.'

Lottie said, 'And were you hurt very much when you banged your head?'

'Enough for the doctor to come and Bobby to be mortified, but I mended.'

'Your brother,' Major Wilder said, 'entered the navy late?'

'Oh, very late. He was nearly sixteen.' Their mother had died and Bobby had gone to sea almost simultaneously: their childhood had ended with a violent abruptness. She said, 'My father hoped he would change his mind. He wanted to send him to Oxford that he might enter the Church.'

Lord Charles thought, Why, we have learnt more about Miss Arbuthnot in the last five minutes than in all the time she has been here. She has character, is quite charming and keeps Lottie so happy. He said, 'Well, we have many a side-saddle tucked away in the harness room, so I hope you won't feel it exceeds your duties to accompany Lottie.'

Lady Charles said, 'But I doubt we will have a suitable horse.'

'Of course we will have a suitable horse,' Lord Charles replied. 'Thomas will find one.'

Major Wilder sat on the grey Andalusian, the reins slack on its neck for it never moved without instruction, watching the antics of Hall and a stable-boy in trying to get his father on to the thoroughbred. He seethed with impatience, though he did his best to disguise it. He wondered at his father clinging to the habits of his youth in insisting on such an inappropriate mount. Every day they had to go through this circus. His father had turned into a feeble old man, whether from his age or the shock of Lyndon's death, who could say? He ought to respect his father, as he respected officers senior to himself, though there had been occasions when that had not been as straightforward as it sounded. Who had not been obliged to obey an order they knew would be countermanded before the day was out?

Why did he, Thomas Wilder, so grieve for his military life, he who was now in the fortunate position of having his future secured? He thought his state one of peculiar imprisonment with two elderly parents, a child and a governess, and he was still puzzled by the dilapidation into which Ridley had fallen. Three days ago he had started to make notes in his pocketbook on the condition of the estate, from small things such as the disintegration of gates and how much of the iron could be salvaged for the construction of new ones to the larger matters of roofs and barns. These jottings slid not incongruously straight on from the need of eight hundred horseshoes and three thousand, two hundred nails; one horse shot for having the glanders and gunner Stevens court-martialled for selling a ration of corn.

Nothing could be done for Ridley without expenditure. He found his father elusive where money was concerned, as he was over any practical matter. It had taken half a day to find a map of the estate, endless shufflings of files and heaps of paper in the office, the opening and shutting of the same drawers ten times over. Sooner or later he must be allowed to look at the books. If he was not to do so, he might as well return to France.

At last Lord Charles was aboard. He apologized. His son made no comment. Together they set off down the drive, the greyhounds trotting behind. Major Wilder's silence made Lord Charles anxious. Though he was delighted with the boy, the way he made sketches of the various farm buildings, his admiration was more than tinged with alarm. He had complimented him on the skill of his drawings, but Thomas had merely replied, abruptly, that it was a necessary part of his job. Lord Charles could see his son found him exasperating, which did not surprise him: his answers to a stream of questions were unsatisfactory. What alternatives were there to saying, 'Yes, indeed, you are right, it was meant to be done last year'; 'It is good you draw my attention to it, it must have slipped my mind'; 'When the agent was here I never had to trouble myself and now it has got out of hand'?

Today Thomas seemed less inclined to ask him questions, perhaps, Lord Charles realized uneasily, because he was coming to see the futility of it.

Major Wilder was actually thinking it would be easier

to go round the estate by himself, but he knew this would disappoint his father, which, despite his irritation, he really did not wish. A watery sunlight illuminated the park. How many trees would they need to replace the ones that had been felled? That had to be done, if only for the sake of appearances, the following autumn. This spring sheep must graze, not horses, for the horses had soured the grass. Unless he stayed nothing would happen, no trees, no sheep. He turned to his father and said, 'Lyndon's horses, was it your intention to keep them for ever?'

'I didn't like to think of them but sometimes, in the summer, I had the idea of Lyndon strolling through the park, of the shadows, the trees and the sunshine, to look over his horses, the chestnuts and the bays with which I particularly associate him; or later in the year setting off for hunting in a red coat, his hat at a rakish angle. Then I knew he would be back, that I had kept faith with him, but later . . . when I knew he was dead, I still had the pictures.' Lord Charles wondered what Thomas would make of that.

Major Wilder considered saying, 'Yet you cut the trees down, bar two or three,' but he knew the necessity of curbing his tongue. Besides, he understood the images as his father conjured them, though it was folly to speak of them. Had he not, from time to time, peopled the guns with ghosts, most of whom, in life, had died before his eyes? It was unwise: was it not necessary to look forward rather than back in order to do one's duty and stare the enemy in the eye? War was, of course, a horrid mistake and inured one to horrid sights: it was with difficulty one kept one's humanity and remembered one's honour, while holding the ghosts at bay.

Finding Thomas made no reply, Lord Charles said, 'But we may not keep the horses, unless you will like to hunt yourself.'

'Certainly, should I still be here.' He wished it were the hunting season for that of all things took a man out of himself.

Lord Charles thought, He has to stay, he has to be here, whatever the cost. He said, 'Would you keep a couple of Lyndon's for yourself?'

Major Wilder was at last seen to smile. 'Lyndon and I were sufficiently different for even our horses not to suit.'

Lord Charles was uncertain of Thomas's taste in horses. He thought the Andalusian, though a pretty sort of creature, peculiar or, at the least, quaint. He could not imagine Lyndon riding it.

'My Andalusian won't do for fox-hunting, he would think it a foreign entertainment, but he will make a fine covert hack.'

Lord Charles felt himself forgiven for the irritation he had caused. 'I suppose Lyndon and I were alike when it came to horses. Lyndon always wanted something that was up to the mark, that had a lot of dash. He liked to be mastering his horses.'

Major Wilder thought his brother had liked to dominate his horses, but he decided against explaining the difference. He said, 'Well, what would you have me do?'

'Under Lyndon's will, they are yours to do with as you like.'

'I suppose they are. We must get the park back in order. If I sell the horses I would be happy to contribute the money to the replanting.' Major Wilder was not sure why he thought this might be necessary. He paused. 'Do you mind telling me why you took the oaks out?'

Lord Charles replied, 'I had a lot of unexpected expense.'

Major Wilder did not consider this an answer but he refrained from further questioning: it was a waste of his breath. Later that day he gave instructions for the horses to be stabled that he might inspect them.

Lord Charles acquiesced with the arrangements. He wished he had taken the initiative and done it himself, but his apparent lack of enterprise was surely the reason Thomas had to be at home. He wondered at Thomas's efficiency. Grass never would be allowed to grow under his feet. Was that what the army had done for him? Where was the little boy who was inclined either to sulk or to lose his temper? Had he sulked, or merely drawn into himself? The metamorphosis from child to man was too much to comprehend.

In the drawing room at Ridley, Mrs Kingston sat with Lady Charles. She had put off visiting for a while, out of delicacy. Was not the return of Major Wilder a momentous occurrence, and his announcing his intention of so doing very sudden? Of course it was easier to return now the army was in France. Her brother had had all the anxiety of coming from Lisbon in a transport ship whereas, she believed, Major Wilder had left from Bordeaux. Poor dear Lady Charles was, not unnaturally, confused: the shock of her elder son's death had so disturbed her, she knew not how she should be with the younger now taking his place. She needed to remind herself it was not Major Wilder's fault he did not lie dead while his brother was gone for ever. It had taken Mrs Kingston several weeks to reach this conclusion, but she was confident she had assessed it correctly, though none of it could be mentioned.

Now she was at Ridley, she hoped she might meet Major Wilder. Would he resemble his brother? She trembled to think that he might. Horatio, who had taken to scampering off across the park on his own the minute his lessons were finished, which she half thought he ought not to do, she had cross-examined. The conversation had run thus:

Mrs Kingston: 'What sort of a gentleman is Major Wilder?'

Horatio: 'Lottie likes him.'

Mrs Kingston: 'She should be fond of her uncle.'

Horatio: 'I'm not fond of my uncle. He wouldn't give me a pony, even if he were rich, and I think he's rather poor.'

Mrs Kingston: 'Your uncle Henry is a sick man. When you are older you will understand.'

Horatio, scowling, had made no reply.

Mrs Kingston, deeming it wiser not to embark upon the subject of her brother's relationship with her son, had returned to her original subject: 'Tell me what Major Wilder looks like. Is he tall? Is he fair?'

Horatio, after much thought: 'He looks like a soldier, more than Uncle Henry. He's not tall or short and his hair is sort of brown, I think. I haven't seen him without his hat.'

Mrs Kingston: 'Does he speak to you?'

Horatio: 'He says, "Good day, Mr Kingston." I say, "Good day, sir," but we don't say anything to each other after that. He goes off on his horse with the long mane and tail. It's a

Spanish horse and he and York talk to it in Spanish and tell it what to do.'

Hence Mrs Kingston had failed to form much of a picture of Major Wilder, and Horatio was more interested in the horse and York, for he launched into a fulsome description of both. While he was doing so, she wondered if Lyndon Wilder had looked like a soldier. Without a uniform there was not a hint of it, and she had seen him in uniform only the once, when he had come to bid her goodbye. At the thought of that interview she would have wept but for the presence of her child. Would Major Wilder remind her of his poor lost brother?

When Mrs Kingston had arrived at Ridley she saw the shutters were all put back from the windows, which delighted her: living in the dark was far from healthy, however much it might have suited Lady Charles's state of mind. She was greeted warmly by her friend, who for the first time embraced her and kissed her cheek.

'My dear Mrs Kingston, I'm so very glad to see you.' Lady Charles said this in all honesty for she had missed any person in whom she felt she might confide and, having already spoken with greater freedom to Mrs Kingston than she had intended, she thought not much more harm could be done. Her husband, never much use as a confidant, she considered entirely under the spell of their remaining son. 'I can talk to no one,' she continued, 'but you I may trust.'

Flattered, Mrs Kingston said, 'Dear Lady Charles, I am sure you can trust me implicitly, but are you not glad to have your son safely at home? He seemed so adamant he wouldn't come.'

'I know, I know. For some reason he changed his mind.

It hasn't been discussed. I dare say he thinks the war will be over soon. He causes rather too much disturbance in the household.'

'I expect he is used to having his own way. An artillery troop is a dreadful responsibility, for they must care for the guns, six, I believe, as well as the men and the horses.' Mrs Kingston had taken care to learn something of the Artillery from her brother and for once he had obliged her. She was not only interested in Major Wilder as possibly resembling his brother, but as a bachelor likely to take up residence at Ridley, which, as far as the neighbourhood was concerned, was short of bachelors, or even widowers.

'Yes, a great many men and horses, over a hundred of each, as well as the Corps of Drivers, which Henry says are a terrible nuisance, and then there are mules, all in great quantity, but perhaps they are not for the Horse Artillery, I forget now, but I'm sure they need them for carrying the forge for the shoeing and the coal, and it must all be got over rivers and up mountains. My brother is very familiar with it, for sometimes the infantry is required to assist in such manoeuvres. There is a deal of bother attached to an artillery troop, Henry says.'

Lady Charles listened to her with as much patience as she could muster. She said, 'He is certainly accustomed to doing what he wants, but as there must always be someone senior to him, you would think he was also accustomed to taking orders. We are very constrained because he insists on Lottie and her governess coming down to dinner. Once the servants had left the room we used to speak freely but now . . . I feel I'm pretending, acting a part.'

'But you will become accustomed to Miss Arbuthnot,

and think how Lottie will benefit from your society. That is surely Major Wilder's intention, even if it's a little awkward at the start.'

'I dare say, but he doesn't mind her learning a very vulgar, common sort of language from his servant. You must watch over your little boy for the same thing,' Lady Charles said, but privately she thought that if Horatio was to enter the navy, it would not matter what sort of language he used. 'As for Lord Charles, he is entirely taken up with riding round and round the estate with Major Wilder until he is exhausted. Our son sets him to fretting about our affairs, which have never before caused us the least concern. You may suppose I am biased against him, but he doesn't understand me. The long years of army life have blunted his sensibilities.'

'Perhaps he needs more time,' Mrs Kingston said.

Lady Charles started to weep. She got a little white handkerchief from her reticule. 'My poor lost boy, he anticipated my every thought.'

Mrs Kingston was ready to be overcome herself, but Lady Charles, once more in control of her emotions, continued: 'The clock is a typical instance of Major Wilder's conduct. I have always taken solace by sitting quietly in Lyndon's rooms, and I used to wind up the clock with my own hand, keeping faith with his likely return. When the news came . . . of his death, I forbade that it be touched. I couldn't bear the chime because he would never hear it now.'

'But does Major Wilder insist on the clock being wound?' Mrs Kingston asked, confused. 'Surely you must tell him you don't have it wound.'

'I went to Lyndon's rooms. The clock began to strike. Nobody went there except for myself. I dusted and swept the floor. To hear the clock . . . When I saw Thomas, I said, "We don't wind that clock," but I couldn't find the words to explain so he just shrugged his shoulders and said he would take it to his own room so I need not be troubled by it. The clock is his. Everything that belonged to Lyndon now belongs to Thomas. I don't go to Lyndon's rooms any more.'

Lady Charles again burst into tears. Mrs Kingston struggled for words. 'There now, dear Lady Charles, you will make yourself ill. Sooner or later one must get along with things. I gave my poor late husband's uniforms to a boy I knew just getting his promotion. It hurt me at the time but I thought, If I keep them for Horatio, the moth will get them, besides which, they are bound to change the detail with some new regulation. I kept his sword for Horatio but even that may turn out old-fashioned.'

Lady Charles sighed, but again wiped away her tears. As she did so the door opened and Major Wilder entered the room. He said, 'I beg your pardon. I didn't realize you had company.'

He made as if to leave but Lady Charles stopped him, saying she wished to introduce him to Mrs Kingston, so he stepped forward, laid on a table a writing box he had had under his arm, and made his bow. He was so unlike his brother, in the eyes of Mrs Kingston, that she was wretchedly overcome. Mr Wilder had been a man with such grace, such address, that Major Wilder, who had not his figure or his inimitable manner of dressing himself, could only be a disappointment. However, she declared, as she must, how delighted she was to meet him, and he dutifully took the chair between herself and his mother.

Lady Charles was preoccupied with gazing at the writing box, which she knew to be the one she had given Lyndon so long ago. Thomas had laid it down beyond her reach but she thought it as well he had not placed it in her lap for she wanted no audience when she again held it in her hands or turned the little key in its lock.

'How relieved you must be, Major Wilder,' Mrs Kingston said, 'to be safely returned from the horrid sights of war.'

'I can't say I am,' Major Wilder replied.

'Oh, but the hardship and the difficulties.'

'Certainly there are those.'

'My brother, who has had to return owing to his poor state of health, feels it extremely.'

Major Wilder was not entirely sure whether it was the difficulties or the return that so affected Mrs Kingston's brother but, deciding it made little difference, he said, 'I dare say it is too much for some.'

'He says half the time you are starved, that you live worse than gypsies.'

'Quite so, but the other half of the time we don't.'

Mrs Kingston correctly suspected him of laughing at her, though she could not tell why he should. She said, nettled, 'I don't see how a gentleman, nicely reared, can put up with it, eating oil and garlic and lying down with bed-bugs or out in a ditch.'

'Oil and garlic is preferable to nothing.'

'And,' Mrs Kingston added triumphantly, for she wished him to understand she knew about such things, 'I hear if one of those guns sticks, even the officers get down in the mud and push at it.'

'Yes,' he replied gravely. 'It's called putting your shoulder to the wheel.'

Mrs Kingston decided it would be expedient to change the subject for Major Wilder might be one of those gentlemen who found it trying to discuss their exploits, possibly distressing, and had he not lost his brother? She said, going off in a new direction, 'I hope my little boy doesn't make a nuisance of himself and take up too much of your servant's time. After all, the pony is Miss Wilder's.'

'That doesn't matter in the least but he should have a pony of his own.'

'That is the difficulty of being a widow. One doesn't know what is best. Who is to advise me on a suitable pony? Besides, it never occurred to me he should have one.'

Lady Charles, who could not take her eye or her mind from the writing box, was still half listening to the conversation. She said, 'As the boy is to go away to sea, is it worth the trouble?'

Major Wilder asked when he was to go and, on hearing it was not for a year, said, 'Let the child have his amusement. I can ask York to look one out on market day. He will know what is suitable.'

Mrs Kingston now thought Major Wilder more agreeable than had been her first impression.

Major Wilder was aware that she was the woman, because his father had told him so, they had rather expected Lyndon to marry. As far as Lyndon was concerned he supposed anything, down that line, a possibility. Mrs Kingston was certainly pretty, like a dove, all soft plumage and pouting bosom. He said, 'I understand from Lottie your son has little fancy for his chosen career.'

'Oh dear me, no, you are quite mistaken. I wonder how Lottie came by such a notion. Horatio adores everything to do with the navy. He knows the names of all the ships that were at Trafalgar and is always studying his book that explains the rigging and the sails.'

Major Wilder gave an almost imperceptible lift of his brow. 'Who could know better than his mother?'

Irony passed with benign impunity over Mrs Kingston's head. 'Ah, yes, we mothers know. Either way, it must be best to settle a boy on his career from a young age so he always has a proper understanding of his future. As to not liking it, what can he know of it before he begins?'

'What indeed?' Major Wilder replied.

They were interrupted by Lottie, her hair squeezed under a cap with a feather in it that had been deemed suitable riding attire by her grandmother, peering round the door and saying, 'Please may we come in?'

It was unusual for Lottie to appear at times other than those allotted. Lady Charles said, 'What is it, dear? What are you doing?'

'I'm going for my ride but we want to see my papa's writing box, which has a secret drawer. Uncle Thomas said so.'

Lady Charles said, 'You run a little wild, Lottie. Where is Miss Arbuthnot?'

'Putting on her boots.'

Major Wilder said, 'Come along in, Lottie, seeing you are halfway in already. I was about to give it to your grandmother, but I will certainly show it to you.'

Lottie tumbled into the room, followed by Horatio, to

the astonishment and consternation of his mother. 'You are a naughty boy! I don't know where you are from one moment to the next.'

Major Wilder, who was of the opinion one should not know where children were from one moment to the next, got up to show them the box, though not before Horatio was made to make his bow to Lady Charles, which he did a little perfunctorily, and Lottie had kissed the cheek of Mrs Kingston.

'Oh, it is a beautiful box,' Lottie said, tracing the brass binding with her finger, but Horatio was interested only in finding out its secret. He diligently examined the various shapes and sizes of the compartments.

'I can see where it must be,' he said, 'but how to get in it?'

'Show us, show us!' Lottie cried.

'Give the boy time,' Major Wilder said.

'Horatio doesn't like it when you call him Mr Kingston. It makes him feel he has already gone to join the navy,' Lottie said.

'That is what he thinks, is it? Well, Horatio, can you puzzle it? Your name is a bit too much to live up to for seagoing folk, but fortunately even your closest friends need never know the H is not for Henry.'

Horatio looked up at him and smiled. Major Wilder told him to remove the inkwells. Pleased, he then located the spring that released the panel. Lady Charles, to whom the box had been sacred, now saw it had become a mere ploy to amuse children, prodded and poked by any passing soul, its connection to Lyndon as remote as though it had never been.

Mrs Kingston, tired of the writing box, said to Lottie, 'What is your pony called?'

'York calls her Pie, because she's black and white, but we call her Jenny Wren, like the pony Miss Arbuthnot had. We think that's a much better name.'

'Better not keep York waiting,' Major Wilder said. 'You'll make him cross.'

Mrs Kingston thought she would go out and see the pony for herself so she left the room with the children. Lottie could be heard saying, in York's voice, 'A more orderly arrangement of them limbs, Master Kingston.' She and Horatio burst into giggles.

Major Wilder, left alone with his mother, said, 'I brought the box down for you.'

She said coldly, 'I no longer want it.'

'In that case I shall give it to Lottie.'

Lady Charles said, 'You don't understand death or loss, do you?'

A moment later she regretted saying this. She saw she had made him extremely angry.

'That is an extraordinary thing to say to an officer, indeed to any soldier, who has been on active service for the best part of five years.' He turned his back and left the room abruptly.

He always left a room rather than allow he had lost his temper.

For a while she sat looking out of the window whence she could see Lottie and the pony, York at its head, Miss Arbuthnot striding along beside them, Horatio scampering about like a small dog and Mrs Kingston trailing behind, holding her skirts up out of the dirt. Yes, she had said something to Thomas that would have been better left unsaid, but Thomas should make more effort to understand her. It was really, she thought, his fault. He had not, when leaving the room, taken the box. She laid her hand on the lid. What if she had received it just as Lyndon had left it, his pocketbooks, which Thomas had so unaccountably destroyed, stuffed behind the panel with his will? Would she have read the will and had the courage to destroy it? Lyndon could only have been in a state of depression, brought on by the horrors of the campaign, when he wrote it, not in a right state of mind, that he took the care of his only child out of her hands. She was sure, had he thought about it, he would have wished her to destroy it and probably meant to have done so himself and retrieve the second copy, but he was always lackadaisical and would have put it off for another day.

Lady Charles ran her hand over the brass plate. She remembered ordering the inscription, 'J. L. Wilder', and declining to have his regiment added, for officers too often changed regiments to get their promotion. When she had purchased the box and fitted it out for Lyndon, she wondered how it had never crossed her mind she might be faced with opening the lid after he was dead.

Inside, under the green baize, there were two broken pens, a candle end and a lump of blood-red sealing wax.

Lottie's bed had flower-sprigged curtains, blue on white: Susan drew them at night, which made her feel safe and warm, but in the morning, now the sun rose early, she felt the curtains to be more of a cage. She tugged them back so she could see out of the window: the weather had become significant. There was no riding on wet days and neither was she allowed the happy alternative of spending her remaining free hours in her newly awakening garden. If it rained Horatio was forbidden to come across the park, but he came all the same, fibbed cheerfully in announcing the wet had only come on after he had left. He would be filthy and his clothes soaking. Why had she not been born a boy?

Miss Arbuthnot had devised a means of amusing her indoors. Together they were making garments for the poor children of the village. Lottie much preferred this to her sampler, it having obvious practical purpose. She was not neat but she improved. Sometimes Horatio was there to assist, proving, when settled, perfectly adept. He said, resignedly, he believed sailors could always sew. Lady Charles ungrudgingly provided the materials for so worthy a project. Miss Arbuthnot patiently taught both children how to attach buttons, gather, hem, lay out cloth and cut patterns. With scraps of discarded lace or ribbon, she added a little charm to garments that would otherwise have been dreary, trying to remember what she had learnt from her mother, who had had greater skill than she in making things pretty.

Lottie lay in bed and looked out of the window. It was quite a good morning, some sun, some clouds. She thought the day not long enough for all her occupations: lessons, sewing, riding, digging her garden, straightening out Horatio's garden, music, Susan doing her hair, changing for dinner, which she now thought rather a protracted activity; and sitting with her grandmother sewing her sampler while Lady Charles read to her, though with frequent interruptions to correct clumsy stitching and other mistakes; and then Susan coming to fetch her, grasping a candle, to put her to bed, as if she could not put herself to bed – as Miss Arbuthnot had pointed out to her, she had done so when Susan had the influenza.

A series of apparently disconnected thoughts started to run through Lottie's head, starting with Miss Arbuthnot, passing to Horatio, the half-hour she had to spend sitting still while Susan untangled her hair and the calico that lay on the schoolroom table waiting to be cut. She got out of bed and paused to take an even closer examination of the weather before opening the door that led from the nursery to the schoolroom. Her books were neatly piled among sundry articles such as thread, thimbles, a pincushion, the calico and a pair of scissors. She picked up the latter. They were long and heavy in her hand, real scissors, not little blunt things for children to cut snips of paper. She carried them back to the nursery and went straight to the looking-glass on the dressing-table, an article of furniture Lady Charles had recently installed in the hope of encouraging her granddaughter to take more trouble with her appearance. It had a variety of ribbons hanging from it and a brush and comb laid side by side as Susan had left them.

Lottie contemplated her face. Her eyes were round and blue and her hair stuck up like a halo before it tumbled right down her back nearly to the point where her legs started. Her grandmother had told her how proud she had been as a child to be able to sit on hers. Now Lottie swiped at her hair with the scissors, but they went wide and cut nothing. It was because, she reasoned, she was looking in the glass, which made you go left when you meant to go right. Horatio had told her the story of Perseus, who had managed to cut off Medusa's head while looking at the creature's reflection in his shield. She thought she would have had to strike out in every direction before getting a sword anywhere near Medusa's head, and Medusa would have had plenty of time to turn her into stone. She tried again, caught a curl or two, but the scissors did not cut. She recalled Miss Arbuthnot instructing her to use the scissors in her right hand. So, she must not look in the glass and she must use her right hand. A moment later, under her left ear, the scissors slithered through the hair, which fell silently to the floor. Lottie gave a little wriggle of satisfaction. Wielding the scissors with even greater care, she worked them as far round to the back of her head as she could reach, closing her eyes in order to concentrate, before starting again on the right, which was more difficult but not impossible. Soon there was a large heap of hair on the floor; her head felt light, her neck cool. She returned to the glass. Her hair was still too long at the top of her head. She ran her fingers through it and snipped some more.

Out loud, she said, 'They can't put my hair back on. It's gone.' She flung the scissors down, waved her arms in the air and jumped about.

It was early yet. Susan would come with a jug of warm water to pour into the china basin. Today, she thought, she had better get dressed without washing and do up all her buttons. She wondered how best to manage the ensuing unpleasantness, but changed her mind about dressing and returned, in her bare feet and nightgown, to the school-room. There was, after all, a useful purpose in being able to write: announcements could be made and people prepared in advance. Here was all she needed, pencils and a sheet of paper. She hesitated before the ink bottle: surely to write in ink was more grown-up, but Miss Arbuthnot always kept the ink at arm's length and slightly more, a pencil being more reliable. Lottie sat down at the table and wrote a letter to her grandmother.

Still in her nightgown, she left the schoolroom and ran along the passage to the stairs, then down the stairs, two flights, and into the hall. The stone flagging was cold to her bare feet and the house was shuttered. She peered at the regulator. There was just sufficient light for her to be able to make out the time, rather a recent accomplishment. Shortly someone would come, light the dining-room fire and lay out the china for breakfast, or so she thought, but breakfast was not until ten o'clock, so it was a little early. She believed it to be only just after eight. Perhaps breakfast was rather too late for her grandmother to receive the letter. As she could not seal it the servants might read it. She thought of the red sealing wax, the wax-jack, on her grandfather's desk, but she could not undertake to master it just now, however omnipotent she might be feeling. No, she would slide the letter under her grandmother's bedroom door.

Lottie skipped out of the dining room and into the gloom of the shuttered hall. As she did so, a housemaid was approaching the stairs carrying a tray upon which was a plate of biscuits, a small bunch of fresh flowers and a cup of hot chocolate. At the sight of Lottie emerging from the half-light in her nightgown, she screamed, dropped the tray with a fearful crash and bolted for the passage with cries of hysteria. Lottie leapt over the broken china and fled upstairs as fast as she could. Stopping only to shove the letter under her grandmother's door, she tore to the nursery and jumped back into bed, disappearing under the bedclothes.

At nine o'clock Lord Charles sat at his desk in the library, ostensibly to attend to his correspondence. He would pick up one letter after another, read them through, put them in neat piles, sharpen a pen, think of this and that, then get out his pocket watch to see if it were sufficiently close to the breakfast hour for it not to be worth while to begin. He could, after all, write letters at another time of day, and should he go out with Thomas, he might see some of his various correspondents, which would render writing them letters a waste of time.

As he was making these customary ruminations, his son strode through the door in the wonderfully brisk manner he adopted from the moment he opened his eyes in the morning. They wished one another good morning before Major Wilder said, 'Today I had better look at the books.'

Lord Charles was unprepared. He said, in a hesitating way, 'The books? Isn't the weather rather too good for those?'

'I am not prepared to put off the moment indefinitely.'

'But surely the books, the accounts, are just tiresome things I should manage for myself.'

Major Wilder thought that if his father were managing the books for himself, it would be a different matter. He climbed the library steps and idly searched the titles under his immediate eye. The library was of his grandfather's compiling. 'If I am not to look at the accounts, I would be better occupied returning to France.'

Lord Charles clenched his hand on the bill he was holding for two months' worth of candles.

'After all,' Major Wilder continued, 'a child could see nothing is right. A considerable sum needs to be spent on the estate, and one of us needs to discover from where that sum is to come. If you will not allow me to assist, why should I stay?'

'Thomas, I used to write and beg you to come home after Lyndon was killed. You wouldn't. You would see the war out. You wouldn't be allowed. Then, quite suddenly, out of the blue, you announced your return. Within days you were here. The war is not over. Why then have you come?'

Major Wilder reached down a book and tapped it on the shelf to shake off the dust. 'My wound.'

'Your wound?' Lord Charles said, bemused. 'What wound?'

'I received a musket ball through the shoulder at Orthez. It passed from front to back without touching the bone. February the twenty-seventh was the date.'

'But, Thomas,' Lord Charles said, appalled at the idea, and shocked at being in ignorance. 'Eight, ten inches lower, it would have gone straight through your heart or your lung.'

Major Wilder laughed, though he was disturbed to see his father so mortified. 'And what about an inch or so to the right? I am afraid eight or ten inches is not a miss to be conjured with. Should you like me to take a measuring stick to it? As for a lung, it can heal well enough.'

'Why didn't you say?'

Major Wilder shrugged. 'It was very trifling.'

'Did you tell Georgie?'

'Certainly not. It healed fairly well but I opened it again. The roads being so deep, everything sticking, a wheel slipped when I was trying to make an adjustment. Our surgeon was cross. He said he would insist on my taking sick leave to give it more time. As nothing much was happening just then, I thought I would return to Ridley as you were so anxious I should.' Now it occurred to him he ought to explain himself a little more. After a moment, he continued, 'I never expected to inherit Ridley. I was always to make my own way.' His mind started to drift and he remained silent, still leaning on the library steps. He could hardly forget the exact minute he was brought the news of Lyndon's death, but he had not consciously registered the implication to himself.

He was having the horses run up, one after another, a tedious but necessary process to check them for any unsoundness. He had felt the back of a big black gelding for an incipient sore, and at that moment a friend of his, a staff officer, Colonel Bowen, from another regiment, had stepped up behind him and spoken his name.

'Why,' he had said, turning round, 'this is an unexpected pleasure. Where have you sprung from?'

'From Roncesvalles. Your brother's regiment was engaged.' This particular officer was one of a few who knew he had a brother.

He had turned his attention back to the horse. Bowen would understand the necessity. He asked, as he did so, 'And how was the engagement?'

'They held the pass and then they retreated. I haven't heard it all. I got leave, as I had other business this way, to see you.'

There was an odd sense of urgency in the way he spoke so Major Wilder had abandoned the horse, summoned his second captain to continue the inspection, and they had strolled away towards the village in which he was billeted. Had his friend any special orders for the troop, he had wondered hopefully, though there was more challenge than appeal in heaving the guns over the Pyrenees and crossing the rivers on the other side.

And then Colonel Bowen had said, 'It is of your brother I have to speak.'

'Is he wounded?'

'He is killed.'

For a moment he had felt as if he would faint and Bowen had grabbed his arm, but then he had recovered and said, 'But, my dear fellow, it will be a mistake. Lyndon is indestructible, positively immortal. You may be sure the French have him.'

'No. I spoke to a very young fellow, seriously wounded though lucid, poor lad, who had crawled back to your brother. He explained he hadn't intended to crawl back, but he didn't know in which direction he was going, and later, absolutely all he could remember was seeing Mr Wilder, who was certainly dead. On the other hand, they didn't bring off the dead. They got the wounded off, they believe, but no one doubted Mr Wilder's death.'

Major Wilder had said to Colonel Bowen, 'I thought I was going to faint, but I never faint. You would think we'd all faint with the things we've seen.'

'I too thought you were going to faint, but you staved it off.'

The staff officer had about an hour to spare. They walked about together, spoke of the war, how the different divisions were placed; and together they looked over the troop horses companionably, speaking little but to comment on any one particular beast. It was a way of passing the time. What a blessing was the friend who knew how little was required of him, but how important that little.

Later in the day he had messed, as was his custom, with a couple of officers from his troop. The conversation was devoted to the action at Roncesvalles and another at Maya, all high in the Pyrenees. They expected orders, at any moment, to move up or to move back. He had retired to write a letter to his parents, but he did not send it until the death was officially confirmed a few days later. It was at this point that it had become generally known, among his associates, that he had lost a brother but as he was reticent on the matter so were they. It was not until then, oddly, tardily, that it had occurred to him the change in his own circumstances. Why had it not struck him before? He never would be able to answer that. It was as though his life were a picture with which he was perfectly familiar, the pleasure he took in his position coupled with the anxiety attached to his income – his father had become erratic in paying his allowance, as had the government in paying his wages – and the subsequent fretting on the subject of promotion. He had always reckoned when his father died he would not get a penny from Lyndon, but it was not his father who had died, it was Lyndon, and the whole picture had spun, as though on an axle.

Now, still on the library steps, he looked down at his father, momentarily as confused by the change in his circumstances as he had been when it had first occurred to him.

Lord Charles was preoccupied with the nature of war. Had he lost both his sons, what then? He could not afford to lose both. What other wounds had Thomas sustained, over the years, and not troubled to mention? He watched him propped on the library steps, his mind obviously adrift, but eventually he said to him, 'Isn't your shoulder painful?'

'Nothing, now, to hold a man up. Sir, I am an authoritarian sort of fellow when it comes to business. Do you see me as high-handed? I dare say you think I am driving you into a corner, but if I can't be of use here, I can be useful elsewhere. You may say I have no right to look at the accounts until I inherit Ridley. This would be so. I wouldn't argue. We must take Toulouse fairly soon, and I should like to be there.'

Lord Charles said, 'Of course you shall look at the books. Today I will fetch them out and put them in order. Shortly it will be Lady Day. I should like you beside me when the tenants pay their rent.'

Lady Charles lay in the half-darkness of her shrouded bed. She thought Jane, the housemaid, late with her chocolate. Her clock had struck the half-hour, or so she thought, but was it half after eight or half after nine? Without drawing back the curtains and getting out of bed, she was left to guess. Had she heard a scuffle in the vicinity of the door?

If it was mice she must remember to tell them to bring up the big marmalade cat from the kitchens.

Now the door opened. She heard the sound of the tray being placed on the dressing-table. Her maid, Sally, said, 'Good morning, m'lady.'

'Is it you, Sally, bringing my chocolate? Is somebody ill?'

Sally drew back the bed curtains and did the same at the window. The sun shone over the park. 'A little disturbance downstairs, m'lady.'

'What sort of disturbance?'

Sally handed her mistress a wrap and propped up the pillows. 'Hardly what you would expect in a respectable house like ours, and Jane not given to fancy, not like that Polly. It was your favourite cup and saucer too, the chocolate cup, all fancy red and gold; and the vase the flowers were in. I picked the flowers myself, last evening. They do brighten up the tray. Though it's early, a bit can be found here and there. Anyway, they're all spoilt, and chocolate and water and broken bits of china all over the floor of the hall. It's cleared up now. By the time it was done and Jane quieted and the chocolate made again, I thought I may as well bring it up myself and get the day started.'

'How careless of Jane to drop the tray,' Lady Charles said, confused. 'She is usually so careful.'

'She had the hysterics. She came into the hall with the tray and she saw this white figure a-coming from the dining room, all gliding along like, though no bigger than a child. She said 'twas a boy in a nightshirt but of course it weren't real. I'd have sooner not told you, m'lady, with all your troubles, but you know what stories will get out, worse than the truth. 'Twas a trick of the fancy, something funny the light did.'

Lady Charles started to drink her chocolate. She did not believe in ghosts or hauntings but she had a momentary vision of a lost child, a little boy. Could Lyndon return to her thus?

'Don't you worry your head,' Sally continued. 'Now, what's this down on the floor? A piece of paper? A letter? Seems I've trod on it.'

Lady Charles took the missive after Sally had attempted to wipe it on her apron. She said, 'How charming, a letter from Miss Lottie. She has never written me a letter before. Let me see if I can puzzle what she says.'

The letter ran thus:

> *Dear Granmamma I am riting this so you dont hav a shok. I jummed from behide the door at Horatio and he went all wite an funny and Miss Buthnot sed this was bad. I hav cut my hare off. It is lovly feel an I am very happy.*
>
> *Your fecshonate granchild*
>
> *Charlotte Wilder*

The writing went in little bursts and scurries until Lottie had got under way. Lady Charles read it through twice before handing it to her maid. She said, 'Dear Sally, do you think it true? Could she be so wicked? All that beautiful hair.'

Sally read it through for herself and promptly burst into tears but equally promptly dried them again. She said,

'Well, it does seem very wilful, but isn't she getting a fine hand with her governess to manage her? It ain't right in all its parts but it's mighty fine all the same.'

Between smiles and sobs, she laid out her mistress's clothes for the morning.

Lord Charles and Major Wilder were eating their breakfast in a not entirely comfortable silence when Lady Charles joined them. Lord Charles knew that if he did not let Thomas look at the books he would lose him; he was filled with forebodings and despair. As for Major Wilder, he was aware of forcing his father to make disclosures against his will, and he was thinking of his artillery troop in France. They were both too preoccupied to pay Lady Charles any attention beyond wishing her good morning and half getting out of their chairs.

She said, 'Charles, I suppose you have heard today's calamity.'

'Slimmer told me some nonsense about Jane seeing a spook in the hall. I'm sorry the silly girl broke the china.'

'Oh dear, not that. It's Lottie.'

'Is she ill?' Lord Charles asked, suddenly anxious.

'I don't know if one would say she was ill. She has cut her hair off.'

He took a moment to digest this piece of information. Then he said, 'Dear me, the little minx, I shan't know her when I see her. What a naughty child. Thomas is her guardian so you must ask him what he means to do about it.' He was glad of the opportunity to remind his son of this other responsibility.

Major Wilder looked suitably grave. He took a long sip of his coffee. 'There seems nothing to do about it. Lottie should be reprimanded and punished, I suppose.' He glanced at his father who was clearly endeavouring to suppress a smile. They both laughed.

Lord Charles said, 'But how does she look?'

Lady Charles was affronted at their mirth. 'I haven't seen her, I couldn't have borne it. I have sent for Miss Arbuthnot to come down and explain the matter.'

Major Wilder said, 'But she may not be able to explain it.'

Lord Charles got up, saying, 'Well, my dear, I shall leave all that to you and Thomas.' He was glad to escape. 'I have the books to get out.' Now he had achieved a sort of resignation, almost a sense of relief.

A few minutes later Miss Arbuthnot knocked and entered the room. Major Wilder stood up.

Lady Charles said, 'Good morning, Miss Arbuthnot. We are very disturbed to hear of Miss Wilder's conduct in cutting her hair. Have you seen her?'

'Miss Wilder and I took breakfast together in the schoolroom, as usual.'

'And what did you say to her?'

'Nothing.'

'Why not?' Lady Charles, irritated, added, 'Thomas, why don't you sit down?'

'Because Miss Arbuthnot stands.'

Miss Arbuthnot looked at him, uncertain whether she should welcome this attention or not. Was he kind to her or annoyed with his mother?

Lady Charles said, 'Yes, please to sit down, Miss

Arbuthnot. Major Wilder will no doubt consider it his part to pour you some coffee.'

Major Wilder did exactly that. As she thanked him he noticed she had eyes of a light green-blue in her half-girl, half-woman face.

'Now, you chose not to speak to Miss Wilder,' Lady Charles continued. 'Did you not reprimand her?'

'My not speaking to Miss Wilder was quite enough for her to understand I thought she had done wrong. She told me she had written you a letter, and that we did discuss.'

'You must understand, Miss Arbuthnot, that as you have the care of our granddaughter, we are disappointed you have not been able to control this excess of irrational behaviour.'

Miss Arbuthnot looked anxious. 'Indeed, I didn't see it. Perhaps I should have done but I didn't.'

Major Wilder said, 'Well, really, I don't see how Miss Arbuthnot could have foreseen it. I doubt Lottie foresaw it herself.'

Miss Arbuthnot gave him an uncertain little smile, but she said, and he liked the way she decorously but firmly continued to fight her corner, 'It certainly was very naughty but I cannot say it was irrational. Her hair took a long time to dress and children don't like to have to sit still.'

Major Wilder said, 'Where is the little monkey? Are we not to see her all cropped and shorn?'

'I asked Polly, who is kind enough to cut my hair for me, to make Miss Wilder a little neater about the head than she managed for herself.' Miss Arbuthnot then added, 'It's very difficult cutting your own hair, because I've tried it.' She could see from Major Wilder's expression that he was amused, but Lady Charles was not and probably considered she had been contradicted.

After a little further discussion Miss Arbuthnot went away and Lottie was summoned. She flew into the room and made a rush for her grandmother, saying as she did so, 'Susan says I've been so naughty Uncle Thomas will take Jenny Wren away from me and I won't be allowed to ride her any more.' She burst into tears.

Lady Charles looked with undisguised horror at her granddaughter, but at the same time she realized Lottie, with her hair cut, more resembled her father than she had ever done before. Despite this fleeting, shadowy vision of Lyndon, the sacrifice of Lottie's magnificent hair was too great a price to pay. She said, 'That would no doubt be an appropriate punishment and one you would not forget.'

'But it would be for Uncle Thomas to decide,' Lottie said, drying her eyes, a little belligerent. 'I don't think it a good punishment because it would last for ever, even after my hair had grown, so that wouldn't be fair.' She thought warmly of the scissors.

Major Wilder said, 'Come here, child, and stop scowling at your grandmother. Let's have a look at you. Well, well, I've seen worse for a haircut.'

'Uncle Thomas, would you take Jenny Wren away from me?'

'Ah yes, that is what you call her. No. She is yours, so I couldn't take her away. Is that what you call her?'

'I call her after Miss 'Buthnot's pony.'

'Quaint, for a little Portuguese mare. You may not ride for a day or two, but it is because I intend sending York to the sales with these surplus horses we have, so perhaps it is timely as a punishment.'

'But what punishment should I have?'

'What made you do it?'

'Lots of things. Miss 'Buthnot has lovely short hair.'

'I am more used to the punishment of soldiers than of children.'

'What do the soldiers do that is bad?'

'Steal, get drunk, sell their kit and wonder why their only remaining shirt, the one they have on, has gone to rags. I spend too much time trying to get them excused punishment.'

'Why, if they're bad?'

'I don't find the flogging they get does them much good.'

'Perhaps my punishment won't do me any good.'

'But if they sell the corn that is meant for the horses, they get flogged. I won't even give them a good character, but as they know this very well, it doesn't happen often.'

'What if they had more money?'

'They would drink it away.'

'Do they like to drink more than you and Grandpapa?'

'Grandpapa and I are very modest in this respect. Yes, I believe a soldier prefers being drunk over any other occupation. All the same, I like soldiers.'

Lottie thought if she could but keep her uncle on the subject of punishing soldiers her own punishment might be forgotten. Such a device would certainly have worked with her grandfather, but her uncle, while he talked, remained grave.

'Perhaps,' he said, 'you should tell me what you would dislike the most, beyond not riding the pony.'

Lottie, who had already decided the time not spent riding could be happily filled with weeding her garden, was puzzled. Eventually she said, 'Doing my sampler.'

'You shall do your sampler one hour a day, under the supervision of your grandmother. It is your grandmother you have most offended, and it will remind you that you may not do things without considering who you may offend.'

Lottie swallowed hard. She saw she had fallen into a trap by so much as mentioning her sampler, and that her uncle was as clever as her governess in getting her to do what she did not want. She had meant to argue how it was her hair to cut off but she could see that no such thing would impress Uncle Thomas.

He now added, 'It will have the advantage of the sampler being finished much the sooner. Bring it to me so I may see it and I will look again in a day or two to ascertain your progress.'

Lady Charles, listening to her son and her granddaughter, had come to the conclusion that Thomas's guardianship of Lottie need make little difference, for why should he bother himself with a child? Now she saw she had been wrong, and she was not even to be consulted: five minutes of Lottie and her sampler was enough to give her a headache, but what could she say?

Lottie returned with her sampler and tried to lay it flat on the breakfast table.

'It is a sorry object,' Major Wilder said. 'How have you got it so dirty? You had better ask Susan to wash it.' He endeavoured to make out the text and, having done so, raised a sardonic eyebrow but made no comment beyond suggesting that if she could get the letters finished she could start on the border.

'I like the carrots and cabbages,' Lottie said. 'Miss Buthnot drew them.'

'I can see the inestimable Miss Arbuthnot's struggles to make it more amusing.'

Lady Charles said, 'It is not meant to be amusing. It is a discipline, an exercise. I'm sure you don't make the drill for the soldiers amusing.'

'Oh, but I do. I give rewards to those who fire with the greatest accuracy and all sorts of praise and prizes for speed and turnout.' He wondered if he would ever be doing so again. His mind went to his father who was, he hoped, laying out the estate books on the library table. How many years would he have to scrutinize before he grasped the whole? He said to Lottie, 'You're not to scowl when you do your sampler. It must be done with a good grace, or it will be very unpleasant for your grandmother. Now it is time you scampered off to your lessons.'

'Uncle Thomas, when you were little, you were naughty. You spent all night in the dog kennel.'

'So I did.'

'But why?'

'I asked the footman to let me out of the house. I think we had company. I remember the noise from the dining-room. I couldn't reach the bolts, so I asked the footman, who must have been drunk, because he kept bowing to me and saying, "Yes, your lordship, anything you say, your lordship." As soon as I was out in the rain, in my night-shirt, he bolted the door again.'

Lottie laughed. 'Why did you want to go out?'

'I had a toy, a dog, of which I was inordinately fond, brown with a white patch on its shoulder. I knew it was outdoors. I was upset to think of it being in the cold and the wet.'

'But how did you come to leave it there?'

'It's all too long ago to get to the bottom of the matter.' Major Wilder said this, but he could remember perfectly well; Lyndon coming into the nursery, snatching the toy from his hand and saying, 'You are too old for this silly thing.' He had opened the window and flung it down into the stable yard. As a child he had tended to fly into a passion, which Lyndon well knew, so perhaps it was owing to Lyndon that he had learnt, on the whole, to button it up.

While Lottie did her sampler, under the eye of her grandmother, Miss Arbuthnot went for a walk. To walk by herself was now a novelty. Her father had never liked her to do so, though she frequently did while he was too busy with his papers and sermons to notice. She thought it an excess of gentility to consider oneself unsafe, or too delicate, to wander the parish. The treeless park was depressing. She hastened down the drive, past the lodge and out towards the stream and the meadows. The interview she had had that morning with Lady Charles made her aware of how vulnerable was the position of a governess. She half thought Lady Charles had been prepared to dismiss her because Lottie had cut off her hair. She supposed she should have foreseen the act. What if Lady Charles declined to give her a reference because all little girls might be considered in danger of cutting off their hair while under her influence?

should Lady Charles dismiss her, she would have to go home in disgrace. What would her father say, let alone her friends and neighbours? She could hardly bring herself to think of it.

Even more distressing, though, would be the sudden parting from her pupil. As a governess she supposed it unwise to become so fond of your charge, who must inevitably grow up and have not the slightest further need of you. She thought Miss Wilder would have some need of her for the next five or six years unless she was sent away to school. After that she would have to find another post, and after that another, and another, until she became too old to work, unless she was required to housekeep for her father. The thought of the latter made her think of her mother. How clever she had been at keeping the household cheerful, counteracting their father's earnest austerity with a light-hearted disregard for the serious and a refusal to be cast down by the makeshift nature of their lives, the lengths to which they were put to stretch a meagre income. 'Saved by the parish,' her mother would say, her laughter filling the vicarage, when a farmer gave her a dozen eggs and a cabbage, or the Hamiltons sent a hare. She was an ingenious housekeeper, which, since she had been brought up in luxury and idleness, was the more remarkable. Her love for her careful, God-fearing husband, for whom she had abandoned family and religion, never faltered, and could only be explained, in the eyes of her eldest daughter, by the attraction of opposites.

If Bobby did well, he would help them, but promotion and prize money would be harder to come by should the war end. Besides, he might wish to marry and set up an

establishment of his own. To return home or to be alway
employed until too old? The prospect seemed cheerless
The spring, the spring sunshine dappling on the grass, al
the signs of spring, from lambs to catkins, which migh
have cheered her, merely served to remind her of anothe
spring, not long past but a hundred worlds away, when sh
had seen with different eyes.

How delightful it was to walk in the blossoming, quick
ening, flower-bedecked spring with your beloved, he s
clever, gentle and tender, irrational and amusing, exacting
excitable and attentive, he to whom you knew you woul
plight your troth. What pleasure there was in the running
laughing chaperones of younger sisters, who took thei
duties not too seriously, as they rambled down Devonshir
lanes in the primrose, cowslip spring. Was there no end t
such happiness? There was indeed.

'Lady Day, Lady Day,' Lord Charles repeated, as he pace
up and down the hall. There were just five days to Lady Da
and he would be caught, fixed in a trap, helpless betwee
his son and his wife, yet he must pretend to command th
situation. Eventually he braced himself to progress as fa
as the drawing room where he knew his wife to be alone
and there she sat, eyes closed, no doubt recovering fron
an hour spent with Lottie and the sampler.

Her eyes opened when he came in. 'What is the matte
Charles?'

'Why do you ask?'

'Because you look worried to death and I have had quit
enough disturbance for one day. Come, sit down, think o

something else. It can't be worse than Lottie's hair. I dare say it is nothing of real importance.'

'I have just been talking to Thomas.'

'So?'

'He has been looking at the books.'

'Why? The way Thomas behaves we may as well both be dead and buried.'

'It was out of fairness.'

'You are always in a fret to quarter day. Things will be better after that.'

'He says we must sell the London house.'

Lady Charles burst into astonished laughter. 'He must be mad. War has given him too great a sense of a perpetual drama. We shall soon have to think of locking him up.'

'He says it will be necessary.'

'Of course it won't be necessary. He is making some ludicrous mistake.'

'He says to keep it is nonsense. It is very large and we rarely use it.'

'Charles, my grandfather purchased that house so that when his family wished to be in town they could entertain, live, appear as befitted their station. Of course we don't go to it out of season, and we haven't been of late because of our circumstances, when appearing in public is hardly appropriate. I expect he thinks us negligent in not having let it, but it is a great deal of bother letting it, and we couldn't have brought our minds to it. If he wants to be useful let him go to London and see if he can let it for a month or two, but we must make sure none of the girls are planning to go. It might need refurbishing before he could get a good price. Let him take those dogs. The Green Park is close enough for him to give them runs.'

'There is nothing spare for the cost of refurbishing. At one time we could have let this house and gone to live somewhere abroad, but while the country remains at war, of course it's inadvisable.'

'Tell Thomas he takes too gloomy a view altogether. Let him look at the books again. They can be got to come out differently if worked on, to be sure. Why should we have no money? Nothing has altered. There was always plenty besides what the estate brings in. Tell Thomas there are no circumstances under which you would sell the London house, no circumstances whatsoever. I don't wish to hear another word about it. Is it not time to change for dinner? I shall be late. My hour with Lottie was a great trial of my patience, but I could see the child was trying to be good. Perhaps it would be better if Miss Arbuthnot saw to the sampler.'

Major Wilder was in his room, changing for dinner. He rather missed the grumpy presence of York, whom he usually saw at this hour. York was no great valet beyond brushing a coat and dangling a shirt in a river before giving it a bit of a scrub, but he was adequate and had a hundred other uses, and was intensely loyal, intelligent and resourceful. He could be trusted to get a bunch of horses to the sale and come back with the money, while years of hard campaigning had taught Major Wilder that he could get himself into a set of clean clothes without a servant standing over him.

Now he thought of his grandfather. Indeed, he had thought of him on and off for much of the day while he had scrutinized the last ten books, one for each year starting with that of Lyndon's marriage. He thought he could have gone back even further without enlightenment. It had not taken him as long as he had supposed it might. The books closely resembled one another, except at the times his father had been without an agent when there had been little more than a pretence of keeping accounts and the pages were interleaved with a mass of bills and other miscellaneous bits of paper. Having ascertained the situation in general, he had asked Lord Charles if he had a copy of his father-in-law's will. He had thought the search for this could take three hours of opening and shutting drawers, but no, Lord Charles knew where to lay his hands on the document but, it being far from straightforward, it took Major Wilder an hour to understand it. His grandfather had had a mind of serpentine complexity, and there was no possibility or rude trick of Fate he had not foreseen. He intended the Ridley estate to belong to a Wilder as long as it could be legally achieved, and there was not a cottage, not an acre, that could be sold. Was it his son-in-law he had not trusted? Was it Lyndon, though Lyndon could not have been more than twelve at the time of his grandfather's death? Had he been the sort of old gentleman who trusted no one? There was a separate trust to provide an income for an eldest son, at that time Lyndon but now himself, and it was arranged so that the capital could not be touched, which he thought, under the present situation, a blessing. He was already in receipt of the income, which was more than sufficient; unaccustomed to it, he considered it a luxury. Lady Charles had a tiny settled income of her own. The London house was the only thing the late Mr Wilder had not seen fit to tie up in a knot: it belonged to Lord Charles. Among other documents Lord Charles had produced with the will, there was a copy of Lyndon's marriage settlement. Lottie's mother had not been poor, and fortunately provision had been made for female children, of which Lottie would receive the full benefit when she was twenty-one, or at the discretion of her parent or guardian.

Major Wilder understood some things that had previously puzzled him. He had wondered why the agent had retired when not so very old and in perfectly good health, and why the man who had followed him had lasted only a few months: they must have wondered whence their salaries were to come. The estate was in debt, not hopelessly so, but it would be if remedial action was not taken in the next instant. There was money for day-to-day expenses, but nothing more.

Major Wilder pushed up the collar of his shirt and quickly tied his neckcloth. Five minutes later, accompanied by his dogs, he went down to dinner.

Lottie had thought she might be excluded from dinner, being in official disgrace, but nothing being said, she and Miss Arbuthnot appeared as usual. They had wondered, separately, if such a ban was to occur, whether Miss Arbuthnot would be expected to share the punishment or whether she should attend dinner on her own. What conundrums there were for a governess. Fortunately Lady Charles had been too flustered by the day's events for it to occur to her until Lottie, a riot of curls all over her head, was seated at the table. Major Wilder thought the illicit haircut a great improvement, but had the wisdom not to say so. He noted she was the only member of the family able to mention the subject of money without palpitations, even if she had not learnt when silence and discretion would be the more sensible course. As soon as Slimmer had left the room, she said, 'Susan washed my hair, I mean the bit of it that's left, because she said it could be dried by the fire and I wouldn't catch a chill. Susan has a sister. Did you know that? She lives in London and she works in a place where they make wigs and hairpieces. They like long hair, like mine, I mean the bit that's gone, specially yellow, so I shall sell it for lots of money.'

Lady Charles was shocked. She glanced at Miss Arbuthnot, but said, 'Lottie, you may not mention money in public and certainly not at dinner. It's very vulgar. Neither may you enter into any financial transaction.'

'But Susan will do it, not me. When may I mention it?'

'Money may only be mentioned when you speak with whoever will deal with your affairs, if he is a professional man. Unless you are widowed you may never have to be worried with such things. Otherwise, when he calls, you must offer him a glass of wine or a cup of tea, though usually the wine seems best. If that is inappropriate to his station, something in the servants' hall will do. No mention of the reason for his call must be made until he has finished it. In the meantime you may speak of the weather or ask after his wife, if he has one.'

'How shall I know his station?' Lottie, despite the recriminations, was still buoyant. 'I shall say, "Finish that tea, my man, so we can talk."'

Major Wilder looked from his mother to his father, the latter looking wretched, and thought the conversation wonderfully ironic. He said, in those effective tones of mild authority, 'That will do, Lottie.'

Lottie said, 'Oh, I will be good, Uncle Thomas, but please may I ask something? If I want to give it away, is it still wrong to talk of it?'

'To me, you may mention money whenever you like, but money being a personal matter, it is best done in private. Charity is another matter. If you had money from the sale of your hair, would you give it away?'

'I thought that as I wouldn't be allowed to keep it, because I have been naughty, I had better make up my mind to give it away from the start.'

'Very sensible. Who is to have it?'

'First I shall put it in a tin and then I shall ask all the grown-ups who have any money, for they don't all, to give me one guinea on my birthday. Susan says she might give me a penny after Lady Day, and perhaps at Christmas too, so that by the time I'm grown-up I can pay a person to teach the poor children to read and write.'

Lady Charles said, 'What makes you think the poor children need to read and write?'

'So they can get on better and look after their families.'

Lady Charles again looked at Miss Arbuthnot. 'I imagine Miss Wilder gets such ideas from you.'

'Miss Wilder and I were correcting the spellings in the letter she wrote to you. When it came to the word "affectionately", Miss Wilder said she envied the poor children in the village because they didn't have to learn anything.' Miss Arbuthnot, who thought she never could do entirely right in the eyes of Lady Charles, decided she must battle on all the same. 'I told her I thought there was always an advantage in being literate and in being able to do simple arithmetic.'

Major Wilder, who appreciated the means by which Miss Arbuthnot tackled his mother, wished his own family could do simple arithmetic. The bookkeeping might as well have been left to Lottie who, Miss Arbuthnot had told him, had an aptitude for mathematics. He said, 'Do you think a man who is skilled in his job, say ploughing, shepherding, hurdling, charcoal-making – I could go on indefinitely for all such things require skill – would abandon these necessary labours if he was literate?'

Miss Arbuthnot took a moment to reply. 'I don't know that he would. It is just that to read is enriching. People can't afford books, can they? My father lends books to the mole catcher. I don't know how he came to be literate, and I'm afraid my father is rather suspicious of him, but he catches the moles very well and presents a neat account. If a child is clever he may aspire to improve himself or he may not, but he has a greater chance if he is literate.'

Lord Charles said, as if coming out of a reverie, 'I often thought I should open a school in the village, but I never did it and now I never shall.'

'Oh, but now, Grandpapa,' Lottie said, 'when I am old enough and have enough money, though I mustn't say it at dinner, I shall start one for you, and I shall ask Miss 'Buthnot to teach in it as she teaches me so well, even when I don't want it. I shall certainly start by getting Susan to sell my hair, because now it's off, it shouldn't be wasted.'

Lady Charles was not reconciled to the idea of a school

because she had never given the matter any thought. She could see that Thomas agreed with Miss Arbuthnot. Eventually she said she preferred the notion of a Sunday school for teaching children their catechism and was cross with her son when he asked, if that were the case, why she had not started one.

As dinner drew to a close, Lord Charles wondered if he could avoid staying to drink a glass of wine with Thomas, as had become their custom, but he knew there was no point in putting off the moment. When the ladies had left and they were alone, nothing was said for a while, but eventually Major Wilder asked if he had given the matter of the London house due thought.

Lord Charles shook his head. 'I have spoken to your mother. I can't do it.'

'The books show the situation well enough. The London house is your only disposable asset. What the books don't do is explain it. Perhaps I don't need to have it explained. After all, the affair is yours, not mine. I shall just have to pick up the pieces at a later date and make my apologies to my grandfather.' He nodded to the portrait at the end of the room, showing a neat, thin gentleman, with the powdered head and the dark frock coat of the previous century. His was a shrewd and careful look.

'Take two days to consider. I can do nothing until York comes back from the sales. I shan't mention it again. If you change your mind, tell me.'

Lord Charles grappled to equate his own affairs with York returning from the sales.

Major Wilder continued, on an almost cheerful note: 'Why wasn't the London house put in the entail?'

'He didn't care for town life. Beyond that, I couldn't say.'

'Well, we shall never know. Let us talk of other things. As far as horses are concerned, I kept one of Lyndon's, the liver chestnut, which seemed my sort of creature. Lyndon must have bought it by mistake. It isn't young, but it's been idle these last few years, which has preserved it. I instructed York to look out for something for you that would stand still while you got on it. If you like it, you shall have it, and I shall be in a nice position to pay for it. I won't have it said I didn't try to keep you alive.'

Lord Charles, who failed to comprehend the working of his son's mind, thought, Is that all Thomas is going to say? Are we to talk only of horses?

Lady Charles and Mrs Kingston sat together in the drawing room at Ridley. Lady Charles had asked Mrs Kingston to come. The spring sunshine poured in at the windows but they were oblivious to it, for they had spread on a table the draft for the monument to commemorate the death of Lyndon Wilder.

Mrs Kingston said, 'In all my life I have never seen such a beautiful thing.' After that she could think of no further words to convey her admiration beyond repeating those she had uttered several times. It was no exaggeration: it was a beautiful thing.

The central tablet was surmounted by the accoutrements of an infantry officer, the cross belt, the gorget, the knotted sash, the hilt of the sword, the breastplate and the tufted shako. The short coatee, with a hint of the lacing and the buttons, draped the left-hand side. It was illustrated in a light marble set against a darker hue, and was suspended in the arms of a pair of tall angels, with sad, serious faces, bending their long wings in an enfolding gesture of protection.

It read thus:

> LT. THE HON. JOHN LYNDON WILDER, ELDER SON OF LORD AND LADY WILDER OF RIDLEY IN THE COUNTY OF WILTSHIRE. HE DIED IN THE THIRTY-SIXTH YEAR OF HIS LIFE, HEROICALLY LEADING HIS MEN IN THE DEFENCE OF THE PASS AT RONCESVALLES, ON THE 25TH DAY OF JULY 1813.
>
> *His joyous spirit made him universally beloved. Death cannot take him for we hold him in our hearts ere we meet again.*

Mrs Kingston, having gazed transfixed for some considerable length of time, said, 'Military gentleman being very particular, ought you not to ask Major Wilder if the detail is correct? You don't want it spoilt by some busybody remarking the hilt of the sword not the regulation pattern, or that sort of thing.'

To Lady Charles, the whole project was so precious that the idea of anyone being in the least disparaging or critical made her uneasy. As she and Thomas were at variance in all their opinions, she hesitated. The concept had been entirely her own, the eminent monumental mason she was employing interpreting her wishes even beyond what she had imagined. The only thing it lacked, in relief, was a profile of Lyndon's head, but she had nothing suitable from which it could be taken. Mrs Kingston having made a valid point, and the fact that Thomas must see it sooner or later, made her ring the bell for Slimmer and ask him if Major Wilder was in the house.

Major Wilder, successfully summoned, entered the room ten minutes later, greeted his mother and made his bow to Mrs Kingston. He studied the draft for some time while both women waited in varying degrees of anxiety for his comments.

At last, he said, 'It certainly is very handsome. You have made no mention of his regiment. Was that deliberate? The insignia ought to be on the breastplate at the least.'

Lady Charles, gratified by his unexpected approval, said, 'I wished to include some mention of his brother officers. I wonder if I may not hear from them when the war is over. Mrs Kingston tells me of a tablet she has seen to a lieutenant colonel which was commissioned by the officers of his regiment, beautifully executed.'

Major Wilder paused. Had it occurred to his mother that there was not the smallest hope of erecting this memorial to Lyndon under their present circumstances? Even to acquire the marble would be too much. He did not say so. He knew how she would reply. How can you grudge a fitting tribute to your only brother? Eventually he said, 'I think Lyndon might have been a little wasted on his fellow officers. It was not an appropriate regiment for him.' Having made such a statement, he went on hastily, 'Just put the insignia on the breastplate. It's here, this small rectangular piece shown, as it should be, attached to the cross belt, but it's been left blank. I have Lyndon's, so it could be copied. That would do very well. The shako is not quite tall enough and the plume a little exaggerated. Now I'm drawing it for you. The regiment was not laced, so that isn't correct, but if you left the insignia off the breastplate, the whole could symbolize the accoutrements of an officer of a regiment of the line, rather than a specific regiment. Perhaps, after all, that's the best solution.'

He looked enquiringly from Mrs Kingston, who was making graceful, confused little gestures between his drawing of the shako and the original, which he realized were meant to indicate admiration for his efforts, to his mother. Not to include an officer's regiment in such a memorial would be peculiar, but perhaps this would not occur to them. Contrarily, he wished he could grieve for Lyndon in a manner of which his mother could approve. He could wear coats in sober colours and black neckcloths, but he was no actor.

Lady Charles thought Thomas never lost an opportunity to hint something snide about his brother but she also saw he was doing his best to be helpful.

He now said cautiously, 'I can see the purpose of the angels, and they make it very fine, but if the monument was intended for any officer of my acquaintance, they would suppose it a little too much.'

Lady Charles said, 'Lyndon, as you well know, was no ordinary officer. If he was here this minute, and God knows I wonder every day how it is he is gone for ever, he would laugh at the angels and laugh at me for conjuring them up, but nothing less is worthy of him.'

At that moment Lottie and her governess could be seen passing by outdoors, Lottie in her sturdy baize smock and

Miss Arbuthnot with a trug on her arm. Major Wilder, thinking them an agreeable addition to any party, especially one comprising his mother and Mrs Kingston, opened the French windows to let them in, saying as he did so, 'I'm sure you think Lottie should see it, as it's for her father.'

Lady Charles said, 'Yes, by all means. Lottie, dearest, come in and make your curtsy to Mrs Kingston.'

Hesitating in the open window, Lottie said, 'Miss 'Buthnot and I have our boots on. They're clean but we don't curtsy in them much.'

'Oh, never mind, darling, come in all the same. Good morning, Miss Arbuthnot. Now, Lottie, I want you to look carefully at this big drawing on the table, for it is the plan for a memorial to your papa to be placed in the church. I should like to think you will always remember seeing it here like this. When you are a grown woman, with children of your own, and you return to visit Ridley, you will take them into the church and show them the monument, and you will be able to tell them how you saw the drawings for it when you were a little girl. I hope you will have some little boys who may aspire to be like their grandfather, little heroes. One or two might even resemble him.'

Major Wilder thought his mother need look no further than the village if she wanted an image of Lyndon, for the lad he had seen on the day of his arrival had looked remarkably like his brother.

Lottie said, 'But must I get married, Grandmama? I rather thought I wouldn't. I should like to live in a house like Mrs Kingston's, and keep cows, if I have enough . . . you know, what I mustn't say in company.'

'Of course you must get married. Whatever next?' Lady

Charles said, but she was pleased with the way Lottie and Miss Arbuthnot turned so earnestly to examine the drawing.

Lottie said, 'I like the beautiful, sad angels best.'

Miss Arbuthnot said, 'It is indeed lovely.' She could not help thinking of her father, who was Low Church and would have been shocked to have anything so opulent proposed.

Mrs Kingston was making a study of Major Wilder. He had initially been a disappointment to her, yet he was not so plain a man. He had an air of steadiness and reliability, of good sense, all qualities it would be foolish to overlook. She said to him, 'It would be a great kindness, Major Wilder, if you could find the time to visit my brother. He is confined to the house a great deal by the poor state of his health. Horatio and I are no proper company for him.'

Major Wilder said, 'I haven't visited your house since I was a child.'

'I hope your memories of it are good ones.'

'Mixed,' he said, smiling.

'Captain Forrester, of the navy, lived there then,' Lady Charles said. 'He was a great friend of Lord Charles and had, I remember, a large tribe of boys, rather riotous.'

Mrs Kingston had not forgotten Lady Charles telling her that Major Wilder had been a warlike child, and had fought a duel when he was only eight. She drew Lottie towards her and said archly, 'How naughty you have been, my pet, to cut off your lovely golden hair. Did you know that your uncle was equally naughty as a little boy?'

'He hid all night in the dog kennel, and even now he won't say why.'

'Hid all night in the dog kennel? I never heard that. It was of something else I was thinking. He fought a duel when he was just a child.'

'Why, so I did,' Major Wilder said, laughing. 'And to think how much I disapprove of duelling now! I have twice refused to act as second. Soldiers have more important things to do than fall out with one another.'

Lottie said, 'Tell us, Uncle Thomas, tell us.'

'It took place in Mrs Kingston's house, she will be alarmed to learn. We were friendly with Captain Forrester's children, I with the younger and Lyndon with the older. My particular friend was Frederick. We quarrelled and I agreed to fight him. Now, the difference between us was that he had been taught, like his brothers, to fence, and this part of my education had been neglected, as outdated. He fetched the foils, took the buttons off the tips, and handed one to me. I hardly knew how to hold the thing, but I was aware that I had to lunge at Freddy, so I did. I took him by surprise and nicked a hole in his arm. Of course there was the most terrible furore, servants running, nursemaids screaming, fathers called, doctors summoned in case Freddy bled to death.'

Mrs Kingston said, 'How very shocking, but it was the fault of the other child.'

'There was a little coolness between our two families as a result,' Lady Charles said, 'and they moved away shortly after.'

'We boys were very disappointed when they went,' Major Wilder said, 'because the duel hadn't spoilt our friendship. I don't know it was Frederick's fault.'

Lottie said, 'Miss 'Buthnot, wasn't Uncle Thomas much naughtier than me?'

Miss Arbuthnot smiled, but she said seriously, 'After such a lapse of time and with too little information, what can I say? It was unfair of the other child to use real weapons if he knew your uncle had had no lessons. That I think really naughty.'

Lottie jumped about impatiently. 'What did you fight about, Uncle Thomas?'

Major Wilder looked reflective. He said, 'Even now, that would be telling.' He got up to go, cheerfully ignoring Lottie's entreaties. Miss Arbuthnot reminded her they were going to put in the peas. Mrs Kingston realized she had not extracted a promise from Major Wilder to visit her brother.

Ridley
27 March

Dear Papa,

In the cedarwood box in the attic I have a riding habit, dark green with velvet on the collar and cuff, that Arabella Hamilton gave me in the hope I might one day have the opportunity to use it, for she never did. She is not as tall as I but she had it let down. Please, please to send it straight away. Fanny will find it for you. It is all bustle here because York came back from the sales minus about eight horses he had taken and returning with a new horse for Lord Charles, a pony for Master Kingston and, you will not believe it, a lady's hack for me so I may ride out with Miss Wilder. Lady Charles said I must have a habit and that Major Wilder had said I was not to be put to any extra expense, so I was glad to explain that I had one. There is a hat that goes with it, which I would like, with a feather. I hope Lady Charles does not think a feather too frivolous for someone in my situation.

This part of the letter had been easy enough. The spring made her restless and reminded her of how young she was but she could not tell her father that. The delicate balance she maintained with him, the harmony, was upset. In her letters to him she liked to speak cheerfully and affectionately, almost as her mother used to do, but now she wondered to what extent she was acting a part, though it was not as if she did not hold him in affection. It was just that he wanted to see her in a particular way and it was not necessarily the way she was.

He had written to ask if she might be allowed home for Easter. She had replied that she did not know and was shy of asking, but she would find it too difficult if Kate and her husband were to be there. He had replied that she was being a trifle ridiculous: she must see that she could not spend the rest of her life estranged from Kate, whom she had a duty to love; she would soon learn to view Mr Langley as the brother he now was. This would be all the easier as the young couple would be full of chatter, tell of their travels to London, Bath and Brighton, and of the plans they had for their house and garden. His dear, sensible Anna would find there was no awkwardness or need to be uneasy. He had decided they had misinterpreted Mr Langley's attentions to her: he had been lonely at his uncle's and was in need of the well-ordered and amusing company he found at the vicarage – he had hinted as much.

This attempt on her father's part to make little of her unhappiness, to suggest she had been foolishly misled, indicated a determination on his part no longer to be in sympathy with her situation or her state of mind. Had he forgotten his own courtship of her mother? He had pursued it with every difficulty to surmount, from differences in religion to her family's natural prejudice against a man with no obvious means of supporting himself. It made her indignantly question the word 'love'. The prayer book instructed one to 'love thy neighbour', but she had never felt for her neighbour anything resembling what she had felt for Mr Langley. Neither did she think Mr Langley was being entirely honest with her father nor her father with himself. As for loving Kate, she retained a sort of sisterly regard for her, but she was jealous. How could she not be? Kate, now all of sixteen, incessantly chattering about her travels and setting up her house, was not calculated to cure it. It was not that Miss Arbuthnot still loved Mr Langley, for that would be impossible. She was in love with the image she had of what she had believed him to be, but she wished she had never met him for he had broken her heart and destroyed her peace of mind. She could not hate him, but neither could she respect him: in the unlikely circumstances of her ever being in a position to love or to marry she thought she would never be able to dismiss him or his conduct from her mind.

Miss Arbuthnot picked up the pen and wrote on:

The horse I am to ride is a pretty grey, all over dappled. Miss Wilder and I have made two little secret sorties to the stables to give him a carrot and make him feel at home. York says he won't go in harness: he was involved in an accident when being driven, and has a few scars. They don't really show, but they brought his price down to something very reasonable. He is, in York's words, proper quality.

And so she went on, though her father was not interested in horses, making no mention of Easter. When the letter was finished, she wrote to Arabella Hamilton, and to her brother, in the hope it might find him at some future date on the wide bosom of the ocean. After that she laid her head on her arms and succumbed to a few tears.

Lord Charles sat alone at his breakfast. He had become accustomed to having Thomas there, so he missed him, but Thomas had preceded him. He felt he was waiting for something, that he was in a state of suspense, and yet he was not sure what form it would take other than it was to do with Thomas and Ridley. Perhaps, after all, they could go on just as they did, despite what Thomas said. If they kept paying the wages and the immediate bills, spending little else, nothing might alter. How was the money to be found to pay for Lyndon's memorial? How could he explain to Eleanor there was no money for it? He would ask to have it costed out in detail and thus delay it. Where was Thomas? Were they not to ride together and he to try that dull-looking horse?

Lord Charles finished his breakfast and took himself to the library. He started doing little sums on a piece of paper from his blotter. He knew immediately what he dreaded when his son walked into the room a few minutes later: Thomas was wearing his uniform. He half started from his chair, saying as he did so, 'Not now, not yet. I can't have you go. Your leave is not up. You can't mean to go today.'

'Why not? I have a few things to discuss and then it's just a matter of giving York time to pack. I'll take a ride out with you. I believe that gelding will do Miss Arbuthnot very well. I've had the side-saddle on it and one of the lads try it out. Her habit arrived today, for I paid the carrier. I had best see her ride it. That deals with the immediate. Otherwise, before I leave for France, it is my intention to visit Georgie and my excellent brother-in-law, for whom anything that pleases Georgie pleases him. Should I decide Lottie ought to go to them, Miss Arbuthnot would, I imagine, be perfectly willing to go with her. It would be in Lottie's best interests. The pony and the gelding could go too. While Lottie has the little Kingston boy in her life, I should prefer not to part them, they are such good company for one another, but once he goes to sea, I must reassess the situation here.'

'But, Thomas, what is to become of me when you are gone? I wish you would sit down. You distress me so.'

Major Wilder pulled up a chair and sat opposite his father. 'I have ordered the trees for the park and paid with the money left over from Lyndon's horses. They won't come until the autumn, of course, and I've made arrangements for the planting. That is the future. There is nothing else I can do. I may as well rejoin my troop.'

'Don't do it.'

'With my troop I know my duty. Here it can't be performed.'

They were both silent. After a while Major Wilder said, 'The only other thing you could do is to apply to your sons-in-law. They might help you. None of them are poor.'

Lord Charles was shocked. 'I couldn't do that.'

'I agree it would be most unpleasant, but I doubt my sisters wish to see you arrested for debt. I can let you have a bit myself, now I have an income as well as my pay, but with the latter, it is hard to know when one may get it, and what I could let you have would be inadequate. Your sons-in-law might club together to do something for you.'

'It is out of the question.'

Major Wilder shrugged. They were again silent. Lord Charles then said, 'Thomas, that wound to your shoulder, I should like to see it.'

His son made no reply. It was almost as if he had not heard.

'Yes, I should like to see it,' Lord Charles repeated.

'Now?' Major Wilder asked, smiling a little at the oddness of the request.

'Yes.' Lord Charles got up and turned the key in the library door.

'Are you locking me in?'

'Slimmer has an uncanny habit of sliding into view when least required. Take off your jacket and shirt, I suppose your sash, all that military paraphernalia. I want to see the wound.'

Major Wilder wished his father was always so decisive. He took off his cross belt and unwound his sash. Stripped to the waist, he said, 'My shoulder was quite black at the front. I suppose it was the same at the back but I didn't see it. There, it was nothing much, as I told you, very trifling.'

Lord Charles thought it terrible, an ugly, jagged mark, indented, barely healed. He shuddered. It was easy to see from the yellowish colouring the extent of the original bruising. 'But who has dressed it all this time?'

'York,' Major Wilder replied, with a shrug.

His father wanted to know what other wounds he had had and not told them of. There was certainly an old scar on his right forearm.

'That one came at Talavera,' Major Wilder said, looking at it. 'I had a wound to my leg, but it healed without leaving me lame. I believe I did tell you of that.'

He started to put his clothes back on. His father watched him, doubting he had been told all, thinking how comfortable the uniform made Thomas, how at home he was wearing it, and how light-heartedly he would embark once more on his military life.

Major Wilder then continued, 'If you applied to your sons-in-law, they would want to know where the money had gone. I should, if I were them. They might, like me, ask to look at the books and, like me, want explanations for the withdrawals, the forty thousand here, twenty thousand there, fifty thousand somewhere else, no explanation.'

'I can't explain it. Can't you see I'm helpless? You are hard to leave me.'

'Yes, I feel it so, but I must do what I can do and not what I can't.'

'Had you a free rein, would you stay?'

'I dare say I should have to, but don't tease yourself with the impossible. We can't agree.'

Lord Charles hesitated, seemed bemused or thoughtful, it was hard to know which, but then his face cleared and he asked, as if with purpose, 'Thomas, if I sent for a lawyer, would you wait?'

'A lawyer? What to do?'

'I want to consult one. Any would do but I recollect the man your grandfather customarily used and I believe his son to be clever. He is a trustee but I have had no cause to deal with him. If I send to Salisbury, I dare say he would come out this afternoon.'

'I intended to leave before dinner. I don't know what a lawyer could tell you that I haven't, but I can wait a day.'

'Yes, that's what I want, and please, don't wear your uniform. Do me the favour of changing.'

'I need you to be clear about my intentions. I don't wish to deceive you.'

'Yes, yes, I understand you perfectly well. Just do as I ask and don't wear it yet. I find it too disturbing. In ten minutes' time, I will try out that horse. You will come with me, I hope. I don't want the time spoilt.'

Lord Charles wrote a hasty note, which he folded, sealed and stamped with the Lyndon crest. He had never cared to use the Wilder, for he felt an impostor should he do so, but when he considered it, he was neither one nor the other, an impostor either way. He rang for Slimmer. There was confusion because he had forgotten he had locked the door and Slimmer was peeved, rattling it when it declined to open.

Major Wilder obliged his father by changing out of his uniform. Slimmer, on seeing the uniform earlier in the day, had said, 'I am very sorry you are leaving us, sir,' but Major

Wilder did not think him sorry. Slimmer was accustomed to being in charge of the servants, in his own way of the entire household, but he had gained no ascendancy over Major Wilder, let alone York, who had no idea of his place, nor any wish to ascertain what it might be.

In the stable yard, York was saddling the pony for Lottie's ride. Major Wilder thought Hall must take her out once they had left for France, but with Miss Arbuthnot to ride as well, anyone would do to come behind and open the gates.

'We had better put Miss Arbuthnot up on the grey,' he said. 'How does Master Kingston? Is he coming with you?'

'Rare old state, he's in. Beside 'isself. A-kissing an' a-canoodling with the pony all day. Just as well it's the sort that'll take it. Taught 'im to saddle an' bridle it. Young gentlemen would be 'elpless if it weren't for folks like me, what makes 'em 'elp 'emselves. Course, little missy was after doing the same, but there's limits. I'll get the grey out. Women an' children, that's me.'

Though York was scowling, Major Wilder knew he would miss his charges. He had not given him the order to pack, but he would be expecting it.

Instructions had been sent for Miss Arbuthnot to appear in her habit. When she did so she was puzzled to see Major Wilder, for before breakfast, when she and Lottie had been coming from the stables, an illicit visit to feed carrots, they had observed Major Wilder running his dogs. Lottie had said, suddenly anxious, that her uncle was wearing his soldier's clothes and that she did not want him to go away. Those were Miss Arbuthnot's own sentiments, because he seemed to have some control over Lottie's life, and was more inclined to approve of herself than Lady Charles. He also took a greater interest in Lottie's education. Was he merely accustomed to giving orders and directions? Surely Lottie's welfare should be the concern of her grandparents. Certainly they had shown little interest in how she managed Lottie: Lady Charles only worried for the outcome, whether she sewed neatly, curtsied, played the piano, spoke French with a correct accent, all of which Miss Arbuthnot could see were necessary accomplishments, but inadequate. Should Lottie not be taught to read books, think and apply her mind? She had woefully failed to instil in her sister Kate these things, and Kate was, as a result, remarkably silly, but Mr Langley preferred Kate's silliness and prettiness to herself. As Lady Charles saw matrimony as the only object, perhaps she was right, but did it not leave a woman with few resources, and few subjects upon which an intelligent comment could be made?

Miss Arbuthnot was thinking these things as she crossed the stable yard. She was wearing not only the green habit with the velvet at the collar, but a neat pair of boots that had also arrived by the carrier, courtesy, she knew, of Miss Hamilton, to whom her father must have spoken. She stopped thinking of Lottie's education when she saw the grey horse being led to the mounting block.

Major Wilder thought Miss Arbuthnot looked charming in a well-tailored riding habit and a small hat. It was not that she was elegant, but she had a certain youthful grace coupled with a purposeful and energetic manner, which he liked. He noted her sudden change of expression. She had seemed studied, almost pensive, but now she was all delight. How should a governess look? Meek, retiring, plain, a trifle desiccated? He had no idea, but he began to see why his mother had said Miss Arbuthnot was too young. He approached her as she was adjusting her position in the side-saddle and arranging the skirt of her habit. She picked up the reins with practised ease. He could pay her no compliment; it was not his place to do so.

He said, undertaking the little duty of checking the girths, 'An excellent habit.' He thought he could praise the garment, if not Miss Arbuthnot, but he found himself adding, with a greater degree of frivolity, 'The hat has no feather.'

Miss Arbuthnot replied, 'It did have a feather, but my father must have removed it before sending it off. I dare say he decided it inappropriate.' She gave a slightly rueful smile but then said, with a lack of feminine wile, 'The habit, everything, belonged to Miss Hamilton.'

'Perhaps your father thought the feather would be spoilt in the packing.'

'My father isn't a practical man. My sisters would have done the packing. I don't need a feather, do I? I appreciate being allowed to ride with Miss Wilder. I shall enjoy it so much that it won't seem like a duty.'

'I can see you are not in the least nervous.'

Miss Arbuthnot smiled. 'I'm afraid I'm not delicate in that sort of way. Women are meant to be delicate.'

Major Wilder thought of the women who had permission to follow their men to war, and the women who followed willy-nilly, cooking, giving birth, minding babies, looting, stealing, starved, drenched, broiled, yet still women, though some of them would stoop to murder for the sake of the gold lacing from an officer's uniform. He watched Miss Arbuthnot ride out of the stable yard.

The Andalusian was already saddled. He brought it out for himself and took the reins of the horse he had bought for his father. He walked them round to the front of the house. Lord Charles was already on the steps and Major Wilder held the head of the brown so his father could mount.

'No grooms required,' Lord Charles said, half laughing. 'What independence. Thank you, Thomas. How still he stood.'

Major Wilder observed how his father's mood had changed. He remembered the horror with which he had viewed his son in uniform earlier, and he remembered the tears of relief, the bowed old man, the day he had returned to Ridley. Now he seemed carefree, childishly happy.

'Where are the dogs?' Lord Charles enquired. 'If they should run right under the legs of this horse, with a hare gone first, I dare say it would remain serene. A man clings to youth, makes no concessions, but sooner or later his age catches up with him. I've had rheumatic pains in my joints for a year or so but I've not acknowledged them until now. I must allow myself to be an old man and plod along on a dull horse.'

'Is it so bad as all that?'

'No, no, I'm enjoying myself. I can talk and think without the worry of staying in the saddle. Look at the primroses. I'm noticing all the things that ought to be done.'

Major Wilder refrained from saying he had been three weeks pointing them out to him.

'I don't want to talk any business today, Thomas. Seeing the lawyer will be quite sufficient.'

Major Wilder had had every intention of running over a variety of matters, including what measures he thought his father should take, supposing he did not return. So far he had been lucky, but that sort of luck could disperse in a second. Did his father believe he would not go? Lord Charles's sudden good humour was of great assistance to his son, for though it did not weaken his resolution, his joy at returning to his troop was very much dampened by the plight in which his father was to be left. To bring Lord Charles back to some sense of reality, he began to describe the officers attached to his troop, their various characteristics, and even to describe the guns, the six-pounders and the howitzer. His father asked how many soldiers were required to man each, how many horses and how many in the Corps of Drivers. Did he always sight the guns himself? He became intrigued by the detail. There seemed nothing he did not want to know, to the very orders given for swabbing the barrels, measuring the powder and setting it all alight.

Having satisfied his curiosity, he said, 'What responsibilities you have.'

The children were not meant to hang around the stables but they did. They liked talking to York and to watch him groom the Andalusian. Stretching to their full height while standing in the passage, they could peep through the bars of the loosebox, but if York was in a sunny frame of mind he would leave the stable door ajar.

'Why is he called "the Andalusian"?' Lottie asked.

'Came from Andalusia, Miss Silly,' York said, without pausing in his task, the soft motion of the brush making an audible swish.

Lottie was not affronted. 'Did a Spanish man sell him to my Uncle Thomas?'

'Nope. 'E give 'n to 'im.'

The children were silent with astonishment. The Andalusian laid his ears flat and made a pretence of nipping York's arm.

Eventually Horatio said, 'Why?'

York contemplated the propriety of repeating his master's business, especially when Major Wilder had committed an act of which he did not entirely approve.

He said, 'Don't you go confusing one of they Spanish officers, prinkin' about, doin' damn-all, daft, useless, never does what they says they will, an' says it's Sunday, an' all manner of excuses; don't you muddle they with yer Spanish guerrilla, for they's a very different kettle o' fish, though you would think careful of risking yer life for sich.' He then added indulgently, 'But there, British officers is full of fancy notions. Now some o' yer Frenchy officers is much the same, but most aren't gentlemen. I never would 'ave truck with officers what aren't gentlemen.'

The children were impatient with what they viewed as an incomprehensible digression.

York twisted a length of hay into a wisp. It seemed as if he would continue but all he said was, 'Mind you learn all them foreign tongues, Master Kingston, afore you get in the navy. I never could get me tongue round 'is name, Don someone or another. Vanity, see. 'E refused point blank to

’ave ’is leg took off, which was what would save ’is life, like. The gangrene set in. Afore ’e died ’e wrote out on a piece of paper the Major was to ’ave the Andalusian.’

York took a hoof pick and the stallion obligingly offered his foreleg.

‘Why? Why?’ Lottie’s patience was exhausted.

‘I’m tellin’ you. Wait.’ York said not another word until he had scraped out all four of the Andalusian’s hoofs but then he continued. ‘That Don Whatever ’ad been in some action where they’d surprised a French picket. Murdered ’em all, I ’spect. Well, the Frenchies sell ’emselves dearly like, an’ this Don got musket shot enough to shatter ’is knee into bits. Serve ’im right, I thinks. Master takes out the brindle dog for a spot o’ coursing, mighty close to the French lines, I thinks, an’ goes down to the creek for water. There’s this Don fellow laid out by the riverbed with a party o’ three French dragoons that chanced on ’im, about to knock ’is brains out after rifling him for this and that. Thing is, the Major, spottin’ ’em, came up mighty close. Course our artillery uniform is blue, an’ they dragoons thinks ’e is a French officer an’ ’e shouts at ’em in French.’ York came to a halt beyond saying, under his breath, ‘Bloody ’eck, what were ’e thinkin’ of?’

‘And then?’ Lottie prompted him.

‘Told you.’

‘Not everything.’

‘Told you. Well, ’ow does I know all of it? Major ’ad ’is pistol loaded up nice. Sort a coaxes ’em along to put the Spaniard up on to this ’ere Andalusian what’s stood like a lamb these two days waiting for ’is master to get up off the ground, coaxes ’em by way of ’olding the pistol agin the ’ead of one an' instructing t'others. So minds you learn French, Master Kingston, for it can get you out o' a scrape. Brought 'em all in, an' not a word more am I telling. What's more, don't you prattle. Chancin' me arm, I am, telling tales to you varmints.'

The Andalusian arched his grey neck, then turned his head and caught the sleeve of York's coat in his teeth. He shook it playfully. York protested. The stallion shook it some more. A catalogue of profanities in a mixture of Spanish and Portuguese, as close as York ever got to mastering foreign languages, reverberated round the stable block as the cloth tore. The Andalusian released his hold and blew an affectionate breath against York's weather-beaten cheek.

Lottie sat on a footstool between her grandmother and Mrs Kingston, the sampler on her lap. Mrs Kingston had temporarily taken over its management. Lottie was saying, 'And with York on a horse and Horatio on his pony, which is not quite so big a pony as mine, and Miss 'Buthnot on a horse, we could go three times further and three times faster without having to wait.'

'Yes, dear, I hope you all went safely and I'm glad you had a lovely time, but look, you must put the needle in exactly where the A is for "abilities", starting at the bottom, or it might end up any old letter, might it not?'

'Oh, yes, and spell another word. Wouldn't that be funny? York said Miss 'Buthnot was proper smart on a horse, and you wouldn't know she wasn't born a duchess, so she can't 'ave 'ung on to its 'ead, not once.'

'Yes, darling, but try to think what you are doing, or it must all be unpicked.'

Lady Charles said obliquely, 'Of course it is all due to Thomas. Do you think a certain person will get ideas not proper to her situation? I never like to give expectations that may have to be retracted. Ah, well, I'm powerless in my own house, and Lord Charles too. We have had to put dinner back three-quarters of an hour. It upsets the kitchen staff. Lord Charles is seeing a lawyer.'

'I hope nothing distressing. I am always uncomfortable at seeing a lawyer. Lottie, the front of that B must be curved, so lots of little tiny stitches, dear. Nothing serious, I hope.'

'I don't suppose so. My father saw lawyers day in, day out. Goodness knows what it was all about. He liked to tie everything up in knots and then to untie them and tie up some different ones. I must say it hasn't been Lord Charles's habit. He worries Major Wilder will go back to France.'

Lady Charles was rather more curious than she would allow. That morning, while she was dressing, Sally had said to her what a shame it was the Major was leaving as his lordship set such store by him. Lady Charles had replied that the Major was not leaving and why did Sally suppose he might be? Polly had seen him in his uniform, taking his dogs out, and Slimmer was alleged to have seen the same. Lady Charles had pointed out they had all seen Major Wilder since and he had not been wearing his uniform: Polly and possibly Slimmer were imagining things. Subsequently she had had the notion of asking Slimmer if the Major had been wearing his uniform at breakfast, but had dismissed it: she did not like Slimmer to know too much of what she did not know herself. It was all tiresomely complicated. Why should Thomas put on his uniform, which was, after all, unmistakable, and take it off again? Had it been a ruse, a blackmail, to frighten Lord Charles into doing something he did not wish, with the threat of his returning to France? This very day Lord Charles had told her how Thomas had received a musket ball through his shoulder and how he had shown him the place. Was that not unnecessary coercion, if not quite blackmail? However, Lord Charles had said nothing of his wearing his uniform. Would Thomas leave for France with such abruptness, without mention? According to Mrs Kingston, soldiers packed in five minutes and were gone as if they had never been, beyond the burnt patches of campfires. Ah, Lyndon was gone as if he had never been but for the scorching of her mother's heart. She thought how Lord Charles hung on Thomas's every word, just as he used to do on Lyndon's. She had been married to Lord Charles for more than forty years without questioning his integrity, but it now seemed their grief could not be shared, for if he was cheerful she felt he forsook their lost son, that he had shallowly transferred his affections.

Lottie, jabbing her needle into the fabric, was saying, 'And I reminded Grandpapa he was not to talk of you know what till the man had finished his biscuit.'

Mrs Kingston, confused, said, half to herself, 'Of what is the child talking?' And then, out loud, 'Lottie, that is three times I've told you to put the needle in with care. You will poke it into your finger next.' She turned to Lady Charles. 'There can be so little purpose in Major Wilder returning to France. My brother says the war cannot last, that Bonaparte is pincered. He has had a letter from his friend Captain Greenway, who is with the army, and he says just the same.'

Lady Charles thought about Captain Greenway, who had been in the same regiment as Lyndon, and that Mrs Kingston did not repeat this fact, as she was wont to do, possibly owing to Lottie's presence. Lady Charles no longer craved information of the sort Captain Greenway could give. She had heard enough of ignoble war, the hardship and the barbarity: she did not wish to associate it in her mind with Lyndon's last years. She knew he must have hated it, his lack of rank and, from the odd hint Thomas chose to drop, his fellow officers. This very Captain Greenway might not be the son of a gentleman but of a successful shopkeeper or a lawyer, like Mr Taplow, who was threatening to do business with her husband and disrupt their dinner at the same time. As for rank, she understood it would have cost a thousand pounds to buy Lyndon his promotion, a subject upon which she and her husband had had much wearying and unproductive discussion.

Mrs Kingston said, 'Captain Greenway told my brother he will visit him as soon as he gets leave, but I dare say he is not to be relied on.'

The truth was Mrs Kingston had been forced to come to the conclusion that she found living with her brother most unpleasant and wished he would go away, but as he was an invalid, what could she do? She feared his friend might be no more pleasant than he was: could he be trusted to tell Lady Charles anything she wanted to know in a proper way? Besides, by all accounts, Captain Greenway was no more rich than Henry, with little above his army pay on which to subsist, so, although he was a bachelor, there was no discernible point to him.

Mr Taplow was a thin, dignified gentleman rather over his middle years. It was probable he did not like to be hauled from his office at the peremptory demand of his aristocratic client but, whatever egalitarian principles he might discreetly harbour, he had no thought of declining. He had arrived as soon as he might in a tidy gig drawn by a smart blood horse, from which he could view, disconcerted, the appearance of neglect as he passed through the confines of the Ridley estate.

Now, having taken the glass of wine he had known would be proffered, he sat opposite Lord Charles in the library, a generous expanse of green leather between them. As a young man, he had visited Ridley in the company of his father that he might listen to and learn from the late Mr Wilder, who knew, his father said, as much about the law as he did. Mr Taplow was pleased to be reintroduced to him via the portrait that hung on the one wall of the room not devoted to books. Mr Taplow's father and Mr Wilder had been, as far as their different stations would allow, rather good friends. Of Lord Charles Mr Taplow knew a great deal less. He believed him to be without the inclination for meddling and altering, had his father-in-law allowed scope for such. Before driving out Mr Taplow had scrutinized the documents pertaining to the family, but there was nothing with which he was not familiar. He was a trustee of the various funds that provided an income for Lord Charles's heir as well as his granddaughter. He had been in correspondence of a nugatory kind with the late Lieutenant John Lyndon Wilder, and had written a short letter to Lord Charles offering his condolences on the death of his son. Now he was glad he had carried out this duty for it saved raising the matter again.

He waited patiently for Lord Charles to speak: he was not a man for idle chatter or made uncomfortable by silence.

Eventually Lord Charles said, 'It is strange how, all day, I have known exactly what course of action I should take and how I should word it, but when it comes to the point it is not so very easy to explain. As a family we have run into difficulties. You may find this hard to believe.'

Mr Taplow was astonished, though he was soon piecing things together and drawing conclusions. He said nothing.

Lord Charles found his silence intimidating, though Mr Taplow did not intend it to be so. Lord Charles concluded, 'Without money a man is reduced and his great name means nothing. I cannot have been intended to make my way in the world, though as the youngest of nine boys, you might think I would have seen the necessity.'

Mr Taplow, though he had little patience with the helpless, was not unkind. He thought Lord Charles looked older than his years and he was mindful of the loss he had suffered. He said, 'Under the terms of the late Mr Wilder's will, our hands are tied.'

'I'm aware of that. My son, Major Wilder, suggests I sell the London property, the house in Stratton Street. My wife sets store by it. I do not like to make decisions and do decisive things. I find they are invariably regretted and turn out mistakes.'

Mr Taplow said, 'It isn't pleasant to have to sell a property that has been in a family several generations and cause domestic disharmony at the same time, but to be of any assistance I must ask why it is necessary.' As Lord Charles made no reply, he added, 'But perhaps it is too painful a matter for you to divulge.'

'Yes,' Lord Charles said. 'Yes, it is, but it is done and can't be undone. You will guess at it. Nothing alters the facts, but I had hoped we could all slide by. My son, who has a good grasp of things, wishes to return to France and I can't afford to let him do so. If I could give him the whole estate today, I would, but he has to wait his turn. It isn't mine to give. It has to be kept for the duration. Can I give him a power of attorney?'

'It is normally given for some particular purpose, such as to allow some transaction to be conducted abroad.'

'Or,' Lord Charles suggested, 'if someone had lost their wits.'

'Indeed, like our poor king, but though you have told me you wish to make no decisions, you will be pleased to hear, my lord, you could not be declared insane.'

'You must draw it up for me in some clever way so my son has a free hand. He will sell the house in Stratton Street, he will repair roofs and barns, he will see tenants and employ no agents. He will be shrewd and economical for he is accustomed to managing.'

'And domestic harmony?'

'It will be ruined. I must hope it will eventually mend.'

'Could you not sell the London house with the same attitude and philosophy?'

'I considered that, but I should still be left with all the troubles of managing the estate, especially as things have fallen behind. Thomas must do it and be chained to Ridley. It is in his own interest.'

'Is he willing?'

'He hasn't been asked.'

'I had imagined you and he had contrived the thing together.'

'Not at all. He is bent on leaving for France tomorrow.'

'He may not consent, but should he do so, his power over you would be too much. I couldn't recommend it. It is most irregular.' Mr Taplow's mind ran rapidly over a variety of contingencies, none of which he liked. 'How are you to live?'

'He must guarantee me some small amount, for the sake of my dignity, that I may tip servants and pay my tailor.'

'Without obtaining your son's consent, we cannot proceed, supposing it were wise. Is he at home?'

Slimmer, never far from the door of a room where he was in hope of hearing things, appeared in an instant. Yes, he could find Major Wilder and say his lordship required his presence in the library.

Mr Taplow hoped Major Wilder was the sort of smart, clever fellow artillery officers were reputed to be, and the second he saw him, he was inclined to think so. They exchanged extremely small bows and, on Major Wilder's instigation, shook hands. Was Lord Charles to initiate his son with the business at hand? No, he did no more than remark that Major Wilder was already changed for dinner.

Mr Taplow said, 'Lord Charles has explained to me his

wish to delegate the management of his affairs. He is tired of them, it seems.'

'That may well be so,' Major Wilder replied, a touch drily.

'He is anxious you should not return to France.'

'Has Lord Charles shown you the books?'

'No, sir. Perhaps there is not the necessity.'

'He either sells the London house or he runs into debts he can't pay unless he sells it. Sooner or later the bailiffs will be in, poking about, walking off with the silver, but it is not my place to force my father to do what is repugnant to him.'

Mr Taplow thought it would be an excellent thing if Major Wilder did exactly that, but he said, 'Lord Charles wishes to give you a power of attorney.'

Major Wilder turned to his father. 'Am I to make the decisions, do the deeds, you don't care to make or do yourself?'

'Don't berate me, Thomas, I do dislike it so. Can't you see what a good plan it is? You are so much better suited to dealing with the estate than I. Troubles came to me too late in life. I am burdened.'

'But I would sell the house in Stratton Street tomorrow.'

'So? The decision would be yours. A lightness of spirit comes over me at the very thought.'

'But what if I didn't spend the money on Ridley or settle the accumulating debts?'

Lord Charles smiled. 'But you will. I have formed a favourable opinion of your character and it is not in your nature to do otherwise. The estate will be yours when I'm dead. Your mother has no influence over you beyond what you see as a duty. You are not profligate. I now do my best for Ridley if before I failed it. I can be at peace. My only discomfort will be the dire disapproval of my wife but I must hope even she will eventually see the logic of it all. But, Thomas, you mustn't go to France. That is the stipulation.'

For a long moment they sat in silence. Major Wilder was preoccupied with a combination of things from his artillery troop to the peculiar nature of his father, who, though life pulled him this way and that, had a clear notion of his real desires, to do nothing and take no responsibilities. Though he was weak, he was wise.

As if to unravel much of what was left to be unravelled, Major Wilder said, 'Those unexplained debits in the accounts. It is my belief they went to settle what Lyndon owed.'

Lord Charles's expression changed from one of cheerful optimism to one of infinite sadness. He started to speak, stopped, and then said, getting the words out with difficulty, 'Ah, my poor dear boy, he couldn't keep out of debt, what between the gaming tables and his friends, for he must always have what they had and a little better. Again and again I refused him, but I always paid in the end.'

Major Wilder said, 'Until you reached the end and he still owed money.' He wished he had not forced his father to tell him the truth for he looked so inconsolable, so weary and broken-hearted. He got up and turned his back on him and the silent Mr Taplow. Time and again, as a child, he had lost his temper, provoked by his elder brother, but slowly he had learnt one thing, and he supposed he had Lyndon to thank for it: to lose it silently. He could not suppress his sense of violent indignation at the folly of his elder brother carelessly forfeiting his future and the fortunes of those unfortunate enough to follow him, but he could disguise it.

Lord Charles was saying, 'Yes, I sold the oaks from the park and bought the first commission I could in a regiment going abroad, no matter where. I sent his measurements to the tailor, prayed the uniform would fit, for he dared not go to London for fear of being arrested for debt, and smuggled him down to Kent, where the regiment embarked, in a post-chaise. Your mother knew nothing, and of course she never must.'

Major Wilder gave a slight sigh: he was aware that whatever his father asked of him, he would do, but he said, 'When Lyndon died, an officer of his regiment sent me a note saying Lyndon owed him a small sum, which he hoped I would honour. I replied that I would honour any debt beyond a gaming debt. You know I have a great abhorrence to gambling. I heard no more. The debt was not honoured. I suppose that shocks you.'

'Why, yes. I would have thought you might feel obliged to pay it.'

'And you honoured all Lyndon's debts, which is why we are now obliged to look at a park with no trees and forgo our London house.'

Ridley
28 April 1814

My dear Papa,

I have a sense of relief, do not you? War just cannot be right, and yet, needs must, to protect ourselves, we fight them. Oh, how wonderful it is over, but I pray they do not put Bobby on half pay, it would mortify him so. I suppose we have not finished with America yet. Of course we can come to no rational conclusions on the subject of war, one thing contradicting another. What will all the poor soldiers do? How can so many find employment, who have given their youth and probably their health in fighting for their country? What will be done for them? Major Wilder drew our attention to this, for initially I could think only of giddy rejoicing. They say four and a half thousand of our soldiers died or were wounded, many of them Spanish, in the vicinity of Toulouse. It is peculiarly wicked if it is true that Marshal Soult was aware Napoleon had abdicated before the battle commenced, that so many should die, his own French soldiers as well as ours, needlessly.

Miss Arbuthnot laid down her pen. She had been about to quote Major Wilder for a second time. He had had a letter that morning, from the officer commanding his troop, and had said he was glad his men had not been engaged in such a useless and costly exercise. He had smiled and added he was not sure how he felt because his opinion was coloured by the fact that he would not have been there to direct it himself. Miss Arbuthnot decided against recounting this to her father, for he might be inclined to read it all out at the breakfast table, and it was possible Kate and her husband were at the vicarage. In the eyes of Mr Langley, Major Wilder would have been displaying the soldier's bloodthirsty desire for action, whatever the circumstances, and would be adept at misinterpreting any doubts the Major might express and use them to fuel his own arguments. Sitting opposite Major Wilder at the dinner table, Miss Arbuthnot knew it was not precisely as Mr Langley would like to see it. She would have liked to ask the Major exactly what he did think, if he examined himself more thoroughly, on all matters pertaining to a professional soldier that might not accord with Christian principles, but she was unlikely ever to be in a position to do so. Mr Langley was not himself moved by Christianity but Miss Arbuthnot was aware he disguised such sentiments from his father-in-law: however good a match he might otherwise be, he would then have found himself quite unacceptable. How was it she herself had not found him unacceptable? She was, she thought, at heart a rebellious creature, but not to the point of eschewing Christianity.

What would Mr Langley be saying now? Napoleon's abdication would devastate him. Kate would be of little comfort. She would pout, put on her baby voice and say that that nasty, wetched Bonaparte couldn't be an empewor any more; or words to that effect. It was strange how this trait of Kate's, so exasperating to her elder sister, had not only charmed Mr Langley but could charm her father as well.

The longer she was away from home, the harder she found it to write. Her father had such a strait-jacket of principles, such strictures upon what were proper subjects for her to discuss, that she was more often than not at a loss. To write to her sisters might have been easier, if she had not known her father expected all letters to be shared.

It would never cross his mind that his daughters might like to say to one another something that could not be shared, so her letters to Fanny or Minette were usually answers to domestic enquiries; to relieve the tedium, she tried to slip in a few little details of her life with Lottie. Their letters to her, apart from asking if it were correct that one pound of sugar was required to set a pint of apple jelly, and why so much, were devoted to descriptions of little supper parties, Sunday school, walks, visits and the parish. Her life had been precisely their lives but hers had been enlivened by taking their lessons: she thought them less demanding than she had been, less questioning, less impatient with the world as it was. She would have liked to tell them her favourite occupation was cantering across the meadows on the dapple-grey horse with Lottie and Horatio flying along beside her, but her father would think this frivolous, though he had no general objection to people enjoying themselves. The predominant moment of the week, he would remind her, must be the Sunday service, but this did not take into consideration that the parson at Ridley was long-winded and dull, and she was preoccupied with ways to prevent Lottie fidgeting.

She took up her pen and wrote,

It was thought Major Wilder would return to the Artillery but perhaps now we are at peace he will prefer to stay at home and help Lord Charles.

She wanted to say, 'There is something uncomfortable about Ridley at the minute. A lawyer comes and goes. Major Wilder asked him to stay to dinner, which Lady

Charles did not like. He is an interesting man. The discussion was whether or not Elba was an appropriate place for Napoleon to be sent or whether it would not be better to allow him to be executed by the French.' She also wanted to say, 'Lady Charles is angry with her husband and her son.' What was it all about? Her own and Miss Wilder's presence at the dining-table kept everyone at their most polite, but it was artificial. Miss Wilder had said, in her inimitable manner, 'I know why Grandmama is cross with Uncle Thomas, because Grandmama told Mrs Kingston. They thought I wasn't listening because I was playing with Augusta. I was teaching Augusta to sew my sampler, like this, "Now, Augusta, use the thimble, put the needle in just there, don't be disagreeable", and then Grandmama said, "It never was considered necessary to sell the London house until Thomas came home and said it was."'

Her father, Miss Arbuthnot knew, would consider this the sort of gossip in which only servants might indulge.

Major Wilder was writing to his eldest sister:

Dearest Georgie,

You are, please, to have faith in my decision to sell the house in Stratton Street. You must know I would not do so if it were not a necessity. You may well ask what has gone wrong and you must accept I cannot tell you. The only person to be asked is my father, but such questioning will only upset him and nor will he tell. Dearest Georgie, can you not guess? My mother is never to know anything. I suppose this is for the best. She is in such a state of grief over Lyndon's death, I doubt she will ever recover. Why can I not feel for her as I ought? There are ways in which I can do my duty by her, and this is one of them. As for my father, he still grieves, yet he survives it all. Now he has given over all responsibility to myself, his spirits are, between times, buoyant. He has no cares beyond having earned the extreme disapproval and outraged astonishment of his wife. I have decided this is nothing to the pleasure he takes in his lack of any responsibility. I am not sure about the state of his health. Physically, his joints are stiff. He is rather lame. I believe him worn out with cares and anxieties but now I shall hope to keep him cheerful. As for the sisters, I dare say they are all very put out. I don't wish to be the root of all evil but I must do what has to be done.

The certain prospect of peace makes my relinquishing of my troop rather easier, though there are all sorts of other places to which I could have been sent, India, America, the West Indies, from which return is uncertain. I find I am confused. War is an abomination, but without it soldiering is dull. There are compensations. I must consider marriage, which I did not previously rule out, but what sort of husband does a soldier on active service make? Who wishes to leave a widow and orphans with no guarantee of their getting a pension, perhaps nothing beyond the few mournful shillings from the sale of their husband's effects? There are a few officers accompanied by their wives but anxiety for the welfare of their families in times of crisis must interfere with their ordinary duties. How could it not be so?

Major Wilder had said as much as he was going to on these particular matters, and went on to enquire after his nieces and nephews, a subject of which his sister was unlikely to tire.

Lady Charles tended to write to her daughters a sort of a general letter and then to fill in at the top the name of which daughter she ultimately decided was to be the recipient. This letter, initially, was destined for Georgie, though it might equally go to Sophia, but as she wrote she hesitated to suppose it suitable. It was difficult to remember her children were grown-up. The years spent caring for them, watching them, guiding them, could not be shaken off in a moment, however many times she had become a grandmother. She was aware of the anomaly for they surely were grown-up; they could hear of unpleasant truths and awkward circumstances, but was it appropriate they should hear of any little thing she chose to say against herself? Lady Charles considered mothers should be omnipotent, that they always knew best. Her devotion to her elder son had not eclipsed her affection for her daughters, whom she had brought up in an exemplary manner, adroit at encouraging and discreetly displaying their better characteristics until such time as they could be firmly, though kindly, led to accept a suitable offer of marriage. Self-doubt or personal inquisition were not failings to which Lady Charles was in the habit of succumbing, but never before had she found herself so awry, even apart from Lyndon's death.

You know how it is, dear, one must try to be rational. Nothing is ever explained to me. Neither your father nor your grandfather considered I need be worried with practical matters. Of course, when things go wrong, one is all at sea. I have been spoilt. I doubt the real necessity to sell the house in Stratton Street, but what do I know? Nothing. I do not think Thomas should have put on his uniform to frighten your father into believing he was off to France while there were still battles to be fought. Lord Charles's health is not up to such alarms. Now he is like a little boy let out of school and Thomas does exactly as he likes.

Lady Charles hesitated. At one time, she would not have spoken so frivolously, indeed disrespectfully, of her husband, but previously she had not had the need.

Well, my dear, he likes to do whatever Thomas says, so how can I say if Thomas bullies him or no? All those years in the army have given Thomas the habit of being obeyed, though there must always have been colonels and generals to whom he was answerable.

Yes, this letter must definitely go to Sophia. Lady Charles paused to consider autocratic behaviour in the male sex. Her own father had been an autocrat, not always pleasant and certainly arrogant, but she did not see such things as sinful because they were of the ingredients that made up her father's position as a wealthy man. He would boast that he could afford for his only child to marry a poor man. He did not mention the status acquired in attaching his family to that of a duke, but it was understood, though perhaps the advantage was lost by their adhering to the name of Wilder: she declined always to be saying, 'My brother, the duke,' especially as she was barely acquainted with him and he was soon superseded by his son, with whom she was not acquainted at all. At the same time, Lady Charles knew her distress at the loss of the London house related to the loss of status, the idea that they could no longer afford such a thing, rather than her desire to go to it. She did not wish to have to start saying, 'My nephew, the duke,' in order to maintain her place in society.

> *I must blame myself for my not having a better understanding of Thomas. He did not receive from me the attention he should have done. I allowed Georgie to take charge of him, and she was but a child herself. Now it seems likely that he will be at home, you had better set about finding him a suitable wife, for I shall not have the energy to do so and we see no company, or very little. He cannot remain a bachelor: there is an obligation for him to marry.*

For a single missive she had included sufficient self-abasement, and she was as angry with her husband as she was with Thomas. Had Charles been mismanaging the estate for years or was it the cost of their daughters' marriage settlements, with the addition of the war tax, that had reduced them to their present situation? She could not, reasonably, blame Thomas for everything: he had been absent. What if Lyndon had not been killed? But this was a journey too painful for her mind to travel.

Was she jealous of Thomas, of his influence over Lord Charles and Lottie? Was it not natural to wish to take first place with those one loved best? It was proper for Lottie to be mindful of Miss Arbuthnot, but she should not bestow on her more affection than she bestowed on her grandmother. Lottie was beginning to view her uncle much as she would a father: though Thomas was very firm with her, he was able to inspire a degree of adulation, which must have to do with his being the able officer of whom much was spoken. If he could win the hearts of soldiers and make them do as he wished, he would not be too taxed by the management of Lottie. Lady Charles assumed there was some sort of knack to it. She was firm in her mind that Lottie must never be allowed to forget her own father, for whom Thomas should be no replacement, whether he was her guardian or no.

Lyndon had always accused her of jealousy, and had used to tease her about it. He would laugh and describe it as the most acceptable of sins. She had been rather jealous of his wife but, though a beauty, during the months she had spent at Ridley she had been frail, fretful and unwell. Her condition had not suited her health and had made of her a sad creature. Lady Charles knew she must acknowledge the necessity of another young woman coming to Ridley as a bride for Thomas. She thought again of Mrs Kingston. Might Mrs Kingston, who had undoubtedly been attached to Lyndon, be prepared to accept what could only be second best? It would seem extraordinary, but even without the London house Thomas must be considered a reasonably good prospect.

The miniature of Lyndon as a very young man, in his uniform of an officer in the Guards, at which, for some time, she could hardly bring herself to look, she had placed on her desk in her sitting room, and she brought herself to look at it all the time. Now, half speaking to herself, half to the rosy image of her son in scarlet, she said, 'You were a mere boy then, but you died a man and a hero.'

Sally came in to lay out her clothes for dinner. The letter remained unfinished.

Lord Charles, like his son, began to see the advantage of having Lottie and her governess at the dining-table, for even when Slimmer had been got out of the room, always a task, the conversation must be kept to the general, no discussions permissible on the sale of the London house or on his own peculiar conduct in absolving himself of further responsibilities. As the days went by, he thought himself not at all peculiar, merely sensible. He saw that, had Lyndon returned, nothing would have been resolved: Lyndon would not have had the tenacity to do anything so unappealing as selling the house in Stratton Street, where he had spent much of his time, and their debts would have increased. Lord Charles had set such store by his elder son that he could not bring himself to acknowledge that the estate was now in more capable hands; he liked to believe that Lyndon had been a little like himself, unsuited to understanding business, altogether too gentlemanly to consider the practical when it was unpleasant. Had Lyndon not run up gaming bills and other expenses, natural to a young man in his position, had he inherited Ridley as he himself had inherited it, Lord Charles liked to suppose he would soon have shrugged off his careless habits. In fact his thoughts were rather confused and contradictory.

With the spring and the warmer weather, with his lack of cares or responsibilities, his spirits lifted. They were not dampened by his wife's continued disapproval, though he thought they ought to be. He had Thomas for company who, though his son might think poorly of him, did not tax him with it. In fact, Thomas did not tax him with anything, doing what he saw fit without consultation. At first Lord Charles had been disconcerted at being of so little use but, having brought it on himself, he had no face for complaining, and had it not been his wish? Perhaps, as in fairy tales, wishes did not necessarily take the shape one had thought they ought, and in his mind he had seen himself as some venerable elder statesman, without, when he thought about it, having qualified for the role. Nevertheless, his spirits had lifted.

Now they sat at dinner and Slimmer had at last been prevailed upon to leave.

Major Wilder announced his intention of going to London in a day or two and from there to proceed to Paris; he would not be away for long. He turned to Miss Arbuthnot. 'Is it not time you visited your family?'

Miss Arbuthnot was disconcerted. She wanted to see Fanny and Minette but the thought of being at home confused her. She had put that life by and exchanged it for this one. Neither did she care to be parted from her pupil. She longed for familiar places and dear friends, but then she must tear herself from them again, which could only be painful, as would be the inevitable talk of Kate and her husband, whom she might even be expected to meet; for that she was not prepared. She did not know how to answer Major Wilder but after a moment she said, 'I haven't been here so very long, just six months.'

'I expect your father misses you,' Major Wilder replied, smiling, 'but I was not suggesting you went against your will.' He was thinking of her situation, aware that to go home might be distressing for her, yet he did not like to withhold the offer.

His words made Miss Arbuthnot wonder if he had learnt of her circumstances. The notion shocked her and she felt all the old sensations of loss: loss of love and loss of youth, and of shame. Why shame? Was it because she had allowed herself to be hoodwinked by the plausible Mr Langley? She did not even know whether the hoodwinking had been intentional. She certainly did not wish it all common knowledge, but Major Wilder looked at her only with gentle enquiry, which told her not a thing. If she could but get over a first meeting with her sister and her sister's husband, nothing could be so bad again, but at that moment it seemed an insurmountable object, so she again hesitated to reply.

Lord Charles said, misinterpreting her silence, 'Why, my dear Miss Arbuthnot, anyone would think you had taken a dislike to your family.'

Miss Arbuthnot said hastily, 'Oh, no, I should like to go home, but perhaps I haven't earned a holiday as yet.'

'I should leave Major Wilder to decide that,' Lord Charles said good-humouredly.

Lottie let her soup spoon fall on her plate with a clatter. She left her chair, put her arms round Miss Arbuthnot's neck and burst into tears.

'Now, Lottie, whatever is the matter?' her grandmother asked. 'This is not very grown-up conduct.'

'But I want to go with Miss 'Buthnot or she mustn't go away.'

'And leave your pony and your garden?' Lady Charles was almost glad to think Lottie could be prised from these.

'They will be there when I come back and Uncle Thomas will take York, and we like to go with York best.'

Major Wilder said, 'Lottie, I think you should consider Miss Arbuthnot. She has not seen her family for many months. They will have much to talk of which will be no concern of ours, and she should be allowed to enjoy a little time without responsibilities. Return to your chair.'

Lottie reluctantly unwound herself and did as she was bid because she found it wise to obey her uncle. 'I would be so quiet and good and I would only speak just now and again, if I should be asked a question, and I could sleep in a little cot in a corner or under the stairs and never miss Susan even if my buttons were on the wrong holes. Miss 'Buthnot's family would hardly notice me. I should be no more than a wee shadow.'

Major Wilder said, 'I can't see you as such.'

Lottie shrank down in her chair in an attempt to look small.

'If nobody minded,' Miss Arbuthnot said, 'I should like to take Miss Wilder with me. I should like it very much.' Suddenly she was smiling. She did not need to be parted from Lottie. Lottie's very presence would be a pleasure to her family and of great assistance in tiding over the inevitable meeting with Kate and her husband.

'You must be quite certain of that, before committing yourself,' Major Wilder said, but he, too, could see the advantage to Miss Arbuthnot of having Lottie with her on this occasion, though he did not, of course, say so.

Lady Charles said, 'Am I not to be consulted?'

Miss Arbuthnot looked at her anxiously. She thought Major Wilder high-handed in as much as he never took notice of his mother, who, she presumed, had the care of Lottie.

'If you think the scheme a mistake,' Major Wilder replied, 'by all means say so. I assume Lottie is not too young to travel.'

Lady Charles could think of no objection that could be declared aloud.

PART III

Does an old house have watchful eyes? Lady Charles, who was not fanciful, was driven to fancy when she contemplated the preceding year. Did Ridley care? Was it conscious of the ghosts that thronged, the dead little children, the stillborn babies, the consumptives, the young soldiers, the lost heirs, those whose poignant ends could stamp their passing on the air by aid of grief? Did it care her son had died? Would Lyndon's graceful form flit from hall to stair once she, who kept him living in the eye of her mind, was gone? What would antecedents know? A sword in a glass case; a miniature of a young officer in the Guards wrapped in a piece of frayed silk and placed in the bottom of a drawer full of miscellaneous things; letters pasted in a book? Who would care, once she was gone, that Lyndon had died? She felt omniscient time remorselessly tugging the world along, crushing and smothering. It was June. Careless spring had come and gone. Soon it would be July. John Lyndon Wilder had died gallantly leading his men in the defence of the pass at Roncesvalles, in the thirty-sixth year of his life, 25 July 1813. It would be the anniversary of his death, the first anniversary, and then would come the second, and the third, and the fortieth, and the fiftieth. His great-grandchildren or Thomas's would say, should they trouble to read the memorial in the church, 'Who was John Lyndon Wilder and what was that war in which he died? Where is the pass at Roncesvalles?' As for the memorial, it would be nothing to catch the eye.

Ridley had long been slumbering as it sank beneath genteel neglect, with empty pond and uncut grass. Did the occasional dream meander through rooms remembered and rooms half forgotten, the lives of those inhabiting the place of little consequence when viewing the long perspective? Had it woken to the pain of Lyndon's death, to the return of his brother, to anger and distress? Did it wake but to sleep again?

Did it open a tired eye on tidiness and vigour? Major Wilder was brisk, his mother thought too brisk, but she could see that what he did had to be done. There were sheep in the park. The terrace was weeded. The leak was found that had caused one pond to empty while the other was full; it had created a quagmire in an unexpected place which, her son had pointed out, must have been obvious to all. Hedges were cut back and borders trimmed. The kitchen garden was shaken, as was the home farm. The long-prevailing habits of indolence were expunged. The estate was to pay its way. It had been agreeable never to worry her head but she was conscious of deliberate ignorance and oversight on her part, of seeing nothing and pretending more. She did not say so. Was she not angry with Thomas on many counts? Her daughters were also angry and confused, apart from Georgie, who made no mention of it, by the sale of the house in Stratton Street, for which no explanation was forthcoming. She had no answers to their questions. They tended, without logic, to blame their remaining brother, who continued in pursuit of what he considered his duty to the estate and his ward, with apparent indifference to other considerations. He was as implacable as the proverbial stone wall.

Lottie was not to wear mourning. Indeed when she had gone away to stay with the family of her governess, Thomas had decreed any new clothes required should be in any shade but black or grey. Miss Arbuthnot said new clothes would not be required for staying in West Staverton, beyond replacing those outgrown. This drew Lady Charles's attention to the fact that Lottie grew, as Miss Arbuthnot said, like Jack's beanstalk, but she sent her away dressed as she saw fit, befitting a Miss Wilder of Ridley, giving way to the dictate that Lottie's official mourning was over.

It seemed there was no end to expense. Lady Charles, who had used to hear, if not believe, that times were bad, now saw money was spent. It was, of course, owing to the ignominious sale of the London house, but nobody could describe Thomas Wilder as extravagant. He was tediously cautious. The monument to his elder brother would be paid for, he had said, but not yet, and he had the mason draw it up again without the angels.

Major Wilder, riding round the estate with his father, was glad of the summer. It altered his mood, and by slow degrees he was learning to become attached to Ridley. He disliked the park: in its treeless state he was ashamed of it. Even when the planting was done, in three or four months' time, it could not look anything but bare, but he would at least have done his duty by it. To love Ridley he needed to be proud of it. He thought cutting down the trees, getting Lyndon's commission and packing him off to war must have been one of the few times in the life of his father when decisions had been made and action taken. Lord Charles, he could see, was ideally suited to the life of a quiet country gentleman of adequate means without tastes more extravagant than fox-hunting. Had he been just so when he was young? Major Wilder did not know. His father looked on all he did with astonished gratification, to the point of causing him irritation, but this he suppressed and, on thinking he had not suppressed it quite enough, he gave him a little dog. It was the sort of exasperating creature with a soft coat and a whiskery face that ecstatically covered yours with its wet tongue whenever you bent over to pull on your boots. He was glad to see how much his father loved it. Lady Charles was not pleased, but then she was not often pleased, and he saw no reason for his father not to have a harmless little dog of his own. And did not the creature love his father? Well, it loved anybody it could reach to give them a washing.

To become accustomed to living at Ridley after the fifteen years and more, if his days at Woolwich should be included, he had spent in the congenial company of his brother officers, he found hard. It was mitigated by the work he had to do, for he liked work, even the tedious undoing of his father's incompetence and the sorting out of muddles. His grandfather's rooms were pleasant and so was the library. Lottie and her governess amused him at dinner. Sometimes he joined them on their rides. He was teaching Horatio how to fish. He liked these aspects of family life more than he had supposed he would, which made him reflect, not for the first time, on the subject of marriage. Georgie had said she and the sisters, even though the latter were still miffed with him, would soon find him a suitable wife. This he knew meant a wife who would not come empty-handed, which point he could appreciate, but how were his sisters, even Georgie, to know what sort of woman he liked? He was obstinate and not easily satisfied.

Mrs Kingston saw that picnics could be viewed in a variety of ways. Lady Charles had used to entertain her family and their friends out of doors. It was sometimes hard to recollect the cheerful past, when the girls and Lyndon were growing up and courting, the informal parties, balls and suppers, Lady Charles a contented wife and mother, adroit at promoting her daughters and enjoying their successes. Picnics she had approved but they entailed earnest preparation, many servants and all the plate. A table would be laid in the shade of the chestnut tree on the front lawn and entailed as much formality as if it had been laid in the dining room, but it did take on a sort of pastoral charm and had an agreeable novelty.

Mrs Kingston, who had listened to Lady Charles's description of correct eating in the garden, had different notions. The purpose of picnics was for a degree of informality. They should be in a wood or a meadow or down by the river. It was important to sit on the ground, albeit with plenty of cushions, so people, she meant men, could lounge about and feel unrestrained in a manner that never could be achieved in the dining room or under the chestnut tree at Ridley. What better way was there of getting to know one another? She would have a white cloth and no more servants than were required to carry the feast, for it must be a feast, though disguised as rustic simplicity: plenty of raised pie, cold meats, sweet pastries and fruit tarts, and always, when in season, strawberries, the latter, so dazzling red, for their very air of festivity.

Mrs Kingston had decided she must be more practical. She disliked living with her brother, but had no immediate means of parting company with him unless his health improved and he was able to rejoin his regiment. Sometimes he went whole days together with the appearance, at least, of normality, but it was never without a relapse. It would be better to live on her own than to live with Henry for the rest of their lives, for he never took pleasure in anything. He was always critical and saw only base motives in the acts of others. She had wished to marry and had been very disappointed by Lieutenant Wilder going away to war without declaring himself, but as he was not to return, she supposed it was of no consequence.

The most sensible thing she could do was to marry his brother. Major Wilder was not so charming or attractive as Lyndon Wilder had been, but she could see he was reliable. It was unfortunate he did not have a warm relationship with his mother, but he was kind to the children and dutiful to his father, who was devoted to him. She thought herself a few years older than him, but she was not too old to bear children, and he must surely want an heir. A woman of reasonable maturity, who had lost none of her youthful attractions, was an ideal wife for a man who had seen so much of the world while experiencing the horrors of war.

As much as she sat with his mother, it was rare for Major Wilder to put in an appearance. She constantly asked after him, but it appeared she was not to get to know him; he must view her as nothing more than a young companion of his mother. Her mind had thus turned to picnics as a means of entertaining. She had prevailed upon him to visit her brother, but it was obvious that no amount of battles they might have in common would make them friends. She often thought how much more comfortable Ridley would be were she in charge of it. In her mind she repainted the rooms and altered the furniture. She knew this process to be unwise. Had she not done it before and with what results? A little daydreaming was, however, hard to resist.

The first picnic Mrs Kingston gave was down by the stream. She started by asking Lord and Lady Charles, who, she thought, would refuse, but the children urged them to accept. She promised them chairs and every comfort. Horatio bore an invitation to Major Wilder. Mrs Kingston was in a quandary as to whether or not she should say her brother was well enough to attend and would particularly appreciate the company of a fellow soldier. Would that induce Major Wilder to accept or encourage him to find an excuse? In the end she wrote that she hoped her brother would be well enough to attend, thereby providing an excuse for the presumption of the invitation. She saw Miss Arbuthnot must attend for she would mind the children. For a moment she thought of suggesting to her she might like to have the time to herself, governesses being so awkward to place, but Miss Arbuthnot had too much self-possession to fall into that category, and she was sure to be useful. She wondered at herself for being so unkind as to wish pleasant, interesting Miss Arbuthnot to be otherwise occupied when the party could only be a pleasure to her. Miss Arbuthnot was too tall, she was not elegant, she had freckles, but she had green eyes the colour of the willow trees that overhung the water and rather a dear, childlike face: what was more, she was twelve years or so younger than Mrs Kingston. No, she could not be so cruel as to exclude her, it would be on her conscience. Besides, Lottie was such an unpredictable little person and Horatio was inclined to be naughty and wilful now he was eleven. The pony, which she liked to make a subject of conversation between herself and Major Wilder on the rare occasions when such took place, was quite a nuisance, for it had given Horatio a delight in independence.

There was some concern that the site for the picnic, with the wide, rushing stream burbling over the pebbles, would be damp, but Major Wilder said it was not damp and if it were, those likely to be affected had chairs. He flung himself down on the ground, helped to spread the cloth and made himself useful. He told Mrs Kingston he had never had so many delicious things offered him as outdoor fare, which remark she treasured for some weeks. Captain Houghton insisted on sitting on the ground too, though it made his sister anxious. He said she could be blamed if he died from it. He was near to Miss Arbuthnot but did not think to pass her anything until Major Wilder, jokingly, pointed out to him the necessity.

Captain Houghton said, 'Beg pardon, miss,' because he had forgotten her name, and Miss Arbuthnot gave a small smile, half amused, half uncertain, at his rudeness.

He was a man in his forties, emaciated, ill health so pervading him it was impossible to feel anything for him but pity.

The children had been allowed to ride their ponies down to the meadow and, as it was not far, they had come on their own, Horatio in charge of opening and shutting gates and looking after Lottie in the unlikely event of an accident. Major Wilder had said there was no harm in giving children responsibility and had shown them how to tie the ponies, with rope halters over the bridles, to the nearest convenient tree, with a particular knot. Lady Charles could not see why Lottie was so devoted to learning things she would never need to put to practical use. Since staying away with Miss Arbuthnot she had come to take a deep interest in domestic matters, which Lady Charles supposed would be useful to her, if only Lottie were not so immoderate in her enthusiasms.

Lottie now sat by her side, her sturdy limbs stuck straight before her, her light blue cotton smock rucked carelessly over her pantaloons, which were intended to keep her decent for riding. She said, eyeing the slice of salmon and the shrimps set in aspic on her plate, for she was suspicious of the jelly, 'Both Fanny and Minette can take the guts out of a fish.'

Horatio said, 'When I catch a fish, which I haven't yet, you can help me to gut it, Lottie.'

Ignoring him, she addressed her grandmother: 'I have been thinking about getting married.'

'I don't think you need consider it yet, dearest, especially while you talk about guts.'

'But I had thought I shouldn't like to be married. Now I

think I will marry but I shall be careful to choose someone without too much of you know what.'

Lady Charles was disturbed. 'Too much of what, darling?'

Lottie mouthed, 'Money.'

'Goodness me, child, I am afraid that is a necessity.'

'But I like to do things. I don't want a housekeeper. I don't want to tell other people what to do and then sit in the drawing room sewing a few things and hoping someone will call. I want to make preserves and roll the pastry and poke the meat with a skewer to see if it's cooked. Fanny and Minette help Mrs Abigael all the time, because there is too much work for one. I want to walk down to the kitchen garden to pick the broad beans and not before they're ready, for that's wasteful.'

'But, darling, in your situation, it won't matter, within reason.'

'I want it to matter,' Lottie said, belligerent and suddenly tearful.

Lady Charles looked at Miss Arbuthnot. 'Inappropriate sentiments, I fear.'

Miss Arbuthnot met her accusing gaze as best she could. 'Miss Wilder is of a practical disposition. I believe, when she is grown-up, she will be able to find useful application for it. It should not be wasted, should it? My sisters grew fond of Miss Wilder, and we were merry as could be. But, yes, a lot of the time was spent in the kitchen.' It would be easier, she thought, to have no opinions, to say yes and no at the proper intervals. She knew Lady Charles must think her argumentative, but she would fight to give Lottie a mind of her own.

Major Wilder, who, Miss Arbuthnot thought, had a mischievous streak, said, 'Lottie, I shall teach you to gut a fish as soon as Horatio has caught one.'

Lord Charles sat with his little dog on his knee to prevent it wandering about among the dishes. Such was its enthusiasm for licking his face he had difficulty in getting anything to eat, but then his dear, managing Thomas scooped it up under an arm, wriggling and squirming, to tie it with the ponies whence it yipped disconsolately.

Mrs Kingston was thinking of the disadvantage of informal entertainment. At least when at home the gentlemen stayed at the table until the ladies withdrew, and could usually be got to join them again sooner or later. Now, the very second the meal was over, Major Wilder jumped to his feet, without a thought for his digestive system, and took the children and Miss Arbuthnot rambling down the stream to see if they could build stepping stones or tickle trout. Mrs Kingston's servants, who had been enjoying a meal of their own, for she was a kindly mistress, appeared from behind the trees to clear away the plates and pack everything in baskets. Lord Charles was reunited with his dog. He got up to meander about, poking his stick in the water and then, more purposefully, into some bramble bushes whence he put up a rabbit for the dog to chase. On hearing its excited yelps, the greyhounds, who had followed Major Wilder, loped back and dispatched the rabbit, Fuente bringing it back to Lord Charles and giving it into his hand like the biddable creature he was. He then looked expectantly at Lord Charles to provide more sport and Lord Charles was happy to prod bushes and the little dog to plunge into the undergrowth while the greyhounds waited, poised for action.

Lottie and Horatio lost interest in doing anything but taking off their shoes and stockings to paddle in the water. Major Wilder leant against the bough of an overhanging tree and was content to watch them until he saw them beginning to tire. His mind having travelled in a variety of directions, he said to Horatio, 'What is it that has so alarmed you about your career in the Royal Navy? Don't you see it as an honour?'

Horatio scrambled out of the water and went to stand beside him. His trousers and jacket were covered with mud, and he said, scowling, 'Do you think I am a coward, sir?'

'I don't suppose so, hence my wondering what made you so anxious.'

'But I should be able to do what other boys do, shouldn't I?'

'Why, yes, and I am sure you will, but what do you know of it? Is it your uncle who is in the navy? Has he talked to you much?'

'Oh, no, I never met him at all.' Horatio looked perplexed. 'It was somebody else. When I tried to tell my mother, she said I imagined it, but I didn't, though it was a long time ago. I know I didn't, nor dream it either. Grown persons always say that when they don't want to believe what you're telling them.'

'Try me with it.'

Horatio considered the matter. His antipathy for his chosen career was not something he had ever attempted to explain, for he thought he ought to be ashamed of it. Eventually, overcome with the temptation to confide, he said, 'All right, but you mustn't tell. You may think, sir, a little boy like me can't remember something happening when he was five or six years old but maybe I was more. I had a little desk in the drawing room at home and I used to sit at it beside my mother and occupy myself with reading and drawing, even when my mother had visitors. There was a gentleman who used to visit my mother quite a great deal but he never took too much notice of me. One day my mother was called away out of the room. I think, though I may be wrong, one of the maids had scalded themselves in the kitchen. It doesn't matter. I was left alone with this gentleman. He said something like, "Well, laddie, how come your mama is so keen to get rid of you that she is sending you into the navy?" I felt quite shocked, and hastened to explain I was going into the navy because my papa had been in the navy. He laughed and said, "You take my word for it, that's what they always say, when they want to get rid of you." Of course, I protested some more. Then he said, "After all, the navy is a dangerous place for little boys and only the strongest survive it." I asked him what he meant. He said, "The captains beat the midshipmen until the blood runs if they do some little thing wrong and ships are generally awash with blood, what with the sailors getting the lash day and night." Well, I knew the sailors did get beaten if they were very bad, so I didn't quite know what to believe. Then he said, "If a midshipman makes a mistake, they send him up the rigging to the crow's nest and won't let him down again. If it's a nice day it's all right, but otherwise he freezes to death from the cold. They have to pop him overboard and write home to his parents to say he had an accident and fell into the sea." He said other things too, I don't remember it all, but I decided straight away I shouldn't like the navy. My mother came back and she laughed in an odd way. She said she was sorry to be gone so long but she was glad to see we were entertaining one another. Now, sir, do you think I made that up?'

Major Wilder said, 'Sadly, I don't. I wish I did.'

'But what he said was true.'

'It was true and yet it isn't.' Major Wilder paused while he thought out what he wished to say. 'Clever, because true enough to seem true yet giving what I believe to be a false picture. If it were totally true there wouldn't be any midshipmen left, would there? Such things are known to happen, but they are rare, and they happen on bad ships with bad captains. I take it you are destined for your uncle's ship?'

'Yes. He is a post captain. My name has been down on the ship's list for a long time, but he will make a proper vacancy for me when I'm twelve. He says he does not like very little boys on his ship. It's the *Prince Adolphus*. He writes to my mother.'

'He is your father's brother?'

'Yes. Because of this, he says, he is looking forward to having me, and I shall remind him of my father.'

Major Wilder said, 'I don't believe you have anything to worry about. You are a good, active lad. It is possible you may even like it. If you don't, you may leave it and try something else.' He had friends in the navy and he thought he would have no difficulty in making enquiries as to the character of Captain Kingston.

'But my mother won't let me leave,' Horatio said.

'In the end, if you are truly unhappy, she will. I am quite certain she loves you dearly.'

Horatio, too, believed his mother loved him. He sighed and then he smiled. He saw he had been right to explain himself to Major Wilder. He said, 'It was a very bad man to talk to me in that way.'

'He was a bully. Such a man will bully and tease any creature subservient to him.'

Together they began to walk towards Lottie, who had settled down to make a daisy chain. Horatio thought how he had been shy of Major Wilder but now there would be no need. He tried to picture himself telling such a tale to Captain Houghton. He caught hold of Major Wilder's hand and said, 'I want to say something else, very quietly.'

Major Wilder obediently bent his head. Horatio whispered breathlessly into his ear, 'Sometimes I think that man was Lottie's papa.' He then added, out loud, 'But that couldn't be, could it?'

Major Wilder did not reply immediately. He then said gravely, 'Let us hope not.'

Horatio ran ahead as if released. He laughed at Lottie. 'That's a very quiet good sort of occupation,' he said.

'I wanted to do it as a surprise for Miss 'Buthnot but I'm not a bit patient and I've broken it twice. Will you do some of it?'

Horatio did not consider daisy chains suitable employ for the male sex but he was a good-natured child. In the end even Major Wilder assisted and they tried it on Lottie to ascertain the necessary fit.

Miss Arbuthnot had spent all this time sitting on the bank above the stream watching the activities of Major Wilder and the children. She decided she would not be required unless Lottie or Horatio actually fell into the water instead of paddling about. She was not exactly happy but neither was she unhappy. She liked to sit in the sun and be entertained by the activities of the little group below her. She had much for which to be thankful.

At home, in the vicarage, she had only had to meet Kate and her husband once. It had been brief. She had not looked Mr Langley in the eye and had busied herself with helping Lottie cut out paper dolls. Kate had talked incessantly, but in that there was nothing new. Mr Langley announced the completion of a play in verse depicting the events of the French Revolution and could talk of nothing else. Once she would have found it fascinating but now she did not: he was too glib in passing over the horror of it all. She noticed Kate took no heed of what he said; husband and wife spoke simultaneously on unrelated matters. She understood she was now expected to call Mr Langley James, which she had not done previously when they were a great deal better acquainted, but fortunately there had been no occasion for her to call him anything at all.

Yet it was early June and in the June of the previous year she had been blessedly happy, innocently so. Mr Langley had dropped hints and she had accepted them at face value. The garden had been full of roses. Kate had come home from a protracted visit to her godmother, who would have liked to adopt her had Mr Arbuthnot allowed it. She had three new bonnets, an endless quantity of ribbons and lace, as well as a length of spotted muslin, which she declared her dear Anna would have to make up for her as she was herself sure to make a muddle of it and cut two sleeves the same way round. The moment she saw Mr Langley she started a flirtation, but that was Kate, and one had no need to read anything into it. Mr Langley had said to her, 'Your little sister is perfectly charming,' and she had been glad he should like her. Well, that was June a year ago. Now there was no elation, no giddy imaginings of unlikely scenarios, no turning of mundane things to magic, no colouring all to a brighter hue.

Miss Arbuthnot watching all the while, wondered what Horatio could have to say to Major Wilder of such gravity as they leant on the low, sweeping bough of a willow tree. How dirty the children were, but how content. She watched them make the daisy chain and then they climbed the bank towards her and Lottie draped her with the flowers. Inexplicably, her eyes filled with tears. They immediately wanted to make another for her hair, and went scampering off. Major Wilder sat down beside her. She sensed he was preoccupied, that something had distracted him. They remained silent.

By the time they got up to go Miss Arbuthnot had a second wreath and a third for her wrist. Major Wilder, deliberately turning his mind from Horatio, thought how unnatural a life it was for a girl, the everlasting company of children, no one of her own age, no balls or suppers, little to disturb the daily round. He knew from Georgie that when Miss Arbuthnot was at home the Miss Hamiltons were her friends and no difference was made between them in their positions. Of course the Arbuthnots were extremely respectable, but the living was poor and Mr Arbuthnot had no other means. Even now, as he strolled beside her, he considered how it was inappropriate for him to offer Miss Arbuthnot his arm because she was Lottie's governess. To do so would disconcert her. He said, 'I hope you are not homesick.'

'No. There are compensations. I like teaching. I like my pupil.' She turned to him and added, smiling, 'I like to be able to ride. My father thinks I like it too much, that I am not sufficiently serious.'

'Oh, you are quite serious enough,' he said, laughing.

Mrs Kingston was talking, a trifle desperately, to Lady Charles. Captain Houghton had gone to sleep with his mouth open. His sister wished, if he must sleep, which she supposed good for him, he could do so more decorously.

Lady Charles was thinking about her mourning clothes. Black was so hot in the summer, but how could she have such a thought when it was not yet a twelve-month from Lyndon's death? Could she not weather a little discomfort in remembrance of her boy? She resolved to wear mourning for the rest of her life. Would she not be for ever in a state of grief and should not the world know it?

Major Wilder and Miss Arbuthnot, who were talking together, strolled towards them with Lottie and Horatio. Miss Arbuthnot was bedecked with daisies. Mrs Kingston wondered at Lady Charles allowing such a young woman in the house when there was a bachelor son. She knew Lady Charles thought Miss Arbuthnot plain; she did not see that Miss Arbuthnot possessed an odd sort of charm. Well, she consoled herself, they must all assume Major Wilder was too sensible a man to disgrace his family by paying court to his niece's governess. A moment later she wondered if any man could be trusted in this respect, and how much of a disgrace it would be. Miss Arbuthnot came from a respectable family, but she was poor and a governess. Mrs Kingston was then annoyed with herself for letting her imagination run away with her. There was no question of Major Wilder being in the least interested in anybody's governess, let alone Lottie's.

Lady Charles said, 'Good gracious, Mrs Kingston, look at the children. They are not only filthy, but wet.'

Lottie ran to her grandmother. 'We've been paddling and then we made daisy chains and covered Miss 'Buthnot all over.'

'But, child, you will catch your death and you are so dirty. Miss Arbuthnot, look at the state of the children. What were you thinking?'

Major Wilder said briskly, 'What does it matter? They will soon dry. It was not Miss Arbuthnot, it was me. We've all enjoyed ourselves and don't want a scolding because of a little dirt and water.'

Lord Charles appeared with a brace of rabbits and all three dogs. He said, on seeing the children, 'What ragamuffins! Thomas, you should see how this little fellow of mine works a covert. He is a grand complement to your dogs.' He slumped down on a chair. His legs ached but he did not care to mention it.

Major Wilder took the rabbits to dress them out. When he returned, he said to his father, 'Will you give the rabbits to Mrs Kingston? I can so easily get more.' Remembering he was Mrs Kingston's guest, he sat down.

Mrs Kingston thought, Better late than never, and was just trying to think of something to say to him when he glanced towards Captain Houghton and remarked, 'Your brother sleeps very sound. I am afraid his complaint is hard to shake off. I have seen many a good soldier forced to take leave and never return for active service.'

'Indeed, it is sad to see his health so ruined.' Mrs Kingston paused to consider her brother. He was fundamentally idle so in some ways, though it could not have been pleasant, the state of being an invalid suited him. It became his character. She continued, 'It is not only in the glory of the battlefield that a man is sacrificed for his country.'

'Quite so. I am never sure a battle is so very glorious, but we need to think so if we win it.'

'And of course,' Mrs Kingston proceeded, 'it is so very dull for Henry to be living with me, no like-minded gentlemen with whom to associate.'

Major Wilder was aware that an appeal had been made, but neither his better nature nor his ordinary good manners would allow him to commit himself to visiting Captain Houghton regularly.

Mrs Kingston then said, 'When Captain Greenway visits, it will be better. You will wish to meet him, I dare say, because he is in the regiment that was your brother's.'

Major Wilder made no immediate reply. His first thought was that he never wished to meet an officer from Lyndon's regiment, least of all Captain Greenway, who believed he was owed forty Spanish dollars. It was out of principle he had not paid them, but now he wished, for the sake of a quiet life, he had honoured the debt.

'And is he a very great friend of Captain Houghton?' he asked.

'I don't believe so. They were at school together but did not keep in touch. They were on the same ship going out to the Peninsula, and then, of course, they became reacquainted. I asked Henry to write to him, for the sake of your poor mother. Eventually Captain Greenway returned a letter announcing a visit when he got leave. I can't say my brother was overjoyed at the prospect, but he gets low and that colours his attitude. However, I know it will do him good.'

Major Wilder would have liked to ask what sort of man Captain Greenway was but he doubted Mrs Kingston knew. If he was not visiting Captain Houghton on the grounds of devoted friendship he was bent on causing mischief, unless he was on a charitable mission to talk to Lady Charles about the loss of her son. What could be said about Lyndon's death? His mind returned to that non-descript, poverty-stricken village in which his brother's regiment had been quartered, the lounging officers, perhaps Captain Greenway among them, indifferent to his approach, verging on insolence, but pulling themselves back from the brink when he gave his name and rank; and the awkward, uncomfortable colonel, thankful to part with him. From there he had ridden the Andalusian to Vera on the Bidasoa and sought Captain Allington, with his company of *caçadores*, in the rain. Together they had stood on the little bridge so gallantly defended by the 95th at the cost of one or two young officers and no doubt many men. There he had taken possession of Lyndon's infantry red coat, that which he had worn at his death.

The recollection made him crave solitude. He had walked to the site of the picnic and now he proposed walking back. Mrs Kingston had not come equipped for walking but she saw her shoes must be sacrificed. She said, 'Of course we must walk.'

Major Wilder sighed while endeavouring to look polite He thought that the best he could do. 'I dare say Mis Arbuthnot would like to walk.'

'Was it not too far?' Lord Charles asked. 'Now it is hot His son had laughed, and replied it could not be much more than three miles. He was sure Miss Arbuthno was accustomed to walking much further. He saw Mr Kingston hesitate and wished he had said the walk was si miles, but she was not to be put off. 'Will you mind goin home by the village?' she enquired.

'Not at all,' he replied, and then, to Miss Arbuthnot, h said, 'Would you like to walk?'

Miss Arbuthnot said she would like it very much an they could start the children on their way. Major Wilde thought it odd that, wishing to be alone, he did not wan the company of Mrs Kingston yet he was content to hav that of Lottie's young governess.

Captain Houghton, who had roused himself, suddenl said, 'Well, Lucy, you won't want your brother as a chaper one, I suppose?'

Major Wilder thought this an offensive remark for i touched on how he might conduct himself. He had know men call each other out for less.

Captain Houghton, apparently realizing he had spoke unwisely, hastily continued, 'Only joking to be sure, n offence meant.'

Major Wilder reflected that the Captain Houghtons o this world were best ignored. He went to put the saddl on Lottie's pony and was pleased to see Horatio busy wit his, carefully checking the girths. York had taught hin well. They set out simultaneously but the children soo drew ahead so he was left with Miss Arbuthnot and Mrs Kingston, one on each side of him. Mrs Kingston tripped along in unsuitable shoes, exclaiming at every wayside flower, stopping to make a bouquet, needing his arm for any rut or uneven piece of ground. Miss Arbuthnot, on the other hand, wore a sensible pair of half-boots, had something of a mannish walk, a long stride, and negotiated stiles without thought of a helping hand.

Mrs Kingston said, 'Oh, Miss Arbuthnot, you took off your bonnet for the dear children's flowers. You must put it on again. Think of your complexion.'

Miss Arbuthnot smiled. 'No one has worried about my complexion since my poor mother died.' She then thought that not entirely true. Had she not herself, on her second or third meeting with Mr Langley, tried to remember the concoction her mother used to make that was to vanquish for ever the errant freckles? Now she could see no purpose in worrying about her complexion but she obediently took off the daisy chains and retied her bonnet, for it would probably be considered inappropriate for her to go about crowned with flowers.

Major Wilder thought of how the daisies had adorned her red hair, even how they suited her. She only ever wore one little brooch, which he supposed was all she had.

Mrs Kingston regretted drawing attention to Miss Arbuthnot's complexion. She said, 'Oh dear, Miss Arbuthnot, you walk so fast you put me to shame. Be careful you don't trip. It's very rough where the cows have been.' It was again necessary to cling to Major Wilder's arm, which he patiently offered.

Miss Arbuthnot could see Mrs Kingston was anxious

for Major Wilder to like her but that she set about it in quite the wrong way and only succeeded in irritating him, though he concealed this with a vaguely good-humoured air. She thought he did not care for small talk or to have someone agree with everything he said. In this he differed from her father, who liked her to agree with his every word. Once she had pointed out to him that if she did not happen to agree with him but made a pretence of doing so, it was as good as a lie. Her father had replied that, before answering him, she should think carefully about what he had said and then she would find she agreed with him after all: not only was he her father but an ordained minister of the Church. This, she saw, was to make him invincible on two fronts. Her mother, she remembered, would defer to his opinion in the meekest possible manner before making a suggestion that indicated she did not agree with him at all, but it was done with such smiles and such laughter, she was forgiven on the spot.

Miss Arbuthnot then thought she ought not to set herself up as an authority on what a man might like. Experience had taught her she was naïve in such matters, and perhaps Mrs Kingston's wiles would prove irresistible to Major Wilder.

With the protracted progress of Mrs Kingston, it seemed to take an inordinately long time for them to reach her front door, though she repeated many a time how short the walk had been, how pretty the countryside, how she wished they could go for ever despite her little shoes near falling apart, how they must all be together again shortly, and how they must be exhausted and would take a cup of tea.

Major Wilder refused the tea with the excuse of having

business to attend but then he said if Miss Arbuthnot was in the least weary he would bide while she took refreshment. Miss Arbuthnot searched for an excuse because she could see he wanted no delay or wished merely to escape, so she said, truthfully, she was not tired.

As they walked across the park, in pleasurable silence, she tried to determine if she was shy of him. Yes, she was a bit. He had led a life of which she knew almost nothing, the foreign places, the hardship, the soldiers and the great brass cannon in which Lord Charles took such an interest, let alone the bloody engagements, the heroism and the sacrifice. How could she know of such things or understand how the mind might work of a man who had been thus employed since his youth? She had barely left home before her present situation had brought her to Ridley.

He said abruptly, 'It takes hundreds of oak trees to build a man-of-war.'

Miss Arbuthnot looked at him enquiringly.

'I was thinking I should not so resent the loss of the oaks out of this park, if they went to help with the building of the navy.'

'I suppose trees must be considered a crop, like any other, but I never knew the park with the trees in it, so of course I don't miss them as you must do.'

'And in the autumn I can put it all to rights, yet I'm impatient.'

'But perhaps that is because they will take so long to grow.'

'I won't live long enough to see it back in its old splendour.' He was astonished at the felling of all the trees. A careful thinning might have provided the necessary funds, but his father, when driven, had gone to extremes.

Miss Arbuthnot said, 'If you extended the garden you could plant a shrubbery with walks and suchlike that would screen the park from immediate view and draw the eye away from it.'

'You have thought about it, I can see,' he said, with a smile.

'My friend Miss Hamilton is very fond of landscaping. I have spent hours pacing out distances and helping to decide if a tree should be three foot from the left or the right and running hither and thither to view it from the different windows of the house.'

'I see you entered into it with great enthusiasm.'

'I did,' she said, laughing a little, but aware of past pleasures and amusements unlikely to be repeated, drifting away, leaving her with a sense of their loss.

Before Major Wilder could make any further comment they saw Horatio trotting towards them on his pony, making for home. He came to a halt beside them and stooped to pat the pony's neck before saying, 'We got back to Ridley first, but it's all right. We didn't need anyone to help us. I took off Jenny Wren's saddle and bridle and put her in the paddock. She wasn't hot, so that was right, wasn't it, sir?'

'Very good,' Major Wilder said.

'And I helped Lottie to dismount. She can do it on her own, but I thought I ought to help her. When she gets down herself she shows a lot of her drawers, which probably doesn't matter but it won't do when she's older.' Horatio looked grave. He then added, 'The trouble is, sir, she weighs a terrible lot.'

Having received the proper commendation for his efforts, he cheerfully went on his way and Major Wilder opened the garden gate for Miss Arbuthnot. As she turned to thank him, she saw he was laughing and she could not help but join in.

He said, 'Lessons in gallantry must be added to Horatio Kingston's curriculum, but he's a good boy.'

They entered the house by the front door. Major Wilder could see Miss Arbuthnot hesitated as if she should not be beside him, should be going to the back, but, having the idea that tutors and governesses should be treated as family, he ushered her in with a smile and followed her upstairs on her way to the schoolroom. He had meant to go to his own rooms but instead found himself, involuntarily, opening the door to Lyndon's.

He thought a picnic should not induce so many peculiarly different sensations in the course of an afternoon, and yet it had started well enough and even ended comfortably, with a quiet walk across the park and a little laughter. There was a change to Lyndon's rooms, not immediately obvious but nonetheless there. They had begun to subside into history. There were no flowers on the table and there was dust. They smelt as rooms smell that are not used. Though he had rarely been in them since the day of his return, he supposed he had broken their spell, as far as his mother was concerned. He was not sure whether this was good or bad but shrines to the dead he saw as a mistake. What was death, after all? A stone over a grave, a tablet to mark what they had been, if worthy of it, was all he could see the dead required. He had known many whose bones were strewn for the attention of wolves and vultures, brave men, gallant and courageous, for whom time had not allowed burial. The officers might get a commemoration in their parish church at home, but what of the poor soldier, whose death was a statistic on an official dispatch? For all that, if they were loved, they would live in recollection, not in the trappings of their earthly presence. Grief was to him a private matter. He wondered if he was hard on his mother: was her excessive partiality for Lyndon perhaps natural in a parent?

He pulled out the drawer in which lay the duelling pistols and took them out of their box. A thought trickled through his head: much as it had done when he was a child. Why can't Lyndon leave me alone? He held a pistol at arm's length and drew a bead on his own reflection in the looking-glass. He found his conduct fanciful and disturbing, but it had been a fanciful and disturbing day.

Within about three weeks, though he had no particular wish for it, Major Wilder pointed out to his mother the need to reciprocate Mrs Kingston's hospitality. Lady Charles said she preferred not to entertain within a year of Lyndon's death. Because it was hot Major Wilder was wearing one of two coats he had had made of a lighter cloth. It was brown.

His mother said pointedly, 'Mourning should be observed.'

'I have marked Lyndon's death. I don't forget it.' He thought he had rather different reasons from those of his mother for not forgetting it.

'Black is expected of you.'

'By whom?'

'By . . .' But she could not say. It was a convention by which the departed were acknowledged, remembered and officially grieved. To ignore it was disrespectful. If Thomas did not know this she had not the words to explain it.

'I don't wish to upset you, but what is a month one way or another? A black coat cannot be dyed lighter when I no longer need it black. I don't forget Lyndon. July the twenty-fifth is the date they were holding the pass at Roncesvalles. What is an anniversary but a date? There is the day you got my letter and the day you will have read of it in the *Gazette*.'

Lady Charles agreed with him. What was an anniversary but a date three hundred and sixty-five days after the event? The figure seemed arbitrary. Was it to do with the moon or the sun or how long one took to go round the other? And had they not altered the calendar? This had been impressed on her when she was a child for her birth had occurred in that period when the start of the year was altered from March to January, and eleven puzzling days dropped from September, puzzling to her, however often her father had explained it. She almost smiled when she remembered her childish bewilderment. So what was time but something with which members of the government might play? It made a mockery of anniversaries, yet the reoccurrence of the date upon which Lyndon had died could only be painful and not as any other day.

Major Wilder resolved to be absent from Ridley on the anniversary of his brother's death. Changing the subject, he said, 'I am wondering if Bath would be of any use to my father. He seems so very stiff and uncomfortable in his joints.'

Lady Charles was nettled. Was it not her task to recognize any ill in her husband and did not Thomas thereby imply neglect? She said, 'I dare say it is seasonal. I'm sure he wouldn't want to go to Bath.'

'He would go if it were suggested.'

'How is he to go? I could not.'

'Why not?'

'It would be full of acquaintance, people who would expect me to know them, who would wish to offer condolences, who would expect me to answer endless platitudes. Of course, Lyndon made the ultimate sacrifice, it is the only thing that can ever console me, but I do not wish to hear it trip casually off the tongues of others. To me it is sacred.'

She thought Thomas looked at her strangely as she spoke. Perhaps he really was trying to grapple with the intensity of her emotion. All he said in reply was that if she did not feel able to accompany Lord Charles to Bath, should it be recommended, he would take him himself. 'After all,' he added, 'he can't go on his own, apart from his valet, it would depress him. I couldn't go immediately but I shall make the time.'

Lady Charles thought it her duty to go with her husband but perhaps it was allowable for Thomas to go in her place. She did not wish Thomas to point out to her any other sort of duty of which he might think her neglectful. She said, 'As for Mrs Kingston, I suppose we should reciprocate in some way or another. Her picnic she made pleasant, though I dare say it was the dampness of the situation that brought on your father's aches. She is certainly very clever and agreeable. Formal entertainment is out of the question but perhaps she and Captain Houghton would like to take tea with us.' Lady Charles began to wonder if Thomas was going to take an interest in Mrs Kingston. Though she would initially find it disturbing, it would certainly be convenient and it would save them the discomfiture of having a stranger in their midst.

Major Wilder said, 'If the evening was warm, I suppose the tea could be served on the terrace, but should that seem inadequate, why not a picnic of our own to include the children?'

Lady Charles supposed he did not want her to do less than Mrs Kingston, though in fact he was barely thinking about it at all, beyond acknowledging the amusement of time spent with the children and Miss Arbuthnot, and the greater ease with which Mrs Kingston and her brother could be circumvented without disregarding what was due to neighbours. He pulled his watch from his waistcoat, aware that it had been Lyndon's, and remarked on the time. It was Sunday, and shortly Hill would come round to the front with the carriage to take his parents to church. They had always used to walk unless it was wet, which had saved the horses and the servants Sunday work. He wondered when this excellent habit had been given up, but forbore to remark on it. Perhaps the walk was too much for his father without the incentive of his little dog beside him, and as his mother took no exercise of any sort, perhaps it was too much for both of them. He would not go in the carriage himself: he preferred to walk across the park with Lottie and Miss Arbuthnot.

Lady Charles continued to speculate on the subject of picnics and, without regard for the spontaneity usually attached to such events, picked a date several weeks off. It was not to be as she used to give picnics, little more than dining out of doors, but in a hollow of the downs overlooking a view in which Ridley, the village and the church could be seen in the distance and also the stream winding this way and that. She had adhered to her son's preference as to the site. It was not particularly close. She thought he might like to drive Mrs Kingston there in the gig. Perhaps that was his intention. It crossed her mind he could take Lyndon's curricle, yellow and blue, an ostentatious and amusing vehicle that lay idle in the coach house, but to see anyone but Lyndon drive it would pain her so she did not remind him of it. When she suggested, in order to give him a little assistance, though she could not see why he should need assistance in such a matter, that he drove Mrs Kingston, he said, 'Certainly not. I should have to drive Captain Houghton as well. There is the landau. Hill can drive you, Mrs Kingston and Captain Houghton. The children would be disappointed if I didn't ride with them. The distance is about right for my father. It is a part of the estate but we rarely go there. He will enjoy it.'

'Oh dear, you will make such a tomboy of Lottie, riding ponies all the day. I don't know what we shall do with her when it is time for her to put up her hair.' Lady Charles stopped to consider how Lottie's hair did not seem to grow sufficiently for it ever to be put up. Was she snipping at it with the scissors? 'It is apparent Miss Arbuthnot was not herself a decorous child. She has managed Lottie's little difficulties very well, but I dare say we shall need a governess more versed in the ways of society in a year or two, one less of a child herself. As Miss Arbuthnot will not be required as an escort, seeing you are all to ride to the picnic, she may come in the landau with us. It would make a change for her to be away from the children.'

'Not a change she would relish. To ride is a treat for Miss Arbuthnot and we should give her what treats we can.'

Lady Charles noted there was an edge to his voice and she was annoyed when he added, 'Please to remember it is I who am in charge of Lottie.'

She could not see why he should trouble himself over something in which he was so ill-qualified to have any opinion. She tried to imagine Lyndon depriving her of the task of choosing governesses, which she had been doing for the last forty years or so. There were times when she simply could not take Thomas seriously, and this was surely one of them.

As he parted from her, stalking off down the passage in the direction of the library, for they had held the discussion in the open doorway of the hall, she wondered why he had not taken the opportunity of driving Mrs Kingston, even if he were not sufficiently inventive to shake off her brother. Lyndon would have got round the difficulty in seconds. Mrs Kingston was such a sweet, accommodating creature and undoubtedly pretty: why did he appear to wish to ignore her? Was it a tactic to gain her attention? A little neglect sometimes had that effect, especially on a woman who was not accustomed to it, but Thomas took it a great deal too far. Had years of soldiering, of male company, left him indifferent to women? Would he remain a bachelor and provide no heir to Ridley? Lady Charles sought reasons. Why was he not charmed by Mrs

Kingston? A woman who had enchanted Lyndon must be of great worth and charm.

Lady Charles did not look forward to the picnic but she saw it had to be done. The ordering of the food was a distraction and this, she knew, was expected to be good for her, she who considered it immoral to be distracted from grieving. Why should one recover from the shock? Was Lyndon of so little note she might reasonably be expected to get over his death? She half hoped the weather would be unsuitable but it was sunny and pleasant, almost hot. Was it not too hot to ride? Would the children get sunstroke? Did Lottie have a bonnet of adequate proportions?

Miss Arbuthnot had succeeded in making a vague imitation of her riding habit from a length of grey linen, sent from home, chosen by anxious sisters. She thought it only tolerably successful but at least it was cool and nobody was likely to notice it.

Lottie had watched its construction. She thought nobody as clever as her governess. She looked at the ribbons that draped her dressing-table but were of no use now her hair was short. Could she give them away? she asked her grandmother.

'Why do you want to give them away, darling? You will need them as soon as your hair grows.'

'It grows very slow,' Lottie answered carefully. 'I think the ribbons will fade. When my hair grows I would like new ones.'

'I suppose that would be pleasant. And who is to have the old?'

'Miss 'Buthnot and Susan.' Lottie was getting wise. Susan would not want ribbons but it was judicious to include her. Why did her grandmother not love Miss 'Buthnot as much as she did? She took all the best of her ribbons and pressed them on her governess though she kept a few for Susan, who would give them to her nieces. To please her, Miss Arbuthnot twisted a narrow blue and a green together for the better securing of her plain straw bonnet.

'You must make a rosette and pin it to your habit,' Lottie said, but Miss Arbuthnot was afraid of being considered too fancy. She thought of her mother who had been able to make something pretty out of nothing. They went downstairs and out of doors. Major Wilder was assisting his father to mount. The grooms had brought all the horses round to the front. Horatio was cantering his pony across the park, the reins flapping: he was, at best, a casual horseman. York was in charge of Jenny Wren. The Andalusian waited on his own, arching his neck and clinking his bit. He was as plump and glossy as the lush English pastures could make his grey coat.

Major Wilder turned to help Miss Arbuthnot but she was already seated on the grey. He immediately noted her habit. The severity of her dress appealed to him yet he wished she might be more frivolous, if only for the sake of her youth. She needed pearls, a brooch or a bunch of ribbons.

Lottie and Horatio were excited to be riding with Lord Charles and to have Major Wilder there on the Andalusian. Normally the business of the estate coincided with their lessons and they did not go out together. Lord Charles thought the sun did him good. He said he was proud to have his granddaughter beside him, happy to have Horatio on his other side, and pleased Miss Arbuthnot was there. Everything pleased him but most of all his dear Thomas sitting so easily on the strange Andalusian with its foreign look and its flowing mane and tail, Thomas, who was introducing order into his father's incompetence and muddle. Lord Charles had given up any sense of shame, merely acknowledging some were more suited to method and organization than others. Occasionally he put it all down to his son's army training.

The picnic was already in place when they arrived, Lady Charles attending to the placing of the last few dishes. She had remembered how she liked to be in charge, directing Major Wilder to sit beside Mrs Kingston, and Miss Arbuthnot to be placed beside Captain Houghton, which arrangement precluded her from having to sit next to him herself. Captain Houghton, rather than have Major Wilder point out his shortcomings, remembered Miss Arbuthnot's name and cut her some pie. After quite a long pause he remarked that he believed she lived in Devonshire.

Elsewhere the conversation was only a little more lively until Horatio said, after careful attention to finish his mouthful, 'Miss Arbuthnot, please would you speak to me in French. When you speak to Lottie it doesn't sound a bit like my mother when she speaks it.'

He looked puzzled when his uncle and Major Wilder laughed.

Mrs Kingston said, 'Why, you horrid boy, my accent isn't as good as it should be, I dare say, but it's not polite to draw attention to it.'

Captain Houghton remarked everything French was

bad. 'And most of all the language. Terrible, artificial, affected noise the French make.'

Lottie was indignant. 'You shouldn't say that. It's rude because Miss Arbuthnot's mother was a French lady.'

Captain Houghton feared he was always going to have to be apologizing to the governess for one thing or another. He thought it a pity she was so tall, for otherwise she had a pretty figure. 'Beg pardon, miss, no offence meant. Besides, French ladies are quite another matter.'

Lottie was not entirely placated. 'Are you going to say they are a different kettle of fish?'

Captain Houghton laughed so much it made him cough and his frail ribs shook. He got the handkerchief from the tail of his coat and wiped the sweat from his brow. Eventually he managed to splutter, 'I can't say those were to be my very words.'

Major Wilder, whose private view of the French was similar to Captain Houghton's, said, 'Of course Horatio should learn French, and any other language he can get hold of. We may not be at war with France now but it doesn't mean we never will be again. Besides, French is spoken in other places and Spanish as well. We are at war with America. He could find himself anywhere in the world. How can he be considered educated if he doesn't speak French?'

Captain Houghton, whose own French was limited to '*non merci*', turned to Miss Arbuthnot and asked her, from genuine curiosity, if she had found it an inconvenience to be nearly French at a time when Britain was at war with France.

'No,' she replied. 'My mother was just another of the

French *émigrés* who abound. I don't believe they are minded.' After a pause she added, 'I am afraid my brother and sisters and I thought our mother some sort of quaint alien but we did not love her any the less for it. As to feeling French, we resisted the idea very heartily.'

'But don't you have relatives to encourage you to feel a little French?'

'None that speak to us.' Miss Arbuthnot thought of the Roman Catholic religion her mother had given up to marry her father. Had she wrestled with her conscience for weeks? Had she really given it up at all? Sometimes, when there were bills to pay and clothes and shoes were wanted, her mother would remark, 'I've said a little prayer to the Virgin, but don't tell your father,' and then she would skip along to the parish church on her husband's arm. Her mother had had a wonderful elasticity when it came to matters of religion and morality. For a moment she wondered if her father could have felt any sense of guilt at wresting her mother from her own faith, but the notion was ridiculous: her father would consider he had rescued her from a faith deeply flawed. Why did she not immediately see it that way herself? She thought she more resembled her father than her mother in doggedly pursuing what she hoped to be right. The difference between them lay in her father's conviction that he was always absolutely right.

Major Wilder was remembering the last picnic. He had been abroad for so long that the verdant green of the English summer had taken him by surprise, but now it was July, though still extremely green, it had altered. He had said as much to Miss Arbuthnot as they had ridden along the edge of the downs. Now he glanced at her and wondered of what she was thinking. It was certainly not Captain Houghton, whose queries she answered at random.

Captain Houghton said, 'Perhaps French connections are not worth the candle and you do best to stick to the good old English.' He wanted to ask why the French relatives of Miss Arbuthnot did not speak but it would be impertinent to ask, even of a governess.

Miss Arbuthnot, as if reading his mind, said, 'It was a question of religion.'

Captain Houghton said, 'Ah.' That was all he could say, for religion was not a proper topic in mixed or, indeed, any company.

Lottie, thinking she might have been rude and, however justified, might still get into trouble for it, tried to make amends. She said to Captain Houghton, 'Have a few peas. They are from my own garden and are perfectly nice to eat cold. I chopped some mint over them for fear that the cook would forget.'

'I'm afraid I don't care for cold peas, dear.'

'That is probably because you haven't grown them yourself. Miss 'Buthnot says it's very healthy to be outdoors digging. As you are not very well perhaps digging would make you better. You could have a little piece of ground just to dig and grow some potatoes for they don't take any management beyond earthing them up. Would you be so kind as to tell my grandmama that I have spoken to you very nicely?'

Mrs Kingston was preoccupied with surreptitiously watching Major Wilder. Had his appearance altered since his return? She deemed the coat he wore to be new but the cut identical to the black he had discarded, presumably owing to the clemency of the weather. Did he feel he had done sufficient mourning for his brother, he who had gained so much by the death? She thought his hair a fraction longer. It softened his appearance, made him look younger, but it was as likely to be an oversight in getting to the barber than any deliberate policy. He remained unmistakably a soldier and now she wondered how she could have wished him otherwise. Though she could not but remember and regret the one who had gone before, what was the purpose of making comparisons?

She said, floundering for some comment that would engage his attention, 'Perhaps picnicking is no novelty to you, Major Wilder, for you must have become quite accustomed to outdoor living in a harsher clime.' She liked her use of the last phrase: she wanted him to understand she knew of the hardship. Lady Charles considered soldiering a romance, but perhaps only when thinking of her lost son. 'Do you not, from time to time, sleep under the stars?'

Major Wilder surveyed her from his brown eyes with a look she could not fathom. He said, 'There are no stars when it's raining.'

'But Spain is hot and dry.'

'It depends upon whether you are sleeping indoors or out.'

Mrs Kingston contemplated this remark before smiling, first doubtfully and then indulgently. 'I begin to think your nature rather a teasing one.'

'It is best to get the men under cover,' he replied, more seriously, 'but not always possible. The army has now been issued with tents.'

‘But did you not have a tent for yourself?’

‘No. Much of the time we could get a billet and the men too, but otherwise we would bivouac.’ He could not imagine why any such detail should be of interest to her.

She considered the word ‘bivouac’ with some uncertainty. ‘Horatio says you are very clever at tying knots.’

Major Wilder laughed. ‘Oh, yes, knots. They are useful.’ He absently took a piece of rope that had been used to hold together the wicker picnic hamper and began to tie the ends up. It was an elaborate knot. He tested it with a sharp tug.

Mrs Kingston said, all wondering, ‘That certainly is clever. Would you teach it to me?’

Major Wilder did not wish to teach Mrs Kingston how to tie a knot but out of politeness he proceeded. Did not the ‘tying of the knot’ have implications?

Lottie and Horatio gathered to watch.

Major Wilder undid one knot and tied several more. Mrs Kingston could not follow the movements of so many.

Lottie said, ‘How did you learn them, Uncle Thomas?’

‘From a man in my troop.’

‘A common soldier, teaching you things?’ Mrs Kingston said, surprised, even shocked.

‘A rogue, but a man who sits beside you on a bit of a rock and teaches you knots is, one way or another, more likely to be your secret friend than your secret enemy. He knew how to keep his place, “sor” this and “sor” that and “Sor should have put the tail end of the string over and not under just the now or it will come out something else.” He was an Irishman.’

‘But how did he learn to tie them?’

'I didn't ask.'

'But why not?'

'Because I guessed.'

'What could you have guessed?'

'He was a deserter from the navy. We should not have had him and he should not have been there. God knows how he got in the troop at all. He was a resourceful fellow, very useful.'

Lottie said, 'Is he there now, in your troop, for you to see again if you want?'

Major Wilder shook his head.

'Where is he, then?'

'He was killed. You know, Lottie, that many never come home from war.'

'Like my papa?' Lottie had assumed, from listening to her grandmother, that her father had been an important person in the war. She wanted to ask if important people and common soldiers died alike. Her grandmother had made it clear that her father's end had been noble, but what was noble when it came to dying? Was the knot-tying runaway sailor noble? Was he brave?

She said, 'Uncle Thomas, you love those soldiers more than you love us.' Inexplicably she burst into tears.

Major Wilder was not a demonstrative man or he might have put his arm round her or given her a kiss. He just said, 'There now, child, there's nothing to cry about. I shan't desert you.'

Lottie went to Miss Arbuthnot and snuggled against her. After a while she said, 'Uncle Thomas won't desert me.'

Mrs Kingston said, in an undertone, to Major Wilder, 'Of course poor Lottie is a very difficult child, the sweet darling.'

'I don't find her so.'

'Oh, but you must see how she lacks a mother.'

'Do you see it as my duty to find her one, though it could only be a substitute in the form of an aunt? We can't put the clock back, can we?'

He had that vaguely teasing look in his eye. Mrs Kingston was flustered. Eventually she said, thinking the topic unsuitable, 'Major Wilder, you have such a beautiful horse. What is his name?'

'He doesn't have one.'

Lady Charles was abstracted by the view. It was so long since she had been going further than the garden. Was the view beautiful or was it merely that she could see a long way? She felt exhausted, unused to an excursion. She glanced at Mrs Kingston. Was Thomas flirting with her or was he being tiresome? What did he mean that the horse had no name? He surely said that to provoke.

Lord Charles was wondering if a match could be made between Mrs Kingston and Thomas. Was she not a pleasing, pretty creature? Would a woman who had been so near to pleasing Lyndon please Thomas?

Captain Houghton was also considering the matter. Could Lucy capture such an obvious prize? She had made herself more than comfortable when she had married Kingston but she would be doing even better if she married Major Wilder and he right on the doorstep. Captain Houghton thought they could all benefit. He was not fond of artillery officers: they tended to be a little too singular, a little too clever. He had not seen anything about Major Wilder to suppose he was an exception: he doubted his sister would suit him.

Major Wilder, in answer to something Mrs Kingston had said, was replying. 'No, I don't tell a fib, as you put it. I dare say he once had a name, but I never enquired what it was.'

'Oh, I should so like to choose him a new name. May I not do that? Moonlight. Wouldn't that suit him?' Mrs Kingston put her hands together in a little clapping motion, indicative of pleased excitement. She was wearing kid gloves in the palest lavender.

Major Wilder was silent while he contemplated the indignities of polite conversation. He then said, 'So long as you are sure to ask him in Spanish if he likes it or no. He might be very fanciful and choosy.'

Mrs Kingston thought if one were married to Major Wilder it would be necessary to make quite a little study of him.

Lottie said, 'Can we play cricket now? We have some stumps, a bat and two balls in the landau.'

Major Wilder got to his feet. 'Of course. Horatio, run and get them. Lottie, go and help him and see he doesn't drop any of it on his toe. Miss Arbuthnot, would you play cricket? The ground is flat at the top of the rise.'

The children set up the pitch. They were happy, released from the restraints of good behaviour that even a picnic required.

Horatio said to Major Wilder, 'Miss Arbuthnot is really good at cricket and Lottie is much better than me, but I tell you what, sir, it isn't quite fair when girls have the bat because you can't see the stumps half the time for their skirts. Still, I suppose it's not proper to say it.'

'I fear we must put up with it manfully, but do not the skirts become a disadvantage when it is their turn to run?'

'Not nearly so much as you would think. Lottie used not to run, I think because she was rather plump, but now she runs like anything.'

'And does your mother play?'

'I expect she will, to oblige, but she's no good at it. I will bowl her out quite quick so she can go and sit down again and I shan't have to worry about her.'

And so the afternoon went by with much laughter and amusement, even Lord Charles occasionally fielding the ball if his little dog did not run off with it. He remembered how once he had been a reasonably good player of cricket and even now his limbs, despite their stiffness, remembered what they were intended to do. He had not played since Lyndon was a boy and the very thought conjured Lyndon's graceful form, his golden curls, his little red buttoned jacket and high-waisted trousers, standing defiant at the wicket, the bat at a menacing angle. What a beautiful child: women would beg to kiss him and total strangers stop him in the street. He realized that to think of Lyndon now the pain was oddly mixed with pleasure. Certainly grief and loss were strange and unpredictable.

Thomas said to him, 'That's enough, sir, or I shan't be able to get you back on the horse.' He wished Thomas would call him 'Father', but he didn't know how to make the suggestion. Lyndon had never been so formal.

Lord Charles returned to sit with his wife but from there he could not watch the cricket. Finding her talking to Mrs Kingston, he thought he could leave her again. She called after him, 'You will be too tired. You must come home in the landau. Someone can lead the horse.' He thought how sensible that would be, but he wanted to ride home with

Thomas and the children, to be young enough to do so, to ride to hounds and walk out with a gun. Thomas had told him he intended to take him to the hot baths before the winter started. He could not exactly say he fancied that, but if Thomas said that was what should be done, they would certainly do it, and Thomas would stay with him there to conduct the operation and see he did whatever the doctors advised. Of course he had loved Lyndon more than anyone else in his whole life but he could only smile at the thought of his elder son taking his father to Bath for the sake of his health. How could it be that his two sons had turned out so very different one from the other?

The ball dropped at his feet. Miss Arbuthnot had the bat. She could hit the ball hard.

Lottie called, 'The ball, Grandpapa, the ball. Don't let Scottie have it because he's chewed up one already. Throw it to Uncle Thomas. He is going to bowl because we can't get Miss 'Buthnot out. She's too clever.'

The old man lobbed the ball to his son. They were all laughing. Thomas was in his waistcoat and shirtsleeves and had loosened his cravat. Lord Charles laughed too. It was as well to laugh at small pleasures and at finding oneself still alive.

Mrs Heugmont, of all the Wilder daughters, could be said to have made the best match. It was not a prestigious one, there was neither title nor estate, but there was an accumulation of several fortunes. Mr Heugmont had made no fortune of his own but he rather thought he could have done had there been a need. His initial circumstances had been modest but respectable. At the age of twenty-one, having been called to the bar, he unexpectedly inherited a great deal of money. A distant cousin, impressed by his sobriety and good sense, had already chosen him as his heir so within a few years he inherited a second fortune, which had made him exceedingly well off. He did not look like a rich man, being a little portly, short and round-faced, very careless in his dress, indifferent to fashion and living modestly. He had a passion for study and his enthusiasms were many, from entomology to ancient history. He was not interested in the land or the countryside except where they might yield up the curiosities of insects, animal or human habits. He considered his house, Finch Hall, to which he had made random additions, perfectly adequate for his needs and those of his family. It had a large garden, a small park, much of it taken up by a big pond, and a single farm. He neither shot, fished nor hunted but, acknowledging his own children could, mysteriously, differ from himself, he allowed his boys a hunter apiece but no more. There had been various attempts to inveigle him into politics but without success. He was probably, at heart, a radical but he had never felt inclined to jeopardize his personal fortune on any great reforming ventures. Hints had been made of his acquiring a title if he could oblige in some way or another but he was not tempted. He had most heartily disapproved of the French Revolution but also of the French monarch and the French aristocracy.

He had every intention, when he died, of dividing his wealth equally between his eight children, a fact made plain to his eldest son who was expected to pursue a career as ardently as his younger brothers. He was glad the issue was not complicated by his owning a large estate but he would philosophically reflect that his principles did not always accord with his own good fortune. He gave generously to charity and was an ardent and industrious supporter of the Abolitionists, the idea of owning slaves abhorrent to him.

He was devoted to his wife. At the time of his marriage there had been speculation as to whether or no it had been a love match or a series of clever manoeuvres on the part of Lady Charles. Mr Heugmont, not one to satisfy the curious, could have told them that all Lady Charles's careful manipulations had suited him and he had cooperated with them as best he could: Georgie, as she was universally known, was exactly to his taste. She was nearly always cheerful, as he was himself, and generous-hearted. She loved the outdoors, gardening and children of all sizes. She had no pretensions to being clever but she was extremely sensible, which he thought of more use. She was as tall as him, still pretty but now plump. He had amiably accepted, from the start, the near permanent addition to his house of her younger brother.

Theirs was a happy house, informal, social, a touch eccentric or perhaps merely original, according to how one might view it. Major Wilder saw it as his own home, but now, towards the end of July, as he rode the Andalusian through the gates, he supposed he must make adjustments: Ridley was his, as near as could be, and he had to live there, not with his sister and brother-in-law or yet with his troop.

When any member of her family was returning, Mrs Heugmont was sure to be found at the door, far too impatient to wait in the drawing room for them to present themselves changed and washed, with the butler to bow them in and announce their name. What did she care for the mud and dust of the road if any beloved was coming home? Thus it was for her brother. Of course, all the rest of her available family as well as her husband were anxious to see him, the boys a trifle nervous they might fall below their uncle's exacting standards, for was he not a hero? They draped themselves in tiers on the steps at the front of the house as soon as it seemed likely he might appear: Major Wilder was the sort of person on whom one might rely to come at the time he had specified.

Mrs Heugmont wished to have her brother to herself but knew she had little hope of achieving that until after dinner. She was anxious about him. She thought of him as if he were still a child and likely to run to her with his troubles, but in whom else was he to confide? There were now things he had indicated that he was unable to confide, such as the reasons for selling the London house, which had infuriated her sisters. They were equally infuriated by their mother telling them Thomas had the equivalent of a power of attorney: he was in control of the entire estate even though their father seemed in good health and in possession of his mental faculties, though he had done rather strange things, such as removing the oak trees from the park.

In the quiet of the evening Major Wilder was able to walk up and down the flower garden and at last be alone with his sister. As much as this pleased him, he was aware of the constraints he felt, as never before, in what could not be told, if only for his father's sake. His father would not allow his mother to know why Ridley had so nearly run into serious debt, and if his mother was not to know, it had to be kept a secret. The image she had of Lyndon was to remain one of perfection. He thought Lyndon's image pretty much perfection in his father's eyes, too, despite the trouble he had caused. He must be forever on his pedestal, as though carved in marble. There had been frequent occasions when Major Wilder had been only too ready to spit out the truth, to abandon his role of chief player in the charade, but he had not and hoped he never would. Other people might speak against Lyndon but not the younger brother. He gave a wry smile. Nothing altered: *Tell tale tit, your tongue shall split.*

His sister said, 'While we were growing up, life seemed to run so smoothly, Papa in control of everything.'

'Smythe, the agent, in control of everything,' Major Wilder replied. 'Besides, what did he have to do but hunt and shoot and say something civil to his tenants when he saw them?'

'But Smythe was not dishonest.'

'No. He was able.'

'And Papa can't manage now because he never had to manage before?'

'That certainly could be said. So long as he has his little dog and a horse to ride out on, he is perfectly happy. He doesn't want responsibilities. He didn't care for my coming away, though he didn't say so. He only makes a decision when he has to, and then it's all drama.'

'Thomas, are you not being rather hard on him?'

'I look after him. He is old.'

'And you have filled Ridley with dogs. Didn't that antagonize Mama on the spot?'

'Why, yes, but my mother is only one. The rest of us like dogs.'

'But what do you do to placate her?'

After some thought, he said, 'Not much.' He could not imagine what he need do to placate his mother beyond not having any dogs. 'We occasionally nearly agree about something. She is mortified Lyndon left Lottie to my care. Why do you suppose he did that, Georgie?'

They did several turns among the flower borders. Major Wilder observed his sister had a cottage approach to gardening, a great deal of pretty things stuffed in to overflowing. Mrs Kingston would have said it was very untidy. He had been required to inspect *her* garden twice.

Mrs Heugmont tried to collect her thoughts on the subject of her late charismatic brother. They had all known their parents had spoilt him, but had she not been accused of spoiling Thomas? She knew she had not spoilt Thomas in the way Lyndon was spoilt. Lyndon had often amused her, he was excellent company, but she had not been bewitched by his charm and her husband had not liked him. As for his sudden entry into the army, she was completely confused by it. What could have induced him to go when there was so little need? Her mother had said it was his sense of duty, but Mrs Heugmont had never thought duty of any sort uppermost in Lyndon's mind. He was more likely to have been in debt or involved with a married woman. It seemed they were never to know.

She said, in answer to Thomas, 'As to Lottie being your ward, you will be head of our immediate family. Perhaps Lyndon saw it as logical.'

Neither of them was convinced by this explanation. She then said, 'How do you find Lottie? Is she like Lyndon?'

'No.'

'Is she literate?'

'She can read and write after a fashion. Progress has been made. Yes, she is almost literate, sings nicely, loves her garden and her pony. I think you would hardly know her. I like to think she and I are good friends. I can't equate her with Lyndon. Miss Arbuthnot, Lottie and Mrs Kingston's boy, who might as well live at Ridley for the time he spends with us, keep me amused in a light-hearted way. Though I am happy to be with my father it would be very dull without them. Mother remains in deepest mourning so we see no one.' Major Wilder frowned. 'I don't think of myself as particularly social but there are limits.'

Mrs Heugmont suggested he was missing his regiment.

Major Wilder shrugged. 'Yes, I miss it, but not so much as I did. I've had plenty to do. I would have returned if we hadn't sold the London house.'

Mrs Heugmont thought how they came round to the London house again. Was Thomas slightly ill at ease with himself, as if he had too much on his mind – too much that could not be divulged? At Ridley all the responsibilities were his, but those of the estate were so well within his capacity, she could not think they troubled him for five minutes a day. She said, 'You had better marry.'

He laughed. 'You are getting like my mother. I think she is realigning Mrs Kingston for me.'

'But I don't enjoy matchmaking. It makes me nervous.' She wondered aloud what sort of wife he should like, but apart from agreeing it would suit him to be married, he said he could not imagine: he only saw women to whom he had no wish to be married. She told him they were bidden, the following evening, to walk across the fields to take tea at the rectory, accompanied by the older Heugmont offspring.

'They always have the house full of people,' she said, 'so you can start looking about.'

'But I would much rather spend the evening alone with you and John.'

'I dare say, but it will do you good. You might meet a pretty heiress of twenty-five years or thereabouts, from a good family.'

'If she must be twenty-five, why has she not married already?'

'Oh, she is of a thoughtful disposition. She is waiting for an officer of the Royal Horse Artillery to seek her out.'

'Must she be that age exactly?'

'You can't marry anyone straight out of the schoolroom, Thomas, they would exasperate you.' She tucked her arm into his and wished things were different and that he was not pretending, probably for her sake, that everything in his life was in order. She hoped a suitable wife and the start of the hunting season would be appropriate tonics but the former might be tricky to initiate. As for the fox-hunting, she knew it to be a cure for all masculine ills, except those of her own husband, but he rarely had need of cures.

The following day Major Wilder spent in dividing his time between his sister's numerous family. His brother-in-law wished to closet him in a little hotchpotch of a room he had, full of things, and his nephews and nieces were anxious to show him anything new, from ponies to rabbits. He did not think of himself as particularly attached to children, and was pleased to see that some of Georgie's had nearly become adults since he had last seen them. For her sake, he took a careful interest in the progress of each one and was not averse to their company. He supposed it was due to them he had acquired the art of keeping children amused that stood him in good stead with Lottie and Horatio, and he now came to the conclusion that they amused him as well as he amusing them.

After dinner they walked to the rectory, which was barely a mile down the road. It was situated at the centre of the large Gloucestershire village to which the Heugmonts' house was attached, the square tower of the Norman church rising above the stone wall of the garden.

Major Wilder, hearing a considerable babble of voices, said to his sister, in an undertone, 'Am I meant to discover the mature young lady of twenty-five years with a small fortune among the rector's acquaintances, and what am I to say to her, should it be so?'

'One never can tell,' Mrs Heugmont replied, laughing, 'but everybody will want you to talk of the war, to be a bit of a hero.'

'I don't believe I have anything to say about the war.'

'Oh, you should tell them an adventure. That's what people like. You could recount how you acquired the Andalusian. It's so romantic.'

Major Wilder looked shocked. Of course he could not repeat a thing that would abound to his own credit, if it did abound to his credit: his colonel had not thought so any more than had York, but then he saw Georgie was teasing him, so he said, 'Certainly not.'

As soon as they arrived, Mrs Heugmont knew it had

been a mistake to bring her brother for he would have been just as happy to stay at home and read the newspaper. The house was full of people, some of whom he knew, but the cause of her immediate concern was the rector's cousin, who was holding forth in his inimitable manner, keeping half the company spellbound.

She whispered, 'Oh, Thomas, I shouldn't have let you come.'

'Why not?' he asked, for he had reconciled himself with having to be social for the evening. He could not complain of meeting no one, then decline what invitations came his way.

'There is someone here absolutely calculated to make you fly into one of your passions.'

'Georgie, you know I haven't allowed myself to fall into any sort of passion since I was about sixteen. It isn't suited to army life.'

They were greeted by their hostess. She declared herself delighted to see Mrs Heugmont's brother again, safe and sound and with Boney put away. Major Wilder replied he could not take personal responsibility for the putting away of Bonaparte to which she said she was sure he must have had a hand in it and would he take a cup of tea or did he prefer coffee? It was put out in the drawing room but many of the young people had gone out on to the terrace.

Mrs Heugmont said, 'I think I spotted your nephew.'

'Yes, he is quite a lion, now, especially since his last poetry book. Everyone hangs on his word, which can't be good for him. His little wife is a beauty and I can't help taking to her, even if the match was a trifle injudicious, but the rector doesn't care to sit next to her at dinner.'

Georgie took her brother by the arm and hastily moved him on. 'Don't go near him, dearest, please.'

'But who is he?'

'He is married to Miss Arbuthnot's sister.'

'The gentleman who Miss Arbuthnot . . .?'

'Yes, yes, but hardly a gentleman, even if he is the rector's nephew, the way I understand he behaved. You won't like him in the least. I have just seen him walk out on to the terrace.'

Mrs Heugmont was accosted by a friend. Major Wilder took the opportunity of slipping from her grasp. He had every intention of seeing what sort of a man Mr Langley was and also of paying his respects to Miss Arbuthnot's sister.

Mr Langley had perched himself on the edge of a garden table amid teacups and coffee cans. He was accustomed to being the centre of attention and took no notice of his shifting audience so long as there was sufficient crowd to listen to him. The rectory gardens spread down to an orchard and a pond but he had his back to the view. He had abandoned his neckcloth in favour of an outsized collar to his shirt and a green silk handkerchief knotted at his throat. He wore a black coat and a striped waistcoat with the buttons half undone. His hair was long and dark, his face narrow and his hands, which he made much use off to emphasize a point, had fingers of a peculiar length.

Waving his right arm, he was saying, 'Look at this ludicrous war with America. Why have we been fighting it? One lot of silly soldiers has proved cleverer than another lot of silly soldiers so now we are to have a treaty. Is it not odd that our soldiers, with all the experience of the Peninsula behind them, can do nothing against the Americans, who have no experience at all beyond getting scalped by Indians? Our pretty redcoats have got stuck in a swamp or fallen in the river. And who do we send to Ghent to make a treaty? A whole lot of nobodies. Who is Mr Robinson? You have to send more than one lord if you are to impress the Americans.' Mr Langley stopped to draw breath but was off again before anyone ventured to interrupt. 'Do we really want a treaty? Do the Americans? Every nation has its pride. Pride can only be gratified by getting men together, dressing them in fancy coats and funny hats, placing weapons in their hands it is a wonder they have learnt to load, and teaching them to go BANG, BANG.' Mr Langley held out his arm and squinted down it as though he were sighting a gun. 'They must see how many thousands can be killed in a day. Those who kill the most are the winners. It's like a sort of tiddlywinks or marbles.'

A girl in a pale blue gown said, 'I think you are very shocking, Mr Langley. How can you say such things about our brave soldiers who have saved us from the French?'

'We poets don't stick to dreaming. We are bold enough to speak the truths that others will not utter. I never said soldiers were not brave. I am sure they are splendidly brave. What must be considered is the nature of bravery. The bravest man is he who least understands the danger he is in. He sees the bullets flying by and assumes they are all destined to hit somebody else. I say disband the army, which is certainly a threat to our freedom, our public liberty, and let the poor soldiers keel pots or grow cabbages, where they will do no harm to themselves or others. Perhaps the officers could do the same.'

Mr Langley again raised his arm in imitation of a weapon. The girl in the blue dress turned away, apparently upset, leaving a gap in the little crowd down which he could fire his imaginary musket . . . but the gap revealed a stranger in the direct line of his aim. He nervously let his arm drop, there being something about the stance of the man, with cropped hair and a distinctly military cut to his coat, that did not appeal to him at that particular moment. There was an anxious silence.

Mr Langley, not liking to be at a loss, said, 'I think we have not been introduced.'

Major Wilder gave a curt bow. 'Major Wilder of the Royal Horse Artillery, at your service, sir. Pray continue. I was listening to you.'

Mr Langley lost his composure. His face was white. He spluttered out, 'Never meant any offence, assure you, sir. They are used to me here and know not to take me seriously. It was just a bit of nonsense. We would appreciate your opinion on the state of things. You have seen much active service, I suppose?'

Major Wilder, not deigning to enter into conversation, said, before turning his back, 'Should Bonaparte ever escape and successfully invade this country I most sincerely hope the first person he thinks to conscript into his army will be you.'

Walking away, he was at first coldly angry, but not to the extent of doing more than disconcert Mr Langley. After all, if you saw things from but one point, there was truth in what he had said. Major Wilder was as aware of the futility of war as he was of the futility of duelling. It settled things but temporarily. Unfortunately other means of protecting one's nation from an aggressor had not been devised and he therefore saw a necessity for it and that the sacrifice of life was not unwarranted. He thought, on behalf of all his friends and the men with whom he had served, clever, good, kind and loyal, who had died and left their bones in Spain and Portugal, he should have given Mr Langley a thrashing, but nothing would have been achieved because it would not have altered Mr Langley's opinion but merely made him a little more cautious. He preferred to leave him in a state of anxiety as to the possible consequences resulting from his conduct. He had seen how white his face had turned and the nervous glint in his hard blue eyes.

Major Wilder's mind then turned to Miss Arbuthnot. Had she really been in love with such a man? No wonder Lady Charles had thought she had radical leanings if she had spent much time listening to him. Well, he supposed Mr Langley could exercise considerable magnetism with his steely eyes and clever, if treasonable, logic. Better, he thought, to be a governess than be married to such a man, for he felt Miss Arbuthnot would have been disillusioned by him five minutes from the altar. She was too sensible. Had she, staunch to the last, remained in love with him? Being in love, unfortunately, had nothing to do with good sense. And was she not very young? He conjured up a picture of her riding along the top of the downs or circumventing a field of hay in the meadows by the river, the long grass brushing the belly of the neat grey horse and her grey linen habit falling in neat folds to the heel of her boot.

Preoccupied, he wandered about among the guests, going in and out of the garden and from the dining room to the drawing room, where the tea was laid out. He thought that when Ridley was his he would not ask so many people at once. He remembered the evenings in London, now long ago, when his mother had been at home to a select number who had sat in a semicircle and discussed, he now wondered what. That would not suit him either.

His hostess waylaid him. She said, 'Oh, Major Wilder, what will you think of us, neglecting you so? I don't believe you have had so much as a cup of tea. Don't listen to Mr Langley, now, he is such a naughty radical. Mrs Heugmont feared he would make you cross. My husband's sister's only child, an orphan now, you must understand we feel a duty to him, but he is getting so famous for his poetry, we hardly know if we are coming or going.'

'And do you like the poetry?' Major Wilder asked.

'Like it? Why, a busy woman like myself with seven children and the parish reads three lines and falls fast asleep, more in danger of setting the house alight for failing to blow out the candle than getting any poetry read. The books look very pretty on the shelf and he inscribes his name really most charmingly on the flyleaf, with so many twirls you wouldn't know for sure it was "James Langley" he had written.'

'It is not my place to give advice, but if he is not more discreet he may find himself locked up, or some serving soldier other than myself will call him to account. Perhaps your husband would drop him a hint.'

'I assure you the rector is forever dropping him hints and rather more, but allow me to introduce you to dear Mrs Langley, such a beauty though a mere child. Does not her sister live at Ridley and look after your niece? I am sure Mrs Heugmont told me that.'

'Yes. It would be remiss of me to go home without a message for Miss Arbuthnot from her sister.' Major Wilder began to walk with the rector's wife out into the garden.

'Indeed, that would be a shame and perhaps you could speak to her, give her warning about the very foolish things James says. She might influence him to greater discretion.'

'I hardly think that my place.'

'Oh, it won't cause offence. Kate is never offended but, come to think of it, nor does she pay heed to anybody. How long does your sister have the pleasure of your company?'

Major Wilder had previously determined on staying until after 25 July, but he said he had as yet made no plans.

The rectory had a rose garden with arbours and iron-work seats. A group of young people, mostly boys, including his Heugmont nephews, were clustered together in a knot but they meekly parted at the arrival of their hostess to reveal, in their midst, an exquisite fairy being: Mrs James Langley.

'Run along, all of you boys,' said the rector's wife, with the ease of one who had known them since they were children. 'Major Wilder must be introduced to Mrs Langley and they are to have a nice little chat about Mrs Langley's sister. Now, Kate, here is Major Wilder and he has just been saying to me your James will get himself into a great deal of trouble one of these days.'

The boys, reluctant, drifted away. Major Wilder made his bow. Mrs Langley raised enormous, childlike, velvety eyes and indicated he might sit down beside her, tucking in the peach muslin of her dress to make room for him with a tiny, delicate hand, upon which glittered a large diamond ring. She said, 'Oh, la, don't pay any attention.

I don't. He doesn't say all that stuff to me. I'm too dim-witted to understand it, but when he says something weally naughty, I disagwee, like his thinking it a pity Bonaparte don't escape. Think of it, the Fwenchies would bob acwoss the sea in their little boats and eat us all for bweakfast.' She hid a small yawn. 'We've been up dancing and it makes me so sleepy.'

Major Wilder wondered if it would be possible to impress anything on her but he said, all the same, 'An old soldier like me, let alone a younger one, but with a more fiery disposition than mine, will call your husband out.'

'Are you a soldier? I wasn't quite listening when we were intwoduced.'

'I am Major Wilder, Major Thomas Wilder. I came yesterday from Ridley.'

Mrs Langley gave a scream, then covered her mouth before frowning as best she could. She then said, with a little dimpling smile, 'I didn't know your name was Thomas. You are Major Wilder of Widley. Fancy, I hadn't put two and two together, but that's just like me. You are Anna's Major Wilder. I am ashamed to think of it.'

'But why are you ashamed?'

'Anna wunning off to be a governess when there wasn't a necessity. Isn't it a disgwace? Whatever was she thinking of? James doesn't like to hear it mentioned. Well, it's twew my papa isn't a wich man, but Anna should be at home, looking after him, not leaving it to the little ones, not that Fanny and Minette are so little as all that. Soon I shall take them away to find them husbands. Isn't that my duty?' She raised her eyes to Major Wilder.

'And what of a husband for Miss Arbuthnot?' His voice

was coldly crisp. At his manner of speaking, any of the junior officers in his troop, or indeed the men, would have recognized it as an expedient moment to give him a wide berth. His sister referred to it as his flying into one of his passions, of which he had just an hour previously denied the existence.

Mrs Langley replied languidly, 'Anna is too tall, more like a man, and she has a twoubled complexion, though not so vewy bad, but then there's the wed hair as well and one can't tell who won't like that. I'm afwaid she is too like Papa. She has sort of a wound face like me, but she makes it so long because she's so sewious. I don't see how I could get her a husband. Maybe she will, one day, mawwy an old widower who wants her to look after his childwen.' She again raised her astonishing eyes to Major Wilder's face and, vaguely registering disapproval there, continued, 'Don't think I'm being unkind. I'm never unkind. I love Anna. I expect she teaches Miss Wilder weally well for she taught Fanny and Minette weally well, evewyone said so. Me, she couldn't teach a thing, I'm so dim-witted – even Mr Langley says it – but I get on vewy well without bwains.'

To her mild astonishment Major Wilder got up and walked away while she was still speaking. The Heugmont boys slipped back to her side. She said, 'Is he your uncle, Major Wilder? I must have made him cwoss or else he's a wude man and I'm sure Anna is odd for saying he's kind. Perhaps he doesn't like women. I hear some men don't.'

Twenty minutes later Mrs Heugmont was walking round the garden seeking her brother, again wishing she had made him stay at home, out of harm's way. She found him sitting on a bench in the shrubbery, she thought pensive, but he smiled when he saw her. Taking the place beside him, she said, 'What are you thinking?'

He was actually thinking he would marry Miss Arbuthnot if he could, but it was another thing he could not tell Georgie, for she would certainly disapprove.

Mrs Heugmont was wondering where he had been. Not at the whist table with her husband, for he never played cards if he could avoid it, or in the drawing room, or on the terrace. Had he been, for the entire duration, here? She then said, scrutinizing him, 'Are you all right?'

He replied, 'Yes, thank you,' in the polite tone he might use if she had asked him whether he had eaten sufficient for breakfast.

Defeated, she told him they could leave. The boys must be dragged away from the alluring Mrs Langley and removed on the spot or they would slide back. The rector's wife would ask them to stay for supper and she would never get them home at all.

All the way back across the fields Major Wilder was preoccupied. His brother-in-law was talking to him about some new-fangled device he wished to acquire and required little attention beyond a periodic earnest nod. His nephews were imitating Mrs Langley's impediment. Was he in love? What was being in love? He had had no sudden rush of blood to the head. Was he behaving irrationally? Possibly, but it did not seem irrational. He had merely come to understand that any activity at Ridley, as far as he was concerned, required Miss Arbuthnot's presence, but it was not until he had listened to her sister's lisping disparagements that he saw the necessity of formalizing arrangements to secure her presence for life. The more he thought about it, the sweeter it became, but how to convince Miss Arbuthnot of this? His family would more than urge him against it, hers would urge her towards it, and her own inclinations might be lost in the mêlée. The idea would not have occurred to her. She was a little shy of him. He could not pay court to her because she was Lottie's governess. He must not compromise her or drive her from Ridley. Should he see her father? Should he write a letter?

For whom did one pray? Lady Charles had never troubled to question her faith or even to give it much attention. On Sundays one went to church. A degree of charity was expected of her within the parish and she had been careful to carry out the necessary duties even in the preceding year, though she had not visited the sick as had been her custom, sending Sally instead. So long as they got their broth, did it matter how it came to the door? After a twelve-month, one was expected to return to normal, as if grief had no right to intrude beyond a given time. Might she not have started grieving for Lyndon from the day he departed? He had been absent for as much as four years, but while she knew he was alive, though she missed him, she had not grieved for him. Perhaps she should have done for had he not been as much removed from her as he was in death? Pray for the dead. Did Lyndon need her prayers? She would pray that God grant her the power to revere every nuance of his life, to forget nothing, to hold every memory dear; and to assist Lottie in understanding her great loss. There was Lottie now, so good and quiet. She had taken off her little bonnet and laid it on the pew beside her, but Lady Charles still could not see her face, for her head was bent in the most earnest reflection, gratifying to observe.

Lottie was kneeling beside her grandmother, her hands pressed over her eyes in the requisite position for praying. The church was empty besides themselves, peculiarly silent and grey, and a little cold, though it was July. Grandpapa hadn't come because he was thinking about Lyndon all day and Scottie wouldn't understand missing his walk. How was it her grandmother kept so still? What did God expect you to say to Him? God always had a capital letter. Dear, large God, look after my papa in Heaven, where he is, so they tell me. Dear God, do little babies who have not had the water from the font splashed on their heads and a cross marked on them go to Hell, which is a horrid place? Dear, large, frightening God, Miss 'Buthnot does not believe that. Is it bad not to believe everything? Will we all go to Hell? I am only going to believe the same as Miss 'Buthnot so we can all be in Hell together. I am going to ask Uncle Thomas some of these things. Where is Uncle Thomas? He went to see Aunt Georgie and he hasn't come back. Dear God, I like having breakfast downstairs and even Grandmama was there today. Uncle Thomas said it was ridiculous servants carrying trays up so many stairs all the way to the nursery. We must think of Susan's legs. If Uncle Thomas had been at breakfast he might have said I could go for my ride as usual, though it is the day, one year on, that my papa was killed in the war, and not with Grandmama to say prayers in the church for ever such a long time. Dear God, please remember my papa in Heaven because that is what Grandmama wants you to do and she will be so sad if he isn't having everlasting life. Grandmama said Uncle Thomas behaves like God. 'Thomas behaves like God. Look at this terrible empty wall where we are to put the monument to our son.' There is a spider on it at the minute and two crooked lines where the plaster has cracked. Uncle Thomas wants a plain slab but Grandmama wants the angels. The angels are very pretty so perhaps Grandmama is right this time, but Uncle Thomas says it will cost too much and he must know because he looks after everybody's money. You would think it must be easy. There either is money for angels or there isn't. 'Miss Wilder has an aptitude for mathematics.' If there is so much money to spend, it could be given to the poor children to learn to read and write so they better themselves, but the rector says God made them poor for the good of their souls. You can't go through the eye of a needle if you are rich. The story in the Bible says you must use your talents if you have some. I don't suppose Grandpapa is worried about not going through the eye of a needle. He doesn't ever mention it, nor Grandmama. Grandmama said we should walk to church. It was more proper. I didn't know Grandmama could walk that far. She was ever so slow. She made heavy weather of it. 'Miss Lottie, you're making heavy weather of it.' That's Susan. I wanted to run but Grandmama said I mustn't because we were going to church to think about my papa. Grandmama said she would be all alone if I didn't go with her. Dear God, if I am good and don't have to go to Heaven until I'm old, will I be younger or older than my papa when I get there? Shall I have a halo like an angel? I must get Horatio to help me cut my hair again, only a teeny bit or they'll notice. He is not very neat at it but Polly tidies it up.

'Polly, you haven't been cutting Miss Wilder's hair?' 'No, m'lady, I just gives it a little tidy-up, nothing what could be called cutting. It grows ever so uneven, Miss Wilder's hair.' Miss 'Buthnot doesn't say anything, though she must guess at how naughty I am. Horatio can't get his peas in a straight line, even with two sticks and a piece of string to help him, but he's ever so good at French, now he does French with me. He can learn lists and lists of words in a minute. He might not get another chance of learning it, he says, before he goes in the navy. Why does his mother want him to go in the navy? Dear God, please don't let Horatio go in the navy. Horatio can't remember his papa. I can't remember mine. I sort of remember a man, but was that man my papa?

Lottie opened her eyes and found her grandmother looking at her with tender affection. Was it all right to smile or must she keep being serious with her face? Well, she had been serious quite long enough. She said, 'Can we go now?'

Miss Arbuthnot's letter was from her father.

My dearest Child,

I cannot believe our good fortune. Major Wilder expressly asked me not to mention it to you as he thought you ignorant of the whole matter, but I take it upon myself to disregard him, for are you not my own child for whom I must know what is best and who I know best? Besides, he seems innocent of women. He does not know even one as young as yourself is always conscious of these things. You must, my dear Anna, be very patient and go on exactly as you always do. I see he is a gentleman not to be hurried nor yet shaken off his course. There has to be opposition from his family, but I understand as the estate is entailed on him, there is nothing they can do. I deplore the idea of your not being acceptable for purely financial reasons, your birth, my dear Anna, being above reproach: such are the ways of the world.

Oh, my dear child, I am so delighted for, besides the practical, he appears most worthy and upright, one to whom it will be an honour to be connected, but how sly you have been, never a word breathed. I find that just a little naughty, but we will not quibble at such a time, and maybe it is so, that you could not believe him in earnest. Major Wilder seemed concerned he might cause you distress. What distress could he cause you, with such a prospect opening before you? How ridiculous even the best of men become when their affections are engaged.

The epistle continued in a like manner for several pages. At first Miss Arbuthnot could not understand it, yet its implication was perfectly clear. She then thought her father must be under a misapprehension, though she could not see what purpose Major Wilder could have in going to Devonshire and visiting the parsonage, unless he happened to be in the vicinity and thought it his duty to pay his respects to her family. This she thought an explanation, though she could not conceive the nature of any conversation her father might have had with him to make him draw such a wild conclusion.

Having thus reasoned, if not with any sense of satisfaction, Miss Arbuthnot was extremely indignant. How could her father assume so much? Did he wish her to be married for no other reason than securing the future of herself and possibly her sisters as well? Put in such a way it sounded reasonable, but was this the man who had defied all and eloped with a French *émigrée*? Though she had always spoken well of Major Wilder, for all her father knew she might be struck with the wildest horror at the notion of declaring at the altar she would love and obey him until death parted them. Indeed, she would have been struck with horror if the whole matter had not appeared so ridiculous and unlikely. She tried to imagine, without success, Lord and Lady Charles's reaction to their son announcing his intention of marrying his niece's governess. It was beyond what could be imagined. Surely her father must see she never could commit herself to any man after pledging her whole heart to Mr Langley. The latter might have proved unworthy, but that altered nothing.

She ended by concluding it was all an illusion, some improbable misunderstanding. After reading and rereading her father's letter several times more, she wrote and told him as much, indicating total bewilderment at all that he had said. As this could be done in a few lines she reverted to her usual accounts of her pupil's progress towards literacy and the child's delight in her garden.

A few days later Miss Arbuthnot received a letter from her sister Kate. As it was the first Kate had written to her since her marriage and, when she thought about it, practically the only letter Kate had ever written her, she was rather astonished. Kate was a poor correspondent but when she settled to the task her undisciplined script was often amusing.

The letter started without ceremony: 'Well, dear old Anna, you good pious creature.'

Miss Arbuthnot sighed and was not taken with this opening. Did she appear thus, staid and ancient, given over to duty, her youth withered away?

> *It will surprise you to get a letter from me but I could not resist writing to tell you how Mr Langley and I stayed with his uncle in Gloucestershire where I assure you I am a great favourite with everybody, and though his uncle is a clergyman, they are very merry all day long and we dance and play at charades, though you can be certain I never guess any of the words, as often as can be. What do you think? We had hardly been there a week before who should attend but your Major Wilder. Of course, I had forgotten his sister lives close by but, MY, isn't he disagreeable? He hadn't a single pleasant thing to say, a perpetual frown on his face. I think the war must have killed him. Mr Langley would not stay another day for fear of meeting him again and he made me get my bags all packed in two minutes and we left the next morning. I thought this reaction very hasty but Mr Langley said it was detrimental to his health to be teased and contradicted in such a cross sort of way and he would not be able to write for weeks unless we made an immediate departure. The poor darling is so*

very sensitive. It is because he is a poet. I am glad I am not one. It is rather inconvenient at times, though people tell me I must find it fascinating to be married to such a clever, fascinating person. They don't know I never understand a word of it.

It was Miss Arbuthnot's opinion that Kate understood much more than she was prepared to divulge. Her constant and careless mention of her husband could not be read with indifference. His name appearing so boldly on the page could only conjure a vision of dreams destroyed and joy trodden carelessly underfoot. At the same time Miss Arbuthnot could not suppress a smile at the very thought of Major Wilder and Mr Langley being in the same room together, and she wondered if Mr Langley's insistence on such an abrupt departure from the vicinity was not more to do with a fear he might have overstepped himself than with the sensitivity of his poet's soul. He would not have known of Major Wilder's frequently stated abhorrence of duelling, despite the custom for gentlemen to call each other out, even to shoot each other dead, for some possibly illusory insolence. She wondered how she could have been so deceived and beguiled by Mr Langley.

Kate concluded her letter with these words:

Well, I like being married. I'm sure it's best. Maybe you will find someone who will like to marry you, even now you are a governess. Goodbye, dear, we mustn't quarrel.

Miss Arbuthnot received no answer from her father. This,

though upsetting, did not cause her surprise. Her last letter home would have displeased him. He was not a man who cared for even a hint of contradiction.

It was the second week of August and the corn was cut and stooked before Major Wilder returned to Ridley, tripping across the park on the Andalusian as if he had never been away. Lottie, spying him from the schoolroom window, dropped her pencil and tore down the stairs to fly into his arms and scold him for being away so long. Miss Arbuthnot hastened after her in order to retrieve her. For a moment she was self-conscious at being face to face with Major Wilder but he smiled at her with his usual good humour as he disentangled himself from Lottie's embrace.

'I am not used to such violent demonstrations of affection,' he said. 'Well, *niña*, I dare say you have been very good and have beanstalks in your garden as tall as a house.'

'Course I haven't,' Lottie said. 'They are just so high but I'm going to dig them up because we've eaten them all.'

Certainly, Miss Arbuthnot thought, as she and Lottie climbed back up the stairs to continue the mundane business of lessons, she could be glad the meeting had passed with such ease.

At dinner, when they were again together, the conversation was given over to his visit to his sister, Lady Charles demanding a detailed account of her grandchildren and Lord Charles wanting to know exactly where else he had been. By the time the dessert was on the table she thought she could be completely comfortable and could meet his eye, when he chose to speak to her, for he had always been careful to include her in any discussion, with composure.

After dinner he said he would look at the gardens and asked if anyone would like to accompany him. The evening sun slanted across the lawns, now so neat and tidy, and they all went out of doors. He walked between Lottie and Miss Arbuthnot, but there was nothing unusual in that. She began to think her father had dreamt the whole thing. It was not until she lay in bed that it occurred to her she was too confused and disturbed by her father's letter to think rationally. Was it not strange, on his part, that he had neither mentioned going to Devonshire nor meeting her sister?

Miss Arbuthnot puzzled over it, but as August slipped by and nothing occurred that was out of the usual way, she began to think of it less. If Major Wilder was courting her, he was biding his time, but in what way could he court her, considering her position? He often chose to ride or walk beside her. Of that she was aware. She did not suppose such acts amounted to courtship, but how could she tell? He spoke of the war. She became familiar with the names of the young officers in his troop and even of the men. She learnt of the landscape in Spain and Portugal and of the habits of the natives, which, as she had never travelled and thought her chance of ever doing so very low, interested her. He was decorous in the extreme. Once she asked him how he had obtained the Andalusian, for surely the possession of a thing so exotic was an aberration in his character, but this it seemed he would not tell, merely smiling and saying it was a long story and he would tell her another day, when they had plenty of time. This she did not believe, for they had plenty of time at that moment, but she knew he had considered telling her from the way he had hesitated before he had replied.

Upstairs, alone in her room, if she glimpsed herself in the little piece of looking-glass, for Miss Arbuthnot had never been one to devote much time to looking-glasses, she thought, Am I plain or not? Is that bridge of freckles over my nose ugly? Was her red hair ugly? Her mother had told her to be proud of it, that her grandmother had had it and she had been considered a beauty. Miss Arbuthnot could not think anyone had ever thought her that.

Life went on as normal but as she had no wish to encourage Major Wilder, was indeed fearful at the thought, she resolved to make clear her view of matrimony for herself, should the opportunity arise in some natural way, though she had to concede that might never be.

In the event the opportunity arose and the consequences were not as she had predicted: they were most painful and upsetting and they also proved her father to be correct. It was a Sunday morning in mid-September and they had all been to church.

Lottie had spent the time in pulling faces at Horatio, who sat in an adjacent pew. He was overcome with uncontrollable laughter and incurred the silent wrath of his mother while Lottie was shuffled along the seat that they might not have such a clear view of each other.

Lord and Lady Charles went home in the landau but Major Wilder walked with Miss Arbuthnot, Lottie bobbing between them. It was a dull day, overcast and a little cool. There were now sticks placed here and there in the park to indicate where the new trees were to be planted and some of the holes were dug. In excess of those trees, forty conkers had been laid in a row in the vegetable garden. They would make horse-chestnuts and grow quickly at no extra expense. Major Wilder had picked up the conkers himself with the help of the children and Miss Arbuthnot. He was thinking of the trees and also of Miss Arbuthnot, who was so patiently and sweetly listening to Lottie's chatter and answering her fifty-five questions.

Lottie then said, 'Why is Grandmama always talking about my marrying? I don't know why she does it. I don't want to marry, but if I have to I had better marry Horatio, because he is my friend. I should quite like to go to sea. Would I be allowed?'

Major Wilder replied, 'I think Horatio would have to be captain of the ship before he could take his wife to sea.'

'That's what Horatio said. We must wait until we are quite old but I don't mind as I don't want to be married. Miss 'Buthnot's brother is a lieutenant. You can be a lieutenant for years and years without being a captain and when you are a captain you might not get a ship. I think it very strange and peculiar to go into the navy.'

'The navy is an honourable profession, Lottie, and of the greatest importance.'

'That's what Horatio says. Still, I'm not sure about marrying and always having to remind someone to change their stockings if they get wet feet.'

'You may find there is a little more to marriage than that.'

Lottie caught hold of Miss Arbuthnot's arm and swung on it. 'Would you get married if a good, kind man should ask you?'

Miss Arbuthnot said, 'No. I am afraid I should have to refuse.'

'But don't you want to be married either? Grandmama tells me everyone wants to be married and she wouldn't like it if I said she was fibbing.'

'I am sure your grandmother is right as a general rule but I have made up my mind against it.' Miss Arbuthnot endeavoured to speak lightly while at the same time wishing to appear resolute, but she was afraid she sounded strange. She was careful to look only at Lottie. At that moment they heard Horatio calling behind them and turned to see him running to catch them up.

For a minute Horatio was too out of breath to speak but he eventually said, 'My mother says Lottie may come to our house for dinner if she is allowed and would like it. Please may she? My mother was cross with me but now we are friends again and I had to run and run.'

Major Wilder said, 'I dare say Lottie would like it.'

'Oh, yes, please,' Lottie said. 'Do I have to ask Grandmama?'

'No, I shall give the permission.'

'I have on my Sunday frock, so that's all right.' At the same time, Lottie was repeating to herself, 'Thomas behaves like God.' She gave Miss Arbuthnot a hug and reached up to give Major Wilder a kiss before running away with Horatio as fast as she could go.

Miss Arbuthnot continued to walk with Major Wilder. She was thinking, It was as well I said what I had to say and now it need not be thought of again, but after a few minutes Major Wilder broke their silence. 'You spoke very firmly to Lottie on the subject of your not wishing to marry.'

'Yes,' she had to reply, 'I did.'

'And would nothing induce you to change your mind?'

'I don't believe so.'

'You see, I have had it in my mind for some time that I would like to marry you myself.'

Miss Arbuthnot looked swiftly into his face and away again, struck with horror: that which she had been so anxious to avoid she had apparently precipitated. How could he possibly wish to marry her, inconsequential creature that she was?

'You do me a great honour but I am certain I should not marry,' she said.

'Are you not rather young to make such a decision?'

'If I am old enough to marry I ought to be old enough to decide against it.'

He gave a short laugh, but she did not think him amused. 'Had you any idea I might want to marry you?'

'I didn't believe it.' She looked at the ground. 'How could you want to marry me? It would cause you so much distress. Your family would dislike it. It would be considered, for you, a disaster.'

'I can be judge of that for myself. I happen to wish it all the same.' He really did wish it, more than he had ever wished anything, but he also knew he sounded unconvincing. What could he offer her, she who had loved, perhaps still did love, a young man possibly intellectually fascinating but, without principles, unworthy of her? He could offer her love but it was of the dogged rather than the romantic, and was he not aged by war? In comparison to Mr Langley he must seem very old. He could offer her security but with youthful defiance she would reject that because she did not return his affections.

Miss Arbuthnot said hopefully, 'I am sure you will come to regret you ever spoke to me, that it was a whim you had, not that I see you much given to whims.' After a pause she continued, but with much hesitation, 'Should I leave Ridley? Should I go away?' She thought, sickeningly, of leaving Ridley and of parting from Lottie, of starting again in another house, among further strangers, and she thought how much she liked Major Wilder with his pleasing quiet brown eyes.

'Would you prefer that?' he asked.

'Not at all. I was thinking of you.'

'It would seem as if I was punishing you, and why should I, who have grown to like you, do that? It would be unfair, and Lottie loves you. Tomorrow I take my father to Bath. It is as well. I don't know how long I shall be away. When I return, no more shall be said and I must learn to live with myself.'

Though his face remained guarded, she knew how much she had offended him and that he would try to make light of it. Was he not a soldier? Had she not sat at dinner when Lady Charles, apparently after some previous conversation with her husband, was berating him for not mentioning the wound he had in his shoulder that it might have received proper attention when he had first come home? He had replied that it was very trifling, yet she understood the ball had penetrated his shoulder and emerged on the other side. It had not, he had explained, encountered too many obstacles in its passage. And when was a wound not trifling, Lord Charles had asked, which had led to a discussion on the need for prompt amputation, when essential, while the patient was still in shock, perhaps still on the battlefield. Lady Charles had complained of it as a topic unsuited to the dinner table, which Miss Arbuthnot supposed it was, though she had found it rather interesting.

She said, 'Please don't think I don't like you. You have always been so kind.'

They had reached the front of the house. Major Wilder knew that being kind and being liked were inadequate sentiments of no particular use. He gave Miss Arbuthnot a stiff little bow and repeated his intention of leaving for Bath the next day but he expected to see her at dinner, which he was sorry could not sensibly be avoided.

Upstairs in her own room, without Lottie to distract her, Miss Arbuthnot sat at the window, looking down on that same corner of stable roof and wall of kitchen garden that she had seen through the rain on her first day at Ridley. She felt weary, dull and empty. Was this all to life, this seemingly dispassionate proposal of marriage from a man she liked? He was not a stranger, yet what did she know of him? She only knew she liked him and that she had very properly refused his proposal of marriage. What sort of person would she be who could give away her heart entirely and then, five minutes later, because it would be convenient, give it to another of quite different calibre and promise to love him until death parted them? The decision made was the correct one, of that she was sure. She thought the pronouncing of it would haunt her, that it would not go away, but that she could safely meet him at dinner without a single person being aware that anything was amiss. After dinner, or perhaps before, she would have to write to her father to apologize for doubting him and explain what she had done.

Captain Houghton, for all his ill health and uncertain temper, was at heart nothing more than a little sour. He was chafed by lack of means to support himself, what fortune there was in the family having passed to his elder brother and on his death to his nephew, a boy of twelve years old, under the strict management of guardians and trustees expressly, it seemed, to guard the lad from impecunious uncles. He was not a man of strong character, easily influenced one way or another, too idle and too ill to assert himself for anyone's benefit but his own. He thought his sister had had all the luck in marrying well and now having only the one child. When she had given him the money to assist him in the purchase of his commission, and at times other gifts, she had tended to remind him she robbed her son of part of his inheritance, which he found offensive: why should these little boys, his nephews, be provided for when he himself was left to struggle on the inadequate pay of a captain in a regiment of the line? Had he had more energy he might have championed democratic causes but had he been more fortunate it would not have occurred to him to give the matter of equality a single thought.

He now saw, as well as his sister, the charm of her remarrying and that Major Wilder was the obvious choice. He was aware she did not care to have it mentioned but he knew perfectly well she was piqued at her lack of progress in this estimable project. Mrs Kingston spent all her time, when in the company of Major Wilder, in what had become jealous observation, though she would not have described it thus. She had reasoned that the only cause of Major Wilder being able to resist her was the presence of a rival but she could see none beyond Miss Arbuthnot and it was simply inconceivable he could prefer Miss Arbuthnot to herself, despite his showing every sign of it. She liked to think it was the company of the children he sought and that Miss Arbuthnot being there was incidental. yet she was uneasy and watched him ever more closely. She thought she herself went quite unobserved and she naturally did not care for it when her brother, one evening when they were lingering in the drawing room after dinner, the teacups on the sideboard and little to be said, burst out: 'I don't know I'm sure, Lucy. I see you set your cap at Major Wilder, but to very little effect.'

Mrs Kingston sat up very straight and dignified.

Captain Houghton continued, 'I dare say I should find living with him pretty irksome.'

This confirmed in his sister the impression that wherever she chose to reside he assumed he would also.

'Yes, it would be irksome,' Captain Houghton ploughed on. 'He is the sort of fellow always on his high horse, sticking to his principles however inconvenient, but the advantages of Ridley would override that.'

'I am quite comfortable as I am, thank you,' Mrs Kingston said.

'No cards, nothing,' Captain Houghton said, ignoring her, and added, obliquely, 'All duty and what would best suit the regiment, day in, day out. They are sticklers to live with.'

'I don't believe you have a proper attitude, Henry.'

'Can't afford one. Now, aren't you wanting a step-papa for Horatio? Wouldn't it do him good? He is getting very wayward and independent for a boy of his age.'

'Only too soon my brother-in-law will be in charge of my child, and he promises most faithfully he will be a father to him.'

'Come now, Lucy, you can't pull the wool over my eyes. You are a little sweet on Major Wilder.'

'Such expressions are suited only to the servants' hall.'

'I may be a sick man but I'm not blind. It would be an excellent thing altogether. I see what's going on.'

'Nothing is going on, as you so vulgarly put it.'

'There's the rub. It ought to be. You're a fine woman, pretty as a picture. Any man ought to be proud to call you his own. Here you are, on his doorstep, and he don't take the bait.'

Mrs Kingston, despite herself, said, 'His affections must have been engaged elsewhere and he is yet recovering.'

'Or his affections are engaged right here.'

'But there is nobody, or nobody he sees, in the vicinity.'

'But there is. You know it as well as I. There is the governess.'

'It simply couldn't be so.'

'A beanpole of a child with red hair and freckles,' Captain Houghton proceeded. 'You would not think her much of a rival, but there, none so odd as folks, and she is not actually unattractive.' He shrugged his lank shoulders. 'I had my suspicions straight away, when I saw that horse he bought for her to ride. Quality. A proper lady's hack and no mistake. I mean, a governess can be put up on any old nag that will plod along and behave itself.'

‘It can’t be so.’ Mrs Kingston reached for her reticule in search of a handkerchief. ‘Think of the disgrace he would bring on his family.’

‘Nothing wrong with the name Arbuthnot. That is her name, is it not? Well, a governess ain’t much, but I expect her papa is a respectable clergyman somewhere or another. They always are. I mean, I don’t believe he’s a linen draper. Where did you say Major Wilder had gone? To take his father to Bath? I don’t suppose he’ll stay there long. I always thought it dull, even in the season. You can’t tell who he might meet. A dangerous place for him to be on the loose. You had better try harder when he comes back, but perhaps that is what puts him off. Maybe Miss Arbuthnot is cleverer than you, ignores him. That can attract a man. It is subtle, you know. That’s what it is, subtle.’

‘It couldn’t be deliberate,’ Mrs Kingston said.

‘Why ever not? A girl in her position can’t afford to pass up any sort of opportunity, however unlikely, you take my word for it.’

Mrs Kingston found herself quite ready to take her brother’s word for it, because secretly it had been her suspicion all along. ‘Oh, what a disgrace it would be. Poor dear Lady Charles, who has suffered so much. I believe it would kill her.’

And so they continued, Mrs Kingston contradicting all Captain Houghton said while, on the whole, agreeing with him, and sobbing into her handkerchief.

Miss Arbuthnot received a second letter from Kate as well as a letter from her father in return for hers. She waited until the evening before opening them, her father's first, and she saw straight away she had been unsuccessful in trying to convey to him her exact reasons for refusing Major Wilder beyond, she thought, the obvious one of not loving him.

Dear Anna,

I am mortified a child of mine could be so selfish. What can you mean by it? My acquaintance with Major Wilder, though short, was sufficient to assure me he was a man of upright principles and strong character. I found no fault with him. He was pleasant and, for a soldier, reasonably educated. I saw nothing in his person for you to take a dislike to him. Your future needs to be secured and you decline to secure it: it is as simple as that. You decline to help your sisters, of whom I always thought you fond. Though I should not expect a son-in-law to support me, one such as myself must dread poverty in old age, and should a daughter have the means of alleviating that circumstance, it is strange to me the means should be rejected out of hand.

Miss Arbuthnot at last gave way and found herself in tears of distress as she struggled through to the end; the letter continued on the same theme for more than a page. She was devastated. How could her father so lack understanding? Had she not recently loved and been rejected? How was she to love again? Or was she expected not to love but merely to pay lip service to love within marriage and at the altar before God? Was the word 'like' to be substituted for 'love'? Was that adequate, true or honest? Was it all that was deemed necessary? Was it not as good as a lie? And indeed there was nothing in Major Wilder's character for her to take a dislike to him, but rather to the contrary.

Wearily, she turned to the letter from Kate and broke the seal.

Now, dear old Anna, won't you be astonished at receiving two letters from me in the month? What a state Papa is in. I never saw the like. He told me all about it. Well, I do think Major Wilder a really cross sort of man so I don't blame you a bit for not wanting to marry him but as I have always trusted you to do what is sensible, your least endearing trait, I was surprised. I am afraid you will have to be a governess for ever. Oh, but Anna, it is so quaint, his proposing to you. I long to know how it was. Mr Langley and I laughed and laughed. Did he go down on one knee and say, 'Anna, my love, my little dove, I adore you and you are breaking my heart'? I can't see him do it, the nasty stiff creature.

Miss Arbuthnot lit her candle and burnt her sister's letter without finishing it. When the last grey wisp of smoke had gone, she lay down on her bed, no longer able to control the violence of her distress.

There was a knock on her door. She tried to compose herself but without success. Lottie called, 'I want to see you.'

Miss Arbuthnot attempted to speak but no words came.

Lottie knocked again but then, receiving no answer, pushed open the door and came in. She took one horrified look at her governess and, bursting into tears herself, ran and put her arms round her, hugging her as tightly as she could and crying out, 'I never knew you could be unhappy and I will never be naughty again, not even cut my hair, or not much. Have I made you unhappy?'

Miss Arbuthnot, the habits of necessity reasserting themselves, rocked the child in her arms and said, 'Nothing is your fault, dearest, of course it's not. It is just a silly grown-up thing that will pass, and it surely must. We won't so much as think of it. It's nearly bedtime. We will go to your room and I shall read you a story. That will make me better in a moment.'

Mrs Kingston had argued with herself for a fortnight and was still in a state of uncertainty when her coachman, on a dank autumn day, pulled up the horses before the portico at Ridley. Was it her duty, as a dear friend, to warn Lady Charles of the danger to her son of his making an unsuitable alliance, or was it none of her business? Was it right to sit by without a word? Would she not be castigated for it later? She was not motivated by jealousy: that notion was ridiculous. She had no ambition of her own: she had quite abandoned the idea of remarrying. That had been a passing fancy. Had she not been indignant with Henry when he had suggested it? Was she not fond of Miss Arbuthnot, who was so clever with the children?

Shown into the drawing room, Mrs Kingston thought it looked as though nobody lived in it, even though Lady

Charles sat there all the day. The shutters, mercifully, were no longer drawn across the windows and one could look out on careful lawns and a park neatly grazed. Lady Charles might still wear mourning but the aspect, even on a dull day, was a deal more cheerful. Mrs Kingston, having kissed her friend affectionately, said, 'And how is dear Lord Charles benefiting from the baths? I pray they do him good. Does he take the waters too?'

Lady Charles thought he did. She was vague on the matter. Lord Charles had written to her but he was not inclined to discuss his health.

'So charming of Major Wilder to accompany his father,' Mrs Kingston said. 'It is not every son who would kick his heels in such a place after the start of the hunting season.'

'He certainly means to hunt,' Lady Charles replied. 'They are getting his horses up. I see the grooms pass the window day in, day out.' She thought, each time, how they should have been Lyndon's horses: there was a dark chestnut she knew he used to ride, but it had not been a favourite so perhaps she must remain indifferent if Thomas rode it.

'How long are Lord Charles and Major Wilder to be away?' Mrs Kingston asked.

'I don't think more than a month. It depends on how successful the treatment is.'

'Yes, dear Lord Charles must be set up for the winter.' Mrs Kingston paused and then added cautiously, 'I dare say it will do Major Wilder good to be gone for a bit.'

'Why?' Lady Charles asked, puzzled.

'I thought him a little preoccupied of late, but it is probably just a fancy.'

'I don't find him given to fancy. Quite the contrary.'

Mrs Kingston laughed. 'No, no, the fancy was mine. Of course, he is more than sensible. However, all men are subject to temptation.'

'I never find Thomas subject to anything.'

'But, close as you are, you might not see what the world sees.'

'And what does the world see?' Lady Charles asked, a little crossly.

'I dare say nothing. It was my brother who drew my attention towards it, but I had thought it, until then, a small delusion of my own. I was overcome to think anything could occur to distress you, you who have had so much to bear.'

'I can conceive of nothing.'

'Of course the connection would be a disaster, though worse has occurred.'

'My dear Mrs Kingston, I wish you would spare my feelings by explaining yourself.'

'You know how men are if they get a notion into their head, it's very difficult to shift. I thought Bath an excellent place for him, out of temptation, and was sorry the hunting season had started or otherwise he might have thought it sensible to stay there much longer.'

'But Thomas shows no interest in any female, as far as I can see. I begin to think he was born a bachelor and I am sure I don't know what will become of us if he should die without an heir.'

'You don't think he could have had his head turned by a young thing in the very heart of your household?'

Lady Charles's mind ran over Polly and Jane, who were thirty and thirty-five respectively. She said, 'Miss

Arbuthnot is the only young thing at Ridley, apart from Lottie.'

'I don't like to name names but I have had my suspicions for a long time and so has Henry. I hated to think you should have to suffer the disgrace.'

'Why, she never takes the least notice of him.'

'Exactly. Doesn't that pique a man so?'

'But you don't think Miss Arbuthnot acts of a purpose?'

'Oh, I don't like to say it. Maybe Henry and I imagined the whole thing. It made me nervous, that's all.'

Lady Charles became speechless with indignation.

'Of course,' Mrs Kingston continued, 'she is very young, but men are so often attracted to youth when it's not very wise and I'm sure they won't be directed. It is just as well Major Wilder has gone to Bath.'

Lady Charles had noticed, in the most casual manner, that Miss Arbuthnot had seemed, of late, not quite her usual self. She had given it no further thought but now she saw it differently. She supposed Miss Arbuthnot was mortified that Thomas had gone to Bath. She burst out, 'Miss Arbuthnot be mistress of Ridley? How ridiculous, but how wicked. She has been deceiving me.'

'Oh, I'm sure it may be unconscious on her part,' Mrs Kingston said, alarmed.

'When is such a thing unconscious? Can you or I say, with our hands on our hearts, we have remained unconscious when some gentleman has taken a fancy to us? Of course, for someone in Miss Arbuthnot's position, it must be all subterfuge and intrigue. She has nothing to offer, neither position, wealth nor even beauty, merely youth. Yes, Thomas always takes her part, he never finds fault and he seeks to make her more comfortable. Did I not hear him say to Slimmer, "Be sure there is enough wood for the schoolroom now the evenings are drawn in, and also for Miss Arbuthnot's room"? Yes, those were his very words. What a catastrophe. I feel Miss Arbuthnot very underhand. One must always be suspicious of cleverness in a woman, and Miss Arbuthnot is undoubtedly clever. But how deceitful, how wicked and two-faced, all innocence on the one and all scheming on the other. To think I only concerned myself with the worry of her having too great an influence on Lottie. I certainly am mortified. However, the remedy is to hand. I shan't hesitate. It will be for the good of all. I am much obliged to you, Mrs Kingston, for opening my eyes.'

Mrs Kingston, further alarmed by the violence of Lady Charles's reaction, said hastily, 'I should prefer you not to take my word for it. We cannot be sure Miss Arbuthnot has done the least wrong thing.'

'But you have told me so yourself.'

'I meant she might not be deliberately at fault.'

'So you are suggesting it is the fault of my son?' Lady Charles thought Thomas was still her son. She would not have him accused of making up to a governess, even if that was exactly what he had been doing. Really, men were troublesome creatures. Her father had not made the entail on Ridley for his heirs to make inappropriate matches, if something so proper as a match was what Thomas had in his mind.

Mrs Kingston was too confused by Lady Charles's question to know how to reply. She said it was time she left. She took a little time to depart, what with her incoherent murmurings and half-expressed anxieties. She then found herself weeping in her carriage on her short journey home while Lady Charles was ringing the bell for Slimmer.

Though several days had gone by since Lottie had discovered her governess capable of tears, she could not quite put out of her mind the idea that something troubled Miss Arbuthnot. She had decided to be extra sweet and good and to have no little temper tantrums over the difficulties she faced in her spelling book or that Horatio learnt French three times quicker than she did; neither would she throw a book at him, though this last resolution was coloured by Miss Arbuthnot having made her sit in another room on her own for forty-five minutes with only her sampler for company, which dread article never seemed to get finished.

When Lottie and Miss Arbuthnot went down to dinner they were surprised to find the table laid only for two.

Slimmer said, 'Her ladyship is indisposed. She is having her dinner upstairs.'

'But Mrs Kingston was here,' Lottie said.

'Her ladyship is not severely indisposed.'

Lottie had been missing her uncle and grandfather at the table but she thought it amusing for she and Miss Arbuthnot to have the whole dining room to themselves. She could not say exactly why it was more comfortable without her grandmother, but it was. She thought it was because her grandmother was remiss in not loving Miss Arbuthnot as much as she ought.

They had only themselves to please. There need be no

formal period spent in the drawing room after dinner, when Lottie was often required to do her sampler or to read aloud to her grandmother while Miss Arbuthnot helped Lady Charles with any other sewing that was on hand, though if her uncle was there they might play Spillikins or a card game, though not one that encouraged gambling for her uncle had an unfashionable dislike of it. Lottie could not understand what fashion was. Her grandmother said fashion was the taste and pursuit of the right sort of people, but her uncle had said it was the taste and pursuit of the wrong sort of people who had nothing sensible to do with their time but concern themselves with fripperies.

Now they went upstairs to the schoolroom where the fire was lit, read stories and played the piano until it was time for Lottie to go to bed but not before she had gone down to say goodnight to her grandmother.

She had expected to find her grandmother, at the least, reclining on her chaise-longue with the smelling salts to hand, but she was seated at her little table apparently not doing much. 'Have you the headache?' she asked.

'Yes, dearest child, just a little one.'

Lottie thought her grandmother looked much as usual. 'You had better take some medicine,' she said, this being a suitable punishment for being poorly.

'I am sure it will be better tomorrow,' Lady Charles said, giving Lottie a kiss.

Another hour or so went by, during which Lady Charles worked herself into a further state of indignation and righteousness. She thought she really did have a headache and it had not been a lie to Lottie. She enthusiastically pictured the perfect governess, one at least forty years old and too sedate for rioting about the countryside on horseback. She would be ladylike and firm, with a great deal of experience. Hall was a model of what a groom should be and he could take Lottie out on the pony instead of York: no other escort would be required. She would tell Thomas, who would no doubt be annoyed but would thank her in the end and ultimately understand how useful his mother had been in separating him from an unfortunate entanglement. He would discover that he must allow her more say in Lottie's upbringing. Was she not a mistress in the art of rearing girls?

When Sally came in to turn down the bed Lady Charles asked her to send Miss Arbuthnot to see her. She felt smug at how carefully she had everything planned.

Miss Arbuthnot, who had been on the point of going to bed herself but had not started to undress, wondered, as she knocked on Lady Charles's door, what irregularity in Lottie's conduct was to be brought to her notice.

Lady Charles was sitting bolt upright in a small armchair by the grate. She said immediately, 'You may wonder why I did not come down to dinner. It is because I am in a state of shock. Indeed, I am so deeply shocked I hardly know myself.'

Miss Arbuthnot looked puzzled but she made no reply, not knowing what was appropriate.

'I believe it to be your ambition to be mistress of Ridley the second Lord Charles is dead and buried,' Lady Charles continued, having already decided how best to broach the matter, even if it sounded a little like something out of a novel.

'It certainly isn't,' Miss Arbuthnot replied, extremely indignant.

'You don't deny a relationship between yourself and my son? If it is not to lead to marriage, what sort of relationship could it be?'

'There is no relationship between Major Wilder and myself.' Miss Arbuthnot endeavoured to keep her voice level though she trembled. She knew Lady Charles to be hinting at something improper or immoral though she understood little about such things. She thought of Major Wilder's proposal. Why should she betray his confidence? That would surely be wrong. Even if she told the truth she could see Lady Charles would not believe it.

'Major Wilder,' Lady Charles said, 'has been out of the country for many years. He is unused to civilian life and the traps that might be set for him now his position is one of eligibility. He knows nothing of scheming young women who have the luck to be placed in proximity to him.'

'I have had no scheme,' Miss Arbuthnot said. 'I never thought of such a thing.'

'Men will be men and you have had a scheme to entrap him. You have thought one thing would lead to another and he would agree to marry you. In that you would have made your mistake. He knows what is owed to his position as heir to his father.'

'Please believe me. There is nothing between Major Wilder and I. I think . . . I believe Major Wilder has had a little inclination towards me, but I have not encouraged him.'

'You can't expect me to believe you. If Major Wilder should take the very smallest interest in a girl in your position, a governess with no future beyond patronage or poverty, can I suppose that girl would be so silly as not to encourage him in some clandestine way? You must think me born yesterday. Had you come to me at the start and explained the difficulty of your position, perhaps something could have been done. Well, it is no use talking. You must get your things together. You are to be taken as far as Salisbury where you are booked on the Exeter coach. From there you must send a message to your father, who will no doubt arrange to meet you. You will need to be ready by five o'clock tomorrow morning. My granddaughter must know nothing. She will be asleep. I have organized it accordingly. When she is older she will understand why I deemed you not a fit person to have the care of her. Slimmer will be up to see you round to the stables where the horses will be waiting for you. He will help you with your box. If you have too much to take at this minute, I will send the rest on. I won't hear another word. You will have much to do. Don't delay.'

Lady Charles opened a periodical she had by as if she meant to spend the rest of the night in the quiet contemplation of it. Miss Arbuthnot left the room and closed the door as if she understood what she did. She returned upstairs and pulled out her box from under her bed. She thought she should be upheld by her sense of the violence of the injustice of it all but the tears ran down her cheeks and she was numb: she hardly knew of what she was accused. She pulled her clothes from the cupboard and, out of habit, folded them neatly, though she could barely see and had little idea what she chose to pack and what she did not.

At length she sat down at the table. How could she part

from Lottie without one word, one last look at the dearest of children? Lottie would think herself betrayed. She would be told a whole lot of lies, innuendoes, half-truths, to make her believe her affection for her governess had been misplaced. Miss Arbuthnot drew the single candle towards her and started to write a letter. She breathed deeply, anxious to control herself, to write clearly. She had energy to defy Lady Charles in this respect. When it was finished, and it was but a short letter, she picked up the candle, went to Lottie's room and drew the curtain back just a little way. She was afraid to shine the light for fear of waking her and could see no more than the outline of her head on the pillow. Was she never to see the child again? Could it be possible she stood there gazing at this shadow of her little pupil for the very last time? How had she come to love her so, when love was always to be betrayed? After a long moment Miss Arbuthnot pinned her letter to the inside of the bed curtain. She returned to her own room but then went again to Lottie's for one last look.

At last she returned to lie down on her bed, fully dressed, sleepless, to await the dawn. There were moments when, distraught and exhausted, she wondered what alternative there was to going home. What would her father say to her? Her heart failed her yet alternative there was none. She must go home disgraced.

Lottie woke quite early. Only a feeble light penetrated the bed curtains. She wondered what she had heard in the night: quiet voices, a bump of something heavy and the sound of horses' hoofs in the yard below, but the latter she often heard when more than half asleep for the grooms took out her Uncle Thomas's hunters early in the morning. She could not tell what was a dream and what was not. She felt unaccountably anxious.

As the light grew stronger she saw a piece of paper, folded in two, pinned above her head. She did not immediately reach for it. She was puzzled, almost suspicious, as to how it had got there. Eventually she sat up, carefully unpinned it and slipped out of bed, laying it on the table in order to draw back the window curtains. She saw it had rained in the night but now there was a feeble sunlight and it was later than she supposed. There was no sign of Susan who usually woke her up if she had overslept.

Lottie returned to the table, briskly unfolded the letter and smoothed it flat. In Miss Arbuthnot's familiar hand, there was not a word mistakable.

My dearest Child,

I have had to go away very suddenly. I wish you to know I will never forget you and I will always love you.

Anna Arbuthnot

Lottie went white with horror. She read the letter again and again in case there was some bit of it she was failing to understand. She then rushed to Miss Arbuthnot's room where the door swung wide and she could see it was perfectly empty, even Miss Arbuthnot's things mostly gone, a few books left and her riding habits abandoned in the cupboard.

In a state of disbelief Lottie returned to her bed where she burst into painful sobs, but after twenty minutes or so of giving way to grief and bewilderment she began to ask questions. Where was Susan? Had she, too, disappeared in the night? No, she thought Susan was hiding. Susan did not like explaining things. Miss Arbuthnot would never have vanished unless she had been made to do so. Miss Arbuthnot would have explained it.

Lottie got out of bed. She reread the letter with even greater care and then hid it in the back of her dolls' house. It was her letter. She looked for her clothes but was only half through dressing when Susan came in.

'Your grandmama wants to see you, Miss Lottie.'

'Where is Miss Arbuthnot, Susan?' Lottie's face had been white but now it was flushed.

Susan, when disturbed, had the habit of approaching matters so obliquely it was not always possible to follow what she was saying. Now she muttered, 'I'm sure I don't understand anything. Such goings on. The horses before daylight. I never heard the like.' She peered anxiously at Lottie's angry blue eyes and red cheeks. 'Quieten, little love, you'll do no good. Let me help you with your clothes. Your shift is back to front. Go down to her ladyship. She must explain it. I'm sure I can't. Jane's taken the chocolate. Seems a mortal shame to me for there never was any malice in her and she gave herself no airs, not like some, and who's to manage the child now? That's what I ask.'

Without waiting for Susan to brush her hair, Lottie scrambled down the stairs to her grandmother's room and entered it without knocking, pushing the door open with considerable violence.

Lady Charles was sitting up in bed, a pretty blue beaded shawl thrown over her shoulders. She had supposed Lottie would be a little difficult, it was only to be expected, but she had lulled herself into the notion that the child, having no choice, would accordingly adapt. Lottie would come to be fond of another governess, but perhaps not to excess. Everything was for their good, for Lottie and for Thomas. She must be allowed to know best and it was a great deal of luck she had been in a position to deal with Miss Arbuthnot while Thomas was not at home to raise an objection.

She said to Lottie, 'Now, my love, that is hardly the way to come in. Look at your hair.'

'Where is Miss Arbuthnot?' Lottie shouted.

'Hush, darling, she has gone home to Devonshire.'

'Why? Is somebody ill? Is her father ill? Is her brother Bobby drowned in the ocean? Why did she go in the night?'

Lady Charles thought how easy it would be if she could say somebody was ill but she had not been brought up to tell lies and it was surely a poor time to begin. 'I knew her going would upset you so I thought it better that way. A parting is painful and, as such, it has been avoided. You will miss her to start with but you will soon have a new governess whom you will come to love just like you did Miss Arbuthnot. In the meantime it will be just you and I, which will be delightful. We will spend lots of time together.' Lady Charles had a habit of seeing a situation as she thought it ought to be rather than as it was likely to be.

'I won't have a new governess,' Lottie said. 'I shan't speak to one.'

'Yes, you will, dearest, of course you will.'

'I certainly, certainly won't. Why did Miss Arbuthnot have to go? You haven't said.'

'When you are older you will understand it better.'

'I want to understand it now.'

'Lottie, you are being very rude and silly. No disaster has occurred. You will certainly need a governess who will expect you to be modest and well bred. What will happen to you when you are old enough to come out? A change was for the best. I was not quite happy with Miss Arbuthnot. There were things you are too young to know of.'

Lottie stared at her grandmother with ice-cold blue eyes. 'You sent her away in the middle of the night because you didn't like her.'

'My dear child, it is never as simple as that.'

'Did you send her?'

'Now, Lottie, let us not have fuss and bother and temper tantrums. You are too old. You must be Grandmama's grown-up girl and dear little companion. Think how your papa would have liked you to behave.' Lady Charles saw, with a pang, how Lottie, with her boyish, curly hair, was like to her father, when as a child he had not got his own way.

Lottie said, 'I shan't speak to you ever again. I won't be your dear little companion. I hate you.' She moved towards the door. 'I hate my papa too. I hate him a lot.'

Susan had brought Lottie some breakfast, a glass of milk, two little rolls of bread, butter, preserve, and an apple. Her first reaction was that she could not possibly eat but sitting down at the table she found she could methodically do so. What, she wondered, would Miss Arbuthnot have advised her? Not to lose her temper. Miss Arbuthnot would have suggested she got on with her lessons, but beyond that habitual advice, Lottie thought, under the circumstances, even her loved governess might be short of ideas as to how she should conduct herself. But Lottie was a mulish child and there was one thing she did know: she would not forgive her grandmother.

Having finished her breakfast, she got out her lesson books. The sight of them made her cry but, resolute, she opened them. Without Miss Arbuthnot they seemed dull and difficult. She did a whole page of sums but she did not know if they were right or not. She tried to learn her spellings but they would not stay in her head. On the other hand, the story book she had been reading aloud was, to her surprise, almost easy: soon she would need another and she would not know how to choose. Throughout she patiently watched the schoolroom clock and occasionally put her head down on her books and wept.

At twelve o'clock Susan came in with some bread and a little cold meat. She had been told Miss Lottie was to have nothing but bread and water, as a punishment, but Susan did not hold with that sort of punishment so she wrapped the meat in paper with a good lump of butter and hid it in her apron pocket.

'But don't you tell on me,' she said, 'and mind you eat it all up so I've only the empty plate to take downstairs. Your grandmother says you are not to have your ride today. You are to stay up here until dinner time and then you are to go down and say you're sorry. You upset her so she was near fainting away when Sally went in to her.'

'I don't care. She sent away Miss 'Buthnot and I don't mean to speak to her if she faints away for ever and ever. I won't go down to dinner.'

'My!' Susan replied, impressed. She wondered what Miss Lottie had said to her grandmother that was too awful to be revealed.

'As for my ride,' Lottie said, going to the window, 'it's not raining.' She thought of York. He had not gone with Uncle Thomas, staying behind to look after the dogs and the Andalusian and to supervise the hunters. Her uncle was to share her grandfather's valet. He thought the greyhounds and the Andalusian would be a nuisance in Bath but he had allowed his father to take his little Scottie. For a wild moment Lottie wondered if York would take her to Bath or even to Devonshire, but of course he would do no such thing. He might take her for her rides against the wishes of her grandmother, but not if it were raining. York took orders only from her uncle.

Later Susan went downstairs to consult Sally, and Sally went to Lady Charles, who was seated in her boudoir with a towel round her head.

'Miss Wilder won't come down to dinner, Susan says.'

'She must. She must come down and make amends.'

'Susan can't make her. If anyone should carry her, she would run back up again. Susan's legs aren't up to it, m'lady.'

'There is chicken, then cherry tart for those who come down to dinner. Miss Wilder must be told that.'

Sally knew a message about cherry tart would not move

Miss Wilder to do her grandmother's bidding. Had not she not seen off any amount of governesses before the arrival of Miss Arbuthnot? She was the most obstinate little thing in the whole world.

'Of course the child is upset,' Lady Charles continued, 'but I never shall forget the expression on her face. I must overlook it. She is all I have of my dearest boy. She is not very old and children say things they don't mean when they lose their tempers.'

Sally thought this not confined to children but she did not say so. She was fond of her mistress but she could see Lady Charles had been, not unnaturally in Sally's eyes, a little jealous of Miss Arbuthnot; though surely parting from Miss Arbuthnot was a mistake, and in such a peculiar manner, as if Miss Arbuthnot had been found stealing the silver. It also made people uneasy: if Miss Arbuthnot, without evidence of wrongdoing, could be sent away in the night, whose turn would it be next?

Captain Houghton was eating his breakfast. The autumn sun bathed the table in a pleasing warmth for so late in the year, adding lustre to the coffee pot, the cream jug and the pink striped curtains at the window. He was reading a letter and, having finished it, he burst out crossly, 'Whatever does the fellow mean? He will see how I do. I don't do well, that's apparent to all, but why should it be any concern of his?' Relenting a little, he then added, 'I suppose he does have the best of intentions and I shouldn't gripe. There's another beau for you, Lucy. Captain Greenway gets leave in February and intends a visit, not that he would be much of a catch. As far as I know he hasn't a bean and he's a bit too fond of a game of cards. There are better prizes and I hear you've done for the opposition pretty much, swift as lightning. I commend you.' He was eyeing his sister with wary respect.

'I am afraid I have no idea to what you refer,' Mrs Kingston replied, carefully pouring her tea into a delicate china cup sprigged with forget-me-nots. They made her think of Lyndon Wilder. How often, in the drawing room, she had made tea and handed him a cup, perhaps this very one from which she drank.

'I understand Lady Charles had the governess put on the Exeter coach at the crack of dawn. No fond farewells or any of that.'

Mrs Kingston stared at her brother. She thought he must be making a joke. She said, 'Don't be ridiculous, Henry.'

'All true.'

'Nonsense. Who told you?' Though Mrs Kingston said this, she knew the answer. Her brother's servant was having a flirtation with Polly, one of the Ridley housemaids. 'It will all be gossip. One of Miss Arbuthnot's relatives will have been taken ill.'

'Apparently not. They are very astonished at Ridley. Of course, Slimmer is the only one in the picture and he won't say. Hall had to take her to Salisbury. He wasn't best pleased at the task. She was in such a state of shock he hung about to make sure she got on the right coach. It was cold, too, and coming on to rain. What a to-do. Perhaps Miss A was found to have stolen something.'

'Of course she never stole anything. Oh dear, oh dear, how very shocking. What can have occurred? Lady Charles must have uncovered a truly dreadful thing to have behaved in such a manner to poor dear Miss Arbuthnot.'

'I thought you had achieved it yourself.'

'It is certainly nothing to do with me, certainly not.'

'So you never did tell her ladyship your suspicions concerning her son?'

'No, no. I dropped her a little hint, just to put her on her guard. I wouldn't have presumed to say more.'

Captain Houghton looked sceptical and laughed. 'Very proud sort of person, Lady Charles. I expect she saw Major Wilder angling to make a connection she didn't fancy and cooked up a story to get rid of the girl while he was safely elsewhere.'

'Lady Charles,' Mrs Kingston said, 'would do nothing that did not become her position.'

'Glad to hear it,' he replied, with another laugh. 'Ain't she human?'

Before Mrs Kingston could leap to Lady Charles's defence for the second time Horatio slid into the room and took his place at the breakfast table.

'Say good morning, Horatio,' his mother intoned.

'Good morning, Mrs Kingston; good morning, Captain Houghton,' Horatio said, without raising his eyes from the table. He started to butter his toast and, reaching for the honey, applied a liberal quantity, more than the toast could reasonably hold.

Mrs Kingston sighed. She wished she understood how best to correct her son's tendency towards cheek. At this particular moment she doubted she had the strength to apply herself to it, so she merely said, 'There will be no point in your going to Ridley today.'

'Why not?' Horatio looked up. 'I must have my French lesson. *Parlez-vous français, monsieur? Oui, certainement, je parle très bien le français.*'

'Miss Arbuthnot is away.'

'Why? She never said. Are you sure? Where has she gone?'

'I believe she has gone home. I have not as yet heard from Lady Charles. I dare say it will be best for you not to go.'

Horatio was silent. He knew something to be wrong and that he was not to be told what it was. He caught the surplus drops of honey from his toast and carefully loaded them back into place.

Mrs Kingston was horribly preoccupied and disturbed. Should she visit Lady Charles or not? Of course, nothing was her fault so it was strange she felt so upset. Miss Arbuthnot was gone. She had surely been too young for the post though a very good sort of governess, it could not be denied, and who else was to have the management of Lottie? It was all a little sudden, which was no doubt what was agitating. She said, 'No, Horatio, you are on no account to go to Ridley today.'

Lady Charles did not waver in her conviction: she had done right. She had salvaged the fortunes as well as the honour of the family. Thomas would be chagrined but time would put that right. If she had a conscience it was because she knew others would think her wrong. Apart from Slimmer, the servants were uneasy, even her own Sally, who would always be loyal. They did not know the truth. What truth? If something clandestine or illicit was being conducted, the servants were always the first to know. Perhaps they knew but failed to grasp the significance. If she had been hasty, it was in a good cause. Had Thomas been at Ridley he would have prevented it and now it was too late. She had also intended it to assist in avoiding the very scenes with Lottie that were now being enacted, so in this she had been unsuccessful.

A letter must be written to Bath. She confessed it made her nervous. After careful consideration she decided on addressing her husband, as head of the family, and allowing him to convey to Thomas whatever he saw fit. She picked up the pen and started a letter to Lord Charles, at first enquiring after his health, the comfort of their lodgings and her hope that the beds had been properly aired. Really, she thought, there was more danger in going away for the sake of one's health than in staying at home. She then said,

Now, my dear Lord Charles, you have always trusted me to make correct decisions when concerning our girls. You know how soundly I judged. It is with regret I decided, something having come to my ears, we should not retain Miss Arbuthnot. She has already departed for Devonshire. Of course Lottie is upset. In fact her conduct is quite unforgivable, but she is Lyndon's child so how can I not continue to love her? We must get over it as best we can. As it is, she declines to see me or to come down to dinner, so a fresh start is not an immediate option. You will find Thomas understands my actions better than you would suppose. He will be very cross but he will see the sense of it. Pray calm him before he comes home. Remind him of his duty to me as his mother.

It now occurred to Lady Charles that Thomas might deny any connection between himself and Miss Arbuthnot whatsoever. He would consider his character maligned and his conduct questioned. What could she answer to that? She never had thought men could resist temptation. She must eat humble pie as best she could under such circumstances, but she doubted the necessity would arise. Perhaps this generation was a little more sanctimonious than the last, for people had become aware of the bad example set by the Regent and his brothers and had grown weary of it, but men could not become saints overnight and she did not see why Thomas should be the exception. On further reflection, she thought she was too harsh on the male sex. Surely she had known many whose behaviour had been impeccable, including her own husband, but were they somehow less of a man as a result? That such a notion should enter her head, against all the teaching of the Church, rather appalled her. Her mind went to Lyndon. Had he not been perfect and yet no angel? As it was, an unmarried woman had to be impeccable and with that there was no arguing. Even if Thomas declared himself blameless and Miss Arbuthnot innocent, the latter was gone and unlikely to return. Innocent? Innocent of what? Lady Charles began to have no clear idea of exactly what she had accused Miss Arbuthnot. If need be, some money must be sent her and a reference written so she could get further employment. Lady Charles was pleased to come to this conclusion. She finished her letter with a few unrelated matters as if the departure of Lottie's governess was some incidental occurrence; she folded it carefully and melted the wax for the sealing of it.

Feeling restless, she thought to put it out on the hall table herself, whence it would be taken to the post. As she entered the hall she saw Horatio about to scamper up the stairs and immediately called him back. He came reluctantly, as far as could be told, but he made his bow as he should. Really, she decided, she found him an unprepossessing child. He was too skinny. Should he not be dosed or purged? She must speak to Mrs Kingston.

'Ah, Horatio, did you ring the bell? I didn't hear it. You should ring the bell.'

'I don't ring it. Slimmer nor the footman don't like opening doors just for a boy.'

Lady Charles thought this very likely. 'You should ring the bell all the same. I meant to write your mother a note. I am afraid Miss Arbuthnot is no longer with us. I take it you are here for your French.'

Horatio screwed up his face. 'When will she come back?'

'Oh, I'm not sure she will. We feel Lottie needs a new governess.'

Horatio looked at the floor and then at Lady Charles. 'Lottie and I like Miss Arbuthnot.'

'I know, but you are older than Lottie and will understand the necessity for the occasional change. Lottie is being rather difficult. You are a grown-up, sensible boy, Horatio. I wonder if you could persuade Lottie to see that a new governess will be no harm, in fact quite to the contrary, and she must settle to the idea.'

Horatio made no reply.

'You and Lottie are such friends,' Lady Charles continued. 'I am sure you are a beneficial influence on her. Of course you are clever and work hard. We will have a new governess who will speak just as good French as Miss Arbuthnot. You will be able to continue your lessons but Lottie must see a little reason first. She must also apologize to me for losing her temper. I expect your mother insists on that when it comes to yourself, but perhaps you don't lose your temper. I believe you to be level-headed and Lottie must learn from you.'

Horatio tilted his head as if he was paying Lady Charles especial attention but he was barely listening to her. He thought she said such silly things. He contemplated and rejected the idea of asking her if Lottie could come riding. She might say no. In the end he just said, 'May I go upstairs now?'

Lady Charles watched him depart. She was wondering how it was she found all children easy to manage but her own granddaughter. A little gentle flattery and Horatio was perfectly biddable.

In the schoolroom Lottie had her books open before her and Augusta propped on a chair. At the sight of Horatio she burst into tears. Horatio trawled about the room, opening and shutting cupboards and knocking into things, hoping Lottie would soon finish. He began to pull faces at her, each more hideous than the last, until she smiled despite herself.

She said, 'I can't do my lessons without Miss 'Buthnot. I tried to teach Augusta in case that would make it easier but I haven't played with her for so long she's got sort of tired and dusty. Will you see if my sums are right?'

Horatio sat down beside her and began to correct her work. Lottie's arithmetic was very good and he wrote 'very good' at the bottom of the page in his best writing. He said, 'Let's teach Augusta French. If Miss Arbuthnot were here we would be speaking French. *Parlez-vous français, Augusta? Non? Tu es très méchante*.'

This occupied them for ten minutes or so but nothing held Lottie's attention for long. Horatio thought she was too sad to think. He said, 'Why has Miss Arbuthnot gone?'

'My grandmother wouldn't say. She just sent her off like she was a parcel.'

Horatio said, 'Put on your riding-habit, Lottie.' He was afraid she might start crying again. 'Can you get it on by yourself?' The riding-habit was new, made for the winter, and Lottie had only just started to wear it.

'I won't be allowed.'

'We won't ask. York will take us. Hurry up. Are your boots here? You can't stay in the schoolroom and not get any exercise. It's bad for you. You would get like my Uncle Henry, moping about on the sofa all day.'

Lottie went to her room and lifted the habit down from its hanger in the wardrobe. She was saying to herself, I'm not helpless. Miss Arbuthnot would say, you need not be helpless. She put on the voluminous skirt, struggled with hooks and eyes, and eventually buttoned the jacket.

'I've done it,' she said to Horatio. 'Now I only have to lace my boots.'

They went down the back stairs and along innumerable

passages, hiding in corners or round doors if they thought they heard any of the servants and twice taking a wrong direction, finding themselves in mysterious pantries and unexplained cubbyholes.

Lottie said, in a whisper, 'When I'm grown-up I shall have a much smaller house.'

Out in the yard they started to search for York but he was soon found at his habitual task of tending the Andalusian. They peeped anxiously through the bars of the loosebox, suddenly unsure of their reception.

York said, 'Wondered if you lot was turning up. Saw Mr Kingston's pony in the stall.'

'We would like to go out riding, York,' Lottie said. 'Will you take us even though Miss 'Buthnot has gone away?'

'Course. Major Wilder didn't say nothin' 'bout your not going out.'

Horatio said, 'Lady Charles might be angry with you.'

'Don't care what her ladyship says. She can't sack me, not like she can some. Cut along an' get Jenny Wren's kit from the harness room, Mr Kingston, young varmint. Now, little missy, you can take this 'ere brush and smarten yer pony up, like you was a lad.'

'Oh, can I, York? Yes, please.' He had never allowed her to do such a thing before.

Patiently, he showed her how to groom the pony, starting behind one ear and working carefully down the body and under the belly.

Lottie said, 'The black bits and the white bits and the black bits again. York, why is she two colours all over?'

'Couldn't make up 'er mind,' York replied.

Lottie continued with the brush while she thought about

this. Eventually she said, frowning, 'I don't think she could choose, York, I really don't.'

Within twenty minutes they were all three mounted and crossing the park. York rode with a child on each side of him and started to tell them things. He talked of bivouacking, of Spanish villages, of how the peasants dressed and of the little boys the officers employed to look after goats. They heard how the pigs were taken out in a herd to graze on the acorns and how they knocked you down in the street when racing back to their separate homes at the end of the day. He described the fierce, wild looks of the Spanish guerrillas and how he had seen mules with their bellies shaved and different patterns decorating their rumps and of the muleteers themselves. They had never known York to talk so much. Horatio began to wish he could join the army but it would be years before he was old enough whereas the navy he could join immediately. Lottie said she would be happy to be a little boy with a goat to mind.

It was not until they were returning to Ridley that York said, 'Seems a waste you varmints learning yer letters.'

'Why?' Lottie asked, this having been her fixed opinion before the advent of Miss Arbuthnot.

'You learns yer letters so as to write things down what others can read. If yer don't do it there's no point to it. Why isn't you writing to my master an' getting 'im to set things right?'

'Write to Uncle Thomas?' Lottie said. 'I don't know how to. My grandmother wouldn't give me his address. Besides, I'm not talking to her.'

'I knows the address, course I do. I learns it off before 'e goes. I can read 'is name. 'Ave to, see, so I knows 'is billet chalked up on a door an' I can fetch 'is post or whatever. Sometimes 'tis just Thomas or the front letter. Don't know what the other letters is for but they crops up from time to time. Major the Honourable T. O. L. Wilder, RHA.' It was only when saying the word 'Honourable' that York condescended ponderously to pronounce the letter H.

'Of course,' Horatio said. 'You must write a letter, Lottie. I can write the address and post it on my way home.'

Lottie thought, Yes, I can write a letter. Did I not write one to my grandmother at the time of my cutting my hair off and she able to read all of it, or so I am told? What would Uncle Thomas say? Might he not be cross and make her do her sampler?

In the stable yard they were greeted by Hall. He said to York, 'There's a fuss and bother you took the children out without permission. Susan panicked when she couldn't find Miss Wilder.'

'Don't need no permission from her ladyship. Master said to take out the little missy an' so I will,' York replied, with unutterable calm.

Hall, whom York filled with alarm, was on this occasion in accord with him, for his sympathies lay with Miss Arbuthnot. He envied York the independence he managed to combine with a dogged attachment to the service of Major Wilder. For a moment he tried to visualize Lady Charles reprimanding York but his imagination would not stretch to it.

York said to Lottie, 'You two cut along indoors an' say your Uncle Thomas wants you to 'ave your ride every day 'cause it's good fer yer 'ealth.'

He helped her down from the pony and winked at Horatio before leading both ponies away.

Upstairs in the schoolroom Lottie got out the ink and paper. Under Horatio's eye she wrote her letter, only a few lines but it took her a good twenty minutes and two fresh attempts, for he saw no reason for it to have any mistakes in it. He said, 'Major Wilder should get this tomorrow. We will see what happens next.'

'People don't always listen to children,' Lottie replied.

Horatio knew this to be true, but he said, 'I think something will happen. In the meantime, if I were you, I should go down to dinner. What can you get to eat up here? What are you meant to eat?'

'Susan brings me bread and gruel, like you get when you are ill. I can't go down to dinner. I said I wouldn't.'

'Go down to dinner. You need not speak.'

Lady Charles wondered if she could face going down to dinner and sitting alone at the dining-table. There was something ludicrous about the proceeding with all the servants aware she was having a battle with her granddaughter, a small girl not quite ten years old, in which the granddaughter showed signs of emerging victorious. Lottie's health, which should not be risked, would suffer if she were kept on bread and gruel. Gruel had goodness in it, but it was more suited to invalids. As for York, taking Lottie out riding as if nothing had occurred, she would have to get Thomas to speak to him for she did not see how she could do it herself. She thought of her son with a determined firmness, not allowing herself to suppose their differences could not be settled in a moment.

What was the point of changing for dinner? The servants expected it of her. She must continue as if she was in command of the situation and, of course, she was in command of the situation, apart from having a very naughty, intractable child on her hands. When she entered her bedroom she found Sally laying out her clothes, carefully smoothing the silk of her mistress's gown.

Sally wished her ladyship would not keep on with the wearing of black for it didn't lift the spirit. However, she smiled and said, 'You will be pleased to hear, m'lady, Susan says Miss Wilder has decided to come down to dinner.'

'Oh, Sally, what a relief. I don't like to confess it but I was beginning to be at my wit's end what to do with the child. Darling Lottie, she has seen sense. Of course I thought she would, sooner or later, but we couldn't be sure, could we? Oh dear, how my poor heart beats, I feel quite light-headed. One should not get oneself in such a state over the antics of a child, but if I am not loved by my Lyndon's little girl . . .'

Lady Charles's voice trailed away to nothing. She thought of Lyndon. Where was he now? How could a personality, a being beautiful, powerful, masterful, loving and charming, be there one day and not the next? How could it be? And yet it was. Surely in spirit he was here at Ridley and not on some unimaginable Spanish mountain. What would the Church say? Something quite else, but it was a little hard to equate Lyndon with the Church. If only one could accept what one told the children.

'There,' Sally said. 'Perhaps all will come to rights now.'

Lady Charles took extra care with dressing. She and Lottie would have a little celebration. She would be careful not to reprimand her. Later, when they were happy and complacent in each other's company, they might have a little talk, on saying things one did not mean when one lost one's temper, but now was not the moment.

In the dining room she found Lottie already standing by her chair. Susan had brushed out her short curls and she looked clean and neat. Slimmer was bringing in soup and there was a pie on the table.

Lady Charles said, 'Well, dearest, it is a great pleasure for me to see you. Grandmama was getting lonely here on her own. How she needs her little Lottie.'

Lottie pulled out her chair and sat down. Slimmer dallied over putting the dishes straight and trimming a candle.

'That will do, Slimmer,' Lady Charles continued, watching him leave the room with his customary reluctance. She picked up the heavy silver soup ladle and delicately transferred soup to Lottie's plate. Lottie seized her spoon but she waited, not very patiently, until her grandmother was also served.

Lady Charles said, 'You and I must forgive and forget.'

Lottie made no answer. She was hungry and her soup was gone in a minute. Slimmer came back and removed the tureen. He disappeared again and Lady Charles cut the crust on the pie. She put a generous amount on Lottie's plate.

Lady Charles repeated, 'You and I must forgive and forget. Come, dearest, let's be cheerful.' She thought, almost uncomfortably, how the child grew more like her father every day.

Lottie, who had decided on saying absolutely nothing, stared fixedly at her grandmother with her round blue eyes. She said, 'I will never forgive you unless you ask Miss 'Buthnot to come back.'

Major Wilder felt responsible for his father in the same manner as one felt responsible for a child. How had it come about? He had been prepared to abandon Ridley and his parents when he was contemplating the return to the war, doing only what he thought appropriate for the management of his niece. The others had seemed like actors on a stage with whom he would have little to do once the curtain was down, especially as he could see exactly how the play was to end. Once his father had given him the power to manipulate the events, the scene had changed: he was stage manager and the responsibilities of Ridley and its occupants had become his. He thought his father exasperating yet he had become fond of him. He watched him now, in the little parlour of their lodging house, eating his breakfast in dressing-gown and slippers, buttering bits of toast and passing them down to Scottie who sat under the table in an ecstasy of tongue and tail. Major Wilder fought in his head for what he and his father might have in common. At best, he could coax from him fox-hunting anecdotes or the eccentricities of his ancestors, though these latter tended to be of the Lyndons, in whom Major Wilder took less of an interest than in his maternal forebears, from whom he received Ridley. Lord Charles declared the Wilders to be rather ordinary and that there was nothing to say about them, which his son, on reflection, considered a blessing. Lord Charles would also discourse on gaming hells, particularly those of his youth, with, as far as his critical offspring could fathom, more mild surprise at the large sums of money that could be lost than with any great sense of disapproval. At those moments the shadow of Lyndon hung between them. To his father, Major Wilder drew no parallels and discussed no business, for it would have served only to make the old man anxious.

Without anxieties Lord Charles's health had improved or he was merely stronger. The warm baths eased his limbs. He was happy in their modest lodgings. At first he had been put out by the smallness of the rooms.

Major Wilder had said, 'We have a fireplace, a window containing glass and a lively view of the street, clean beds without bugs. What more could be wanted?'

'When you were in the Peninsula,' his father asked, 'is that what you hoped for in a billet?'

'If we found any one of such things in a billet we would have thought we had been cut in two by a cannon ball and gone straight to Paradise.'

Lord Charles had laughed and become quite content. He endeavoured to imagine himself on campaign but without success.

He liked to spend time in the Pump Rooms, more to chat to old acquaintances than to take the waters. He inveigled his son to attend the Assembly Rooms of an evening and got satisfaction from pointing him out to all and sundry. Lord Charles thought how Thomas might not remotely cut such a dash as Lyndon had but there was something very fine about him, though less discernible, even without the, to his father, chilling appearance of the dark blue jacket and the red facings of an officer in the Royal Horse Artillery.

Major Wilder could see his father had come to dote on him much as he had doted on Lyndon, though he could not think to quite the same excess. The tiresome aspect of the Assembly Rooms was Lord Charles's assumption that his son would be happy to stand up and dance with the daughters and even the granddaughters of those he knew. Major Wilder thought he might not have suffered such hideous boredom at the execution of this duty if his mind and his heart had not been elsewhere. He noted Miss Arbuthnot's refusing him, which he considered absolute for he could see no reason why she should change her mind, did not alter his feelings towards her. He felt that it should, that rejection was injurious but that the wound ought to be considered trifling and that it should not be allowed to impede ordinary life. He saw he must oblige his father and dance with all those young ladies of various age and appearance, some of them pretty, prettier than Miss Arbuthnot, but without whatever it was about Miss Arbuthnot that he particularly liked, some characteristic he was unable to identify, apart from her sensible boots and her red curls and even her freckles. Perhaps all the females with whom his father required him to dance had sensible footwear when not in their dancing slippers. He wondered if Miss Arbuthnot had dancing slippers and how much opportunity she had had for wearing them, and should she have them, how he would like them perfectly well, and how he was to abandon his attachment to her while she remained at Ridley.

Major Wilder pulled out his watch. It would soon be the hour for his father to go to the baths. Having established a routine, Lord Charles could be safely ensconced in the right place with his servant to attend him while his son would be handed the leash of the frantic Scottie that he might take the little creature for a walk. The walk he made to last several hours because it was as much a necessity to himself as it was to the dog. He was about to urge his father to go and get dressed when the servant came in with the post. There was one letter for Lord Charles and several for himself. The first of these to catch his eye was written by a child, but he thought the hand too neat and careful to be Lottie's. On unfolding it he saw the letter itself was Lottie's and it ran thus:

Dear Uncle Thomas,

Please come home. My grandmother has sent Miss Arbuthnot away and I am very unhappy.

Your affectionate and dutiful niece,

Charlotte Wilder

Major Wilder's initial reaction was that such a carefully spelt little missive could not be Lottie's and was some sort of hoax. He hastily shuffled through the rest of his post in the hope of enlightenment. Seeing a letter in an unfamiliar hand that had been redirected from Ridley he opened it and read the following.

Sir,

It is with deep concern that I beg you to explain the extraordinary conduct meted out to my daughter. I understand she has been dismissed without tangible explanation, or certainly not an explanation I can believe or even contemplate for it is unthinkable and, as you will be aware, totally defamatory. She was deposited on the coach within hours of receiving her notice, indeed was required to leave at dawn, ill-equipped for the journey. As you may imagine, she arrived, having been stranded some hours in Exeter, in a state of great shock, cold and fatigue which I sincerely pray may not do lasting damage to her health.

I understand you were not at home, but I cannot help feeling, all the same, this whole sorry business results from my daughter not acceding to your wishes. Should this be the case I wish I was not in Holy Orders and, old as I am and unaccustomed to such things, could act as a father should and demand from you immediate satisfaction. My son, when not at sea, will feel obliged to do so on my behalf.

I am, sir, your servant,

Samuel Arbuthnot

Major Wilder laid this letter down on the table. He then picked it up and read it again, with an odd mixture of violent indignation and bewilderment.

Lord Charles, reading the letter addressed him by his wife, ignored her instruction to convey to Thomas what he thought appropriate, and handed him the entire content. As he watched his son skimming the pages with an expression on his face he did not think he had ever seen there before, he said, extremely confused, 'Whatever has your mother done? Why does she say you will understand it? I'm sure poor Miss Arbuthnot has done no wrong.'

Major Wilder gave him Lottie's letter and also the one from Mr Arbuthnot. Lord Charles became increasingly distressed. 'What can it be about? Why doesn't Eleanor say? Miss Arbuthnot might have caught her death on that coach. I hope she was not sitting outside, but maybe it was the mail, where there is no outside. Oh dear. We must go to Ridley. We must go home. It must be sorted out. You will have to go to Devonshire and make some explanation. I doubt Miss Arbuthnot will come back after such treatment, and nobody else managed Lottie. I can't understand how your mother came to behave in this extraordinary manner. What can she have heard?'

Major Wilder said, with a discouraging coldness, 'Whatever she may have heard, or chosen to believe, it is certainly lies.'

'I must return to Ridley. You had better go straight to Devonshire. No, you must speak with your mother first. I don't know what's for the best. What if Miss Arbuthnot is very ill?'

'What indeed?' Major Wilder replied. He then said, in his usual tone of calm authority, for he saw all the signs of his father's renewed health vanishing as if they had never been, 'You will stay here. Get dressed. Johnson will take you to the baths. You must finish your course.'

Had his father not had troubles enough in his latter years that he had been ill-designed to manage? Lord Charles's exasperating helplessness always reasserted his son's sense of it being his duty to soothe and care for him. 'There is no need for you to leave but I, obviously, shall. No, much as I desire it, I must not go to Devonshire before going to Ridley.'

'But should I not come with you?'

'Certainly not.'

'But, Thomas, what will you do? What will you say to your mother? I'm afraid of your quarrelling dreadfully. I'm sure she will have acted as she thought best, even if it seems strange to us.'

'It is more than strange to me and I have every intention of quarrelling dreadfully. You shall remain here, out of the way of it all. Now, I have a letter to write. You would be obliging me if you would go and get your clothes on.'

Lord Charles called for his servant and went away to the bedroom, Scottie clutched under his arm. Major Wilder sat down to write a hasty, furious note to his sister Georgie. Suppose Miss Arbuthnot was really ill and it his fault? Ultimately he saw it as his fault for not foreseeing in some way how his mother might act. It never had crossed his mind, though he had seen she was jealous of Miss Arbuthnot, that she might go to such extremes, or even that she might suspect some impropriety between himself and Lottie's governess. Did she not understand him better? No, she did not, she understood nothing. He was not another Lyndon, to be leaving bastard children for all to identify, should they care to do so, let alone abusing his position by one who was in his employ. He had every intention of doing rather more than quarrelling with his mother.

In a state of extreme anger combined with despair he mechanically set about arranging his departure, packing his belongings himself in order not to distract Johnson from assisting his father, and ordering a post-chaise and horses as the quickest means of returning. It was certainly not the cheapest and, amid it all, he reminded himself of the luxury of affording such things, for it was hard to shake off the habits of perpetual care and economy. He thought if there ever was a moment to overlook economy it was now, and the good-natured keeper of their lodgings did not see it as her place to ask him what took him off so white-faced and abrupt.

Lady Charles received a letter from Georgie. Slimmer brought it in on a salver while she sat in the drawing room and she made no attempt to open it until he had gone away. She had expected a letter from Lord Charles in answer to hers or, worse, from Thomas. At least the distance between them would allow Thomas, no doubt after an irrational outburst or two, time to consider the wisdom of his mother's actions. She opened Georgie's letter without enthusiasm because she recalled, at that moment, the close connection between her daughter and Mrs Hamilton, who had recommended Miss Arbuthnot in the first place. Lady Charles, conveniently overlooking her initial lack of success with Lottie's governesses, thought how unfortunate it had been that her state of mind at the time had not allowed her to choose a suitable governess herself.

My dear Mama,

Whatever is the meaning of all this? I have received a dire letter from Mrs Hamilton describing the abrupt return of poor Miss Arbuthnot to West Staverton.

There is much indignation, the whole thing so injurious to her character, sent away without notice or indeed obvious reason. She herself is in a sad way and apparently unable to comprehend, let alone pronounce, her misdemeanour, so I await with dread some really terrible pronouncement from yourself that I will feel bound, under the circumstances, to repeat to Mrs Hamilton. Oh dear, please do not delay but answer this by return.

Georgie

Lady Charles disliked this letter just as much as she had thought she would. She supposed to a married daughter it was possible to explain, but she did not feel ready for explanations, though even a besotted Georgie could not condone anything between her precious Thomas and the governess. Perhaps Georgie would think her mother had been too hasty. Could she be got to understand the necessity of parting Lottie from Miss Arbuthnot in a manner least likely to cause scenes and tantrums and without allowing Miss Arbuthnot time to appeal to Thomas? Though Lottie had not reacted in the way she had hoped, Lady Charles thought how well she had herself managed things but there was to be a difficulty in convincing others of this.

She was in need of a confidante but Georgie seemed not the right person just now and she considered Mrs Kingston, who had paid her no visit since the departure of Miss Arbuthnot. Was this by design? As Mrs Kingston had precipitated the whole incident one would have thought she might come round with her congratulations, and Lady Charles was in need of someone with whom she could discuss Lottie. She had forgotten – or, rather, had thought her granddaughter had outgrown it – how obdurate the child could be. Lottie came down to dinner, ate but would not speak. Lady Charles forbade her to come down to dinner unless she could behave herself. Lottie came down to dinner all the same so Slimmer laid a place for her. If she was to be forcibly removed, who was to do it? Could she be locked in her room? She would soon get round Susan and escape in a minute. What would the servants say? Lady Charles was aware of the undignified nature of the deadlock. She forbade Lottie to go out on the pony but York took her all the same. She had summoned Hall and told him York was not to take Miss Wilder out, but Hall had replied he had as much control over York as he had over the city of the same name, a comment Lady Charles thought impertinent. She was not accustomed to servants who did not do as they were asked, but York was Thomas's man so what could she do? It was peculiar to have come to such a pass with a child, to whom neither threats nor pleadings made the smallest difference. Was not Lottie the most precious thing remaining to her?

After a great deal of rumination she decided she must send for the carriage and call on Mrs Kingston. She might do this with gracious condescension. She would suggest Mrs Kingston had been indisposed for she disliked to think there might be the smallest misunderstanding between them. She laid her hand on the bell but before she could ring it the door was thrust open. Thomas stood before her, white-faced, tired and without having gone to his rooms to make himself respectable before greeting his mother, dust on his clothes, mud on his boots. Her first reaction was to note how extremely angry he looked, which confirmed in her mind that he was not in the least innocent and that she had caught him out. He had flown, as Georgie would have put it, into one of his passions, and though she had half expected it, the reality alarmed her more than she had supposed it would.

He said, with extreme abruptness, 'I have a letter here from Mr Arbuthnot. You had better read it. Should his son wish to shoot me dead, I would let him. There would not be an ounce of justification in my defending myself. Still, that's all of little moment. Our conduct, as a family, has been dishonourable, and that I do mind.'

Lady Charles, pale herself, took the letter and read it, as she was bid. She felt faint with horror. She had foreseen nothing of such further consequences of her dismissing Miss Arbuthnot.

Major Wilder then said something else she was not expecting. 'What you have overlooked is that Lottie is my ward and her governess is paid by the trustees of her mother's estate. You have no authority to either choose or dismiss her governesses.'

Lady Charles said, 'Oh, but, Thomas, I was merely doing what was expedient at the time.'

'On what ground was your decision made?'

'You surely know.'

'I can think of no reason whatsoever for anyone to be dismissed in the manner I understand Miss Arbuthnot to have been dismissed.'

'But it was for your own good, Thomas, and for Lottie's.

There should be nothing clandestine or irregular about the person in charge of a child.'

'You make an assumption I find extraordinarily offensive.'

'You cannot, I believe, deny there is some sort of relationship between yourself and Miss Arbuthnot.'

'I can deny it, though I wish it otherwise. I asked her to marry me. She refused me. Beyond that, there is, and never can be, anything. She asked me if she should seek another post. For Lottie's sake and for hers, because she loves Lottie, I said no. I told her I was going to Bath and that by the time I returned she was to have put the incident behind her. You, in one stroke, have ruined her name and formed a wholly defamatory opinion of my character.'

Lady Charles was too stunned to reply. Eventually she almost whispered, 'How could I have known? How could she refuse you? How could you so disgrace your name by endeavouring to make such an ill-considered match?'

'How can you talk of disgrace? It was not in the least ill-considered. Miss Arbuthnot's misfortune is poverty. That is certainly viewed as some sort of sin, but one I was prepared to overlook. Have I not known myself how to live on a shoestring?'

Lady Charles still could not believe what she heard. It was inconceivable, for a start, that Miss Arbuthnot could have refused him. Did they not tell her Miss Arbuthnot was clever? There could not be the least clever thing about her. She said, 'How could she possibly have refused you?'

'For exactly the sort of reason I wished to marry her. A sort of independence of spirit. The idea I might wish to marry her had not occurred to her, and it had no particular appeal, however practical. She was not prepared to marry me for the sake of it. She had the courage to refuse me.'

Lady Charles could not understand independence of spirit and did not see it as a necessary commodity in a wife, but rather to the contrary. Neither did she think it likely Miss Arbuthnot could have refused him, though it was not the minute to accuse him of lying. She said, 'How could I guess or believe such a thing? She didn't tell it me.'

Major Wilder shrugged. 'And would you have believed her had she done so?' He paused for a moment to consider Miss Arbuthnot's failure to defend herself with the truth: he dared not suppose it was done for his sake. He said, 'Your treatment of Miss Arbuthnot was unforgivable. I am not likely to forgive it myself.'

Lady Charles wavered momentarily in her conviction, her sense of rectitude, and was slightly appalled, if every word he spoke was true and she supposed he believed it, at the injustice she had done Miss Arbuthnot. Despite this she was thankful she had acted as she had: Miss Arbuthnot was unlikely ever to consider returning and Thomas's desire to marry her she viewed as much worse than anything else she had visualized.

Hoping to sound contrite, she said, 'I now see I misjudged Miss Arbuthnot, for which I am sorry, but I never could have foreseen the circumstances. What should be done?' She wondered what he might suggest in the way of compensation and found it difficult to remember they were discussing the woman he professed a desire to marry.

'Of course I must go down to Devonshire but here and now I know what I intend to do.'

'And what is that?'

'You will see.'

Nervous, she watched him ring the bell for Slimmer, who, as ever, was not far away and now bobbed obsequiously in the doorway.

Major Wilder said, briskly, 'Send me Susan, York and after that Miss Wilder, in that order.'

'In here, sir, Susan and York?' Slimmer asked, incredulously.

'Now.' Major Wilder had only to raise his voice a little.

They were silent while waiting for Susan, Major Wilder turning his back on his mother and standing at the window while she wondered, not without some vague apprehension, why he should wish to speak to Susan. Within minutes Susan appeared, worried and abject.

Major Wilder came away from the window and said, 'Good morning, Susan. Miss Wilder's clothes must be packed and any toys or books she likes particularly. I am sending her to Gloucestershire. I believe Mrs Heugmont was a favourite of yours.'

'Oh, yes, sir, thank you, sir, Miss Georgie as she was, or so I called her, always sweet-tempered. Be I to go with Miss Lottie?'

'Would you like to?'

Susan, who was not often given choices, hesitated, confused, but then she said, 'Seems I should mind Miss Lottie like I always have, be the house strange or no. Miss Lottie doesn't take to everyone, sir, so I 'spect it's for the best.'

'Thank you, Susan. How long will you need to pack?'

'If someone do get the boxes down for me and I starts now, an hour or so.'

'Could you be ready by midday?'

'Yes, sir.'

'Pack for yourself first and say nothing to Miss Lottie until I have seen her.'

'Yes, sir.' Susan bustled away, musing on the abrupt manner in which a life could be turned about, even at her age.

Lady Charles rose and stretched out pleading hands to her son but he seemed not to see her. York entered the room as Susan left it. He had kicked off his boots and there was a hole in the toe of his left stocking.

'Thought of the carpet, see,' he said, eyeing Major Wilder with a certain reproach but ignoring Lady Charles.

Major Wilder said, 'Ah, York. All well?'

'Yes, sir.'

'Unpack my portmanteau and start again with clean shirts and suchlike, what I might require for five or six days. I am going to Devonshire. I need you to take Miss Wilder and Susan to Gloucestershire. Take the carriage but it must come straight back. The pony must go and the grey Miss Arbuthnot rode. The Andalusian and the dogs had better be here for the time being. Put someone you trust to mind them. Decide how best to do it all and don't squabble with Hall. I am, by the way, very pleased to see you. We shall all leave at midday. You have the route for Finch Hall, I think.'

York said, 'Yes, sir.' He pulled from his pocket a silver watch he had stolen from a dead Frenchman, eyed it carefully, put it back, grunted and left the room. He found Lottie hovering on the other side of the door.

He said to her, 'Well, little missy, here's a fine to-do.'

'Is my uncle Thomas cross, York?'

'Why, yes, 'e certainly is cross all right. Mighty fine temper Major Wilder 'as, somethin' special. I've always 'ad an admiration for it, fair made them gunners an' drivers 'op, an' them captains and the Mr Thises an' Thats, but 'e don't shout nor nothin'.'

'I'm afraid to go in.'

'Don't be daft. Get on in an' give 'im an 'ug.'

'But I've been so naughty,' Lottie said, but York was already halfway across the hall. Cautiously she pushed the door open.

Major Wilder said, 'Don't skulk, Lottie. Am I to have no kiss?'

Lottie ran across the room and flung herself against him, bursting into a passion of tears. He picked her up and sat her down on the nearest chair. 'Uncle Thomas,' she said, between sobs, 'I did something so bad.'

'And what was that, *niña*?'

'I don't like to tell.'

'I don't mean to be here all day, so you had better get on with it.'

'I burnt my sampler. I put it on the nursery fire, which I'm never to touch on my own, case I get cooked to a turn, like Susan's aunty. When it was all burnt I thought of those carrots and things Miss 'Buthnot had taken care to draw for me and I wished I could get it back off the fire but it was too late.'

'The things we do in haste we tend to regret.'

'So will you think up some really bad punishment?'

'No, certainly not. There is quite punishment enough. Besides, I am sending you to Finch Hall, to your aunt Georgie, so you must help Susan pack your clothes.'

Lottie looked astonished. 'What will happen to Jenny Wren and my vegetable garden?'

'Jenny Wren is to go with you. You must ask your aunt for a new piece of ground for gardening.'

'And Miss 'Buthnot? York said if I wrote you would make everything right.'

'I can make no promises but I am going to Devonshire in order to see her. I can't say more. You must settle down and do what your aunt tells you. You will have lessons so you must be good. I don't expect to hear of any nonsense.'

'But can't I come with you to see Miss 'Buthnot?'

'No.'

'When am I to go to my aunt?'

'Now.'

'Will you be there?'

'After I have seen Miss Arbuthnot I shall pay a visit. Susan is to go with you. Now, run along and help her.'

Lottie, torn between excitement and misgiving, was glad to think Susan would be there. She left the room with a doubtful skip, not once having addressed her grandmother, as if, indeed, her grandmother did not exist.

Lady Charles said to Major Wilder, 'You are taking the child from me, the one being I have reason to value above all else in this world.'

'Yes, I am,' he replied. 'What did you expect?'

'You are punishing me.'

'The punishment is incidental. I believe it best for Lottie. Georgie has always been prepared to take her. I don't think there could be a more appropriate moment for her to go.'

Lady Charles thought, If I write to Georgie and say how sad and unhappy I am, Georgie will send her back, but it was wild thinking and she knew Georgie would not send Lottie back. She would just add her to her own innumerable brood and barely notice the extra child.

The Reverend Samuel Arbuthnot, seated in his study, his feet stretched, almost hopefully, towards the empty grate, for no fire was lit until the evening fell, was at none of his usual occupations of writing letters or sermons. He was a tall man with large, severe features and a quantity of white hair. He was a little too tall to be quite at home in his vicarage. The rooms were on the small side and the kitchen arrangements hugger-mugger with the parlour and the dining room; his study, entirely lined with books and completely dark, was about two foot too small in all directions, his desk too close to the door and the one window overlooking a modest square of grass and the cabbage patch. Despite these disadvantages, for Mr Arbuthnot had been brought up in more spacious surroundings, he thanked the Lord each day for what he had, his girls making a neat and tidy home of it, as had his wife before them. Even now Minette had placed some sprigs of briar rose in a jug, where their bright autumn hips cheered the side table beneath a youthful portrait of his father in clerical bands and a white-powdered wig.

His thoughts were of his eldest daughter. Her too sudden and mournful reappearance was a source of anxious concern to him. At first he was only anxious for her health but in his endeavours to understand her situation he had become increasingly enraged not only on her behalf but on the way this episode would reflect on the reputation and standing of his family. The loss of her salary, which she had always so dutifully sent home, would be felt, but he did his best to console himself on the ground that they had managed before and they would manage again: it ought to be but a small part of the damage done, yet he was more than aware of its significance.

His relationship with her had not been the same since he had been so violently disappointed by her disinclination to marry Major Wilder. He accused himself of worldliness, of putting Mammon before all else, but she surely could have settled to making Major Wilder a dutiful wife. Why would it have been such a sacrifice when her general prospects were so dismal?

Now, since this disaster had come upon them and the likelihood of his daughter getting another post was small, he began to think his Anna a sounder judge of character then he would ever have believed. The less they had to do with the Wilders the better. Whereas before he had pointed out all of Major Wilder he knew, on brief acquaintance, to be good, now he thought his name must never be mentioned, though Anna herself declared she did not suppose Major Wilder had known anything about it. Mr Arbuthnot certainly did not believe her right and had sent off his letter, though he did not judge it sensible to tell her of it. It was a question of honour and it had had to be done, but honour was not a thing understood by women. Much as he wished honour satisfied he was at the same time deeply grateful to the Lord for Bobby being on the far side of the Atlantic.

As several days had gone by without his receiving an answer, his opinion of Major Wilder had sunk yet lower, so he was taken by surprise when his only female servant pushed the door open and said, 'That gentleman what came to see you before, sir. He's stood in the hall.'

No one was ever refused entry to the vicarage, however inconvenient the moment.

'Which gentleman?' Mr Arbuthnot asked, looking up.

'The military gentleman what came before but I didn't get his name.' Mrs Abigael was rather deaf but she was aware of some peculiar significance attached to the visitor so she spoke in an exaggerated whisper.

Mr Arbuthnot rose hastily from his chair, full of consternation. He had intended, should Major Wilder appear, to refuse him entry but he said, 'You had better show him in.' He thought it odd, the difficulty of adhering to the strategy he had thought would be best. For a tiny second he recalled himself, a very young man, turned away from the door of his wife's family to whom he had gone to plead for a reconciliation. Perhaps turning people away was not an answer.

Major Wilder looked composed but Mr Arbuthnot thought him not so, that appearing composed was second nature to a soldier. It certainly would be a mistake, in military circumstances, to be seen to be disconcerted at times of crisis. Major Wilder did look tired, very tired, and that could not be disguised.

They made no attempt to shake hands and neither spoke until Mr Arbuthnot, finding the silence too much, said, 'I am surprised, sir, at your temerity in coming here.'

'It was necessary. I have come to apologize.'

'What good will that do?'

'It seems churlish to refuse an apology, it being part of

repentance. You see, I must take the responsibility, though I was in ignorance of it. I did not foresee something going so wrong, but I should have done so. I hope you will believe the circumstances mortify me and I see an apology as inadequate, though it is the best I can do.'

'The best you could do is to write my daughter a reference so she may get other employment. You must see it is very disagreeable to me that she needs employment. Otherwise I will, I suppose, have to believe what you say.'

'I should like to speak to Miss Arbuthnot myself.'

'Certainly not. You ask too much. I believe her in a delicate state. Anything you wish to say you must say through me.'

'Unless I see her, how can I be satisfied she is well or as well as can be expected? I wish to make amends, as much as I can.'

'It would be inappropriate. I can't allow it.'

Major Wilder said, with perfect smoothness, 'In which case I shall stay at the inn and come here every day until I do see her or you change your mind.'

Mr Arbuthnot was alarmed that he might be as good as his word: he thought of the embarrassment it would cause him in the parish, of the gossip. He then thought, with a lightening of his heart, Is it possible Major Wilder intends to renew his proposal and Anna see some sense? He said, 'Stay here. I will speak to my daughter.'

Major Wilder, alone in the little study, paced about. He wondered, for the millionth time, how his mother could have done as she had and the exact nature of the conversation between herself and Miss Arbuthnot, the slurs, the implications, some of which he hoped might, through sheer innocence, have been lost on Miss Arbuthnot, but he burnt with indignation while the prospect of seeing her made him anxious. What if she should decline to see him?

Mr Arbuthnot returned. 'My daughter is in the parlour. You may not, of course, see her alone.'

Major Wilder thought of what he wished to say to Miss Arbuthnot and that he would not say it while her father looked on. They went through to the parlour, which he saw to be a family room, sewing spread about, silks and a skein of wool, a book open on the table, a Paisley shawl laid over the back of a chair, a spinet, and French windows, with blue and white striped curtains, overlooking the modest garden. In the midst of it, Miss Arbuthnot rose to greet him, pale, rings under her eyes, and nervous, naturally, at the sight of him but not, he opined from her expression, holding him to blame, yet he felt to blame for everything.

Miss Arbuthnot said, as she saw something had to be said, 'I was not expecting you.' This was very true: she had not expected him.

Major Wilder, apart from giving her a small bow, said nothing. Mr Arbuthnot thought Major Wilder did not mind silences. He watched him cross to the windows and then, looking back at Anna, he did say, 'You have a pretty garden.'

Miss Arbuthnot said, 'It was my mother's. It isn't very big. Would you like to see it?'

'Yes.'

Mr Arbuthnot said, 'Now, Anna, don't tire yourself. You ought not to go out.' It again occurred to him that Major Wilder might wish to renew his proposal, yet he did not wish to leave them alone together. He thought, under the circumstances, that to be improper, yet he hesitated to offer to take Major Wilder into the garden himself. He could also see Major Wilder would out-manoeuvre him, and Anna too: he had a sensation of helplessness to which he was unaccustomed.

Major Wilder said, 'You mustn't go out without a shawl.' He reached and took the shawl from the back of the chair. 'Perhaps this is yours.' He noted it was worn and thin.

Miss Arbuthnot wrapped it round her shoulders. Major Wilder was frowning to himself because he thought the shawl inadequate.

Mr Arbuthnot, in a dilemma, said, 'You will get cold, Anna. I can't allow you to go out.'

'It isn't cold,' she replied. 'Please close the windows after us to keep the warmth in the house.'

Miss Arbuthnot thought that, despite her situation, she no longer did exactly as her father bid. Stepping briskly through the French windows with Major Wilder behind her, she watched him push them to himself before he said wryly, while still turned half away, 'If you did not expect me to come you must have a very poor opinion of my character. No wonder you declined to marry me.'

The grass was frosted but the sun was out. Miss Arbuthnot endeavoured to think of an appropriate reply but he saved her the difficulty by hastily continuing, 'I must, however, take the blame for what occurred.'

'But why is that?' she asked.

'I should have foreseen it, or something like it.'

'I don't see how anyone could have foreseen it.'

'I never thought my mother so observant as to notice any change in my attitude towards yourself.'

This, Miss Arbuthnot thought, though she made no comment, was not surprising, when she considered he had been sufficiently discreet for her not to notice it herself. He looked tired, even exhausted, and she wondered at herself for being concerned at his possible suffering.

'Also,' he continued, 'I should have reminded Lady Charles that Miss Wilder is my ward. She has no jurisdiction over her or her governesses.'

'I had no idea of that.' Miss Arbuthnot was startled but did not think she could have made use of the information at the time. 'But how is my dear little pupil? That is what haunts me most. One should not, I know, in the position of a governess, become quite so fond of one's charge, but I did.'

Major Wilder suddenly smiled. 'Lottie took her revenge on her grandmother in more ways than one. She burnt her sampler on the nursery fire.'

Neither of them could help a little laughter, but Miss Arbuthnot said, 'Well, that was indeed naughty, and so I would have told her.'

'But she regretted it because you had drawn the carrots in the border.'

He noticed Miss Arbuthnot had hastily to wipe away tears.

He then said, 'I cannot ever expect you to return to Ridley but I have removed my niece to my sister, Mrs Heugmont, in Gloucestershire. They have a large nursery there and several governesses. My sister is perfectly happy for you to join them and continue in charge of Lottie. There is a little girl roughly Lottie's age whom you might not mind to share her lessons. I don't know if you would even contemplate this proposal, but if you should, my sister is anxious for you to speak French to all her children. The other governesses are older than you, very pleasant, but their French cannot have the polish of one brought up to speak it. You see, my sister is full of schemes for your employ, but I am afraid, after what occurred, it is wrong even to ask it of you.'

They had walked side by side to the bottom of the garden where there were a few crooked apple trees and a damson. Miss Arbuthnot picked up a windfall apple where it had been missed in the long grass and turned it over carefully in her hands. She seemed lost in contemplation.

Major Wilder said, 'I dare say you will need time to think about it.'

'Of course I don't,' she said, meeting his gaze and nearly laughing. 'It would make me so happy.' She paused before adding, with what he saw as a perfectly natural awkwardness, 'The only thing that would be of concern to me is that I should prefer Mrs Heugmont to know anything there is to know about me, in regards to yourself, that is.'

'When I wrote to my sister, I told her all. I had to.' Major Wilder thought of the letter he had written to Georgie, which had been as abrupt as he could make it considering the topics to be covered: Lottie, Miss Arbuthnot, his mother, his father and the fact that he had precipitated the whole disaster by his desire to marry his niece's governess. Georgie had written back even more briefly, for she knew when not to waste words on her brother, but starting, 'My dearest Thomas, What confusion. By all means send Lottie, though my mother may never speak to me again, Susan, Miss Arbuthnot if she cares to come, for the latter is surely better here, out from under your eye.' She had gone on to express astonishment at the conduct of Lady Charles, but her general tone was the one she had been prone to adopt when he was a small boy and had got himself into a scrape.

Major Wilder then said, putting his sister's correspondence out of his mind as well as he could, 'There was a necessity to tell my mother. I had not intended to tell anyone, but there we are.' He shrugged his shoulders dismissively.

'I will trust you to do all that is best,' Miss Arbuthnot said. 'It need not be of account. Why, I could start out tomorrow. Of course I shall speak French and do whatever is required of me.' Her mind ran on, full of joy.

Major Wilder thought of the long evenings at Ridley without Lottie or Miss Arbuthnot. He settled into despondency but the happiness in Miss Arbuthnot's face was a reward of a sort. 'You must take a proper rest before setting out for Gloucestershire.'

They returned indoors, where Mr Arbuthnot awaited them. When he saw the radiant look on his Anna's face and the way she ran up to give him an affectionate kiss, he assumed his earnest desire for her happiness and, he admitted, his, was accomplished. When the truth was revealed that she was still to be employed, to be shortly reunited with her dear little charge, and that alone made her so joyful, he was a little grumpy and inclined to make difficulties, all of which were brushed aside by his daughter. He realized he must be civil to Major Wilder and asked him if he had breakfasted, but after settling the details of Miss Arbuthnot's immediate future, Major Wilder declined to stay.

Miss Arbuthnot stood in the porch of the front door to watch him go, to watch his back as he walked down the straight path to the little gate leading on to the muddy lane that constituted West Staverton's high street. She had the sense of saying goodbye to him. Of course it was not that she would never again see him, for she knew he visited his sister from time to time, but she felt a parting of their ways, for Ridley, sparsely inhabited, invited intimacy, whereas at Finch Hall, thronged with family, staff, governesses, tutors and nursemaids, it would be very different. Apart from taking a proper interest in the progress of his niece, he would not, she thought, seek her out, but would school himself to direct his attention elsewhere. His fancy for her was surely a passing thing but she ended her reflections with a sense of confusion and loss. She thought of running after him, of calling him back so she might say something more, but what more could be said?

Lord Charles, disconsolate, wondered if anything could ever be exactly right again. Yes, he was agreeably free from anxiety concerning the estate, he had complete faith in his son's management of all their affairs, but the domestic dramas that had taken place while he was in Bath had left him disagreeably at odds with his wife. Now, hugging Scottie in his arms for comfort, he tried to puzzle why Eleanor had acted towards Miss Arbuthnot in the way she had. She would only tell him, reluctantly, that she thought Thomas had become too fond of her. Why, if that was the case, had she not spoken to Thomas? Thomas, he was sure, would have denied all. The result of the whole horrid business was his being deprived of Lottie, whom he missed extremely, and Miss Arbuthnot, whom he found, inexplicably, he also missed. He had taken to writing to Lottie and she answered his letters in a big, round, careful script, which delighted him. Her letters had many mistakes but what did it matter? They were charming. Miss Arbuthnot did not inhibit her pupil by correcting every word. He could not help reflecting on his age. Would he see the child again before he died? It was a question he could have put to Thomas but Thomas had a soldier's attitude to death, both brisk and practical, which made his father hesitate to make so maudlin an enquiry.

His wife and his son remained furious with one another, though the civilities were just maintained. Thomas, understandably, in apparent desperation at the general unpleasantness of his existence, threw himself into fox-hunting, and all that could be seen of him was a glimpse in passing. He was rarely home in time for dinner though when he was he devoted his hours to his father, allowing him to win innumerable games of chess or draughts, only winning himself when his mind was elsewhere. Once or twice a week, when he was not hunting, Thomas would ride out with him, the business of the estate uppermost in his mind.

On one such occasion Lord Charles ventured to ask if Lottie was ever to come home.

Major Wilder replied, 'While she needs Miss Arbuthnot, no. We cannot expect Miss Arbuthnot to return to Ridley.'

Lord Charles said, 'No, indeed,' for he did see this clearly, but then he suggested Lottie might come while Miss Arbuthnot visited her family.

Major Wilder shrugged. 'Perhaps Lady Charles had better make it up with Lottie first.'

'But she doesn't write to Lottie herself, she just writes cross letters to Georgie.'

'Perhaps she doesn't know what to say. What could she say? "I am your grandmother and it is your duty to be fond of me"? I suppose a reconciliation between Miss Arbuthnot and Lady Charles would bring Lottie about, but I don't see why Miss Arbuthnot should ever forgive her treatment. I am aware it is wrong for the child to be estranged from her grandparents, but there is no reason why you should not see her at Finch Hall. I would take you there myself.'

'Your mother would never forgive me.'

Again Lord Charles thought of his relationship with his wife. He concluded she blamed him for Lyndon's death but had previously not allowed such a notion to take hold of her. It had always been underlying, he supposed, hinted at, and now, deprived of Lyndon's child, God alone knew how her mind worked. Would she ever forgive him anything? Was he to live the rest of his life in this horrid disharmony? If Thomas was home for dinner or not, it was the time of day he had to encounter his wife and pretend some sort of normality: he was thankful when it was over and he could creep into his favourite chair and get Scottie up on to his lap.

Major Wilder was aware of making his father wretched. He thought they were all wretched and he saw no end to it. A few days later he further reflected on the matter while hacking back from hunting. He decided he must, one way or another, contrive to get his father to Finch Hall for at least a month; to stay at Ridley under the present circumstances must be detrimental to his health. He pursued various options in his mind until reminded of the route home by his horse taking a correct turning, without instruction, which might otherwise have been missed. He was riding the liver chestnut he had retained from those horses that had belonged to Lyndon. To his surprise, it had turned out a capital hunter, perhaps his best, though Lyndon had not favoured it. If Lyndon could have seen him now, astride the horse, watching the same pair of long ears and floppy ginger mane with which he must have been familiar, jogging along the dirty lanes in the direction of Ridley, he would have been first annoyed, if only that his younger brother was alive to ride the horse and he was not, and then scornful: in Lyndon's eyes, getting a tired horse home from hunting was a job for a groom. It was hard to imagine Lyndon dead. Major Wilder had no conception of his brother haunting him but he saw that Lyndon's death would shape the lives of those he had left behind, and it was this that made him ask why Lyndon could not leave them all alone.

He reached Ridley in the dusk and rode straight round to the stable yard. York appeared and led the horse away. Major Wilder was pleased at how well York had adapted to looking after hunters, of which he had no previous experience, while still being prepared to mind his master's clothes. He followed him into the stables to talk to him and immediately noticed Horatio Kingston's pony tied up in a stall. He said, 'Is that child living here? Does he ever attend his lessons?'

'Lonely,' York replied, beginning to unsaddle the chestnut by the light of a lantern. 'As for lessons, 'e don't need 'em, what 'e 'as in 'is 'ead already. Blimey, 'e 'mazes me entirely with 'is chatter, ancient Romans an' suchlike folk, the 'orse what was all of a fright at its own shadow. Couldn't never 'ave turned out any good, I say, not worth nothin'. I puts Master Kingston to work, quieten 'im for a while, an' 'e shapes well as a stable lad, though I don't fancy it's what 'is ma wants for 'im, poor mite, small for 'is age an' gentry too, no shortage of rations. Gentry is peculiar with their brats, sendin' 'em off to school an' such, some 'orrid ship. Don't she love 'im? If she knew what you an' me knows about ships, she wouldn't never do it.'

Major Wilder listened patiently to what was, for York, whose vision of the Royal Navy was coloured by his being interminably seasick, an extremely long speech. When it was over, he said, 'I dare say it does seem odd.' His own mind went back, with an uncomfortable jerk, to his first day at school, the bewildering passages down which lurked, somewhere, Lyndon's study. He then said, 'Where is Master Kingston now?'

'At work on the Andalusian. I lets 'im. I know the 'orse is choosy but 'e minds out to the lad.' York spoke carefully, in case Major Wilder was to question his actions. He then said, puzzled, 'The Andalusian is more of a 'uman than what 'orses are of a general run.'

Major Wilder agreed with him. He walked through the stables to find Horatio, under the light of another lantern, his jacket off and his sleeves rolled up, industriously grooming the stallion, the rug folded back on its loins. The boy looked up when he saw him and smiled.

'Well, Horatio,' Major Wilder said, 'don't you go home for dinner?'

‘I have been home, sir, and come back again.’

‘It’s dark.’

‘I don’t mind the dark . . . or not too much. The pony knows the way. I like it better here with York and the Andalusian.’

‘But what of your lessons?’

‘I don’t do them. I’m teaching myself French. I practise on the Andalusian. I believe him to have a little French.’ He ran the brush down the grey flank of the stallion, who did his normal trick of swinging his head round in mock ferocity, making a grab at Horatio’s seat but not actually engaging his teeth in the cloth.

‘*Monsieur l’Andalusian, je vous en prie de ne pas manger mes pantalons*. Mr Andalusian, I beg of you not to eat my trousers. Could it be done in Latin? O Andalusian . . . no, I don’t believe he has Latin.’ Horatio turned back to Major Wilder and added, confidentially, ‘Sometimes I think I’ll run away.’

Major Wilder was standing within the loosebox now, his back leant against the railings. He said, ‘It can turn out a mistake.’ The Andalusian, pleased to see him, stretched out its nose and blew in his face.

Horatio said, ‘Do you think so? They would catch me and send me back.’

‘Very likely. Perhaps you shouldn’t tell me where you intend to go.’

‘But you are my friend.’

‘So I hope, but if one sees a friend committing some act one knows to be unwise, is it not one’s duty to prevent it if one can? If I thought you were going to jump in the river, should I not pull you back? Still, it’s a difficult one, for I'm sure such acts have spoilt many a friendship.'

'But, sir, I should only run off to Gloucestershire to see Lottie.'

'Certainly my sister would welcome you, but her conscience would make her relieve your mother's anxiety by returning you.'

'But perhaps not immediately.'

'Perhaps not on the same day.'

Horatio was silent.

Major Wilder then said, 'And it was I who sent Lottie away.'

'You were not thinking of me at the time.'

'No, though I have thought of you since. I mean to go to Finch Hall myself for a month or so, take my hunters if I can find accommodation for them. I have already helped fill the stables of my long-suffering brother-in-law.'

'Why, I could come with you . . . I could disguise myself as your stable lad and make myself useful.'

'You're a fanciful boy. Why should it be necessary?'

'So I could go with you.'

Major Wilder thought, If I am to find a means of taking my father, why not the child too and anyone else who cares to go? 'Would your mother allow you to go?'

Horatio studiously bent to brush under the belly of the Andalusian, keeping his face averted. He said, 'If you asked her . . . she would.'

Lady Charles thought her life had become intolerable. There was nothing to lift the greyness of each day. Under the excuse of mourning, she had let it be known she saw no one but her family, with the exception of Mrs Kingston and the rector, for the latter one could not escape. She had decided it was the state she preferred and it was a homage to her son, but now she wondered if it remained preferable. To see people would be painful, but maybe after the first ten minutes old habits would reassert themselves and she would converse much as she used to. Would it not help relieve the tedium of the day? Should she order the carriage and call on neighbours? They had, in fact, few neighbours from which to choose.

She saw the late-autumn-early-winter sunshine streaked across the lawns. She would go outside. She would walk in the garden. That was what people did, they walked in the garden. Was it not the purpose of a garden? It was rare for her to take advantage of it. She had used to go out of doors to watch her pretty children playing on the grass, but her pretty children grew up and departed. The gardens had lost their appeal and, unloved, they had decayed, though tended, she supposed, in a rudimentary fashion. Without an agent, Lord Charles had managed little. He had become inept and childlike.

Lady Charles rang the bell for Slimmer. Sally was to bring her a cloak and some half-boots. It was probably wet underfoot.

Once in the garden she noted what she had previously not cared to acknowledge: things had changed and there was no longer evidence of neglect. There were no weeds on the terrace and the fountains worked. A gardener was at that moment sweeping up the last of the leaves and heaping them, a rich dark russet, into a barrow. The edge of the carriage sweep was neatly chiselled from the soft turf and fresh gravel had been laid. She wished she had a purpose for being out of doors beyond aimless wandering. Such had never been her habit. A walk should have direction. She used to think the garden mourned for Lyndon, but that was fanciful for it had taken only another hand to dispel that sorrowful neglect. She was disturbed to find herself comparing how it would have been had Thomas died and Lyndon returned. Surely such thoughts were wicked. Lyndon would not have so arbitrarily usurped his father's place or sold the house in Stratton Street, and it was mere daydreaming to imagine him organizing the day-to-day business of the estate, which would have driven him to paroxysms of boredom. Another agent would have been employed, but what was the harm in that? A gentleman need not be suited to business: much of it must surely be beneath his notice.

Lady Charles, methodically going from one part of the garden to another, found herself crossing the strip of ground given over to currant bushes and hazelnuts and opening the small door in the wall that led to the kitchen gardens. There, among the cordoned apples and neat squares, was Lottie's vegetable patch. It was still in good order, much as she had left it, a row of beans a few inches high, to take their chance over winter, and some cabbages. Lady Charles chided herself that she had not spent more time with her granddaughter, had not better entered into her enthusiasms, but Lottie's enthusiasms were so bizarre. She would, of course, have grown out of them and come to something more decorous, but perhaps not under the influence of Miss Arbuthnot.

She again thought how right she had been to part with

Miss Arbuthnot, although she would not have done so, had she foreseen the consequences, Miss Arbuthnot's influence now paramount. Under Georgie's management, so many children, who was guiding and supervising? Thomas was Lottie's guardian, but of what use was he, with this extraordinary partiality he had for the governess? Lady Charles hesitated to say he was in love. It was too emotive and romantic. It had nothing to do with reality and rang of excess. There was something vulgar about it, too extreme, not quite gentlemanly, though she acknowledged the condition overtook the most unexpected of people and they seemed unable to adjust. She tried to remember herself at seventeen. What had she felt for Lord Charles? A proper sense of affection and respect for the man to whom she had plighted her troth. The choosing of her trousseau, the bustle of her wedding day here at Ridley, her husband's kindly and indulgent disposition, had all aided in confirming to her how fond she was of him. She had learnt to love him dearly. Had she put aside romantic and tender thoughts of other suitors, perhaps younger than Lord Charles? No, she thought not. It had been easy. Was he not handsome and the son of a duke? What was more, he had been a faithful and devoted husband.

Now all was awry. Since Lyndon's death she and Lord Charles had not understood one another. She knew he was confused and upset by her treatment of Miss Arbuthnot. She could not explain to him those dire thoughts that had assailed her at the time, the wrongful conclusions to which she had leapt with such alacrity. He would be too mortified at the direction in which her mind had run. She still felt justified when she considered the matter overall. Was not Miss Arbuthnot removed from under the eye of a strangely vulnerable Thomas? Was this not a triumph? But, as it was, Thomas was vengeful, her husband estranged and Lottie gone.

She began to calculate what she had to do to get Lottie back. It was absurd that Lottie's fondness for her governess separated the child from her own grandmother, or was it Thomas's inexplicable fondness for Miss Arbuthnot that caused the separation? Lady Charles was aware her parents, her husband, her children had all loved her, had all striven to please her, but not Thomas, who behaved like God and, though she was his mother, did little to accommodate her wishes beyond a dutiful compliance with matters of minor importance.

If she could not influence Thomas, she must engineer a reconciliation with Miss Arbuthnot, but short of making an apology, humbling and humiliating, she did not see how it was to be done. Turning her back on the kitchen garden she returned, more purposefully, to the house.

Twenty minutes later she was seated at her bureau with a pen newly sharpened in her hand. After a great deal of careful thought she wrote:

Dear Miss Arbuthnot,

You may be surprised at my writing but it has come to my mind that I must make you a sincere apology. I made assumptions that were incorrect and therefore acted in a manner that was misguided. The truth was withheld.

It took Lady Charles some time to get thus far for it did not come naturally but, having got over the worst, she was able to continue in fine style:

Of course I could have no idea of my son's intentions towards you and you behaved very sensibly in refusing him. It must have been a sacrifice but I dare say you could see how his father would disown him and how disruptive it would have been to the family, so, in the end, perhaps not to your advantage. You are a sensible girl and will understand how a man returned from a long sojourn abroad, without civilized female company, indeed the only females foreigners or those without rank or morals, is going to be vulnerable to the charms of the first reasonably educated woman his eye falls on. Such an attraction is but fancy and you were wise in seeing nothing lasting could come of it. We of the weaker sex must be realistic over such things.

To be separated from my granddaughter is very painful to me and surely unnatural. I hope you will not feel it your purpose to prolong such a separation while it is in your power, for Miss Wilder is the only remaining link Lord Charles and I have with our late son, so gallantly killed in the course of his duty to his country.

Lady Charles signed her name. She thought it the best she could do. She folded the letter and put it away, not having the intention of posting it unless she was driven. At that moment Slimmer came in with another letter, but this was addressed to Lady Charles by her daughter Sophia. She opened it eagerly.

Sophia and Emily had decided their parents would be miserable at Christmas without Lottie and they were making the suggestion their two families should converge on Ridley for the season, bringing all the other grandchildren to amuse and occupy them. They would be happy, if this arrangement seemed too much, for Lord and Lady Charles to travel to whichever of their daughters' houses seemed the most convenient, but they would, Sophia said, prefer to be at Ridley and they were assuming Thomas would go off to Finch Hall for they were very indignant at his conduct and had no wish to see him.

Lady Charles was delighted by this letter. All the same, her first instinct was to refuse. How could Ridley be so thronged with children bent on enjoyment, all the upheaval of the festivities, when her heart was broken? How could there be celebrations if Lyndon was dead? It was unthinkable. While she considered it, Mrs Kingston was shown in.

Lady Charles was quite reconciled with Mrs Kingston, not that they had had exactly a difference, but there had been a little distance, a certain coolness, which they had conquered by rarely referring to the matter of Miss Arbuthnot's dismissal and, for whatever each might be accused of, to find excuses. Much of their conversation ran on the sad absence of Lottie and the cruel refusal of Lady Charles's eldest daughter to give her up, blame for which Lady Charles could lay at the door of her remaining son. Mrs Kingston did not enter too heartily into such recriminations on the grounds that, with Miss Arbuthnot safely at Finch Hall, Major Wilder might be inclined to seek other feminine company closer. It was a trial for poor Mrs Kingston to be in the position of most sincerely wishing to agree with everything Lady Charles cared to say while not castigating her son. This act of keeping both ends of the seesaw in the air at once took all her attention.

After greeting her guest, Lady Charles's mind reverted to what had previously occupied it: Thomas, Lottie, her unposted letter to Miss Arbuthnot and then the letter from Sophia. She thought it rather troublesome of Mrs Kingston to arrive when she was so preoccupied but really she was quite pleased to see her.

She said, 'I have just received a letter from my daughter Sophia. She and Emily are determined to bring their families to Ridley for Christmas. They were always very close, Sophia and Emily, always together.'

'But how delightful that will be,' Mrs Kingston said. 'What joy. What quantities of little ones you will have at your knee, their dear shining faces.'

'I have by no means accepted. I only received the letter this minute. I may not be strong enough, after all. I had not given up hope of seeing Lottie.' She was wondering, with distaste, whether she need Thomas's permission to have these families for Christmas. Would he or Lord Charles object to the expense, which must be considerable? She added petulantly, 'The needs of others are put before mine.'

Mrs Kingston was not sure to whom Lady Charles referred. She hoped not Miss Arbuthnot. She said piously, but with suitable, she thought comfortable, vagueness, 'We are all equal in the sight of the Lord.'

Lady Charles, who had been referring to Miss Arbuthnot, said, irritated, 'One does wonder, in that case, why He was so discriminatory when He first conceived of the world and the humans on it.'

Mrs Kingston was slightly shocked.

Lady Charles then said, 'Thomas has such a very strong character, one can't move him in the least. One can't win him round or over.' It was strange how this thought came to her. At one time she would have pronounced him pig-headed and obstinate but she had decided she should present him in a better light, especially in front of Mrs Kingston. He was, she realized, the only person over whom she had no influence. This, though novel and unpleasant, was also intriguing. Thomas's only weakness seemed to be for Miss Arbuthnot.

At that moment the door was thrust open and Major Wilder strode into the room, the greyhounds fast to his heels.

He wished his mother good morning with mechanical politeness and, bowing to Mrs Kingston, remarked on having seen her carriage draw up.

A faint glow of satisfaction suffused Mrs Kingston's face. Never before had he given even such a slight indication as this that it was his intention to see her. He had, she thought, overridden his disinclination to see Lady Charles in order to see her, and she was further delighted by his pulling up a chair and sitting down beside her, the greyhounds biddably settling at his feet while pushing their noses against his knee in the hope of having their ears pulled.

Mrs Kingston said, 'No hunting today?'

'The meet was right across the county. I don't want to knock my horses up. I've had some good days. I would become a bore if I was to hunt every day.'

'Indeed, that couldn't be so, Major Wilder. A man so travelled as yourself, so full of experience quite beyond the ordinary, could never be dull.'

Major Wilder laughed. 'I've known some mighty dull soldiers.'

Mrs Kingston was tuning herself to drop him some other little compliment but Lady Charles intervened: 'I have just had a letter from Sophia. She and Emily would like to bring their families here for Christmas.' She watched his face, sure he would not raise the matter of expense in front of a visitor, though since the sale of the London house expense had seemed less of an issue.

'Very good,' he replied cheerfully. 'So long as they don't bring too many servants, they should fit in.' He wondered if his mother would break her taboo and use the empty rooms once devoted to Lyndon.

'You have no objections?'

'Certainly not. I would see it as a duty to entertain the family at Christmas if they seemed disposed to come. I myself intend to go to Finch Hall and take my father with me.'

Lady Charles was entirely taken aback and far from pleased. For a moment, when he had first entered the room, she had thought he had seen, at last, her good sense, would forgive her, forget all about governesses and pay some attention to Mrs Kingston, but she saw she had been deceived by his mildly conciliatory manner. She said, drawing herself up from a position already elegantly perpendicular, 'Take Lord Charles? Surely not.'

'Yes, I believe he would like to go. He won't be of the least use here, and you so busy.'

'But he won't see Sophia or Emily's children.'

'You will see them and he will see Georgie's.'

Lottie's name hung between them, unspoken.

Lady Charles, momentarily defeated, said wanly, 'Who will sit at the head of the table?'

'I dare say one or other of my brothers-in-law would be happy to oblige. My father can sit in a corner by the fireside at Finch Hall with Scottie on his lap and no one trouble him with a single question. Emily and Sophia will miss him but he can't be everywhere at once. How long do they mean to stay?' Major Wilder, without giving time for a reply, turned to Mrs Kingston and continued, 'What of that boy of yours?'

'Oh dear, yes, he has become a great anxiety to me. Indeed, he is a worry. He minds me not at all and Henry less.'

'But what do you intend doing about him, other than allowing him to roam the countryside like some little vagabond?'

Mrs Kingston could not help but feel criticized. 'I think you don't understand the trials of widowhood. If only his poor father were alive . . . I would, of course I would, do anything to resolve the dilemma I find myself in. Horatio used always to be such a good little boy.'

Major Wilder raised an eyebrow. 'What sort of sacrifice would you make?'

'Sacrifice? Why, any.'

'You must part with him. I feel a certain responsibility towards the boy. I deprived him of the companionship he needed, let alone the French lessons he so much enjoyed. Allow me to take him to Finch Hall. My sister and brother-in-law will hardly notice another child. Indeed, they think the more the merrier. I will undertake to see he gets some lessons.'

Tears started to course down Mrs Kingston's cheeks. She thought Major Wilder just as unkind as Lady Charles was always indicating. How could she part with Horatio when, within a few months, she would be parting with him for good? At the same time she was gratified by the interest Major Wilder was taking in her child and conscious of what a perfect stepfather he would make. If only Major Wilder could be prevailed upon to become Horatio's stepfather she thought she might change her mind on the subject of her boy entering the navy.

Lady Charles, less pleased than ever, said, 'I had just decided to invite Mrs Kingston and her little boy to spend Christmas here at Ridley. There will be plenty of children to occupy him.'

Major Wilder said, 'By all means invite Mrs Kingston and Captain Houghton. It will cheer them up, under the circumstances. Allow me to take Horatio to Finch Hall. I will keep a good eye on him.'

Lady Charles said, with the intention of making him uncomfortable, 'What business is the boy of yours?'

She only succeeded in making Mrs Kingston uncomfortable because he replied, with the greatest of ease, 'I have already explained it.' He then turned to Mrs Kingston. 'Why not allow Horatio to choose, but let him do so freely?'

He got up to go, bowing with equal politeness to Mrs Kingston as to his mother.

Mrs Heugmont was writing to her friend Mrs Hamilton,

something she did approximately once a month. She sat at her bureau in the drawing room, at a moment carefully chosen when the children were occupied with their lessons and would not interrupt her. Much as she liked to be interrupted, it was no aid to concentration, and writing letters to Mrs Hamilton was one way she might clear her head from the many distractions that beset her and put two consecutive thoughts together. The letter was dated 10 December.

> *I know you must be wondering a thousand things, but most of all, how we go along with Miss Arbuthnot. Why, she is a dear girl, honest and direct, wise beyond her years. Miss Smith and Miss Campbell, those doyennes of the schoolroom, I thought could be jealous, especially when Miss A goes out riding with the children, a thing they never learnt and view as dangerous, and considering Miss A's youth, but I was banking on their good nature and it has turned out safe to do so. We all speak French at table. This is our new regime. Miss Arbuthnot must correct us, even John, at which she is quite overcome and mortified, but she adheres to our rules and steadily steers her course,* Monsieur, je suis extrêmement gênée d'être obligée de vous corriger, *indicating how painful she finds it to have to correct his French . . . yet again. Of course, the children are delighted and we are very merry. I thought my own French quite good until now.*
>
> *My brother Thomas has arrived with my father and a small boy about his person, various dogs, horses, a pony attached to small boy. It is as well my John views*

Thomas in such a brotherly light, though Thomas is very anxious on the subject of not putting us to extra expense and would take the horses off to the Crown except John will not allow it. As for the child, who is most remarkably skinny, he is the son of that Mrs Kingston, a widow, whom my mother always thought Lyndon would marry, though really I have no idea if he had any serious intention. Lottie burst into tears of joy at the sight of him and then ran away and hid behind the sofa. He has the prettiest French of all of us, sits beside Lottie or Miss Arbuthnot at dinner, very decorous, but he has sparkling black eyes and a mischievous look . . . My mob can't wait to abscond with him. They envy him the journey here, riding much of the way with Thomas, but when considered tired he was popped in the carriage with my father, who assures me his entire reading matter was The Young Sea Officer's Sheet Anchor, *which he is industriously getting by rote. Surely less enviable. We have the best navy in the world upon whose altar we sacrifice these little boys.*

My mother is very cross at Lottie being here but puts all the blame on Thomas. And what can I say of Lottie? She is certainly quaint but I rather love her. She is growing to resemble her father; she used to be such a stout little person. Poor Lyndon. My parents spoilt him. He was full of charm but, well, there were buts. I wonder why one should not speak ill of the dead. It seems as good a time as any. Such was he, it is hard to think him gone for ever.

Mrs Heugmont laid down the pen. She wished she could discuss the whole business of Lady Charles and Miss Arbuthnot, but Lady Charles's conduct simply could not be explained, without repeating the unrepeatable, even to such a friend as Henrietta Hamilton. Lady Charles had leapt to strange conclusions, but what of Thomas? Was he wise to come? He was civil to Miss Arbuthnot, beyond that spoke to her but little. He certainly made no attempt at courting. He might have given up the whole idea, as she herself would urge him should he allow her the opportunity, but Thomas would not give something up light-heartedly: he would ruthlessly expunge it. She supposed one should know a brother well whom one had loved since he was an infant, but Thomas had left home as a boy. They had seen him, of course, now and again, but his real journey from boy to man had unfolded in letters, long letters, short letters, lost letters, letters months old arriving in the wrong order, and thus he had gone from small, rebellious schoolboy to major in the Royal Horse Artillery, competent, authoritative and . . . and exactly what? Still her beloved Thomas but with a puritanical streak. Men were strange creatures, particularly soldiers, their personal courage synonymous with their honour and their honour rarely separated from the honour of the regiment. What could a woman know of the campaigning that had forged her brother's growing years, the tedium, hardship and discomfort interspersed with the horrors of the battlefield?

Thomas had an austerity about him, his dislike of gambling, his intolerance of duelling, and now, she observed, an increasing antipathy to drunkenness, all of which were more than acceptable to his peers, even, surely, his fellow soldiers. Now she knew him to be unhappy, his suit scorned by a young girl not in a position to refuse him, but who had, nevertheless, done just that; and barely on speaking terms with his mother. Ah, her beloved Thomas, she wanted, above all things, his happiness. Ridley must be, at the moment, a deeply uncomfortable house. And would he be happy if he had Miss Arbuthnot for his wife? On reflection, she rather thought he might. The Miss Esmonds, sisters, cousins of her husband, were to be with them at Finch Hall over Christmas. The elder, Margaret, was twenty-five years old, very anxious for a husband and handsome. Would she distract Thomas? Might he like her? Why had she no husband already? She was of independent means, always advantageous. Well, she could not speak of it, even to Mrs Hamilton, but of Lottie she could speak:

As I mention Lottie, to what extent may a child judge a parent or, in this case, a grandparent? One might say never. A child does not understand what lies behind mysterious, grown-up deeds, or so we like to think, but Lottie sees her grandmother as having been cruel to Miss Arbuthnot, which, indeed, she was, so how does one advise? As a Christian, you will say. Is it not hard to forgive when there is no obvious repentance or making of remission? What can I say to Lottie? She and I walked round the kitchen gardens. She is very interested in the growing of vegetables but I managed to wean her from the subject of potato varieties on to the subject of her grandmother. She told me she no longer included her grandmother in her prayers or, she said, her papa, because she could not see he needed them now he had gone to Heaven, and she had all her cousins to pray for, and their dogs and ponies and her uncle and aunt, who had not been included in previous lists, so she was very glad to be able to drop some names off. Dear me, give me the potatoes. I said she must pray to find it in her heart to forgive her grandmother. She replied that her grandmother must say she was sorry to Miss Arbuthnot and then she would give her a kiss, or she thought she would but she was not quite prepared to commit herself. She said her Uncle Thomas, who is high on the list of prayers, was cross too, and did he forgive, and was it the same rules for grown-ups as for children? Dear, oh dear, and here am I against feeding platitudes to children.

Mrs Heugmont wondered in what manner she had answered Lottie. She felt to nobody's satisfaction, but she had told Lottie she would think about it, and here she was thinking about it but without coming to any conclusions.

At the end of the following week Miss Arbuthnot wrote to her father. It had been decided the frost was too hard to allow the children to ride. They were playing hide and seek, wrapped up in muffs and hats, in the garden and the wood. There was no hunting. She saw Major Wilder and his two eldest nephews from her window, which was high under the roof, crossing the carriage sweep with the greyhounds. They strode along purposefully.

20 December 1814
Finch Hall

My dear Papa,

This is only my second letter to you since I have been here, but I am so busy, two pupils, all the children for French, little Master Benjy to be started on his Latin, and every other activity besides. Of course I am happy. Miss Smith and Miss Campbell are very kind but they are amused at the studies I have made and are not in the least impressed with my reading matter. Rousseau, Miss Trimmer, Hannah More, the Edgeworths are nothing to Miss Smith and Miss Campbell. They recommend common sense and any doubts to be referred to Mrs Heugmont. So much for my efforts! Perhaps they are right. No theory has been of assistance to me in teaching Miss Wilder.

This is a liberal household, the tone set by Mr Heugmont. He is a philanthropist, a member of the Abolitionists, and concerns himself with restricting the hours children may work in factories. There is much discussion on the subject of our war with America, the ending of it, and whether we should have gone to war in the first place, which he feels to have been a great error of judgement Mrs Heugmont reminds me of Mrs Hamilton. I am quite under her spell. I could not have a more thoughtful or kindly employer. Here I am, in the smallest bedroom you could think but made attractive with quilts and fresh curtains and a little grate with a fire in it, very necessary if I am not to freeze solid while writing to you. My toes are on the fender and this letter on my lap, which does nothing for neatness of handwriting. Mrs Heugmont constantly apologizes for the smallness of the room, saying no governess should be expected to share one with their pupil and it is the best she could do for me, for the house is quite full. However, it is a dear little room and I like it.

French is spoken at dinner, which I am required to correct. It would make me uncomfortable, if they were not so merry about it. Mr Heugmont makes many mistakes but I try to correct only the most obvious.

Miss Arbuthnot paused. What else might she tell her father? Lord Charles had arrived, and Horatio Kingston, but could this be mentioned without saying Major Wilder had accompanied them? It seemed ridiculous, now, to be shy of mentioning his name to her father. He had arrived and he had asked her how his niece progressed. She was not sure he had listened to the answers, but she thought he had, though all the children were clamouring for his attention. He had asked if she was well. After that he had not taken notice of her beyond the ordinary courtesies. He was exactly as she had predicted he would be. He was preoccupied and absorbed by his family, hunting or shooting with his nephews, taking long walks with his sister, shut up with Mr Heugmont or helping the younger children with their ponies. If they rode out together, they were all of a group and he was never beside her. He had, she saw, cut her from his mind. Did this mean her attraction for him had been an idle fancy? Perhaps it did, but again, perhaps it did not. Where was the violent and undying passion one read about in stories? Had she an undying passion for Mr Langley? Major Wilder was allowed to cut her from his mind, it was only sensible that he should do so, yet she found it difficult to be coldly practical when she considered it. She tried to puzzle how it was, since she had rejected him, she felt a sense of loss. Surely that, too, was ridiculous. Was she no better than her sister Kate, who had been peevish at the very thought of any one of her admirers, dismissed out of hand, turning their attentions elsewhere? Was she just as frivolous? Should she not rejoice in Major Wilder's ability to dismiss her from his mind, which was what she assumed he had done? She thought human nature very frail, and hers particularly so – epitomized when the eldest of the Heugmont boys, near to herself in age, had laughingly teased her at dinner for failing to correct his uncle's French, when the rest of them were not spared. She had brushed the remark aside by saying Major Wilder spoke his French too rapidly for her to be able to correct it, and he confused her with the addition of a little Spanish. She thought, but did not say, she could bring herself to correct Mr Heugmont and, reluctantly, Lord Charles, and even Mrs Heugmont, Miss Smith and Miss Campbell, but she could not look Major Wilder in the eye and correct his French. Perhaps to silence young Nicholas Heugmont, Major Wilder had thereafter taken to asking her for the odd word and, when she had given it, continuing with what he was saying with scarce a break.

Miss Arbuthnot resumed her letter.

I wish I had had the teaching of all of them from the beginning. Miss Smith has the most terrible accent which the girls have copied, but we are mending things.

Miss Esmond, Mr Heugmont's cousin, gave the impression of extreme good health. She was a tall young woman with a magnificent figure, abundant brown hair, a high colour and careless self-confidence. Major Wilder, his vein of austerity at war with ordinary masculine inclinations, found her a little overwhelming, especially when she sat next to him at dinner, the fashion of the day, to which he was not quite reconciled, being for a peculiar scantiness in female dress. Miss Esmond walked into every house as if she owned it, with her young sister, Miss Molly, trailing along behind.

Mrs Heugmont, who had not seen Miss Esmond since she was a child, wondered if she was going to like her. If she turned out to be kind at heart she might be a distraction for Thomas, or even something more than a distraction, but who could say? The sisters, orphans, had been brought up by their married sister living in Edinburgh. They had a faint Scottish burr, though Miss Molly's voice was not heard. Mrs Heugmont decided she was too young and shy to distract, or yet attract, anyone, but she then recalled Miss Arbuthnot was barely nineteen and that had been no bar to her brother's partiality. He might feel a protective tenderness to the pretty, shy, slender Miss Molly, which was as good as falling in love, but she hoped he would have more sense. Why she hoped any such thing she could not imagine, for when had love to do with sense? The disadvantage of the arrival of the Misses Esmond was its ill timing: it was too soon. Thomas, she doubted, could be fickle: he might cut Miss Arbuthnot out of his mind but the business would be painful, or so she thought. The Misses Esmond could be a distraction but, she concluded, nothing more, though one could live in hope.

Major Wilder thought seriously on the subject of flirting when he saw Miss Esmond was ready to find him attractive. He was accustomed to flirting but, under a soldier's circumstances, never likely to be in the same place for very long and more a form of occupation than anything else. With the idea of inheriting Ridley in his head, mere flirting seemed frivolous and unappealing: he wanted a wife. He had fixed his affections and been rejected so did he not have to start again? He was confused, in his present state of mind, as to how that was to be done.

At Finch Hall another leaf was put in the dining-table and, out of respect for Miss Esmond, the adults no longer spoke French. Miss Esmond could speak French, she said, even quite good French, but she could not be bothered with it. The younger children suspected her French to be poor and continued to speak French to each other, to Miss Arbuthnot and to anyone else who could be got to listen to them, so there was a little babbling undercurrent of French. Miss Molly was not heard to speak in any language whatsoever. Miss Esmond was shocked at the number of children and governesses at table. She was introduced to each in turn, spoke politely but saw no reason to address them again, either children or governesses.

Miss Esmond was also interested in riding but she was startled to discover there was not to be a riotous gallop across the countryside but a sober excursion to include Lord Charles, who anyone could see was too old, and even the youngest of the children. At first she declined, saying she would be unable sufficiently to curtail her natural high spirits. She then suggested they could be split into two parties, which would increase the amusement for all, each going at their own pace. She looked hopefully at Major Wilder to agree with her and to direct operations, but she found his gallantry did not stretch so far for he replied it was their pleasure to go together, the exercise did them good and the ground was too frosted for much of a gallop. Miss Esmond was affronted, however politely he told her this. She again considered declining the ride but when she found the alternative was to take a stroll with Molly, who had no taste for horses, Mr and Mrs Heugmont and possibly Miss Smith and Miss Campbell as well, she thought anything preferable and was resigned to having a spare carriage horse, which was accustomed to take a side-saddle, made over for her use.

On the first ride they took, Miss Esmond rode between Major Wilder and Nicholas Heugmont, the eldest of the Heugmont boys. Major Wilder had a young nephew on the leading rein, the child having fallen off the day before; his confidence was in need of restoration. Miss Arbuthnot and Lord Charles rode side by side at the back. There was a considerable gaggle of other children, all of whom Miss Esmond thought would have been better off at home in the nursery, especially as Major Wilder constantly broke off what he was saying to address the little boy.

Miss Esmond admired the Andalusian, but she said, 'He is such an elegant creature, I would have thought he was more of a lady's ride.'

Major Wilder replied he did not know what made her think that. The Andalusian was a powerful horse and used only to one rider. He had himself worked hard to gain the stallion's acceptance. He had then said, 'No, Benjy, don't hold your reins so tight or Prince won't like it.'

'But where did you get the horse?'

'In Spain.'

'Did you buy him from a Spaniard?'

'I acquired him, one way or another.'

Nicholas Heugmont, who was fascinated by the ample proportions of Miss Esmond's figure, said, 'It's no use to tease my uncle on that subject. He never will tell how he got the Andalusian, though I believe my mother knows.'

'Perhaps he stole him,' Miss Esmond said, laughing.

'Certainly not,' Major Wilder replied. He then said, 'Benjy, if you lean forward like that, your legs will go back and tickle Prince in the sides, making him think you want to go faster when you don't.'

Miss Esmond said, 'But in a battle, might you not take a French officer's horse?'

'In a battle I might take anyone's horse, had I lost mine.'

'And have you lost horses that were killed beneath you?'

'Twice.'

'And what were the circumstances?'

Major Wilder turned to look at her and then turned away. He never talked about such things. They were not a subject for idle chatter. It was pitiful when a good horse died. He said, 'That's right, Benjy, sit up straight,' and after a little pause, he turned the subject: 'Of course the Andalusian is not a charger or even a horse for fox-hunting. He's an agreeable companion.'

Miss Esmond, thinking herself snubbed, gave the carriage horse a sharp dig with her heel and jerked its head up. She said, 'I am used to something a great deal more sprightly than this.'

And so the ride went on. Miss Esmond thought it and Major Wilder dull but she suspected he would not be dull if she could draw him out in some way. On failing to draw him out at all on a subject she assumed must be of interest to him, they started to discuss other things, the war with America and the Catholic question. Miss Esmond was forthright in her opinions but she was pleased, although or perhaps because they did not agree, that the conversation became lively. Major Wilder seemed not so dull after all. She dogmatically refuted his considered opinions and saw herself as a woman of spirit, which she assumed must appeal to a military man.

It was the first of many rides and they followed much the same pattern, though Major Wilder, even if he did not have a child on a leading rein, frequently chose to ride alongside his father for at least part of the procedure, and Miss Esmond had to content herself with the admiration of young Nicholas, though she could not influence him away from his father's egalitarian principles, which she found too shocking and peculiar. She chose not to ride when the men were hunting for she found if she walked with Mr and Mrs Heugmont there were pleasant little visits to be made to friends and neighbours, even if Major Wilder were not of the party.

Christmas approached. There was a party for the servants. The children entertained them with their own personal version of *Romeo and Juliet*. It was even more tragic than the original, nearly all of the cast falling on their swords, except Juliet, who for some reason not clear had not died after all. Miss Arbuthnot helped with the dressing-up and with the learning of lines. She was in constant demand and kept very busy. After the play had drawn to its grisly conclusion there was dancing. Mr Heugmont danced with the cook, which was a tradition at Finch Hall, much enjoyed by the children, as neither their father nor the cook was in the least good at dancing. Major Wilder, besides most often dancing with Miss Esmond, did his duty by Miss Smith and Miss Campbell and all of his nieces. Miss Arbuthnot danced with the Heugmont boys, even Master Benjy, when not required to play the piano. She wondered she was not quite indifferent to what Major Wilder did. She hoped she wished him well and that it was of no importance that he chose never to speak to her unless on the subject of his ward, and that not often. She turned her mind from repeating to herself the conversation they had had in the garden when she was at home in Devonshire, because it seemed like the last conversation she was ever to have with him.

As for Miss Esmond, so much family life, so much attention given to children, it was not at all to what she was accustomed. She found Major Wilder cautiously flirtatious but was irked at perceiving what she took to be his underlying indifference, his preference for fox-hunting over her company, though she knew fox-hunting always to be the most serious of rivals. Nevertheless, Miss Esmond was not used to indifference and thought it had best be conquered one way or another. She also, frequently, considered matrimony. Did she want to give up her independence? Married women took precedence over her. Suppose Molly married, the shy little goose would need to parade through an open door ahead of her elder sister: the very thought was a mortification. Why was she, Miss Esmond, not married already? She had had several offers but she had declined them. She was always waiting for a better but now she supposed to be unmarried at twenty-five was one thing but to be unmarried at thirty would be another and she had heard Ridley was quite a fine place. At one time the Wilders had had a house in London but they had sold it, which was unfortunate, but Major Wilder was still the sole heir and, despite his apparent indifference, she thought him vulnerable. In such matters, if not in others, her perceptions were acute. She also considered the eldest of the Heugmont boys, Nicholas, who was only six years younger than her, which was not so very much. She assumed he would inherit Finch Hall, which was not large, but pleasantly situated and she liked it, though it was not entirely safe to assume anything, her cousin having such peculiar notions. Their very peculiarity struck her afresh on a sunny day when she had decided to abandon a walk to the rectory in order to ride, for though Major Wilder was hunting, Nicholas was not. Benjy had regained his confidence, so his brother was unencumbered by the leading rein but he did spend a tiresome time joking with Miss Arbuthnot while leaving Miss Esmond to make conversation to Lord Charles. At the appropriate moment she gave the carriage horse a hearty kick in its unreceptive ribs and manoeuvred it alongside her quarry.

'Have you no second hunter?' she asked. 'Is it lame? Why don't you hunt today?'

'My father allows us only one hunter each.'

'I would never have thought him so mean.'

'It isn't meanness, it's principle. James would want two, and then Christopher, and even little Benjy would get there in the end.'

'But you are the eldest.'

'So?' he said, laughing. 'Do you suppose my father thinks that significant? I have never been allowed to consider myself of more importance than my brothers and sisters, and nor do I. I shall read for the bar. If I do well and can afford it I shall get a seat in Parliament. I am interested in parliamentary reform and of course to carry on the work of the Abolitionists. We all, secretly, wish to emulate our uncle and spend some years in the army, but though my father loves him, he won't hear of it. Perhaps, now we are not at war with France or America, it wouldn't be so interesting.'

'But you will inherit Finch Hall?'

Nicholas shrugged. 'Who's to say?'

Miss Esmond rapidly cooled on the idea of attaching herself to a young radical whose rightful inheritance might be divided between seven. Her mind reverted to Ridley. She wished she knew more of it and had cross-examined Lord Charles, but the old gentleman was not precise and it was a little indelicate to be too direct. She wondered about questioning Miss Arbuthnot because she understood she had lived at Ridley with Miss Wilder before coming to

Finch Hall. It surprised her Miss Arbuthnot was so young but she supposed even governesses had to be young at some point. When Nicholas rode ahead to open a gate she held her horse back until she was level with Miss Arbuthnot. In her experience governesses were flattered to have attention paid them. She said, 'I understand you have recently come from Ridley.'

Miss Arbuthnot agreed she had.

'And Miss Wilder is your pupil?'

'Yes, that is so, but at Finch Hall I have more than one pupil. I am starting Master Benjy on Latin and I take all the children for French.'

'My, you are accomplished. Fancy knowing Latin.'

'I learnt it with my brother.' Miss Arbuthnot thought of adding, 'Astronomy and navigation too,' but decided against it.

'And if Miss Wilder was to return to her grandparents, I suppose you would go with her. I hear Ridley is a fine place.'

'It is considered so, I believe.' Miss Arbuthnot had no wish to discuss Ridley with anyone.

'Don't you think so yourself?'

'I'm no judge.'

'Anyone can judge if one property is finer than another,' Miss Esmond said, cross at Miss Arbuthnot's reserve. 'Are the reception rooms good? Is the park fine?'

Miss Arbuthnot thought the park might have been fine before the trees had been cut down but she did not say so, merely remarking the rooms were just as rooms were in houses of a similar size, that being about a third as much again as Finch Hall.

‘Ah, well, you would like to return to the larger property, I suppose.’

Miss Arbuthnot did not see quite why this assumption should be made. She said, ‘Miss Wilder must do whatever her guardian requires of her, and I also.’

‘But her grandparents would be her guardians?’

Miss Arbuthnot let this go uncorrected and turned to say something to one of the children, who milled about on their ponies, chatting and laughing with one another, but Miss Esmond was not satisfied. She said, ‘Whatever harm is there in my knowing such things? Why are you so button-mouthed?’

Miss Arbuthnot thought Miss Esmond vulgarly curious but she had to be answered all the same, so she said, ‘Major Wilder is his niece’s guardian.’

‘Major Wilder? Fancy that. Well, if he should get married, maybe the child will go to live with him and you will go too.’

Miss Arbuthnot looked down at her gloved hands on the reins, which she found she had clutched unnecessarily tightly. Cloudy gave a protesting shake of his shapely head. She slipped one hand down his neck and twisted her fingers in his mane. Such a situation as Miss Esmond suggested she knew could never be.

Miss Esmond’s attention was drawn, not for the first time, to Cloudy. How was it Miss Arbuthnot had this pretty, dark grey gelding to ride? It was an expensive lady’s hack, far superior to what she had been consigned to. She said, ‘You are rather lucky to be going riding, are you not?’

‘Oh, yes, I’m very lucky.’

‘Most people . . . er . . . most people in your situation are not so fortunate as to keep a horse. It must be something to do with my cousin's egalitarian principles.'

'Cloudy isn't mine,' Miss Arbuthnot said, suddenly smiling at such a ridiculous assumption.

'He is Mrs Heugmont's, perhaps, and she no longer rides?'

'No. Major Wilder bought him so I might accompany his niece.'

Miss Esmond spotted an irregularity. Why had such a quality horse, so expensive, been purchased for the sake of the governess, and since it belonged to Major Wilder, why had she not been offered it for her own use? She thought Miss Arbuthnot, as ever, looked guarded. Really, until this moment, she had paid the girl no attention, but now she cast her eye over the well-cut riding habit, though altered, so probably somebody else's originally; and the hat, which looked as if it had once had some further ornamentation, and the red curls that peeped out from under it; and the face, which, had it not been for the freckles across the white skin, might almost have been pretty, the brows well shaped and the eyes expressive. As for her figure, she was too tall, taller than Miss Esmond herself, and a great deal too lean. Miss Esmond concluded, knowingly, that Miss Arbuthnot would be scrawny by the time she was thirty. Though there was no accounting for masculine taste, the girl was a lesser being when compared to herself, even without taking her position as a governess into consideration.

The necessity of crowding through another gate that Nicholas Heugmont had opened for them gave Miss Arbuthnot the opportunity to drop back beside Lord Charles. He smiled at her companionably and they were happy not to speak. He was admiring his grandchildren: he loved to see them out riding together and in such cheerful spirits. Miss Arbuthnot returned his smile but she was thinking of Miss Esmond, whom she thought to be interested in Ridley because she was interested in Major Wilder, who was an eligible bachelor. This was of no concern to herself, of course, yet it made her uneasy. The suggestion Major Wilder might marry and take Lottie to live with him also made her uneasy, though she saw no prospect of it. She thought he would leave his niece at Finch Hall. Her mind wound about in circles: could Major Wilder be contemplating marrying Miss Esmond for the reason he was anxious to be married? Could he not see she would make him unhappy?

Lord Charles said, 'Miss Arbuthnot, I know it would be out of the question for you ever to return to Ridley but I want to tell you it's a dull place without you and Lottie, and Major Wilder so busy. He doesn't forgive his mother. It makes me very unhappy we live in such disharmony. You might think I make excuses for my wife but she can't get over the death of our eldest son.'

Miss Arbuthnot said gently, 'You, too, suffered that loss.'

'I did indeed, but I seem better able to count my blessings.'

And then Miss Arbuthnot, who wondered if he had intended to say rather more, was distracted by the children. Benjy had dropped his stick and in getting off to pick it up Prince had trodden on his toe. She hastily slipped down from Cloudy to comfort the child and, in the middle of a field, had no means of remounting, but Nicholas came cheerfully trotting back to assist her and to admonish his little brother for such loud wails. Miss Esmond remarked she never wanted to go out with children for even if they did not fall off their ponies they were bound to need attention just at the moment someone had something interesting to say, but silently she was now also preoccupied with what she perceived as a slight.

The notion of this slight she harboured all through Christmas, which came and went amid much festivity and dutiful walks to church; even Mr Heugmont attended though he had Quaker leanings, which Mrs Heugmont was happy were only leanings, nothing more. After Christmas there was no riding or hunting because the fields were again frozen. Major Wilder contemplated his return to Ridley without enthusiasm and concerned himself with the state of the roads. He did not care to risk an accident if he was to have his father with him. He was aware that Miss Esmond's manner had become a little abrasive, though she still made up to him with arch smiles while hinting at something he saw he was meant to understand but was as yet a mystery. She was, all the same, pleased the bad weather kept him at Finch Hall.

At the end of December Miss Arbuthnot caught a cold. Mrs Heugmont confined her to her room, insisted on fires all day and nourishing broths. Miss Arbuthnot protested she was not so ill as all that but she was not allowed to come down to dinner for Mrs Heugmont feared the Siberian draughts that haunted the Finch Hall passages. It was this that prompted Miss Esmond to make her grievance public. She was aware a complaint, however she might be feeling, must be delivered light-heartedly, as if a slight to herself was of no consequence but yet must be acknowledged as a slight. She waited until all the candles were lit, the soup on the table and the servants out of the room before remarking on the absence of Miss Arbuthnot, as well as that of Miss Campbell and Miss Smith, who had both gone away to their relatives for Christmas. Miss Arbuthnot had thought she would much prefer to stay at Finch Hall and help with the children.

Miss Esmond continued, 'Of course, Miss Arbuthnot is an estimable creature and treated better than a guest, even a relative, but I do find it so pleasant to sit down with just the family, no staff, no prying eyes, no silent observation. Is it not refreshing?'

There was a moment of unhappy silence before Mr Heugmont took it upon himself to reply. 'I'm afraid you don't understand the principles upon which we run this house. I entrust the education of my children to others and there can be no more important persons in the house than those others. They are a part of the family.'

Lottie, who thought Miss Esmond had said something rude about Miss Arbuthnot but without quite understanding what, was ready to be cross. She said, 'They're not slaves.' Thinking it time Miss Esmond had a good lecture, she went on loudly, 'And slaves are real people just like you and me, even if they're black. There's no sugar at Finch Hall because of the bad men who make the slaves work in the sugar plantations. I'm telling Grandpapa when he goes back to Ridley he is to tell the cook she mustn't use any sugar. You have to be like John the Baptist and eat honey and locusts. Did you know that, Miss Esmond? You have to eat honey but we don't have any locusts. I am going to be an Abolitionist as soon as I'm old enough.'

Lottie was not cautious when embarking on a subject of which she was fond and she was a willing receptacle for her uncle's views.

Mr Heugmont said, 'My dear Lottie, you do put it so succinctly, but you mustn't shout at guests. It isn't polite and it doesn't make them agree with you.'

Lottie subsided but then she said quietly, but not so quietly she could not be heard, 'And it isn't right to make little boys go up chimneys. I hope Miss Esmond doesn't allow that where she lives.'

Miss Esmond laughed. 'The child would have us all turned to kippers or burnt to death in our beds, I can see, for want of sweeping the chimneys.' She thought if Miss Wilder was to live with her guardian when he got married, it would be detrimental to his chances of securing a suitable bride. She had no reforming zeal and thought her cousin extreme, for it was apparent to all that only the slaves would work the sugar plantations, and should they not, the economy of the horrid West Indies would collapse and everyone would starve, slaves included. As for chimney sweeps, she had never considered them. She turned away from Lottie, who was too forward a child and ought to be put much more firmly in her place, to continue what she had originally intended to say.

'Well, with the frosty weather, I don't miss riding so much as I thought I would. It's really very dull.'

Major Wilder, thinking the remark addressed to him, said, 'You want a more exciting life than we can offer you.'

'I am used to a better horse. Everyone, but everyone, is better mounted than me. Isn't that rather teasing?'

Lord Charles said cheerily, 'But, Miss Esmond, your horse is no worse than mine, but my son insists on my riding it.'

'It is to preserve you,' Major Wilder replied.

'Well, we must preserve Miss Esmond too,' Lord Charles said.

Miss Esmond said, 'Oh, I don't need to ride anything tame. I'm very able. Aren't I able, Molly? Say yes. You have a better horse in your stables, Major Wilder, a perfect-looking horse with impeccable manners that I have never yet been offered.'

Lord Charles said, 'Dear Miss Esmond, I hope you are not asking Thomas to let you ride the Andalusian.'

'Of course not. I thought I might have been offered a ride on the horse Miss Arbuthnot has. I understand it belongs to Major Wilder.' Miss Esmond delicately helped herself from a dish of rabbit fricassée that happened to be before her.

Major Wilder, who did not allow himself to dwell on the subject of Miss Arbuthnot, was forced to consider the justice of what Miss Esmond said. He had, indeed, never offered her a ride on Cloudy; he had never so much as considered it. He was saved any immediate reply by Lottie, who said, 'You can't ride Cloudy, Miss Esmond. He's Miss 'Buthnot's.'

'But I understand, little miss, from your governess herself, the horse belongs to your uncle.'

'You couldn't ride Cloudy. He's had an accident. If you feel on his neck and his quarters, which Miss Smith told me is not a good word for little girls, but you have to call it something, he's all scars. They're from some bloody fool what never ought to 'ave 'ad an 'oss, driving 'im too bloody fast.'

This statement silenced the whole table but while the adults sought an appropriate reproof, Miss Esmond said, 'And why may I not ride him as well as Miss Arbuthnot?'

'Because you're too stout, not like Miss 'Buthnot.' Lottie looked her most belligerent.

Mrs Heugmont said, 'Lottie, that is very, very rude.'

'But why? It's good to be stout. Grandmama always told me it was healthy and she didn't like it when I got thinner.'

Major Wilder said, 'You must not comment on people's appearance.'

Lottie was working herself into a passion. 'I don't understand it, I don't, when it's a different rule for children. Grandmama always told me I was stout and everyone tells Horatio he's all skin and bone, which is true. Miss Esmond is stout, 'specially at her top.'.

She was not prepared for the strange, startled looks on the faces of all the grown-ups at the table, and the servants who had come back into the room to clear the dishes went out again in a hurry as if there were no dishes to collect. She looked anxiously at Major Wilder, who beckoned her to him, actually not trusting himself to speak, so she reluctantly got down from her chair, knowing it was a mistake not to do what her Uncle Thomas said she must.

He put his hands on her shoulders and said, gaining sufficient calm, 'There are different rules for grown-ups, there are and there are. Grown-ups are upset by personal remarks. And, Lottie, how many times have you been told not to copy York?' He turned her round to face Miss Esmond. 'Now, say you are sorry.'

Lottie said she was sorry but without much enthusiasm, though she could see her uncle was right: Miss Esmond did look upset.

Suddenly there was a curious muffled squawk from the other end of the table. It came from Miss Molly, hitherto so silent, who had her hands stuffed into her mouth but was at last heard to gasp, ''Specially at her top.'

As she showed every sign of having hysterics the hartshorn was sought and Lottie forgotten. The children, though they had not yet had their dessert, made a bolt for the nurseries. Christopher and Horatio, realizing this was a mistake, crept back amid the confusion and helped themselves to the apples. Miss Molly was supported away to the drawing room. Eventually only the men were left. Mr Heugmont silently filled their glasses. Nicholas got up and carefully closed the door. He was only the first of them to break into uncontrollable laughter.

The children at Finch Hall loved the big pond in the park. In summer it was used for boating and in the winter they could skate. Now Lottie and Horatio were side by side pushing chairs across the ice while Lottie's more accomplished cousins, as well as the children from the village, shot up and down with cries of joy.

Lottie was pleased to have Horatio to herself. 'Was it something so very bad I said?'

'Oh, yes, very bad. You mustn't refer to the bosom unless you're a poet.'

'Why is that?'

'It is the seat of the emotions.'

'It's what?'

'When poets say it they mean it's where they feel things.'

'Is your heart in your bosom? I feel things up here.' Lottie nervously took a hand off the back of her chair and pointed to her head.

'Well, I dare say we feel things in a more ordinary way as we aren't poets.'

'And I didn't say bosom, I said top.'

'But it's what you meant. Anyway, it doesn't matter now. The important thing is not to tell Miss Arbuthnot about it, or she might think she has to offer Cloudy to Miss Esmond, if Major Wilder allowed it, and we don't want that, do we?'

Lottie agreed they didn't. 'Uncle Thomas was not as cross with me as he seemed. He was shamming.'

Christopher Heugmont came up to them at racing speed and executed a neat halt so that he fell in beside them. 'I bet you could do better, Horatio. Leave that old chair. Take my hand. I'll steady you.'

Lottie watched them go. Horatio called back, 'We'll come and help you later,' but she was not sure they would. Despondently, she attempted to go a little faster, slipped sideways and fell over, taking the chair with her.

Major Wilder walked across the ice and picked her up.

She said, 'I was just going to be really cross.'

'What with?'

'The chair, the ice, Christopher, who has taken Horatio away, me.'

'And have I saved you the trouble?'

Lottie smiled. 'Nearly you have. I wish Miss 'Buthnot were better. She would teach me quickly and I could go with the other children. Why isn't Miss Esmond skating?'

'Miss Esmond tells me she doesn't skate.' He knew Miss Esmond thought everyone was laughing at her and that she could not wait to leave Finch Hall. If it had not been for the weather she would have left already. He had done his best to placate her.

''Spect the ice would crack if she got on it.'

'Lottie!'

Lottie grasped hold of the chair in a more determined manner and he walked along beside her. She said, 'But you can skate.'

'I have to borrow Nicholas's skates and he's using them. Why is it you dislike Miss Esmond quite so much?'

'She doesn't like children.' Lottie thought there was something else about Miss Esmond that made her uneasy but she was not sure what it was. She then said, 'I quite like it when you're cross with me.'

'It certainly isn't my intention you should like it in the least.'

'When I'm here, Grandpapa is everyone's grandpapa and you are everyone's uncle, but when you're cross with me I know I belong to you for you to be cross with.'

Major Wilder puzzled through this last sentence. 'I hope a guardian has more purposes than just to be cross.'

'If anyone should ask me who I am, I can say I'm Major Wilder's ward. I like that. Nobody else is, only me.'

'Lottie, would you like to go back to Ridley, where you are the only child?'

'Not for ever and ever, but I miss my garden. I like it with my cousins but I liked it when it was just me and Miss 'Buthnot. I would like to visit Ridley but not to stay there for a long time and I wouldn't like to go without

Miss 'Buthnot and Miss 'Buthnot can't go to Ridley in case Grandmama sends her away in the night.'

'That was a mistake and would not occur again.'

'I would be lonely at Ridley without Miss 'Buthnot.' Lottie suddenly thought, What if Uncle Thomas made me go to Ridley all on my own? As she slid along with the chair in front of her, a few tears cascaded down her cheeks.

Major Wilder noticed them. 'Have I made you cry? Why is that?'

'Don't, please, make me go anywhere without Miss 'Buthnot. Please don't, Uncle Thomas.'

'My dear child, not if it upsets you so, though indeed it had not crossed my mind. I hope I shall always look after you.'

'But what if you died?'

'Your aunt and uncle here would look after you.'

Major Wilder thought soldiers and children were much alike, never consulted, nothing explained. Well, here he was with Lyndon's child and he did not like to see her unhappy.

Lottie, impatient, pushed the chair to one side and shot forward. For half a minute she glided confidently in a smooth arc before descending to the ice with a thump. For a moment she thought of being cross but then she laughed.

Miss Arbuthnot emerged from the sickroom that very day and everyone was kind, the children offering her a place nearest the fire in their best French. Even Major Wilder asked after her health, but she thought his manner off-hand. She saw Miss Esmond had an aggrieved air and that

Major Wilder was solicitous of her. She had no idea he was trying to make amends for the great insult Miss Esmond considered Lottie had inflicted on her.

Major Wilder could not help feeling a little to blame because he had not offered Miss Esmond a ride on Cloudy. Now, she told him, she would not ride the horse if it were offered. Major Wilder took her at her word and did not make the offer but, as there was no riding, it was academic. He thought she took herself too seriously and wished, despite the splendour of her person, she would go away. Miss Esmond would have gone away had the roads been better, for she was not accustomed to staying in a house where she thought people were laughing at her. Such a thing had never happened to her before and she could not forgive her sister who, though she had lapsed into her habitual silence, Miss Esmond suspected laughed when no one looked. Miss Molly had also taken to running about with the children and had been seen to climb a tree, so the sooner she was removed from Finch Hall the better it would be. Should the roads improve, one other thing made Miss Esmond wonder if she was not being unnecessarily hasty, for Major Wilder's attempts to placate her led her to suppose he might be falling in love with her after all.

At Ridley Lady Charles was entirely alone and had been so for a fortnight. Her daughters and their families had departed before the new year. Now the roads were so bad Lord Charles did not return and neither did Thomas. She could not remember being alone for so long and she disliked it more and more. She had found her life intolerable before, but now it was worse. The rituals of the day barely altered, starting with Jane or Polly bringing up the chocolate on a tray. She dressed and then she wrote letters about nothing, for she had exhausted the subject of Sophia, Emily and their children. She had asked Georgie if Thomas was likely to propose to this Miss Esmond, whom Georgie had initially spoken of with favour, but Georgie, having become better acquainted with Miss Esmond, had replied she hoped not. Lady Charles would go downstairs, take breakfast in the austere splendour of the dining room, though she thought it only splendid for the number of chairs it contained, and then see the housekeeper. After that she might do a little sewing and while away the time until her luncheon was brought in on a tray.

She did not go out into the crisp white frosts: she thought the cold too unpleasant and that she might slip on the garden paths. Mrs Kingston did not visit because it was not safe to take the horses out. They wrote each other an occasional note. Mrs Kingston was expecting a guest, Captain Greenway. Lady Charles did not know whether he had braved the roads and arrived. At one time she had been anxious to meet him but no longer: she had given up the idea of knowing more than she did of Lyndon's death. She had come to believe Lyndon's fellow officers were jealous of him, he being so very much finer than the ordinary run of man, and certainly of the ordinary run of army officer. If Lyndon was not to be praised she would hear none of it.

At last she would go upstairs and change for dinner, though to what purpose she could not imagine, with only the servants to please. Darkness fell and she must kill the hours before she might reasonably go to bed. It made her consider the future. Was this to be her life? Lord Charles was old and would die before her. Thomas would spend only that time at Ridley he considered sufficient for running the estate. While he remained unmarried she could probably stay at Ridley as a widow, but it was a sad, dull life. She wondered if she could rent a house in London but Thomas would consider anything respectable too dear. She had used to think her future bound up with Lottie's, but now there was no Lottie. She took to reading and rereading Lyndon's letters, as if she might find something new in them: even repetition could not quiet the gaiety of his loved voice as it echoed from the sprawled lines and dashed notes, but the process only made her sadder.

When January was more than half gone she took from her desk the letter she had written Miss Arbuthnot and sent it to the post.

Miss Arbuthnot received two letters on the same day but as one was from her brother it was some time before she came to open the second. It was not often she had a letter from her dearly loved Bobby because he considered his letters to be family affairs, shared by all. As no one was closer or more attached to him than the eldest of his sisters, she longed, she supposed selfishly, for some communication from him that was entirely hers. As the nature of his occupation made any communication a mere toy of current, wind and wave she was generally just glad to know he was still alive when heard from last. The letter she had in her hand had been a month or so in coming. It had been addressed to her at Ridley and forwarded from there. Lieutenant Robert Arbuthnot had neat handwriting: she often wondered how he kept it so even when the ship was rolling, which he often mentioned that it did. He also thought to be economical with the space so though neat the words were a little small and squeezed, also crossed, belying the generous nature of his character.

My dearest, dearest Anna,

What a peculiar letter I received from Father, dated August, but only received now, November, and two from you written earlier. One gets glimpses of the lives of those one loves, snatches and patches, topsy-turvy as to order of events and troublesome to make sense of. Now, dearest sister, what is this of your declining to marry the most eligible of bachelors, the uncle of your little pupil? It is monstrous of Father to expect you to do so if you do not like the fellow, however convenient it might be for the rest of us, and I am shocked he considers it. I know you were attached to the man we now must now call brother, though I'm d----d if I will because he only sounds fit to be married to that little minx Kate, but you were deceived, and it is easy to be deceived in midsummer madness. It is no point to dwell on it. You may start again with a clear conscience and sounder judgement. You must not marry a man you do not like, respect, etc., nor if he is very fat, old and ugly, though ugly can turn out charming and take one by surprise. If he is weak and vacillating, boorish, a bully or drunk, I forbid you to marry him. However, artillery officers tend to be quick, sharp fellows, adept and ingenious: they have many obstacles to overcome in keeping the guns on the road. Now if Major Wilder is, as I suspect, nearer thirty than forty and can add kindness to quickness and perception, and has the ability to see something humorous and to laugh, but not maliciously, I suppose he may have the qualities to make an excellent husband. If you do not like him, never, and I do trust your judgement, my dear Anna, despite that Langley fellow, but should Major Wilder have qualities you can admire, you can betrothe yourself to him and he will be yours and you will love him dearly,

Ever your affectionate brother, Robert Arbuthnot

Miss Arbuthnot read this letter through three times. She wondered if it would have influenced her had she received it at the appropriate moment. Bobby's cheerful good sense came too late, but what was right and what was not? He certainly made it clear she should no longer dwell on the matter of Mr Langley, of whom she could see he had formed a low opinion, and this made her take note of the fact she had scarcely given her brother-in-law a single thought in months. So much, she thought, for true love, the poets and the ballads. One was a mere human after all, and her dearest Bobby thought none the worse of her, which was a comfort, though, on the whole, his letter did not comfort her, or his apparent assumption she would be able to put things right if she so wished.

She then turned to her second letter, which she found to be from Lady Charles. She skimmed through it, various phrases catching her attention: 'making you an earnest apology ... misguided ... wrong. My son's intentions towards you ... refusing him ... a sacrifice ... his father would disown him ... such an attraction is but fancy ... you were wise.' Miss Arbuthnot was so disturbed by the first part of the letter she could hardly bring herself to read the conclusion in which Lady Charles spoke of her pain in being separated from her granddaughter, with some idea that it was in Miss Arbuthnot's power to rectify the matter.

For a whole day Miss Arbuthnot puzzled over the two letters, aware that the first, had it come sooner, would have failed to influence her, so convinced had she been at the time of doing what she felt to be right; and the second, in which she could not make out what Lady Charles had meant to convey. She supposed it was an apology, though it was inadequate, and the rest of it made her assume she was a creature of such insignificance it was a wonder she had been noticed. Should this letter be answered? She had no wish to answer it and there was nothing she could possibly say that Lady Charles might understand. Eventually she recalled Miss Campbell advising her to take any problem to Mrs Heugmont without further ado. The difficulty would be to catch her alone for sufficient time to have a proper conversation. When dinner was over she managed to indicate to Mrs Heugmont how much she would like to speak to her, though she disliked the conspiratorial air she had to adopt to convey this, as if she was to make a confession or had some drama to report. Mrs Heugmont, however, led her away to her own little sitting room and sat her down by the fire.

Miss Arbuthnot produced Lady Charles's letter because

she did not, otherwise, know how to begin, and she knew Major Wilder having asked her to marry him was no secret from his sister. When Mrs Heugmont had read it, Miss Arbuthnot said, 'I didn't know how to respond.'

Mrs Heugmont said, 'I should think not.' She then said, after a pause, 'I have never known my mother admit, even to the smallest degree, she might have been wrong. Her parents, my father, always assured her she was perfect. My sisters think it. My poor lost brother certainly kept up the myth, whether he thought it or no. When I married Mr Heugmont he taught me, in a kindly way, no one is always right, and certainly not my mother. I don't hesitate to say, though Lady Charles is my mother and I am fond of her, her treatment of you was abominable and I shall always be ashamed of it. Even had you committed any of the sins she attributed to you, it wasn't justifiable.'

Miss Arbuthnot, despite Latin and astronomy and her excellent, sensible management of small children, was young and unworldly. The violence of Lady Charles's conduct to her remained mysterious: she never could entirely believe that Lady Charles had accused her of having some clandestine relationship with Major Wilder. It seemed too impossible, so far had it been from her mind, and indeed his, as far as she knew. She supposed she never would guess exactly what went on in his mind but she was certain it was nothing dishonourable.

Mrs Heugmont read the letter through again and then said, in her forthright way, 'Of course, you will have had your own reasons for declining my brother's proposal, and they certainly won't be the ones cited by my mother. What my mother wants is Lottie back at Ridley.'

'But Lady Charles must know it is not my position to decide.'

'Why Lyndon chose to make Thomas Lottie's guardian, as they were not at all close in the way one should like brothers to be, in fact quite to the contrary, we seem destined never to know, except that Thomas will be the head of the family. My mother thinks if you, the one who was wronged, forgive her then everyone will forgive her and Lottie will go back.'

'I have it on my mind that Miss Wilder is separated from her grandmother, but the decision must be Major Wilder's. I . . . I can't discuss it with him. Here Miss Wilder has a proper family. She is easily distracted and may not learn so much and I can't give her quite the same attention as I did at Ridley, but all the same, she is doing very well. She is no longer afraid of her books. As for myself, I never expected to go back to Ridley.'

'Nor should you. My brother would never ask it of you.'

'My father always taught us we should forgive, but I'm not sure even he has seen his way to forgive my return home. Lady Charles's letter is an apology. It is difficult to view it in a proper light. I see, from what you say, Lady Charles is not accustomed to apologizing. She doesn't know how it's done. Nevertheless, it is hard to forgive. Miss Wilder's best interests should be my main concern, whatever my personal reflections.' She knew she would make any sacrifice for the little girl she loved like her own child.

Miss Arbuthnot then began to wonder if being with her grandmother was in Miss Wilder's best interests, but certainly a permanent feud was a poor thing. A reconciliation with her grandmother and a series of visits of not too long a duration would do no harm. She remembered what Lord Charles had said, that Ridley was dull without herself and Lottie, and how he had said Major Wilder could not forgive his mother. If the last was on her account, she thought she stood between Lady Charles's reconciliation with her son as well as with her granddaughter, which could be construed as a just revenge and a cause for satisfaction, but it made her uncomfortable.

Mrs Heugmont said, 'Lottie probably should make it up with her grandmother. A long-drawn-out quarrel is bad for the soul. She would need supervision, which my mother would never undertake for more than an hour or so. Lottie would be distressed at going without you and I don't see why you should go.' She then added, with a smile, 'Besides, we rather like having you here.'

'You are very kind to me.'

'As for my mother's letter, leave it unanswered. I will speak to my brother.'

'I don't wish to go to Ridley, but if it were best for Miss Wilder, of course I should consider it. I can't imagine how it would be, but if it were only for short visits, I would face up to managing it somehow.'

Mrs Heugmont, having undertaken to speak to her brother, did so at the first opportunity. She was perfectly aware the very mention of the matter would make him cross. He had no wish to think about Miss Arbuthnot except in her capacity as governess to his niece and he considered Lady Charles had forfeited her right to the child. Mrs Heugmont also knew her brother was not blind to reason and could be coaxed, though she was herself doubtful as to what might be best. Her underlying wish was for reconciliation, however undeserving her mother, for permanent enmity, constant bad feeling, would render all of Ridley a deeply unpleasant place and Thomas, let alone his father, now so obviously in his declining years, had to live there. As it was, they would both be miserable the moment they set foot in the place and they would remain so. She pointed this out to Major Wilder, who replied that he was perfectly aware of it. He said he thought his father, to whom the children were always running with some little task or another or questions to be answered, was much happier at Finch Hall, but he conceded Lord Charles would consider it imperative he return to his wife. He himself had already decided he would have to be more civil to his mother in order not to render his father still unhappier but, he added, he did not know how it was to be done.

Mrs Heugmont told him it was not good for Lottie to be estranged from her grandmother. Major Wilder replied that he had reassured Lottie he would not separate her from Miss Arbuthnot, and as Miss Arbuthnot could not go to Ridley, the matter would have to wait until the child was older. Mrs Heugmont told him she thought Miss Arbuthnot would go to Ridley if it was for Lottie's sake, but he had replied she should not be expected to make such a sacrifice as to return to a place in which she had been so ill-treated. Mrs Heugmont tended to agree with him but she also wondered what effect it would have on her brother to have Miss Arbuthnot under the same roof as himself in the more intimate circumstances of Ridley, where there were five of them to sit down to dinner rather than the ten or twelve that could be mustered at Finch Hall, but this she thought better of mentioning. She definitely supposed any visit Lottie might make to Ridley should be of the shortest possible duration.

Major Wilder said he would speak to Miss Arbuthnot himself for not to do so would be shirking his duty, by which means his sister knew, however cross and irritated he might sound, he had listened to what she had said. She put her arm through his and gave him a kiss.

Miss Arbuthnot could skate but there never were quite enough skates to go round. Having helped Lottie to a greater expertise, she contented herself with walking among the frozen reeds and the willows. It gave her proper time for reflection but skating would have been more amusing, especially when she merely let a variety of notions ramble round inside her head as aimlessly as her footsteps led her round the pond and in and out of the little wood.

Major Wilder, seeing her thus occupied, was glad to think he might catch her alone, though he had got out of the way of talking to her at his ease. As he approached her he began to be concerned that she would be cold, walking about in the snow and then standing to wait for him. On reaching her, he said, ignoring what else he might be thinking, 'I have been speaking to my sister. She tells me, for the sake of my niece, you would consider going back to Ridley. I am doubtful I should allow you to do such a thing. I don't see how you can even consider it.'

He sounded extremely cross. Miss Arbuthnot looked at

him shyly but she was, she thought, always able to say to him what she thought necessary. After a little contemplation, she said, 'I don't suppose I ever will understand what made Lady Charles think so ill of me. I ought to be too proud to go back, but what is pride? Is it good or bad?'

'Some self-esteem is a requirement,' he replied.

'My father would preach Christian forgiveness, though he certainly forgot that at the time. It is hard to live up to every principle, though I used to think him capable of it. Lady Charles has apologized to me. Though I didn't care for her letter, it was an apology. I don't like the idea of returning, but perhaps, in the end, it would be better for everyone. Miss Wilder ought to see her grandmother. I don't imagine we should go for very long.'

'Oh, no, just enough time to make the journey worthwhile, I suppose, and to bring Cloudy and the pony back and forth.'

Major Wilder frowned to himself. She could see his mind had gone to the complexities of travel, but he said, 'I feel you are sacrificed for Lottie. I'm not comfortable with it. You must be free to change your mind. Why should you be at the mercy of my mother's freaks and fancies?'

'I don't think it the sort of thing that would happen twice.'

'Certainly not.' He would be there to see it did not happen, or anything resembling it.

He could hear Miss Esmond calling, 'Cooee.' She was looking for him. He had agreed to take her on the ice. She was striding across the snow, magnificent in a fur-lined scarlet cloak with a bonnet and a muff that matched it. She looked three of Miss Arbuthnot, with her red cheeks and her bright eyes: he only wished he liked her. She made Miss Arbuthnot look like a child.

Miss Esmond thought she had interrupted something. Had she not, all along, considered there was an irregularity? She gave Miss Arbuthnot a cursory glance but did not address her because she was only a governess and need not be addressed.

Major Wilder, his arm seized by Miss Esmond, said, 'Nothing can be done until the weather breaks, so you have time to think. Don't allow yourself to get cold.'

Miss Esmond took him away. 'Oh, dear, I fear you are far from gallant, leaving me at the mercy of so many children and dogs in order to talk to the governess.'

Lady Charles had had instructions from Georgie that she did not much care to receive. Surely it was for the mother to give instructions on how best to make amends, but she complied. She made a stately visit to the schoolroom and the rooms that it was customary for governesses to call their own, accompanied by both Jane and Polly. She decreed Miss Arbuthnot should have a change of quarters, the room across the passage being sunnier and having a better view. The two maids measured the windows and Lady Charles chose the fabric for fresh curtains. She had the pictures changed around and added more but she did not return to see the finished result.

She could not reconcile herself to the fact that Lottie and Miss Arbuthnot were merely paying a visit. Would they not stay? Was it not for the best to continue as if nothing unfortunate had occurred? Thomas had made clear that it was just a visit. He considered it better for Lottie to be with her cousins. Lady Charles thought that if all went well Lottie could visit with regularity. When the child was sixteen or seventeen they would take a house in London and give a ball for her. She adjusted her image of Lottie, with her gardening, her boots, her baize apron, her cropped curls and her solid figure into the graceful being she was to become in time for her launch upon society. She must be worthy of her father. She dwelt so heavily on the matter she half expected that when she saw Lottie she would have started on the necessary transformation.

Lady Charles, waiting anxiously in the drawing room for her granddaughter's arrival from Finch Hall, wondered how their greeting would be. She did her best to expel from her mind Lottie's conduct when they had last been together. Of course children said dreadful things when they lost their tempers but Lottie had carried it to excess. She was surprised by how nervous she was, a sensation to which she was unaccustomed. There was also the question of Miss Arbuthnot. It was all very tiresome. She could not even be sure how Thomas would behave.

For once, seeing the carriage come briskly through the park with Thomas riding and leading Lottie's pony, Lady Charles went into the hall to greet them. Slimmer opened the door and through it she saw her husband climb from the carriage, assisted by York, swiftly followed by Miss Arbuthnot. Lord Charles turned to her and took her arm, as if he looked for her support. Lady Charles immediately thought, Does he need her arm to come up the steps? Is he so frail?

Before such a question could be answered, there was

Lottie, cheerfully greeting her grandmother as if she had seen her the day before. Lottie had not forgotten that Miss Arbuthnot had been sent away in the night, but the intervening months had served to dull the memory of much else, so she just said, 'I hope you are well, Grandmama. One of the carriage horses lost a shoe. Uncle Thomas let us watch the blacksmith. Miss 'Buthnot has been reading a story to Grandpapa and me.'

Any ideas that Lottie might have altered were quickly dispelled. Lady Charles was faintly disappointed. She greeted her husband after kissing the child, and said, 'Miss Arbuthnot, how kind of you to be looking after Lord Charles. I have given you a different room. It has a better aspect. I hope it will suit you.'

As Miss Arbuthnot was not expecting any further apologies or explanations from Lady Charles, she saw this as a peace-offering. Doing her best to expunge from her mind her last encounter with Lady Charles, which, unlike Lottie's, had remained vivid, she replied politely, if awkwardly, that she was sure the room would suit her perfectly well. Lord Charles, who still had her arm, gave it a little pat. Lady Charles then realized he had made himself Miss Arbuthnot's champion: should he not support his wife? Why could he not agree she had done what was right at the time?

Major Wilder then appeared. He greeted his mother civilly, if perfunctorily, and reckoned his performance adequate, while his father was considering all life a good piece of acting.

Slimmer hovered in the background, fascinated; for once no one remembered to send him away.

Lady Charles thought how unpleasant everything was, but recalled that disagreeable topics would fade away if ignored. She turned back to Lottie and decided the child had grown. With the correct help, she would yet be pretty and elegant. Even now the dear little girl was not plain and had still a look of her father. She drew Lottie towards her to give her another kiss, delighted to think they really were reconciled. 'Why, darling, I declare you have grown quite a bit.'

'Children do,' Lottie replied. She wanted to run round the house and into the garden.

'Your manners haven't improved.'

'No, but I have to grow, don't I? I didn't mean to be rude.'

'Well, we won't squabble. I hear from your aunt Georgie you have been very good.' Lady Charles still had an arm round her. 'I hope you have remembered your prayers. I am sure Miss Arbuthnot reminds you.'

'I don't need reminding.'

'And you remember your dearest papa?'

'Oh, sometimes,' Lottie replied airily, 'but they take ever so long to say, what with all my cousins and the sad slaves and the chimney-sweep boys that oughtn't to be made to go in the chimneys.'

'Whatever next? Slaves and chimney sweeps! You've been listening to your uncle John Heugmont,' Lady Charles said, attempting to sound indulgent, but Lottie had already gone.

Mrs Kingston arrived two days later. Slimmer ushered her into the drawing room. She was sufficiently agitated to be ready to propel herself there without his assistance, her little feet hastening across the marble flags of the hall. She greeted Lady Charles with a flood of apologies for her tardiness in not coming sooner.

'I have so much to distract me. It is very tiresome having Captain Greenway in the house. I had hopes, once, it would be appropriate for you to meet Captain Greenway but he is not at all the sort of person I had supposed he might be.' Inexplicably, Mrs Kingston burst into tears, but then she said, 'Of course, Horatio took the most instant dislike to him and I said to Henry, "You must tell him to go away," but Henry said how could he? And Henry is quite right for I believe Captain Greenway to have an uncertain temper.'

Mrs Kingston accepted Lady Charles's invitation to sit down and seemed to soothe herself by the careful smoothing of her lilac skirts. She said, 'I'm delighted to have my boy returned to me, though it won't be for long. I see he ran a bit wild at Finch Hall . . . so many children.' Mrs Kingston had chosen to forget that Horatio running wild at home was the reason he had gone to Finch Hall. 'However, he was happy there and got on with his lessons, I understand. Now, I have had a most disturbing letter from my brother-in-law, Captain Kingston of the *Prince Adolphus*. It was, of course, written months ago. I have kept up a correspondence with him, as well as one can. I believe I had hinted, as a widow, I was finding my boy rather a handful, but I only said it in play. However, the *Prince Adolphus* will be coming into Plymouth some time next month, Captain Kingston will go to London to the Admiralty and on his return he will call on us and expect to take Horatio away with him. Horatio's name has been down on the ship's list since he was seven. He must be measured for his uniform, and I have a list as long as anybody's arm as to what he will need. He must have his father's spyglass: I've kept it by all these years. Captain Kingston says he likes a lad with spirit.' Mrs Kingston again resorted to tears. 'I said to Horatio, "You don't want to go, do you?" He said, "Yes, I do, I'm going to go." I'm so distraught, I can't think what's for the best.'

Lady Charles, composing her features to indicate proper concern, said calmly, 'Why, you must take his measurements and send them to London. Then, when you go, he will only need a fitting. You must have the coat made roomy for he will certainly grow. They must make it so the sleeves let down. In the meantime he had better take his lessons with Miss Arbuthnot to keep him from mischief.'

'But is she not to return to Finch Hall and Lottie too?'

'All in good time, I suppose.'

'And Miss Arbuthnot has got over any little difficulties?'

'It is all water under the bridge. Besides, Miss Arbuthnot must know she has an excellent position here, considering her age. Others might hesitate to employ one so young, or only as an assistant. I know you acted as you thought best when you spoke to me that day, but we were both a little too hasty in our judgement.'

Mrs Kingston could never understand why she had to share the blame for Miss Arbuthnot's abrupt dismissal but, having no wish for a dispute with Lady Charles and with other things more pressing on her mind, she said nothing.

Major Wilder came across Horatio on the stairs. He felt

the child was waiting for him, waiting for his door to open, and he asked him as much.

'Yes, sir.'

'And why was that?'

'I wanted to tell you I'm to go to sea now. My uncle is coming to fetch me when his ship comes into Plymouth. First he goes to London and then he comes here on his return.'

They paused on the stairs, neither going up nor down. Horatio then continued, 'My uncle wrote me a letter. He is looking forward to my being with him in the *Prince Adolphus*. I would remind him of my father and of all the naughty things they did when they were boys together. He told me I must expect treatment no different from that of the other midshipmen, but even when he was stern, I was to know he loved me, for my father's sake. Well, I shouldn't like any special favours: it would make me disliked by the other boys. It is a very kind letter but I should like to be able to tell him I hope he may love me for my own sake. He reminded me my father died doing his duty. I hope I may do mine. I know now it doesn't matter if I'm dead or wounded or drowned so long as I do that. I hope I may not disappoint my uncle.'

Major Wilder looked at Horatio and wished he was more than eleven years old and more than four foot tall. He said slowly, 'If you do your duty you will never disappoint Captain Kingston.'

Horatio said, 'I shall be twelve next month, so I'm old enough now. I wanted to ask you a favour, sir. Will you do me one?'

'If it is within my power.'

'I asked Mr Heugmont if I might give my pony to Benjy. He said, "Hasn't Benjy a pony already?" I said, "Yes, but my pony is better than Prince and won't give Benjy a fright." He said, "Yes, yes, child." He was studying papers about the telegraph system. He wasn't paying attention. You see, I want to know where my pony is, when I'm gone, and giving him to Benjy would be like a little brother of my own having him. I told my mother and she said the pony was mine to give but I don't trust her to remember, once I'm gone, and he might just be sent to market so, when the time comes, I'll leave him here, and if you would be so kind, you would take him to Finch Hall next time you go.'

'Of course, and when you are on leave, you can go to Finch Hall and see him. I know you will always be welcome there.'

'Yes, I shall come here and I shall go to Finch Hall.'

'But the *Prince Adolphus* is not yet here, I hope.'

'No, no, not yet. I have to get my uniform and other things and I'm to have my father's telescope.'

Below them they could hear Slimmer crossing the hall and opening the drawing-room door.

Horatio said, 'I expect my mother is about to leave. I think I'll run up to Lottie and Miss Arbuthnot before she sees me and tells me to come home. Miss Arbuthnot says she can teach me some astronomy before I go.'

Horatio scampered up the stairs and Major Wilder continued on his way down, deciding not to be deterred by his almost certain meeting with Mrs Kingston, seeing how sad a time it was for her. She was about to go out of the front door when she turned and saw him. She said, 'Ah, Major Wilder, I was hoping to see you. May we take a turn on the terrace, or in the gardens? Yes, I would prefer that. Have you time?'

Major Wilder thought she looked ill. He could see she had been crying. Was she not to lose her only child to an uncertain future in the *Prince Adolphus*? He gave her his arm.

Once they were among the bare borders, a few snowdrops all that was to be seen, Mrs Kingston said, rapidly but quietly, 'I'm so glad we met. I have been so agitated and distressed I haven't known which way to turn. It's a terrible thing.'

Major Wilder, seeing how genuine was her state, said, 'It is certainly a sad thing to see the boy go. It is not as if you had other sons. Perhaps, now, it is late for changing your mind if Horatio himself is expecting to go. It would turn his world topsy-turvy, but you should discuss it with him because it is not actually too late to retract.'

For a moment Mrs Kingston looked puzzled. She then said, 'Oh, to be sure, it's not Horatio I'm talking of. No, I shan't like to see him go, but it has been arranged for years. To change our minds at the eleventh hour would be very havering and inconsistent. I'm sure my brother-in-law would take a dim view of it and I am always hoping, as he is not a married man and has no heir, he will think of Horatio. It is another thing entirely.' She started to weep and wring her hands. 'It is Captain Greenway.'

Major Wilder sighed. He had been certain, ever since he had heard of Captain Greenway's visit, that the gentleman had only one intent, and that was to cause trouble to himself. Had he been a little cavalier in his treatment of Captain Greenway? He had not, at the time, given it much thought. He supposed if Captain Greenway had come to him in person with Lyndon's IOU, he would probably have paid it, as he had told the Colonel at the time, but there had been no IOU, merely a note, and that written in a manner more likely to cause offence than anything else. Well, if Captain Greenway cared to come to him with the IOU in his hand he would be disposed to give him the eight pounds fifteen shillings that should cover his forty Spanish dollars, but he had an idea Captain Greenway wanted more than the settling of an old debt.

Mrs Kingston, recovering her composure sufficiently to speak, said, 'If it should get to poor Lady Charles, it would kill her, yes, kill her, though it's a lie, as Captain Greenway must know. The lies he tells . . . it can't be anything but lies. I can't bring myself to repeat it.'

Major Wilder said, 'I dare say it is best not to repeat it.'

'But he will repeat it, he says he will, he doesn't care who knows it. He has no heart. Henry can't stop him. I believe he frightens Henry to death.'

'I take it, as they were in the same regiment, Captain Greenway talks of my late brother.'

'Yes, it is all about your brother, the kindest, the most noble, most true-hearted of mortals, who went to war from a sense of duty.'

'And is that the reason he gave for going?'

'Yes, certainly. He can have had no other reason for going, no need at all . . . it was all duty . . . He told me as much himself.' Mrs Kingston could not help but cry. 'You cannot imagine the terrible thing that Captain Greenway says.'

'You are mistaken. I can.'

Mrs Kingston was horrified. 'It would be impossible to imagine it.'

Major Wilder shook his head. 'I don't want to discuss it. I know what he will be saying, that it was not the French who shot Lyndon.'

Covering her eyes, Mrs Kingston said, 'I don't see how you guess it.'

Major Wilder wanted to say, Has it not occurred to you that, if you wished to preserve my life, I am the last person to whom you should speak? But he thought Mrs Kingston a woman of limited intelligence.

She then said, 'I know you will want to deny everything, to scotch it. Your brother's honour is at stake.'

'So it may be. There is probably only one way to settle such a business and it is the one way of which I most heartily disapprove. My own honour will be at stake, let alone Lyndon's.'

Mrs Kingston began to understand what he was talking about. She said, uncertainly, 'Of course, your own honour is unquestioned, but you seem as if you were expecting . . .'

As she seemed disinclined to continue, he said, 'I have had it in the back of my mind that Captain Greenway would cause me trouble.'

'He is very hot-tempered, very difficult . . . I shouldn't have told you. I couldn't think what to do. If such a scandalous lie should reach the ears of your parents, I should never forgive myself. I had to tell you. I'm sure you would not have liked it had I kept it from you.'

Major Wilder led Mrs Kingston back to her carriage. She was alternately silent, then pleading, then weeping, then making excuses. He was relieved when her coachman jumped up on the box and drove her away. He called his dogs and walked out into the park. His mind was filled with that rainy day at Vera de Bidasoa and with the disgust, the shame and the ignominy from which it could not be detached.

It had been late September. He had left the drab little village that was housing much of Lyndon's regiment, the lounging, insolent officers and the awkward, ill-at-ease colonel who had not the grace to offer him dinner. He had left his servants to make their way back to his distant billet with the white greyhound and as many of Lyndon's effects as he deemed reasonable to keep, leaving instructions for the rest to be auctioned according to practice. Mounted on the Andalusian he had ridden in the direction of the Pyrenees. He had been glad to be alone. In his mind he composed a letter to Georgie. This was a means he often used for clarifying a situation in his head. On the day that he reached Vera, at the foot of the mountains, it was pouring with rain. The village, with its narrow, wet streets and deep, jutting eaves, more alpine, he thought, than Spanish, stood on the very banks of the wide, rushing, tree-clad Bidasoa. He asked for Captain Allington, who was to return to him those articles that had been looted from Lyndon's body.

As directed, he rapped at the door of a tall house on the main street and it was immediately opened by a diminutive, neat little fellow, a soldier's servant. He showed him into a large, low room. An officer wearing the brown uniform of the Portuguese service was addressing four or five *caçadores* in rapid, fluent Portuguese. He had his back to him and did not immediately notice him, but the servant drew his attention to his visitor and he turned round and said several things, most likely an apology, but continuing to speak in the foreign language. He was a young man, perhaps as much as ten years younger than himself, with such black eyes and dark hair and such a tanned complexion that Major Wilder took him not to be an Englishman at all and that he had been given the wrong direction.

Allington, seeing his bewildered expression, said, 'I beg your pardon. You are Major Wilder of the Horse Artillery. I was not expecting you so soon, sir. You are very wet. Allow my servant to take your cloak. He will dry it. Pride, take the Major's cloak and see what you can do with it. Have you dined?'

Afterwards he concluded that Captain Allington had applied a ruse to know if he spoke Portuguese but this did not occur to him at the time. He said, 'You are very kind. No, I haven't dined, but I dare say you have.'

'Yes, but Pride will rustle you something up.' He turned again to his *caçadores* and dismissed them with a few further instructions in Portuguese before saying, 'I'm sorry for your misfortune.' He then went to a small trunk and unlocked it.

While Captain Allington was thus occupied, he was himself hesitating, though he was hungry, in accepting the offer of being fed. He knew very well the slender means of some of these young officers but the servant who had taken his cloak was already laying bread and cheese on the table, half a bottle of wine and then a bowl of soup.

'Rabbit, sir, in the broth. The Captain's yellow dog got it yesterday. We've plenty of it.'

Captain Allington said, 'Thank you, Pride, that will do.

Leave us be, now.' He turned to his guest and added, 'It's not exactly a whole dinner.'

'It is very welcome, thank you, and more than sufficient.' He tasted the soup. 'Your servant is a good cook.'

'Yes. He has his faults, is sometimes not very bright, but he is solely devoted to my interests.' As Captain Allington spoke he was laying on the table a spyglass, a gilt snuff box, the regimental buttons from a jacket, and a gold watch with the chain, seal and key still attached. Alongside them he carefully laid a sword. He then withdrew to the other side of the room, as if to leave his guest alone with his brother's possessions.

Major Wilder remembered how he had picked each article up in turn, even the buttons, but particularly the watch. It was a gold hunter, with a beautifully chased outer casing that sprang open at a touch to reveal the face behind its glass. He had said to Captain Allington, for he saw the awkwardness in having to hand over to an officer senior to himself, and a stranger, these objects that must be assumed to be of a deeply personal and affecting nature, 'I am extremely grateful to you for the trouble you have taken. Acquiring them may have been tiresome.'

'Not in the least. I don't care so much what the men take from the French, but I won't have them looting British officers, not if I can help it. I don't punish them but I go through their kit if I'm suspicious of them. They would prefer to be looting than getting their own wounded off the field. I suppose it was ever thus. British soldiers are no better, as I don't need to tell you. The officer from the 95th who was killed defending this very bridge at Vera had the ring stolen from his finger by a man from his own regiment, who showed a sad lack of wisdom in trying to sell it back to the other officers of the same regiment.'

'He will be flogged?'

'Yes, he will be flogged.'

Their manner as they spoke indicated they thought the punishment would be ineffectual.

'As for your brother's things,' Captain Allington said, 'we were in the action at which he died, and having my usual suspicions, I was able to retrieve them, among other things, but these seem to belong together. The snuff box is inscribed.'

'The watch I have often seen before and, of course, the seal.'

Major Wilder clearly recalled the exact conversation he had had with Captain Allington, and as he walked across the park he put his hand to the pocket of his waistcoat and felt the smooth, rounded shape of his brother's watch. It kept excellent time. He thought Lyndon would not have cared for him to have it, whatever he might have written in his will. He had then said to Captain Allington, 'Do you have brothers?'

'No, sir, I was orphaned at an early age. I have a step-family who might or might not take note of me.' He suddenly laughed. 'I live by my wits. I entered the Portuguese service for the extra pay, but it suits me. I am a natural linguist.'

Though Captain Allington appeared to speak freely, yet there was something enigmatic about him. It was at that moment Major Wilder recalled what had been teasing at the back of his mind. It was this officer who, despite his youth, had a reputation for being extremely clever. He was frequently used for surveillance, for which, with his foreign appearance, he was probably well adjusted.

Major Wilder then said, having finished his meal, 'I must thank you again. I have a long way to go as yet but I shall take a look at the bridge before I leave. Will I find it easily?'

'It's only a short way. Allow me to take you there. Your cloak won't be dry but I think it's stopped raining.'

They left the house together. Major Wilder checked that his horse was still standing where he had left it, with loosened girths, half an old blanket across his loins, the halter rope flung casually over a railing.

Captain Allington said, 'An Andalusian, I see. He's very pretty. How did you get him?'

'Oh, it's one of those stories,' Major Wilder had said, with a laugh, and then added, not strictly truthfully, 'I would tell you if we had all day.'

So they had walked to the bridge together, discussing horses. The Bidasoa was swift and wide, murky green and dark with rainwater. It was overhung with large trees. The bridge itself was of a modest size with low parapets and a passing bay. As Major Wilder was giving it a cursory examination and paying a mental tribute to the men who had lost their lives defending it, he turned to see a Portuguese lad of about fourteen years old running towards him with a red infantry jacket over his arm. Smiling, he proffered it to Captain Allington, who spoke to him, extremely sharply, in his own language.

The boy seemed to be protesting. He indicated Major Wilder, then thrust his hand into the pocket and produced a small key of the sort used to open a writing box.

Major Wilder had said, 'Is that my brother's jacket?'

Captain Allington replied, 'I believe so. I had not intended you should see it. It is too emotive a thing, blood-stained, but this lad belongs to the house in which I'm staying. I had suggested they dispose of it but he is telling me I had overlooked this key, which he is sure you will need for something.'

Major Wilder said, 'Ah, well, now it is here I shall look at it.' He produced a tip for the boy, who ran off delighted.

Captain Allington said, 'I don't think you are obliged to have it so much as in your hands.'

'Possibly not but, odd as it is, I find it difficult to believe my brother died. Half of me wonders if he is not wounded and a prisoner with the French, though there is no evidence to support the idea, not a shred. He was seen by an Ensign Parker, who, though wounded, crawled back to look at him. Unfortunately Parker died of his own wounds before I could speak with him. It has left a small part of me unconvinced. Wounded, yes, looted, stripped, yes, but then, possibly, picked up by the French. Allow me to see his coat.'

He had sat down on the parapet of the bridge and held out his arm for the jacket, which Captain Allington gave him with evident reluctance. As he laid it across his knees, he said involuntarily, 'God knows, I didn't love him, but one wishes this on no man, even while one sights the guns oneself.'

The back of the jacket was entirely shot away in a ragged patch about eight inches across but when he turned it over he could see the front was only slightly damaged. What bullets there were, and they seemed considerable, had for the most part lodged in the body. Major Wilder thought they had been fired at comparatively close range. He said, almost without thinking, 'What was he doing, so close to the enemy, and with his back to them?' As he spoke he understood the truth. He thought he understood everything, even to the reluctance of Lyndon's colonel, or anyone else from his regiment, to speak to him. They knew the truth and were covering it up. He felt himself to lose all colour in his face, indeed he felt ill with shame and ignominy, with utter disgust.

Captain Allington had moved away from him and gave the appearance of studiously studying the Bidasoa. So he, too, knew the truth. Major Wilder said, keeping his voice as steady as he could, though it sounded strange in his own ears, 'My brother was not shot by the French. He was shot by his own men.'

Allington said slowly, 'It is a conclusion one could draw, but perhaps one you leap to without sufficient evidence.'

'But you know it's true.'

Perhaps at this juncture Captain Allington saw there was no point in evasion but he said nothing.

Major Wilder said, 'You see, there was something about the character of my brother that makes it perfectly likely. It was not good to be in a subordinate position to him.'

Captain Allington still said nothing, still gazed at the river.

Major Wilder then said, 'If this is my brother's jacket, if the blood is his, one would certainly be surprised if he lived, but extraordinary wounds are got over from time to time. There is nothing about the jacket to say it is his. It belonged, we can say, to a man from his regiment. The facings are correct, no lacing, the buttons you gave me are correct, but he was not the only officer from his regiment who died that day. I should be glad if it were not his.'

Captain Allington said, 'It was far better not to know it.'

'I thought doubt the more tormenting, but if my surmise is correct, the shame of it, one's own brother, is worse. What can you tell me?'

'Remember, it was the men from my company who stripped that jacket from the body. They saw him shot.'

Major Wilder got up from the parapet of the bridge. He said, 'Tell me all.'

'He had the face of an angel, my *caçadores* told me, very fair, very handsome. Once I had confiscated their spoils, they told me how he died, how they had seen it. They told me the English soldiers shot him and ran away but not very far, for they rallied and started to fire on the French. They knew he must be dead and they said they went to look, but it would have been the looting that was on their minds. They promised me he was dead and I do believe that. The face of an angel, so they said, and they were . . . I was pleased to note . . . a little shocked and confused. I had not intended anyone should know any of this, least of all yourself. I had thought, if I was careful, when you came, it could all be neatly passed over.'

'And you chose not to report the matter further?'

Captain Allington shrugged. 'And get my Portuguese, who speak a minimum of English, to stand as witnesses at a court martial, their word against the word of the English soldiers whose very officers might not speak the truth? I believe it is a poor regiment, that one, with low morale. What would be the point? My own *caçadores* would be court-martialled for making mischief. Only his regiment can do it and if they don't choose to . . .' Captain Allington paused; and then repeated, 'The face of an angel . . . that is what they said.'

'My brother was very good-looking, very blond,' Major Wilder said. 'You have quashed my doubts. I feel strangely sick. That swathe of bullets might be in my own back.'

'It is the effects of the shock.' Captain Allington spoke coolly. 'If you wish to take it further, I will, of course, support you.'

'No, thank God. Why should I, of all people, make it public?'

'But you believe some of the officers, the Colonel, know it?'

'Yes, I do. He longed to be rid of me. I felt it in every bone. There was no question of my being invited to dine with Lyndon's brother officers, who would be delighted to meet me, such a loss to the regiment et cetera, et cetera.' Major Wilder managed a wry smile. 'You and I know you don't necessarily see much of an action more than clouds of smoke, but if those other officers didn't see what happened, it occurs to me that Parker did, and that was perhaps his main purpose, though badly wounded, in going back. I don't suppose he kept the information to himself. And the men who did it, they'll be pipe-claying their belts and cleaning their pieces, polishing their buttons, washing their linen, and will they raise their heads and meet each other's eyes? You may bet they won't.'

'But it was murder.'

'What is war but murder on a grand scale with a fine excuse? It is my profession all the same.'

'Well, it had been my intention nobody should know it, least of all yourself. The officers of your brother's regiment may know it, some of them, but they can have no purpose in disclosing it. Look, it is starting to rain again. Don't go tonight. It's getting late. I can make room for you and your Andalusian. I think you would be unwise to travel tonight.'

Major Wilder then thought how, at this moment of revelation, he and Captain Allington had lost all sense of rank or age. Captain Allington had ceased to address him as 'sir' and he had ceased to think of him as a younger man of more junior rank. Indeed, he saw him as a man in every way equal to himself. His instinct was to flee into the oncoming darkness, to accustom himself to bear the truth and to accept the burden of it as something that could never be told, that must weigh on him until he died, the shame, the disgust and the ignominy, but now he changed his mind. He was tired. Had he not made a long journey?

Miss Arbuthnot was puzzled by her father's last letter. He was agitated by the thought of her returning to Ridley. He told her it did not become her dignity or that of the family for her to return after such treatment, but then he had talked of Christian forgiveness and humility, so she was left wondering if he wished her back at Ridley or not. She supposed he could be divided on the subject, decidedly thinking she should not return yet, she suspected, still hoping she might marry Major Wilder, which he must think a greater possibility if they were living under the same roof, even if only temporarily. Miss Arbuthnot thought his principles, when applied to his children, became pulled out of shape, like old clothes, and then wondered at herself for questioning her father's judgement. At one time she would not have dreamt of doing so.

She began to think of forgiveness. Lady Charles was not the sort of person who would go down on bended knee, like the Prodigal Son, and beg it. Miss Arbuthnot was fairly sure Lady Charles's knees had not the capacity for bending. Lady Charles was capable of a meagre apology and fresh curtains. The new room was much prettier than the old, lighter and with a fine view across the park, though Miss Arbuthnot was sufficiently perverse to miss the quaint irregularity of the vegetable gardens and the stable roofs. She had made the sacrifice, swallowed her pride, because she thought it best for Miss Wilder to move freely between the two houses and her various relations, and did she not love the child? She tried to delve further into her own mind, to judge herself honestly for other motives, but she was no longer clear about what she thought or felt. The one thing she was certain of was her lack of vulnerability as far as Lady Charles was concerned. Lady Charles could do no worse than she had, and was now conciliatory and polite, but Miss Arbuthnot believed it all an act and the best Lady Charles could do. She was herself polite and, whether false or no, an air of civility pervaded the place. Her new life at Ridley differed from the old in as much as she now led a life less segregated from the family than had been previously the case. This was due to Lord Charles. He had wished to make amends for what he saw as his wife's inexplicable conduct with solicitude and kindness, but now he had come to require her company as well as Lottie's. If she read aloud to Lottie, he liked to listen, sitting between them with Scottie on his lap. Sometimes she read him the newspaper, and if he took the little dog for its evening walk, he would ask her to go with him, take her arm, and encourage her to talk of her family and her vicarage childhood, tales of which he was happy to exchange with those, a little disjointed, of his own distant past and his father's grand house, six times grander than Ridley, and its magnificent estate. When she suggested Ridley was possibly adequate for the needs of most, he would say, a trifle wistfully, 'I dare say you are right, my dear.'

Not knowing how to describe this change to her father, or indeed any of her reflections, Miss Arbuthnot asked him to send her the books he had had for teaching Bobby astronomy to aid her in teaching Horatio before he entered the navy. She then settled to answering the letter she had had from her brother, trying to visualize where he might be and how he might receive the epistle. After the customary salutations and necessary enquiries into his health, all of which would be irrelevant by the time a reply could be remotely forthcoming, she said,

Much as I appreciate your opinion, you make it sound too simple. It is odd, my dear Bobby, how I have gone along always thinking I could manage things, the death of our oh-so-beloved mother, the taking on of our little sisters, and the managing of them, though ill-managed where Kate was concerned but, then, I defy anyone to manage Kate and cannot help wondering how Mr Langley does. Then there was the kitchen and the housekeeping, the garden et cetera, with the very minimum of servants and they looking to a girl of fourteen for instructions. When it comes to the management of my own heart I am as much at sea as you are but in the less literal sense: I am a dismal failure. As for Major Wilder, you must not run away with the idea I could still marry him. He has taken me at my word and gives his attention to another, or I believe he does. I cannot accuse him of fickleness. He never declared an undying passion for me, merely that he had grown to like me, though I think my refusing him was hurtful to him. He wishes to marry and he is entitled to try elsewhere. I dare say it is a great deal easier for a gentleman not to marry the governess of his ward who has neither money nor position. He must, after all, be practical, for he needs an heir.

Miss Arbuthnot put down the pen and wondered if she was telling Bobby what she felt or what she thought she ought to feel. Having decided quite enough had been said on the subject, she went on to ask her brother what would be the most useful things for Horatio to be taught before he went to sea, and did Bobby know anything of the *Prince Adolphus*? It made her shed tears to think the child would most likely be gone before she received a reply.

Major Wilder sat at his grandfather's desk before breakfast. He needed to write to Captain Greenway though he was reasonably certain it would be to no avail. He could only hope to make a dignified appeal to the man's better nature, but did he have such? After much careful consideration, he wrote,

Dear Captain Greenway,

It has come to my hearing that rumours circulate as to the manner of the death of my brother in the action at Roncesvalles on 25 July 1813. Should such rumours come to the ears of my parents it would cause them great agony on top of the grief they already have to bear for the loss of their elder son. Such speculations never abound to the credit of a regiment, and that regiment being yours, I should feel deeply obliged to you if you felt able to dismiss these conjectures or at least discourage those who wish to repeat them.

In the aftermath of my brother's death, I believe I recall your name in conjunction with a gambling debt of my brother's. You may think me absurd or a radical evangelist, but I have nurtured a horror of gambling since I was quite young. However, should you recall the details and wish to discuss the matter further, wait on me at your convenience,

Your obedient servant,

T. O. L. Wilder

He regretted that he could not put 'of the Royal Horse Artillery' after his name, but he no longer felt entitled to do so. He regretted even more having to indicate he would settle the gambling debt but he saw, of two evils, it was the lesser.

He thought of Lyndon's duelling pistols upstairs, so neatly packed in their mahogany box, and of how he had taken aim at his own image in the looking-glass. He then thought of the evening he had spent with Captain Allington, after they had returned from the bridge in Vera de Bidasoa. Captain Allington seemed to live a solitary life. He had told Major Wilder he had recently lost a close friend. Such matters not being suitable for discussion, they had left it that and, for similar reason, they had not further discussed the death of Lyndon Wilder, though it was never far from the mind of his younger brother. They had talked of the war, of soldiers, and of the merits of the Baker rifle over the musket and if either could be improved. Major Wilder could see his companion was very clever: he had a sort of fiery brilliance, he was full of notions. If luck favoured him he should have an astonishing career but he told Major Wilder he would have as soon been a barrister, where it was more probable to gain a living. They acknowledged to each other the difficulties of being kept short of income. Captain Allington then announced he supplemented his own by gambling. Major Wilder, anxious to disguise his true feeling, had said lightly he had always thought that the route to certain penury. Captain Allington had replied he had misunderstood him: he played no games in which luck played the significant part, he preferred chess, in which there was no chance involved, and he played only to win. He wanted to know if Major Wilder considered that ungentlemanly. Major Wilder had replied he supposed even the most besotted of gamblers preferred to win than otherwise, but he should not care to ruin anyone, however foolish they were. To this Captain

Allington had agreed, though he confessed to having won, at times, quite large sums of money, but he hoped from those who could afford it. His brother officers, being well acquainted with him, were inclined to bet on the results of his game, so money passed from hand to hand. Major Wilder, being well aware that to have a wager on something or another seemed the breath of life to much of his fellow man, was not surprised, and neither was he inclined to disapprove of anything Captain Allington might choose to do, one who had treated him with such consideration and who was so alone in the world.

He had absolutely declined to take Captain Allington's bed, which the younger man was anxious to offer him, and had settled on the floor with his cloak for a blanket and a bundle of clothes for a pillow. Having spent many a perfectly good night under far less comfortable circumstances, he considered himself well off. He had left early the next morning but had subsequently written to Captain Allington to thank him for his adroit and tactful handling of what could only have been a distasteful occurrence. Captain Allington had chosen to answer the letter, though this was not strictly a necessity. He had pointed out he had been insufficiently adroit, for Major Wilder had been intended to know nothing. Thus, one way or another, they had continued to correspond. Subsequently he heard more about Allington, that he was indispensable as an intelligence officer, which made Major Wilder nervous on his behalf, for there was nothing more dangerous. He came to value the correspondence and the man himself. Captain Allington was full of information and had a better idea than anybody else of what was going on and, to

Major Wilder's astonishment, was nearly the first to reach his bedside when he had received the musket ball through his shoulder. Captain Allington had examined the wound himself for he had theories on wounds, as on most things it seemed, and had cursed the surgeon, in his absence, for bleeding him.

As Major Wilder reached for a fresh sheet of paper, he did not pause to analyse the nature of his friendship with the singular young infantry officer. One gained a friend through proximity or through being like-minded, and his friendship with Captain Allington did not fit either criterion. He had gained him as a friend through the death of his brother, and though they were rarely together and not particularly like-minded, they had an affinity. Perhaps the nature of Lyndon Wilder's death was a bond between them, but it was not a subject they discussed. This, Major Wilder now thought, he would rectify, but he opened his letter with other matters. Captain Allington had recently written to him. He had long since left his *caçadores* and rejoined his own regiment, which was just returned to England. He was wondering whether or no he should stay in the army. He did not consider himself too old to undertake studying the law. Were his chances of promotion, without his having sufficient funds for the buying of his majority, rather too slender, with the declaration of peace? He then put in the notion, to tease Major Wilder, of raising the money through playing piquet, which Major Wilder, though aware of being teased, thought Captain Allington quite capable of doing.

It was not until Major Wilder had given due consideration to Captain Allington's affairs and discussed a variety of other military matters that he raised the subject of Captain Greenway, his willingness to speak on the issue of Lyndon Wilder's death, hitherto so careful a secret, and the forty Spanish dollars. He said that he had written him a letter in the hope of placating him, but he felt in his bones the fellow wished to make war on him. Had his parents been dead, he would have let Captain Greenway say what he liked and borne it, however unpleasant for himself and the rest of his family, but such was not the situation. He then said perhaps, on further contemplation, he would find it all too unpalatable and his reaction would not be what he supposed. He concluded that Allington might see he was in a sad quandary and he hoped he might find the time to apply his brain to the matter and write his conclusions.

On the following day Major Wilder received an answer from Captain Greenway.

Sir,

I see it is your intention to be conciliatory. You have failed to understand my grievance. When I applied to you to honour the debt of your late brother, you informed Colonel Smythe you would not do so without an IOU. Thus you accused me of telling a lie in stating the money was owed me. The reason I did not produce the IOU was because I had had the ill luck to have my baggage stolen by my own servant, which I never recovered, during the very action in which Lieutenant Wilder met his unfortunate demise. At such a moment, minus most of the necessities of life, to have my word doubted caused me outrage and has since rankled with me as something I should need to resolve. You now add to your calumny by accusing me of spreading rumours. However painful it may be for you to hear, I speak only the truth.

G. F. Greenway

Major Wilder was depressed by the nature of Captain Greenway's letter. He saw him to be a man always determined to nurture a grievance for an indefinite period and probably immune to logic. Nevertheless, he knew he must write a rational reply and, after leaving the matter for two uncomfortable days, he returned to his desk and made his answer.

Dear Captain Greenway,

As I knew not a single officer in my brother's regiment at the time of his death, any number of dishonest persons might have approached me for unpaid debts. It was far from my intention to accuse you personally of a falsehood. As you interpreted it thus I can only offer you my most heartfelt apologies.

Your obedient servant,

T. O. L. Wilder

He was compelled, with many misgivings, to leave it at that. Within a few days he received another letter from Captain Greenway.

At the end of this short period, one mid-afternoon,

Slimmer opened the drawing-room door to say to Lady Charles, 'A strange gentleman has arrived, m'lady, a military gentleman.'

'And who is he?'

'He didn't exactly say, m'lady. I asked if he would send in his card, and he said no, he didn't have a card.'

'Oh, really, Slimmer, no one is without a card. Where is he?' Lady Charles was aware that Slimmer was now slightly deaf and that was the most likely explanation for his not having the name.

'He's in the hall. I believe it's the Major he's after seeing.'

'I dare say he is an artillery officer, a friend of Major Wilder's.'

'No, m'lady, begging pardon.'

Lady Charles had a sudden conviction. She went pale. This was some officer from Lyndon's regiment, wishing to speak with her. Was she to have, at last, some affectionate sad reminiscence of her boy's last days? Ah, she had long since given up hope of that but the desperate, suppressed longing for some essence of his being rose in her yet again. It would be a pure, sweet agony, precious but painful. She then wondered if it could be Captain Greenway, escaped from Mrs Kingston, she having indicated he was not fit to be in Lady Charles's company. What had Mrs Kingston meant? Perhaps Captain Greenway was not quite a gentleman. What would she mind if he were a little rough at the edges, his language a trifle coarse, if he would speak feelingly of her lost son and conjure an image of him?

She said, 'I insist on his being sent in.' She thought, He is probably diffident and wishes to speak to Thomas first.

Slimmer disappeared but returned shortly. 'He says, m'lady, he'd as soon not trouble you.'

'Slimmer, make it quite plain I leave no gentleman unattended in the hall. It is my wish to see him.'

So Slimmer disappeared again and reappeared with a strange young man dressed in the red jacket of an officer in the infantry. Not wishing to admit that he had missed the young man's name, he said, 'Captain . . . the gentleman, m'lady.'

The young man bowed and the silver lace across his chest dazzled Lady Charles with hope. Not knowing what to say, and the young man only bowing and looking as if he would say nothing, she said, 'I'm wondering that you did not write to say you were coming.'

He replied, with more ease than she expected, 'Oh, I didn't write on purpose. I have just disembarked from France. I came in a hurry. I haven't been in England for years.' He looked disparagingly at his dress and added, 'I haven't any clothes except my uniforms. You must excuse me.'

Lady Charles looked at him carefully. Though he had no accent she thought he was foreign. He might have been as much as fifteen years younger than Lyndon but he held the rank of captain. Could such youth have had seniority over her son? She had a moment of renewed bitterness towards her husband. She then remembered Lyndon's regiment was without lacing, or unlaced, as they called it, so this boy, as she now, derogatorily, referred to him, might be of no connection whatsoever, so what purpose had he in coming? He had come in such haste. What urgency did that indicate? Her mind see-sawed from one idea to the next. It meant nothing that his uniform was not Lyndon's:

officers skipped from one regiment to another in order to take up promotion. She said, though hope had died in her, 'Perhaps you came to speak of my son.'

He had glanced away from her while she had been contemplating him so intently but now he swung back abruptly. 'Your son? Nothing has occurred, I hope?'

Lady Charles said, 'I see we are at cross purposes. Why have you come?'

'To see Major Wilder.'

'Ah, I didn't understand.'

'I have leave. I am on my way to Devonshire. It suited me to call on Major Wilder. I hope the wound he received at Orthez healed as it should. He never mentions it, but then he might not.'

Lady Charles had assumed the wound had healed but now she realized she had not enquired. She should, of course, have done so. She said, 'It is quite a long time ago now.'

'A year,' he replied, 'but wounds can be troublesome. His was very clean and neat, but it only takes some little bit of fabric to be left behind in it for it to fester.'

'You were not acquainted with his brother, my elder son, I suppose?'

'I didn't have that honour,' he answered. He spoke with a mechanical politeness for which she did not much care.

Slimmer returned to the door. 'Major Wilder is come indoors now.'

And then Major Wilder strode in. His mother, not in the habit of observing him closely, thought a whole range of expressions passed over his face at the sight of the unexpected visitor, pleasure, dismay, even anger. He said, shaking the officer's hand with what appeared to be warmth,

'Why, Allington, you Jack-in-the-box fellow, it was never my intention you should come.' He turned to his mother. 'Please be so good as to have a room prepared for Captain Allington.'

Lady Charles had gone away to order the airing of the bed and the other tasks requisite with receiving company, including the laying of an extra place for dinner. She had also sought out her husband to complain of being made to endure a stranger in the house when the state of her mind did not allow of it. Lord Charles had said there was nothing that could be done about it short of sending the young man away, which was out of the question. Later, when he came to meet him, he thought him a gentlemanly young fellow, for he had asked if he might send his horses to the inn. Lord Charles had told him that any friend of his son's was welcome and his horses too. He had added to himself that it was not as if he were in control of such matters, but it was pleasant to pretend and Thomas had looked at him approvingly, as he might at Lottie when she said the right thing.

At dinner Captain Allington had sat down very cheerfully and been introduced to Lottie and Miss Arbuthnot, and Lottie, fascinated by the brilliance of his scarlet jacket and shining buttons, his silver lace, had asked him if he had been a soldier for ever and ever because she did not think him nearly as old as her Uncle Thomas.

Major Wilder said, 'Lottie, I thought we had told you it is not polite to make personal remarks.'

'But I haven't said anything rude,' Lottie replied, 'not this time. Have I?'

Captain Allington had laughed at her, but she decided not to mind it.

Miss Arbuthnot remembered how the sight of a uniform used to make her uncomfortable but that seemed a long time ago: she could not afford to be so fanciful. She thought Captain Allington must have foreign blood, with his black hair and dark eyes, and he was only a little older than herself. She was intrigued by his swift wit and his exotic, alien appearance. He amused her by recounting how he had instructed his servant to go round to the stables to find York, when they had first arrived, but the man, who had met York many months previously, was too terrified to do so, and had been found cowering behind the stable wall still clutching the horses some considerable time later.

It was not until the evening that Major Wilder and Captain Allington were alone together. They sat one on each side of the fire, the greyhounds at their feet, in the room once exclusively occupied by Major Wilder's grandfather. For a while they drank their wine and were silent, but at length Captain Allington said, 'You are preparing, sir, to scold me.'

'I had thought of it.'

'But why not proceed?'

'I should never have mentioned the matter in the first place, so am I not to blame? Had you written I should have made light of it and told you not to come.'

'So I surmised. You spoke of it to me because it is my belief there is no one else to whom you may speak of it without explaining the full circumstances. To whom could you do that? I am sure you have plenty of friends.'

'Yes, scattered all over the world and not one who knows

what you know. I didn't want you to sully your hands with it, so much my junior, and I already under obligation to you. It makes me feel as if I corrupted you.'

This made Captain Allington laugh. 'You are full of every correct sentiment. Allow me to look after myself. Now, let us get down to business. We may not, I suppose, make light of it. With the reductions in the army, Captain Greenway will shortly be put on half pay. There is little to his credit. He likes a quarrel. He has been in arrest twice and brought to court martial twice and only exonerated by the skin of his teeth.'

'But do you know him?'

'Certainly not.'

Major Wilder decided against asking how this information had been obtained. He went to his desk and got out the correspondence, which included copies of the letters he had written, and handed it all to Captain Allington. He had received that morning Captain Greenway's challenge.

> *Sir,*
>
> *An apology will not satisfy me. A gentleman cannot easily recover his character once it has been besmirched by accusations of dishonesty. However often the truth is stated, people will choose to doubt it. Captain Houghton will call on any friend of yours you care to name. In expectation of hearing from you in the immediate future,*
>
> *G. F. Greenway*

Having read the letters, Captain Allington said, 'The man

is disordered in his brain. You have given him a full apology. What more can he expect? You would be justified in refusing to meet him.'

'I have drafted a reply, not so much because I think it will be of the least use, but to gain time and also, in fairness to myself, to give my opinion, one I have long held.'

Major Wilder handed him a final sheet of paper. He had started 'Dear Captain Greenway', insisting on retaining the polite opening.

> *I regret you cannot find it in yourself to accept my apology. The conception that a duel is the only means of settling a dispute is quite alien to me. What does it settle? Our forebears believed Providence favoured the righteous and the better man won. Anyone can see this is contrary to the evidence. The man most skilled with the chosen weapon wins, regardless of the merits of his case. Where is the justice in that?*

Captain Allington said, 'By all means send it off. It gives us a little more time and it indicates the extent you have gone to in order to placate the fellow.'

He knew that Major Wilder would have to fight the duel and he knew Major Wilder was bound to be aware of the fact. Duelling was commonplace, if illegal, though many spoke against it, and no jury would convict a man who killed another in a duel, unless it was proved it had not been conducted according to the accepted procedure, in a manner fair to both parties, and with seconds in attendance. To evade accepting a challenge and to come out with a reputation unscathed was impossible. Captain Allington had known of men ostracized by all the officers in their regiment for declining just such a challenge. He thought Major Wilder's reputation and his known abhorrence of duelling would probably carry him through, but there would be many an old messmate who would give him the cold shoulder. Besides, it was not the only issue.

The following day Major Wilder sent the letter by one of the grooms from the yard and received the reply shortly after breakfast.

> *Sir,*
>
> *Your late brother, whatever faults I found in him, was no coward. You wish to protect his reputation for the sake of his parents. I dare say Lord and Lady Charles Wilder will be interested to learn how one son died and how the other is too cowardly to defend his own honour or that of his brother.*
>
> *G. F. Greenway*

Major Wilder said to Captain Allington, 'It is one insult too many.' He noticed, after that, how easily they fell into their allotted roles. It was his to appear calm and detached, to take but a cursory interest, and to allow Allington, like the groom's man at a wedding, to conduct the practical aspects of the proceedings. The word of the seconds was sacrosanct, for they were in charge. He regretted having to involve the younger man in something he viewed as sordid, in something with which he had been as good as blackmailed into complying, but he realized Allington did not view it in the same light.

Captain Allington stood in the rooms once occupied by Lyndon Wilder. His expression, which had been enigmatic, had changed. He was grimly, furiously indignant that Captain Greenway should force Major Wilder, intelligent, upright, honest, an irreproachable officer of the first quality, an example of how to behave both on and off the battlefield, to stand up to be shot at. He looked around the room with irritation and curiosity. There was a faintly depressing smell of disuse. Feeble midday February sunshine made squares on the Turkey red carpet. He opened and shut the drawers of the desk, which were full of the detritus humans left behind, and he cursed Lyndon Wilder in his mind. Was he not as much at fault as Captain Greenway? Without him Captain Greenway would have had no power over Major Wilder. The face of an angel, Allington's *caçadores* had said, impressed with his fair good looks.

In the second drawer down he found what he was looking for: Lieutenant Wilder's duelling pistols, snug in their mahogany box, smooth, sleek, perfect. Everything was in its allotted place: balls, powder horn, flints, leather, wad cutter, wad and ramrods. He picked out one and peered down the barrel. It lay comfortably in his hand: he doubted it had ever been used. After replacing the gun he put the box under his military boat cloak which he had laid over his arm. It would not do to be seen leaving the house carrying it, nor yet to walk through the village of Ridley with such an easily identifiable article.

Within half an hour he had crossed the park and was ringing the bell of Mrs Kingston's house, which was prettily set back from the green. A maidservant opened the door. He sent in his name and asked to speak with Captain Houghton. A moment later he was shown into the parlour.

Two officers were seated at the table playing a game of chess. They got up as he came in. Captain Allington's eyes slid to the chessboard and then to the faces of the officers: his expression had resumed its enigmatic, immovable indifference. He bowed but slightly, making no attempt to indicate he might shake hands, and said, looking at the taller of the two, because he had been given a description of him, 'Captain Houghton?'

Captain Houghton looked flustered. He had not expected Captain Allington to be so young, perhaps as much as twenty years younger than himself. He had been trying to remember what he had heard of the man. Was he an intelligence officer? Was he foreign? Was he in the direct employ of the Duke of Wellington? Captain Greenway had asked why it could matter, but to Captain Houghton it did.

Captain Greenway, who was a short, bald-headed man with a high colour, muttered, not quite audibly, 'Wilder has sent us a child.' He, too, was surprised.

They proceeded with the introductions. Captain Allington was minded again to examine the chessboard but this seemed to irritate Captain Greenway, who shut it, scattering the pieces.

Captain Allington said, 'I have brought the pistols.'

Captain Greenway said, 'That was unnecessary. We will use mine.'

'Certainly not,' Allington replied smoothly.

'And why not?'

'I assume you are familiar with your own. You will know if they pull a little to one side, how they fire. This would give you an unfair advantage. These, I believe, have never been used, and certainly not by Major Wilder. They are Mortimers, so you can have no reason to complain of them.'

Captain Greenway looked aggrieved. 'Have you tried them?'

'No. If Captain Houghton is agreeable, he and I will try them. We have to select a place for the meeting. There are woods near by in which we could be discreet.'

'I shall come with you.'

Captain Allington smiled amiably. 'You must know Captain Houghton and I have a great deal to discuss. Your presence would prevent that.' He turned to Captain Houghton. 'You will, I am sure, be in agreement with me. If Captain Greenway is to be with us, we must take time to be together at a later date, and we have agreed to see each other now.'

Captain Houghton said anxiously, 'I'm afraid he's quite right, Greenway, you can't come with us. It would be most irregular.'

Captain Greenway could be seen to comply with reluctance. The other two left the room together. Within a few minutes they had departed from the house and were walking through the village.

Captain Allington said politely, 'Your health is poor, I think. I hope it won't be too much for you.'

'It's all a great deal too much for me.'

'But what made you consent?'

Captain Houghton shrugged uncomfortably. He was afraid of Captain Greenway but it had not occurred to him to refuse.

'It is as well we establish exactly what we consider our duties on such occasions as this.'

Captain Houghton was bemused. He said simply, 'Honour must be satisfied, I suppose.' He was thinking that his sister would never forgive him and he was almost totally reliant on her charity.

'Of course. That was not what I meant. Honour must be satisfied but I would consider myself a poor friend to Major Wilder if I did not see it as my duty to mitigate the damage he and Captain Greenway might do to one another to the very best of my ability. I hope we are in agreement on that.'

Captain Houghton had not considered it in such a light. Being the man he was, he had not been the foremost choice, among his acquaintance seeking satisfaction, as a second. He only knew Captain Greenway would kill Major Wilder if he could, and he, Houghton, had not the least wish to be embroiled in the aftermath. Why, he might even have to go abroad and he had so little money.

Allington said, 'We will load the pistols and neither Major Wilder nor Captain Greenway should see us do it.'

'But Greenway said to me, "Don't stint on the powder. I'll be watching you."'

'If he watches while we load, we will halt the proceedings. We are entitled to do so. What is more, we will stint on the powder. I see that as my duty.'

'Are you sure that is our duty?'

'Absolutely. We are here to prevent a death, not to entice

one. The weapons must have, however, enough powder. I am afraid the ball must fly. We will ascertain the quantity needed. Duelling is against the law and strictly forbidden in the army. I believe Captain Greenway to have already overstepped the mark in this respect. He will be cashiered and I don't think him a rich man. You must protect him from himself. I imagine you see that as your duty?'

'Why, I suppose it is. As far as I know, he has little beyond his commission that is of the slightest value.'

They had now reached the gate into the park.

Captain Allington said, 'So I thought. We must now decide the distance they are to be apart, how many shots are allowed, who will take first shot or if they are to fire simultaneously, and where they shall stand should the sun be rising.'

'Greenway has already demanded twelve paces and that they will continue to fire until a conclusion is reached.'

'I see he takes advantage of your more equable nature, and he is a little too experienced in the matter for our taste, a little too demanding altogether. It is his duty to place himself in the hands of his second, not to dictate the conditions. Major Wilder has instructed me to do whatever I deem fit. Twelve paces? Certainly not. There is a common belief that the closer the guns are to each other the less damage is done. It is to do with the trajectory of the weapon. I don't believe it myself, though I have heard of men being only six paces apart and doing each other no harm: they possibly meant no harm in the first place.' Here Allington embarked on a short treatise on the subject of trajectory, rifling, the lack of it, and flintlock pistols in general, of which Houghton understood about half, before he concluded by saying, 'Twelve paces is very dangerous, positive murder. I would prefer twenty-five, but in order not to over-excite your friend we could settle for twenty.'

'In a poor light, at twenty-five paces, they would hardly make one another out. We must settle for fifteen. Should I dissatisfy Greenway, he will pick his quarrel with me. He likes duelling.'

'Rely on my ingenuity. Fifteen? Eighteen, on the condition I measure them out myself. I have reasonably long legs. As for the powder, there will be sufficient but we won't overload.'

Captain Houghton thought Captain Allington very managing for one so young. He viewed him with suspicion, but he did not see what he could do. They were now walking down through the park. He said, 'And who should fire first?'

'Major Wilder should fire first because he is the damaged party, but maybe Captain Greenway considers himself the damaged party. He thinks Major Wilder accused him of lying. Major Wilder apologized. That should have been the end of it. Captain Greenway is the challenger and left Major Wilder no option.' Captain Allington thought it likely Major Wilder would decline to fire at all. Duelling was against his principles and he had hinted it would be hard to fire on a man for telling the truth. If he was to fire first, declined, or fired in the air, it might leave Captain Greenway to do, at his leisure, whatever he felt inclined. After some consideration, Allington continued, 'I think it best they fire simultaneously. What do you say?'

Captain Houghton was glad, at last, to be asked his

opinion. 'I agree. We will drop a handkerchief. They must have their right arms at their sides and they may not raise them a moment sooner.'

'Yes, that will do. And they may have one shot. It is adequate to satisfy the honour of both.'

'Greenway will harangue me on that.'

'Tell him if he can't abide by the decisions of his second, he must find someone else for the task. Have you spoken to the doctor?'

'Yes. He was not enthusiastic but I swore him to secrecy. He wants four pounds. It seemed a lot to me but he is a real doctor, not just an apothecary. Greenway was angry. He's short of the readies, but we must have somebody there.'

'Yes, we must, not that he will be of the slightest use,' Allington replied dismissively.

Being now at the furthest part of the park from the village, they looked about for a suitable spot.

Captain Houghton suddenly said, 'Do you suppose the . . . the dire, unpleasant thing that Greenway says about Major Wilder's brother is actually true?'

'I assume Captain Greenway thinks it is, or the repeating of it would make him beneath contempt. It is irrelevant, is it not? The fault is in the repeating of it. Lieutenant Wilder is dead. Why mortify his family?'

Captain Houghton agreed, but he made no reply. At heart he was not a bad man and the situation in which he found himself he considered very unfortunate.

Between them they selected an appropriate spot. Major Wilder had said any place on the furthest side of the park would do, but Captain Houghton, feeling he must assert himself, pointed out the distances from the village, the house itself and the little lane that could be seen to twist along on the opposite side of the park railings, at times running parallel and at times hiving off and screened by hedges. There was something over half a mile of ground from which to choose but they made their decision promptly. Allington measured out the ground according to his own light, while Houghton rested. A man on a horse came into view, slowly wending his way along the lane. Captain Houghton knew, and Allington suspected, it was Captain Greenway endeavouring to spy on them. Hastily, they walked over to the copse where they were hidden from view. Here they could confirm the working order of the weapons and discuss, as they went, at what time there would be sufficient light.

Captain Allington pointed out the usefulness of there being insufficient light. Though his companion was unaware of it, he retained his extreme anger at the entire idiotic, illogical situation. Captain Houghton, who was now overtired, did not impress him. By the time they were ready to part with each other, the older man had broken out in a sweat. He said, gloomily, 'You are right to be anxious for Major Wilder. I am anxious for him myself.'

Captain Allington looked at his grey face but he was not disposed to feel sorry for him. As for anxiety, it was not a thing he allowed himself but, on this occasion, it was not for himself and he was, with good reason, anxious. He reached into his pocket for his watch, a Vulliamy, that he had won, among other things, in a game of piquet. The gentleman who had lost it to him had asked to buy it back but Allington had laughingly declined, unless he was to be provided with a watch of similar quality. He saw it was twelve o'clock.

It was with reluctance that Horatio returned from Ridley in time for dinner. He thought it would be easier if he could live at Ridley instead of going backwards and forwards all the time. Dinner at his own house was at five o'clock whereas at Ridley it was at half past six. He explained to his mother this stole an hour and a half from his day but she could not see that this was so. He had no enthusiasm for sitting down to dinner with his mother and his uncle but the addition of Captain Greenway he really disliked. At first he had thought, an idea scarcely to be borne, Captain Greenway wanted to marry his mother, because he seemed to go out of his way in paying compliments, declaring her abounding with feminine insight, exquisite beauty and other such nonsense, or nonsense in Horatio's eyes, but his mother seemed indifferent to these blandishments and was barely civil. In fact it was obvious she had taken a great dislike to him. Captain Greenway would laugh off her curtness and say to Horatio's uncle, 'Well, Houghton, your sister's very hard on me. I'm sure I don't know why.'

Mrs Kingston, if she replied, would indicate he must understand in what way he had met with her disapproval and he would say he would never again offend her in that manner.

Horatio, to whom all this was mysterious but of no particular interest, did not think Captain Greenway meant anything he said and any pleasantness was all pretence. He seemed to make Captain Houghton nervous and he certainly made Horatio nervous: it was as though he was always on the brink of losing his temper, of suppressing some violent inclination, and Captain Houghton was always placating him.

However unpleasant Horatio found the company at dinner, he was, nevertheless, hungry. He peeped into the kitchen to see why the dinner was not yet on the table. The cook was there and also a kitchen maid. The former, on seeing him, said, 'Well, Master Kingston, you'll be after your victuals, I'll be bound. Now don't you come in getting under our feet 'cos Betsy here left the fish out and the cat had it, and it ever so lovely an' fresh, up from the coast this day.'

Horatio, recognizing a kitchen crisis, backed away and entered the little morning room where they had breakfast on fine days. He had taken from his mother's bookcase *The Romance of the Forest* and though he thought it an unlikely tale he had been surreptitiously reading it during the meal and had left it there in case he was tempted to read it when he had to attend to his studies. Now he supposed he might as well pass the few intervening minutes before he was allowed to eat in reading it.

His uncle's writing box was on the table. Captain Houghton often wrote his letters there because the room had the morning sun but he usually took the box away again when he had finished. Horatio was reminded of the one Major Wilder had shown to himself and Lottie, the writing box that had belonged to Lottie's father. It was superior to this. His uncle's was shabby and it had less brass at the corners, but did it, too, have a secret drawer? Could he ask his uncle? There was no point in having a secret drawer, he supposed, if you told where it was. Would it be like the secret drawer in the box that had belonged to Lottie's father? He eased the lid a little. It was not locked. His uncle frequently complained that he had lost the key.

Aware that he was doing something he should not, Horatio lifted the lid and the desk folded out neatly enough into its two hinged halves. Lying on the scuffed and ink-stained green baize was a letter, written in a neat copperplate script. It was a single sheet and it was signed 'R. Allington'. Anxiously, guiltily, Horatio closed the lid but, curious, he opened it again. Why should Captain Allington, whom he knew to be staying at Ridley, write a letter to his uncle? His uncle had gone for a long walk in the park and it had made him poorly, Horatio knew from his mother, but his uncle never went for any walk further than the post office.

There the letter lay. Horatio knew he should, on no account, read it, but it was not very long and it seemed the work of a moment to do so.

Dear Captain Houghton,

I believe all to be in order but we arranged the meeting for 6.30 a.m. Major Wilder tells me he would prefer to leave the house before 6.00 so as not to attract the attention of the servants. As it will take barely ten minutes to cross the park, I hope you will agree to come earlier. If I were you I should not disclose details of any importance to Captain Greenway. When he is on the site is quite soon enough for him to know how far apart we intend them to be and I shall be there to reinforce what you say. I dare say he will bully you. If he will retract, of course Major Wilder will do so, but I understand this to be unlikely. I send this letter with my servant. He is reliable and will wait if you tell him you wish to reply but there may be no necessity to do so,

Yours etc.

R. Allington

At first Horatio was shocked at his own wickedness in reading his uncle's private correspondence. In great haste he shut the lid of the writing box but then the very contents of the letter began to do battle for supremacy in his mind and he quickly opened it again to see when the letter had been written. Did it have a date? Yes, it was dated 28 February, in fact that very day. It was clear to him what it meant but he could not believe it.

A footstep behind the door made him jump away from the writing box. They were going in to dinner. He was frightened, extremely so. He could hear his mother call him. He must go into dinner. How could Major Wilder do such a thing?

Horatio joined his mother and Captain Greenway at the table. The thought of food made him feel ill but he knew he must eat or they would ask him what was the matter. He might be sent to bed and somebody sit with him. There was no sign of his uncle. He was declared too poorly to come down. Horatio stared, fascinated, at the ruby red countenance of Captain Greenway. He knew what his uncle was doing: he was avoiding Captain Greenway in order not to disclose details. Captain Greenway and his mother kept up a desultory conversation but Horatio was frantic. Captain Greenway would kill Major Wilder, he knew he would, he would kill him. It was an affair of honour, but Major Wilder had a great dislike of duelling and had said he would never partake in one; therefore Captain Greenway had tricked him in some way and would undoubtedly kill him.

Mouthful by mouthful Horatio forced down his dinner. He could do nothing. He could do something. He could do nothing. He could not tell his mother. She would have hysterics. He would tell Miss Arbuthnot and she would think what was to be done.

As soon as dessert was on the table he asked to be excused. He said he wanted to look at the stars.

His mother said, 'But it's barely dusk, dear.'

'I know. I want to see the evening star just as it appears, and write the time down.' How easy it was to lie once one got into the way of it, but what was telling his mother a lie compared to reading his uncle's correspondence?

Mrs Kingston, who did not like to be left alone with her unwelcome guest, was reluctant to let him go but she said to Captain Greenway, 'He is studying astronomy with the governess at Ridley.'

'What would a governess know of astronomy?' Captain Greenway replied, with a laugh.

Horatio wished to defend Miss Arbuthnot but now was not the moment and he was sliding from the room before he could be stopped while his mother was patiently explaining about Miss Arbuthnot having a brother in the navy.

The stable yard was empty. In the harness room Horatio

lifted his saddle and bridle down from their pegs and took a rope halter. He carried them as far as the paddock and rested them on the fence. He felt as if he had only just put the pony out to grass but, ever obliging, it walked towards him and he slipped the halter over its ears. He put the bridle on over the halter, looping and knotting the rope of the halter round the pony's neck and then saddled up. Though he felt his hands to tremble it was all done in a moment. Anxious to be neither seen nor heard, he did not leave through the stable yard, where the pony's hoofs would have clattered on the cobbles, but crossed the paddock from which a gate led on to a narrow green lane, a back way, not much used, but a perfectly swift route for a boy and a pony. He wished to reach Ridley before the family went in to dinner. He could avoid the lodge and the drive by entering the park via a little wicket gate and a small wood. It was not yet dark. The pony went along at a swift canter but once they were through the wood and into the park Horatio loosed the reins and let it gallop. He knew it sensed his agitation. Fifty yards from the house he pulled it up and tied it, with the rope halter, to a low branch of one of the few remaining large trees in the Ridley park to have escaped the axe. While he loosed the girths he thought the pony was well tucked in: with the broad trunk of the tree shielding it from the sight of the house and with the dusk falling it would, with luck, not be seen. He knew, without reasoning it out, neither he nor the pony must be seen.

He approached the house as rapidly as he could for the ground was open. Would the door be locked? He thought not. He turned the big brass handle carefully and pushed the door sufficiently wide to peer inside. The hall was empty. He took off his boots and, carrying them in one hand, eased himself round the door and closed it carefully. There was a three-branched candlestick on the chest, already lit, and he could see by the regulator it was twenty past six. In his stockings he crossed the hall and made for the stairs, running up them as fast as he could. It was as well he knew Ridley as he did. He went up more stairs, down this passage, along that. Polly was going away from him with a jug of water. He froze against the wall until she was out of sight.

At last he reached that part of the house containing the schoolroom, the old nursery where Lottie still slept, various bedrooms and linen cupboards. Outside Miss Arbuthnot's door he paused a second before opening it a crack and whispering, 'I've got to come in.'

Miss Arbuthnot was seated at her table writing a letter. She jumped up at the sight of him as he slid into the room, his finger to his lips.

She said softly, 'Horatio, whatever is the matter?'

Relief at having arrived made him, for a moment, want to cry, but he could not do that, and then, echoing through the house, came the sound of the Ridley dinner bell.

He said, 'I have to see you alone. Don't say a word. It is dreadfully important. Hide me here. Nobody will come in, will they? Come back after dinner, soon as you can, make an excuse. Don't let Lottie see me. It's not for girls.'

Miss Arbuthnot went down to dinner. She was alarmed by Horatio's conduct. Had he run away from home? Had his Kingston uncle appeared to take him off to sea and Horatio taken an immediate dislike to him? She thought him very undecided on the subject of his chosen career, and this as likely an explanation as any. As it was impossible for her to hide him overnight, she thought, having spoken to him, she must turn to Major Wilder for assistance.

Her mind rather constrained by the fugitive upstairs, in the years following she thought it strange nothing appeared in the least out of the ordinary at dinner. There was the customary flow of conversation, perhaps eased by the presence of Captain Allington. He was lively-minded and yet she did not feel she had come to know him. He had a peculiar reserve and, though he spoke freely on innumerable subjects, remained an enigma. He mentioned neither family nor friends nor place, so one was left supposing he had dropped out of the sky, and, as far as Miss Arbuthnot could make out, his visit to Ridley had been entirely unexpected. On Major Wilder mentioning Mr Heugmont's interest in the telegraph system, Captain Allington was able to explain how it worked and of what assistance it had been to Napoleon, who had been able to communicate from one end of his empire to the other. The English telegraph system, a deal more modest, had been closed down on the grounds of expense, which Captain Allington considered short-sighted. The telegraph system became ever connected in Miss Arbuthnot's mind with that dinner at Ridley and the subsequent events.

As soon as dessert was over, Major Wilder declared, with an apology, he had business to attend to and he and Captain Allington left the room. Lord and Lady Charles and Lottie went to the drawing room and Miss Arbuthnot made some little excuse to return upstairs.

Horatio was sitting at her table. He had taken a book

from her shelves but it lay unopened: it was apparent he had not been able to settle to reading it.

She said immediately, 'Horatio, have you run away?'

He replied crossly, 'No, of course not. Why should I do that? I should only have to run back again. It's much more dreadful a thing. Look, I have copied down on a piece of your paper the exact words, as far as I can remember them, and I remember them pretty well, of a letter Captain Allington wrote this day to my uncle. I shouldn't have read it, but I did.'

'I didn't think Captain Allington knew your uncle.'

'I don't know that he does particularly.' Horatio was glad Miss Arbuthnot did not seem inclined to examine the matter of his reading his uncle's letter.

Miss Arbuthnot took up the piece of paper and read what he had written, then read it again. She said, 'Are you absolutely certain this was exactly it?'

'Yes.' Horatio burst into tears.

Miss Arbuthnot went to comfort him, but she was as appalled, as devastated as he was. He said, sobbing, 'Major Wilder doesn't approve of duelling so what has made him do it? Captain Greenway will kill him, I know he will.'

For a few moments they clung together, but then Miss Arbuthnot said, 'We will go to Lord Charles. That is the only thing we can possibly do. You must go down to the library. Does your mother know where you are?'

'No. I told a lie and slipped away after dinner. I have my pony tied to a tree. If I have an excuse to be here, it's that we are looking at the stars, but I expect I can get to the library without being seen.'

Miss Arbuthnot thought a duel could be postponed or

located elsewhere. Without the time to contemplate, she too thought it best Horatio was not seen. She went ahead of him down the numerous passages and staircases and turned to see his small figure, still clutching his boots, disappear through the library door.

In the drawing room, Lottie was reading to her grandmother. This was her latest accomplishment and though she made many mistakes she persevered in a loud voice.

Lord Charles was sitting by and would occasionally say, when he considered it appropriate, 'Well done, darling, well done.'

Miss Arbuthnot whispered to him, 'I need to speak to you. Something has occurred. It's urgent.'

The old man looked surprised but he got up quietly and they left the room together. In the library Horatio was standing in the gloom.

Lord Charles said, 'It's late for you to be out, young man. We need Slimmer to light the candles.'

'Don't call Slimmer,' Miss Arbuthnot said. 'I can light a candle. Please sit down. I have to tell you something Horatio knows and it will shock you dreadfully.'

Lord Charles took his customary chair. He looked anxiously from one to the other, bewildered, the light from the single candle leaving their faces shadowy.

Miss Arbuthnot said, 'We know Major Wilder is to fight a duel with Captain Greenway.'

'But that is ridiculous. You must be mistaken. My son is, in principle, against duelling.'

'I know but, nevertheless, it is so. Horatio has seen a letter written by Captain Allington to Captain Houghton, confirming the arrangements.'

Lord Charles clasped his head in his hands and groaned. He repeated, 'It must be a mistake. Thomas would never do it.'

Horatio, again bursting into tears, said, 'You have to believe it. It's not a mistake, it's not. Captain Greenway is a very bad man. He will kill Major Wilder, I know he will. He will have tricked him into it. You must tell them not to do it. You must go to Major Wilder.'

Lord Charles rallied himself. He said coldly, wearily, 'I can't interfere. I shall lose my son. To go to him would not avail. If he has agreed to fight, he will do so. It is, you see, an affair of honour.'

Miss Arbuthnot said, as firmly and authoritatively as she could, 'Sir, you must interfere, you must. Horatio and I don't care about honour.'

'You are a woman, my dear. Horatio is a child.' Lord Charles looked dignified but the tears were running down his cheeks. He said, 'Ah, my dear boy, my Thomas. How can this have come about? You, who are so strong and managing, what is the purpose of it? What does it solve?'

Miss Arbuthnot said, 'You must inform on them.'

'My dear, you don't know what you are saying. It is an affair of honour.'

Horatio said, still sobbing, 'Captain Greenway will kill Major Wilder. I know he will.'

Miss Arbuthnot said, 'Lord Charles, you are not a young man; I am a woman, not much more than a girl; Horatio is a child. Honour is not for us. We can and we will inform on them.'

Lord Charles was silent. He then said, 'Do you know when it is to take place?'

'We assume tomorrow morning but we know between six and half past at the bottom of the park,' Miss Arbuthnot replied. 'We are not sure exactly where.'

'Tomorrow? So soon. Within hours. Dear God, what have I done to deserve this? My sons. First Lyndon, now Thomas, who I have come to love so dearly. Tomorrow? It cannot be so.'

'If you love him so much,' Horatio said, 'you must stop it. I shan't believe you love him otherwise. I'm glad I never had a father if he was to teach me honour because I mind about love more.'

Lord Charles looked at him as if in surprise. After a moment he said, 'Sir John Richards is a magistrate. He lives at Monkton. He is violently against the practice of duelling. Should I write to him, how could the letter be conveyed? It is dark now. There is not a servant I could send. The whole world would know. Thomas must never, never know what I did. How can I send a letter?'

Miss Arbuthnot said, 'I will take it.'

'What? Walk all through the dark to Monkton, and you a young woman? Alone? Certainly not. I haven't lost all sense. I should prefer to go myself but my old bones wouldn't carry me and I can't have a horse saddled at this time of night. The smallest suspicion would end all.'

Horatio said, 'Write the letter. I will take it.'

'But how can you, my little lad?'

'I have the pony here. Monkton is only a few miles on from Ridley. I know which is Sir John's house. Write the letter. I will take it.' He leant forward, picked up a quill from a selection already on the table and placed it in Lord Charles's hand. 'Here is the ink. Where is the paper?'

Lord Charles opened his blotter and obediently started to write. He thought how strange it was, he knew what to say.

Dear Sir John,

My good friend, God forgive me, I believe my son is to fight a duel tomorrow, six or half past six, somewhere at the lower end of the park, here at Ridley. What devilment persuaded him I know not. He is as against the practice as you are yourself. Pray stop it if you can. Save his life. I beg you not to let him know it was his father who informed on him.

Your humble and obedient friend,

Charles Wilder

Horatio tipped the candle for the sealing wax while Lord Charles folded the letter and took his seals from his pocket. He said, 'Sir John will know it is from me.'

Horatio put on his boots, saying, 'They mustn't see me. No one must see me. I can get out through the window.' He almost snatched the letter from Lord Charles and thrust it deep inside his jacket.

Miss Arbuthnot asked him if he was quite sure of the way, and he replied he had been there with his mother. She said, 'Shall I come with you?'

'No, you would hold me up.'

Miss Arbuthnot could see that this was true.

Lord Charles said, sliding up the window sash, 'What a mission to trust to a child.'

Horatio slipped over the sill and vanished into the garden.

Lord Charles took Miss Arbuthnot's arm. He said, 'Come, my dear. We will go to the drawing room. We will tell a lie. One gets accustomed to doing wrong. I shall say we were looking for a book. Should I yet go to my boy and beg him not to go tomorrow? Of course not. What could he do? He would be dishonoured. The officers would disown him, his friends would turn their backs and walk away. I . . . I am dishonoured, but I don't care. It is done. Will the child get there safely? Will they let him in? What will he do?'

Horatio fled across the garden and into the park. There was a moon and now a fitful little wind that made the shadows leap and change their shape. What if the pony had broken loose and gone home? No, the pony was still as he had left it. He tightened the girth and scrambled on to its back. He turned it away from the house and towards the village. He must go the way he had come. When he entered the wood he was afraid. It was dark. The pony cantered along, glad to be going.

He remembered he would soon be at sea. He was not a boy at all, he was a man and men were not afraid of the dark. He started to repeat to himself, in time to the rhythm of the pony's hoofs, 'Mr Midshipman Kingston, yes, sir, no, sir. Climb to the crow's nest. Look at the stars.'

Major Wilder, sitting at his grandfather's desk after dinner, was aware there was a prescribed manner of conducting oneself when awaiting a duel. It was necessary to appear calm and detached. As it was, he felt calm and detached. It was no worse than the night preceding an engagement. He had faced death so often. He had run risks. He considered the occasion that had led to his acquiring the Andalusian. You knew your hour might come but what did it matter? At time of war you were never indispensable. There was always somebody else to fill your shoes, indeed quite anxious to do so. You did your duty. Now he supposed he was less dispensable, but that distant cousin who bore the name of Wilder would no doubt be delighted. Before an engagement the sensation was of shared experience. Now he stood alone and his death served no purpose beyond satisfying one man's desire for revenge, so it did seem pointless, but all the same, not of great moment. He did mind for his father.

He would write a letter to Lord Charles. He was not sure he had been a good son. He had deprived his father of the dignity of office, yet it had been what his father had wanted. Had he bullied him? Was he another Lyndon? He hoped not. In the letter he would explain what he felt and apologize if apologies were required. He would give as much practical advice as he could. He believed the tenant of the home farm would make an able and honest agent. He recommended his father to spend as much time as he could at Finch Hall as it would help to keep him cheerful. He would ask him to give the Andalusian to Captain Allington.

Having written that, he would write to Georgie. He would tell her he loved her and thank her for her care of him. He would explain his will in which he gave her and John custody of Lottie. He would ask her to see York always had employment. He would beg her, for his sake, to look after Miss Arbuthnot.

He thought of Miss Arbuthnot. Now it was plain to see his folly in asking her to marry him. Suppose he had left her a widow? She would have been destitute. Without his marrying her she was destitute. The family, he hoped, would have looked after her, but she would have ever been the poor relation. If they had been married and she had borne him a son, the whole picture would have been different. How much harder it would have been to face the oncoming event had Miss Arbuthnot returned his affections, how much harder indeed, for he had, he knew, never succeeded in entirely expunging her from his thoughts, but to have married her he now saw would have been an act of selfishness. On the other hand, it would probably be better for Miss Arbuthnot to have been married than otherwise, but at least, as it was, he caused her no heartache.

Having written to his father and to his sister, he wondered if he should write to his mother. Unfortunately he could think of nothing to say. He had ordered and paid for a tablet to be placed in the church commemorating Lyndon. He thought it plain, dignified and sufficient but he had not consulted his mother. Perhaps he should have done so but as they did not agree he had acted as he thought best. Should he tell her that? He saw he was a little high-handed but he remained, towards his mother, unforgiving. He decided to write her no letter. Was he not engaged in this duel, against every proper inclination he had, that both his mother and his father should remain in ignorance, should retain their rarefied image of Lyndon's death, even of his character? It was even more for his mother's sake than his father's, for he thought he could have told his father the truth, though he certainly would not have cared to do so.

He turned his attention to his will. His personal possessions were not much. He could leave Lyndon's gold watch to his nephew, Nicholas. Any wealth he had enjoyed was tied to the estate. He supposed he owned all the articles in Lyndon's rooms. They could be divided between his three Heugmont nephews. Otherwise he had his books and his uniforms, the remainder of his horses, his saddles and bridles, some of which his nephews could have the use of, except those pertaining to the Andalusian. Captain Allington must witness his signature, so he must not appear as a beneficiary, in however small a capacity.

Captain Allington was sitting by the fire, upon which he occasionally threw a log. He had the greyhounds at his feet, which reminded Major Wilder they, too, must have a home. The will and the letters took him longer to write than he could have imagined.

Eventually, when all was done, he said, 'Allington, when this is over, one way or another, what is to stop Captain Greenway speaking out on the subject of my brother, just the same? His tongue may never be curbed.'

'I shall see to that.'

'How?'

'I have no intention of telling you, but you may rest assured Captain Greenway will wish he and I were perfect strangers.'

'But should I allow you to undertake anything further on my behalf?'

'It would depend in what way you intended to prevent it.'

'However I juggle things I find myself in debt to you.'

'And I so young and impressionable that you consider it should be in the reverse,' Allington said, smiling.

'Why, yes, that is exactly it, but I must draw the line at impressionable. No one in their right mind could call you that.'

'I will tell you the truth. My rearing was a strange one. I had little guidance. I value the friendship of a few I consider to have integrity, whose opinion I can draw on.'

'But I never knew you to draw on anyone's opinion,' Major Wilder replied.

'Ah, well, in my own way I do. And I trust you.'

After that they were silent, both oppressed by the situation, but eventually Major Wilder said, 'I must ask you to witness my will.' They returned, briskly, to matters of a purely practical nature.

Major Wilder wondered how to close the evening. It was his inclination to see no one but Allington and to go to bed, but to act in any way that was out of the ordinary struck him as cowardly. Ought he to go downstairs, eat a little supper and wish them all goodnight, particularly his father? To do so seemed a deceit, because would he not be wishing them goodbye?

Eventually he and Captain Allington went down to the drawing room but only his mother was there.

She said, 'I don't know how it is, but everyone is tired tonight. Your father went up very early and Miss Arbuthnot went with Lottie.'

Major Wilder realized he was to be let off lightly and, after saying goodnight to Lady Charles, retired to bed himself. Captain Allington said he would wake him in the morning. Major Wilder could not envisage oversleeping under the circumstances, but he said nothing. He had been brought hot water for washing so he washed and shaved as well for good measure, undressed, pulled on his nightshirt, blew out the candle and lay down on the bed. At first he thought about days previous to likely actions, checking equipment, talking to the men, always appearing cheerful and calm. He had never analysed it: it came to him naturally. On such occasions he said the Lord's Prayer on going to bed. He did not see himself as religious but he practised a sturdy Protestant ethic and was inclined to say a prayer in a crisis, but more to keep himself calm than in expectation of immediate succour. He was aware of good and evil as separate forces and respected them as such. The Lord's Prayer was, in fact, the only prayer he said and he turned to it now, repeating it slowly line by line. He paused at 'Thy will be done.' He wondered what was God's will in relation to himself. He passed over being given his daily bread and paused again at having his trespasses forgiven him. He supposed, in the eyes of some, that must include an indeterminate number of Frenchmen blown to bits, but war and Christian principles were too difficult to reconcile and he did not attempt it. Had not Napoleon to be kept in check, had not those very Frenchmen to be kept from British soil? He hoped if he had wronged his father, his father would forgive him. He forgot about his mother but was reminded of her when it came to 'As we forgive them that trespass against us.' Well, he didn't mind forgiving his mother, he supposed, because he thought she could not help herself, but he found it a tall order to forgive Captain Greenway. He assumed he would get his just deserts and he was glad he was unlikely to be responsible for administering them. He ended, thoughtfully, on 'Deliver us from evil.' That, he considered, he needed most of all. He said, 'Amen,' closed his eyes and listened to his own breathing, slowly, slowly, slowly.

Thomas Wilder fell asleep. His dreams were disturbed by the diabolical roar of artillery, the screams of wounded men, the need to shout his orders, to re-sight the guns, but he slept all the same.

Miss Arbuthnot, alone in her room, thought initially of Horatio. It did seem, as Lord Charles had said, an unsuitable mission for a child. Monkton was about three miles, perhaps four, from the village of Ridley, which in daylight was not so far, but at night it was surely a different matter. Horatio had also to return and explain his absence in some convincing way, and they had had no time to discuss how the letter was to be delivered. Was he boldly to knock at the door? Would Sir John receive him? Would a servant take it and consider breakfast the following day as good a time as any to hand it to his master? Miss Arbuthnot thought there was too much to go wrong and that Horatio would hold himself to blame.

The image of Lord Charles came to her next, so distraught, so tired and old in his face, overcome with contemplating the possible death of his only remaining son. Would he sleep? Never. What agonies he would suffer the night through before the morning would bring its news, good or bad. It was impossible not to feel indignation at the conduct of Major Wilder, that he could not only risk his life but abandon his principles. Duelling might be common practice but it was illegal and served no useful purpose. It was some absurd and inexplicable aberration in the male mind. How could he have allowed himself to get into such a position? Was it not a betrayal of all who had respect for him? Would her brother Bobby ever fight a duel? She prayed not, but Bobby, she knew, even if reluctantly, would defend what he saw as his honour if he thought he had to do so.

Though she prepared for bed, washed, hung up her clothes, brushed a little mud from a hem acquired while inspecting the kitchen gardens with Lottie, she saw no prospect of sleep. One could lie down, draw the bed curtains, close one's eyes, pretend, but that was all. She saw in her mind every image of Major Wilder and tried to turn herself away from that of his death, sudden, bloody and violent.

As the weary night proceeded, she dozed a little, always waking with a start to renewed anxiety. She thought of poor Lord Charles, alone in his rooms, more anguished even than she. Several times she left her bed and went to the window to see if the sky would gradually lighten. At last, after many tired hours, dawn began to break. Miss Arbuthnot waited some while longer before dressing herself. She pulled a shawl round her shoulders and went noiselessly from her room. She knew where Lord Charles slept though she had, of course, never been there. The idea of his being alone and without comfort only added to her distress.

Softly, very softly, she tapped on his door and whispered his name. If he was asleep, which seemed unlikely, he would not hear her but she was immediately aware of his footsteps as he crossed the room.

'Who is it?' he asked quietly.

'It is I, Miss Arbuthnot.'

He opened the door. She could see, looking past him into the interior, that he had one candle lit and he had placed it on the chest of drawers of what was obviously a small anteroom. There was a grate, a couple of chairs and a wardrobe. She said, 'If you wouldn't mind it, I would keep you company.'

'Mind it? My dear child, we can but keep each other company. Come in. I'm afraid you will be cold. I let the fire out. They leave me wood for the fire. Old men don't necessarily sleep well. Sometimes I get up, light the candle, get the fire going, sit by it and think of days gone by, days gone by and I was a lad, scrambling after my brothers, always the smallest, always the youngest. Most of them are dead now.'

'Let me light the fire again.'

'How practical you are. Neither my wife nor my sisters would ever light a fire for themselves. They wouldn't know how.'

Miss Arbuthnot knelt down and attended to the fire in which there were yet a few hot embers. She said, 'I suppose they never had the need. If we didn't do things for ourselves they weren't done, but Kate was never to light the fire in case she burnt herself.'

Lord Charles, anxiously watching her, said, 'Yes, there are always the favoured ones. So we were with Lyndon. We spoilt him and spoilt him, we loved him so, the precious heir at last and such a beautiful infant, such a beautiful boy.

Let us watch the window. We will move the chairs thus. Sit beside me, child, and let me have your hand in mine. Ah, yes, there are always the favoured ones. I was closest in age to my brother John. He was my playfellow but he wasn't strong. It was his lungs. I took his death badly. He didn't make eighteen, God rest his dear soul. Why court death when it hovers round the corner? Is it light enough to see my clock? Do you suppose it a little after five? I haven't been able to sleep. I haven't been able to sleep, thinking of my boy and thinking of John. I don't think of John very often, it's all so long ago. I think of Lyndon too. How would the estate have been if left in Lyndon's hands? Gone to rack and ruin, I dare say. How love blinds. What delusions I allowed myself, how soldiering would bring him home ready and practical, willing to undertake his responsibilities. Well, we now understand the presence of that young man at Ridley, Captain Allington. But why should Thomas choose so young a man? He must have older, experienced friends, who would have known how to get around the whole business. I keep trying to remember in what context Thomas spoke of him. Was it he, in the Portuguese service, from whom Thomas fetched Lyndon's things? Captain Greenway is in what was Lyndon's regiment. What have I overlooked?'

Miss Arbuthnot, her arm tucked into his and his hand on hers, saw it eased his mind to talk, to spill out unguardedly whatever crossed his mind. She had no idea how long they sat gazing out over the park, which imperceptibly grew lighter as the hour wore by, a grey, clouded, sunless dawn.

At length two figures could be seen, side by side, walking

steadily away from the house and across the park, one with a flat, oblong box under his arm.

Lord Charles watched them go. Miss Arbuthnot saw the tears flowing unchecked down his cheeks. He said, 'Those will be Lyndon's pistols. He had a very handsome pair from Mortimer. Should I go after them, even as I am, in this quilted dressing-gown, and beg them to return? No, it would do no good and make it harder for Thomas to do what he has to do.'

Miss Arbuthnot said, 'But maybe it would make a difference, that he would listen.'

He replied, 'You must see it will be a question of honour.'

As Major Wilder and Captain Allington crossed the park, leaving a trail of their footsteps in the dewy grass behind them, Major Wilder said, 'They say history repeats itself. Last time I was engaged in an affair of this nature, I was all of eight years old. My closest friend lived in Mrs Kingston's house. He had brothers, some younger, some more Lyndon's age. One day he and I had some little quarrel and he said, "Your brother is a beastly, horrid bully and us little boys hate him." Now these were exactly my own sentiments but I was mortified. I told him I would fight him. We were in a room at the back of the house where I believe Mrs Kingston now has her kitchen. It had a billiard table and other such things for amusing the family. My little friend got a couple of fencing foils down from the wall, he had to stand on a chair, and we took the safety buttons off them. Freddy had been tutored in using them but, my father thinking it archaic, I had not, and being aware of this I thought the only thing to do was to take him by surprise. I fell on him without any of the niceties attached to the proceeding and, much to my own astonishment and his, I nicked a hole in his arm. Can you imagine the furore? I got a terrific hiding from my father. There was a coolness between our houses after that, though Freddy and I remained the best of friends. They moved away and I lost touch with him. He entered the navy at a young age. I used to spot him in the navy lists but he was killed in an engagement with an American privateer, or so I believe.'

While Major Wilder was recounting this tale, much as he had told it to the children but including the one detail he had previously left out, they were every moment getting closer to the allotted site. Captain Allington, though listening to Major Wilder, was glancing in the direction of the village in the unlikely hope of their adversaries never appearing or, perhaps more likely, Captain Greenway coming unattended, Captain Houghton either declining to come or being too sick to do so. Under such circumstances Major Wilder could honourably refuse the engagement. However, they had barely reached the designated spot before they saw three figures making towards them. Captain Allington could not delude himself they were labourers taking a short cut across the park, but they seemed to take a long time to arrive. Captain Houghton walked slowly and was using a stick.

As soon as they were within speaking distance Captain Greenway, evincing every sign of extreme impatience with his companions, called out, 'Good morning, gentlemen. We've crept along. Houghton's a bit knocked up. You're devilish early. It's scarcely light.'

'Quite light enough,' Allington replied.

'I will introduce Dr Peasbody. I dare say he is already known to Major Wilder.'

Dr Peasbody, a small, stuffy, middle-aged gentleman carrying a leather bag containing his instruments, tersely acknowledged the introductions, 'I will retire to some distance. I don't wish to be associated with the action, you must understand.'

Major Wilder was looking at Captain Houghton. He considered Captain Greenway extremely thoughtless to put such a sick man through the ordeal ahead of them and he saw, more clearly than before, that Captain Houghton would not live: he had death in his face and was as likely to need the services of Dr Peasbody as he was himself. It was a sad thing his principles forbade him to fire at Captain Greenway for he would surely be doing the world a service if he shot him dead.

Captain Greenway, pacing about, hectic, said, 'I don't consider it sufficiently light. Let me see the weapons.'

Captain Allington opened the box. Greenway took out first one of the pistols and then the other, cradling them in his hands before holding them at arm's length to align them.

Allington said, 'Allow us to have them back. Captain Houghton and I will load them now.'

'Ah, I shall see you do that.'

'Sir, I am sure you are aware that that contravenes accepted practice. You are joking, I assume.'

'How is the ground marked? I understand it to be marked.'

'We marked it yesterday.'

‘Houghton tells me it was you who paced it out.’

‘By mutual agreement, I did. Is that not so, Captain Houghton?’

‘Why, yes. We agree very well on all the points.’

Captain Greenway went off to stamp up and down in an effort to locate the second marker, Captain Allington having shown him the stick that marked the first.

Major Wilder took no notice of the others. He had wandered off to examine his young trees, which he did with some satisfaction, thinking he might at least go down in family history as the man who had replanted the park even if he was to be remembered otherwise for selling the London house and then getting himself killed in a duel, always, in his eyes, a disreputable thing, even if commonplace.

Captain Allington called out that they were ready. Captain Greenway was still grumbling about the light. Major Wilder took the pistol in his hand. Allington directed him to a stick stuck in the ground and he biddably stood by it.

Captain Houghton said, ‘I can’t find the other marker.’

Captain Allington had not intended Captain Greenway should know where he was to stand until the last conceivable moment so he had merely placed a stone in the correct position but he was able to find it himself.

Greenway said, ‘That is never eighteen paces, upon my life. It’s more like twenty. What nonsense is this, Houghton?’

‘Of course it is eighteen. I watched Captain Allington pace it out at the time.’ In fact, Allington had instructed him to take a rest and he had lain down on the grass, not taking the least further notice, but he did not care about the lie.

Major Wilder, in the calm tones of one who is obeyed without question, said, 'I'm not going to wait all day. If you can't agree with your second, Captain Greenway, I don't know what you are doing here.'

Captain Allington said smoothly, 'Every man's pace will be a little different. I must have a long stride. Major Wilder, would you oblige me by taking off your coat? Should you be wounded . . . Now, Captain Houghton stands just there. When he drops his handkerchief you may each raise your arm and fire. You are to fire but once. We will not reload. Captain Houghton and I are in perfect agreement.'

Captain Greenway, who had thought he could manipulate Captain Houghton, as well as one so young as Allington, was indignant and frustrated. He would have liked to prolong the moment but saw he could not delay. Thinking little of death or injury, he fed on the drama of the moment. Major Wilder took off his coat and handed it to Captain Allington. He stood with his right shoulder towards his opponent and he knew that when the handkerchief dropped he would raise his arm and point the weapon well to the left of Greenway's head, thus using his arm as a shield for his body. At the same time he would lower his own head a fraction to make it less of a target. In the random manner of thoughts at such times, he considered how a soldier was chided if he ducked a ball but in duelling a little subterfuge was acceptable. As for firing, the pistol was cocked and his finger was on the trigger but he came to no decision as to whether he would fire it wide, if he was able, or not fire it at all.

Captain Houghton, perspiration running down his pallid face, held his arm aloft, with the handkerchief in his hand. He let it drop.

Major Wilder had one second to confirm in his mind that Captain Greenway meant to kill him. The handkerchief dropped and Greenway's arm came up smartly, though no more smartly than his own, and the barrel pointed exactly at him while his was well to Greenway's left. Greenway fired but as he did so there was the loudest possible shout, which distracted his aim and his arm involuntarily jerked.

Major Wilder heard the shout, also the blast from the gun, and he saw the puff of smoke. He let go his own weapon and it fell harmlessly to the ground as he registered the ball ploughing up the length of his arm and embedding itself in the top of his shoulder. Blood immediately started to seep the length of the wound. He was vaguely pleased and relieved to realize he was not going to die.

Captain Allington rushed up to him, a delighted smile on his face, displaying rather more emotion than was his custom. He said, immediately lifting bits of Major Wilder's shirt away from the wound, 'Thank God, not deep.'

Captain Greenway, beside himself, screeched, 'Someone informed. Where's that Peasbody? Did you inform on us, sir?'

The doctor hastened up. 'Certainly not. I gave my word. But informed on you are. Here is Sir John Richards, the magistrate from Monkton, and a couple of constables. Allow me to go to the patient.'

Sir John, aboard a stout pony, the two constables running beside him, was as red in the face as Captain Greenway. He drew up by the little group and said, 'By God, in the name of the law, I arrest the lot of you.' He pointed to Greenway. 'You, sir, if you have committed murder . . .'

He got off the pony and approached Major Wilder.

The doctor, embarrassed, said, 'Good morning, Sir John.' Then, addressing Major Wilder, he said, 'If you would lie down it would be more convenient.' He was rummaging in his bag for his fleam but when Captain Allington saw it, he said, 'Don't bleed him. I won't have it. He will lose plenty of blood. Put that instrument away. It makes me ill to look at it. I take it you have bandages. We will bind the arm for now.'

Dr Peasbody was disgruntled, muttering just loud enough to be heard.

Sir John said, 'What is the damage? We arrived a moment too late. By God, Major Wilder, I thought you knew better than to get mixed up in this sort of thing. I must take you in. I have my carriage on the road. You will all oblige me by getting into it. Can you walk? How bad is it?'

'The wound is superficial,' Captain Allington said, 'but the ball is lodged in his shoulder, I should say not deep.' He could not help smiling he was so relieved.

Sir John turned to Captain Houghton. 'As for you, and you a sick man, I don't know what your good sister will have to say when she hears of this.'

Captain Houghton was gloomily reflecting on this matter for himself but things were better than they might have been.

Sir John then said to the doctor, 'I intend to arrest these gentlemen. You should have informed, rather than comply with their ill-judged demands. However, I don't intend to arrest you, but you had better call in at Ridley in an hour or so to remove the ball from Major Wilder's shoulder, unless this young fellow intends doing it himself.'

Allington, taking the suggestion seriously, said, 'The doctor will have the correct instruments.'

Sir John said, 'Major Wilder will have to wait for the attention.'

The wound was bound up and Major Wilder's coat dropped over his shoulders. Sir John, before getting back on his pony, escorted them to his carriage and instructed his coachman. He was terse, for none of his staff had shown the necessary alacrity at turning out so early in the morning, hence their being ten minutes later than had been the intention. The coachman said, when his master was safely out of hearing, 'If the gentry want to shoot each other, let 'em.'

Captain Greenway, unaware of the irony in settling down into a coach opposite a man he had just done his best to shoot dead, could only consider the circumstances of the engagement. He turned accusingly to Captain Allington. 'I don't believe you loaded more than a morsel of powder: I could tell.'

'There was a sufficiency,' Allington replied. 'Is that not so, Captain Houghton?'

'Indeed, yes, it was a very adequate amount of powder. You are quite mistaken.' Captain Houghton was wondering how he had allowed himself to be so bullied by Greenway and was overcome with peevish irritation. His life was worth so little, a deal less than Major Wilder's, he wondered he had not stood up in his place to be shot at. He was, after all, used to enemy action and had taken quietly the whirring of musket balls and shrapnel about his head. He now said, 'Never mind all that now, Greenway. I believe we are in a pickle. I'm not accustomed to being arrested.'

Captain Greenway glared round the small confines of the carriage. 'Who informed?' He wanted to think it could have been one of the other three, or even Peasbody, but had that been so the arrest must have taken place sooner. It was apparent Sir John had not had the information long.

They were all perplexed except Major Wilder, who did not trouble himself to think about it. The carriage, lurching over the ruts of what was little more than a cart track, made his arm uncomfortable, but it was nothing, very trifling indeed.

Within a quarter of an hour they were filing into Sir John's place of business, like, Major Wilder observed to himself, so many naughty schoolboys. He was the only one permitted a chair.

Sir John, sitting down at his desk and taking up a pen, demanded from Captain Greenway his name, rank, regiment, the name of his colonel and where the regiment was situated. Captain Greenway, an element of reality at last penetrating his head, gave these details with reluctance. Sir John then asked Major Wilder for his full name and the date of his birth. He took similar information from Captain Allington and Captain Houghton but he did not ask for their regiments or the names of their colonels. He could not see Captain Houghton ever returning to his regiment. When he had all the information he required, he laid down the pen and said, 'Well, gentlemen, you have broken the law. You, Captain Greenway, have maliciously wounded Major Wilder. What do you suppose I am able to do about it? If I had my way I would have you strung up for attempted murder but, as you are no doubt aware, even should Major Wilder develop a fever and die from his wound, should I send you for trial no jury would convict you. Juries will not convict duellists, yet the law has been broken, and nothing, no, nothing, makes me so angry as that. Suppose, just suppose, they spotted an irregularity in the manner in which the duel was conducted, why then, I might have my way and I should be delighted to see you hanged. I know not the cause of your disagreement, nor do I wish to know it. Being acquainted with Major Wilder, I am satisfied he will have entered into the engagement with extreme reluctance. I doubt it was his intention to fire that pistol, though I can't be sure of it, and nor is it my intention to ask. Despite this, he is not exonerated of the crime.'

Sir John paused. He felt responsible for the fact that he had not been able to arrest all the participants five minutes earlier. Receiving the information after dark and his servants lacking the necessary sense of urgency had nearly been at the cost of Major Wilder's life, and when Sir John considered all the dangers of foreign campaigning through which that life had been preserved, he was mortified at what he saw as his own inefficiency. Given the little time he had had, he supposed he had done his best. Slightly confused, his mind went to the previous evening when he had been sitting alone in his dining room enjoying a solitary glass of wine until he had become disgruntled at a constant light tapping at the window. At length he had got up, taken the poker in one hand, in case of intruders, and drawn back the curtain. Initially he had seen nothing, but the tapping, which had momentarily come to a halt, then continued more frantically and he could see something resembling a letter purposely being applied to the lowest portion of the window. The windows of his house were rather high from the ground and he deduced that whoever was in charge of the missive, for it surely was a missive, was not very tall. He had cautiously raised the sash a few inches and a small hand had slid the letter though the gap. A little voice had whispered, 'Read it now, Sir John, it's very important.' The hand had vanished into darkness and there was the merest hint of retreating footsteps, the clink of a shoe against a stone. He had, of course, immediately recognized the seal and the handwriting of his neighbour at Ridley, but even while he was digesting the contents he was wondering at the peculiarity of Lord Charles finding a small child to deliver a message in the night.

Captain Greenway was musing over the apparent intention of the magistrate to write a letter to the colonel of his regiment, an idea causing him quite a degree of discomfort, but he was also considering the inconclusive nature of the duel. It was unsatisfactory. He wondered why Sir John was taking so much time in deciding what to do with them if he did not intend to send them for trial. Perhaps, being a neighbour of Mrs Kingston and of Major Wilder, he would let them off with a caution.

Major Wilder was thinking that to be alive was more than he had expected and Captain Houghton was thinking about his sister upon whom he was so dependent for, with his health, the army would surely place him on half pay, and then where would he be? Captain Allington hoped they would be allowed to return to Ridley sooner rather than later.

Sir John said, 'Major Wilder, I shall bind over you and Captain Greenway to keep the peace for the sum of fifty pounds each. Captain Greenway, you shall stay in the vicinity until you have found the means of raising the sum.'

Captain Greenway stared at him. How was he to find fifty pounds from the ten shillings and sixpence a day he received as his army pay? He heard Captain Houghton gasp with horror.

'Considering the offence,' Sir John continued, 'it is light. You must remember, Captain Greenway, in the eyes of the law, you attempted murder. I could bind you over for the sum of one hundred pounds or even two, but what is the point if you can't produce it? I hope you have some long-suffering relative who will help you out. I shall certainly be writing to your colonel.'

Within half an hour they were all back in Sir John's carriage. For a while they were silent. It then occurred to Captain Greenway that the fault of the whole business lay with Major Wilder. If he had paid the forty Spanish dollars none of them would be where they were at that minute. He leant forward and said to Major Wilder, 'Of course, the affair is not finished. You never fired.'

'Neither I did,' Major Wilder replied, with every appearance of complete indifference.

'We will go to France.'

Captain Houghton said, 'Really, Greenway, I don't see how you can expect Major Wilder to consider the matter in his present condition. If you can't find the money, you'll end in prison.'

'Oh, his arm will soon heal. I doubt it's much. As for the money, it is a ludicrous sum to ask of a man serving his country. Nevertheless, I don't feel honour is satisfied between myself and Major Wilder.'

Captain Allington drew his gold watch from his pocket and dandled it in his hand. He seemed in no hurry to look at it. Eventually he said, 'Let us not discuss it now. I shall attend on the doctor. Major Wilder must be made comfortable. Suppose I call on you in an hour or so?'

Captain Greenway's eyes were fixed on Captain Allington's watch: he knew an expensive article when he saw it.

Dr Peasbody had gone home to breakfast before ordering his gig and setting out for Ridley. Slimmer spotted him coming up the drive and was at the door in an instant, for he knew the doctor's gig when he saw it, though Peasbody was only called to Ridley when a second opinion was required. Slimmer had been aware, all the morning, of something being amiss, out of place, but he had been unable to detect what it was. Ushering Peasbody in, he said, 'Fancy you coming, Dr Peasbody, all unannounced.'

The doctor grunted. He thought Slimmer impertinent and was disconcerted to discover he had arrived before his patient.

'Are you come here particular?' Slimmer asked.

'Of course, idiot. Why should I be here otherwise? I am to see Major Wilder.'

'As far as I know he went out before breakfast and isn't back in yet.' Slimmer was affronted.

'I shall wait here.' Dr Peasbody made a move towards the

only chair in the hall but did not care to sit in it: it looked as if it had been put in place for a servant.

'I don't see anything could be wrong with Major Wilder. There must be a mistake.'

'Major Wilder has an injury to his arm.'

'What sort of injury? Is it broken?'

'It is not my place to say.'

Slimmer hastened into the dining room. Breakfast was on the table but Lord Charles and Miss Arbuthnot were standing by the window. Lord Charles, who, Slimmer thought, looked ill, immediately turned and said, 'Whose gig was that, Slimmer?'

'Dr Peasbody's, m'lord.'

'Did he not say why he had come?' There was a curious, weary note in his voice, which Slimmer did not understand.

'He says the Major's hurt his arm.'

'His arm? Just his arm? Send Peasbody in.'

Dr Peasbody came with reluctance. He saw he could not avoid explanations.

Lord Charles, who, the doctor thought, had vastly aged since he had seen him last, said, 'I hear my son has injured his arm. How bad is it? Don't spare me. Tell me honestly.'

'I should say the wound is unpleasant but not dangerous.'

'Ah, it was a wound, but it isn't dangerous.'

'Yes, my lord, I am sorry to say it was a wound from a pistol. The ball is in his shoulder.'

Miss Arbuthnot came forward. 'I would so like it, Lord Charles, if you would sit down.'

The doctor noticed she, too, looked white, indeed quite unwell, but the news was shocking, after all.

Lord Charles said, 'Why, yes, my dear, it would be best. And the other gentleman, the one who shot him? And where is Major Wilder now?'

'Sir John Richards arrived and took them all into custody. Major Wilder never fired at the other gentleman.'

'Thank God, thank God it is no worse. Sir John will send him shortly. We must be prepared. What will you require?'

'Major Wilder has a very interfering, ignorant young gentleman about him.' Dr Peasbody suddenly wondered why he did not withdraw his services if Captain Allington would not allow him to conduct the matter as he saw fit, but it would, he supposed, be hardly worth his while to offend the most influential family in the neighbourhood.

Horatio, though he had woken twice in the night, had gone back to sleep again. Now, lying awake, he could see the morning was well advanced. He got up and opened his bedroom door. The house was completely silent. He thought about the previous evening. He saw that if you were on a mission you had to think well ahead for, having supposed he had done everything he could, he had had no explanation for his mother, whom he had found waiting up for him after he had slipped the pony back in the paddock and surreptitiously crept indoors.

Anxiety had fuelled her indignation: his statement that he had forgotten the time did not appease her. She accused him of running wild with the boys from the village, poaching, stealing, housebreaking and any other crime of which she could think.

'That my only child should treat me so, and he, just a

little boy, already a hardened criminal, his only destination Botany Bay.'

At this Mrs Kingston burst into tears and he was genuinely upset at the distress he had caused her. He would have liked to tell her the truth, but he suspected she would rouse his uncle and Captain Greenway and they would postpone the matter of shooting Major Wilder dead to another occasion. He also thought he would have to tell her how he had opened his uncle's writing box and read a letter in it, which he did not fancy doing, though it was heavy on his conscience, so he hung his head and said he was sorry and that he would not do it again and had fallen asleep while she was talking to him, snuggled into a chair, and she had woken him up again to remind him she had been going to take him to Salisbury as a birthday treat. She would now go to Salisbury without him and visit their elderly cousin Alexander, who would surely have died before she was able to visit him again in the company of her son, and tell him how extremely bad Horatio was, which would cause the old gentleman much disappointment because he was very fond of Horatio and always put out his curios with which to amuse him and had all sorts of treats to hand. Her parting words, as Horatio had dragged himself to bed, were that he was not to leave the house, even once, in her absence.

Horatio now started to pad about the house in his nightshirt. He saw by the regulator in the hall it was nine o'clock. His mother would have left for Salisbury. The breakfast table was laid for three but there was no one at breakfast. He heard a carriage in the drive and ran to the window in time to see his uncle and Captain Greenway getting out of it. He skipped back upstairs before they could reach the front door and began to dress, scrub his face and comb his hair. By the time he returned he found them pouring coffee and sitting down to breakfast.

Captain Greenway, ignoring Horatio, said, 'I can't raise such a sum. Your sister wouldn't loan it, I suppose?'

'Not worth asking. After this morning's activities, you will be more than beyond the pale, and myself also. You never should have told her all that stuff about Lieutenant Wilder because she was bound to tell Major Wilder, and it made her take a great dislike to you.'

'But I told her on purpose, so that she would repeat it.'

'I dare say, but it wasn't sensible.' Captain Houghton sounded at his most peevish. He felt very ill and no longer cared if he offended Captain Greenway.

'It was most unfair. After all, Major Wilder can easily raise it, but it's nearly a third of my salary and I owe my tailor as much. Suppose you asked your sister for the loan and you lent it on to me? Of course I would pay you back, if I starved to do it.'

They both glanced towards Horatio but he was intent on drinking a large glass of milk.

Captain Greenway continued, 'If he writes to my colonel, as he threatens, I shall be finished.'

'Should have thought of that before,' Captain Houghton replied, pleased, rather than otherwise, at the other's discomfort. 'I shan't ever agree to second anyone again. Being taken up before the magistrate, like a common criminal, is very disgraceful, and his wife a friend of my sister.'

Captain Greenway, further irritated, said, 'Shouldn't you mind your tongue in front of the child?'

'My nephew's but a lad. He won't understand. Where is your mama, Horatio?'

Horatio looked up. He had a rim of milky froth on his upper lip. 'She's gone to Salisbury to see Cousin Alexander.'

'Oh, yes, I had forgotten. Weren't you to go with her?'

'I overslept and Mama was cross with me for staying out so late and looking at the stars.'

Captain Greenway, impatient, said, 'Well, I've not finished the business, but who could have informed? We couldn't have been more discreet. I don't trust that young whippersnapper Allington, too pleased with himself altogether, with his theories about this and that. Who is he, anyway? His name rings a bell.'

'He has a stepfather in Devonshire, Lord Somebody. He told me he was on his way there. It is my belief he is one of those officers employed to gather intelligence. He speaks several languages and was in the Portuguese service. I believe people talk of him.'

Greenway said, 'Ah,' abruptly, and was then silent before leaning forward and saying, in an undertone, 'I am beginning to remember. He had a company of *caçadores* and it was they . . .' He looked at Horatio before continuing. 'Never mind what, but it was he Major Wilder went to see after he left us. I remember the very village we were in. Now I understand the connection. Among those *caçadores* there might have been witnesses.' Captain Greenway shrugged. 'I wonder what Allington knows. Either way, what's a stepfather? Might it be something polite for another relationship of a closer description? There's money behind him. Look at his watch. That's no ordinary watch.'

Captain Houghton agreed it was no ordinary watch

and that Captain Allington seemed particularly attached to it.

'It would be my pleasure to take the young fellow down a peg,' Captain Greenway remarked. 'Just to see him a little crestfallen would do. You let him hoodwink you.'

'No, I didn't. We were very agreeable.'

At that moment the parlour maid opened the door and said, 'Captain Allington to see you, sir.'

Captain Allington showed no sign of the exigencies of the morning. He had changed his linen while the others looked tired and dishevelled. The maid brought in a tray and cleared away the breakfast. When she was gone, Captain Houghton said, 'I hope that ball came away cleanly.'

Horatio looked up, startled. He had been sure nothing would have occurred. He said, 'What ball? Is somebody shot?'

'Now that was careless, Houghton,' Captain Greenway said.

Captain Allington said, 'It can't remain a secret. You had best explain it, Captain Houghton.'

'Explain it? I don't think I can. Things don't sound good when explained. It was like this, Horatio, Captain Greenway had a . . . a polite disagreement with Major Wilder. Major Wilder received a wound in his arm.'

Horatio was completely shocked. He turned on Captain Greenway and said, 'You shot at Major Wilder.'

'So I did. It's what happens, you know.'

Captain Allington said, 'Fortunately, the wound is not serious. The magistrate arrived and put a stop to proceedings.' Being aware that Greenway's aim had been put out, he added, 'In fact, the arrival of the magistrate was very opportune, very opportune indeed.'

Allington was conscious of Captain Greenway glaring at him, flinging his head back, his colour deepening.

'But did Major Wilder fire another gun?' Horatio asked.

Allington said, 'No. I don't believe it was his intention to fire at Captain Greenway.'

Horatio, turning to Captain Greenway, said, 'You are a bad man. If I was older I would make you leave our house. My Uncle Henry should do it, but he's too poorly, and you take advantage of that. You are a really bad man.'

Captain Greenway shrugged. 'You don't understand these things, but you had better keep a more civil tongue in your head when you join the navy.'

'If you went to Ridley,' Captain Allington said, relieved Greenway had not chosen to strike the child, 'you could talk to Miss Wilder. She is in perfect agreement with you but she is very upset.'

'I expect Lottie is upset. I'm not meant to leave the house today but I will go to see her. My mother will have to understand. I can comfort Lottie.' Horatio sighed. He had meant to do as his mother told him, just this once.

Captain Houghton, anxious, said, 'You cut along, Horatio. This is not a good place for you at the minute.'

As soon as Horatio could be seen to leave the house, Captain Greenway said, 'I don't mean to give up the business. I admit I'm in a scrape, but the conclusion was very unsatisfactory.'

Allington said, 'You believe Major Wilder accused you of lying. He had no intention of so doing. He apologized. He accepted your challenge. What more do you want?'

'We did not complete the affair. We must go to France.'

'Major Wilder will never consent. I consider it unreasonable of you to expect it of him,' Captain Allington said, but he was calm and civil.

'We are back to where we started, in that case.'

'Even suppose Major Wilder changed his mind, for all he means to ride to Monkton this afternoon to pay his fine, it will be at least six weeks or more before he could be fit. Will you not have rejoined your regiment by then? I would have thought you might yourself be occupied with pecuniary matters. I thought the magistrate very lenient,' Allington replied.

'Lenient?' Greenway started to walk up and down the room. 'It may seem lenient to you but it's more than I've got.'

'Why, as Sir John said, the figure could have been two hundred pounds or more. You must have plenty of friends who could lend it to you.' Allington smiled. He was sure Captain Greenway must have outworn all the friends he had.

'My friends would consider it a very large sum.'

'You are, in that case, in a scrape. You may have to sell your commission.'

'Sell my commission? And then where would I be?'

'You must know your own affairs,' Allington replied indifferently. 'It's no use discussing it with me. It's not as if I'm to lend you the money.' He pulled out a chair and sat down, as if he had no intention of leaving. 'It's useless to talk about it. Can't we do something more amusing? If I go back to Ridley now, Lord and Lady Charles will wear me to death with their questions. Have you no cards?'

Captain Greenway's attitude subtly altered. He became amenable. He thought of Captain Allington's watch. 'What would you play?' he asked.

'Piquet, I suppose.'

Captain Houghton declined to join in. He went to the window and lay down on a daybed that had been put there for his convenience. He was extremely tired and he did not suppose Captain Greenway had any good intentions towards Captain Allington.

Greenway and Allington proceeded to play piquet. Captain Greenway at first won ten pounds and then another fifteen. He looked for some sign of his opponent becoming anxious but he laughed it off and did not even seem to pay much attention. Greenway won a further twenty pounds and began to think he might be in a position to pay his fine, like Major Wilder, that very afternoon, but, to his chagrin, Captain Allington suddenly won the whole sum back and declined to play another game.

Captain Greenway was trying to puzzle out exactly how the last game had been quite so much to his disadvantage. He even wondered if Allington had cheated, but if he had, he could not see how. He said, 'You are afraid of not getting your money back another time, I suppose.'

'Not at all, but we are now in the same position as when we started, bar you owe me a pound. By the way, were you aware one of Sir John's constables is watching this house? Seems uncivil, but I dare say you were not intending to leave. I thought we might play something different. I seem to recall a chessboard the last time I was here.'

Captain Greenway could not help smiling. He knew himself to be excellent at chess. In fact, he was rarely beaten. What would he care for the arm of the law? He got up and fetched the box and the board, immediately putting the pieces out.

'I will play you for your watch,' he said, 'for a start.'

'Certainly not. What if I lost it? It is of sentimental value to me. I don't mind playing you for the value of my watch but I don't know what it's worth. Still, that's a little tame. What shall we say to three games at . . . at a hundred pounds each?'

'Three games? We'll be here till midnight.' Greenway saw it was a very high risk he was taking but he was in love with risk and surely Allington, a mere boy, was a complete fool to throw his money about in such a fashion.

'I never find a game of chess very long, and there isn't much else to do,' Allington said.

'And why not a hundred pounds' bonus should one of us win all three games?' Greenway suggested, placing the board between them.

'Why not?' Allington replied, putting his hands behind his head and stretching out his legs in their regimental overalls. 'Do you prefer the red or the white? Shall we toss for the first move?'

Miss Arbuthnot was writing to her father. She had started as usual with 'My dear Papa' but what was she to say? She could imagine few things more likely to shock her father than the bald truth: Major Wilder fought a duel with a Captain Greenway. Nobody knows why. He has a long thin wound up his arm and into his shoulder, from where the doctor has extracted the ball. The doctor was assisted by Captain Allington, who likes everything to be boiled: water, instruments et cetera, because he has theories, but the doctor was much teased by him. Despite all this Major Wilder has gone off on his horse to pay his fine at the magistrate, instead of biding quietly at home as Lord Charles suggested.

Miss Arbuthnot wondered if she wrote all that whether it would at last make her father think Major Wilder was not such a suitable match for her as he had first considered, for she was aware, though her father did not say it, he still harboured a few thoughts in that direction. She would have liked her father to know Major Wilder now never considered her as anything more than his niece's governess. But would her father be as shocked as she thought he ought to be? After all, though he was a clergyman he was also a gentleman, so might he, too, suggest it was a matter of honour? She began to dislike the word 'honour' altogether. Was she not herself mortified by Major Wilder's failure to adhere to his own principles? Horatio had said, 'But we don't know the reasons for it,' and that Captain Greenway was a bad man. It was true they did not know the reasons so she thought she should be less judgemental but she was still upset, angry, disturbed and anxious. What if the wound should fester? Captain Allington had said there was no piece of the shirt left in it, which he viewed as important. All the same, it might still fester and Major Wilder run a fever. Why did he not rest? Why treat such a wound as if it had not happened?

Miss Arbuthnot began to think of herself and Lord Charles so long awaiting the departure and subsequent return of Major Wilder and Captain Allington. Would

Lord Charles, of whom she had grown fond, ever get over it? Oh, the blessed relief when Slimmer had announced the presence of the doctor and said Major Wilder had hurt his arm. The doctor, accepting a cup of coffee, had drearily recounted the event. And then Major Wilder had walked in of himself and his poor old father had staggered towards him. Major Wilder had caught him up with his left arm and his coat had slipped from his shoulders, exposing his blood-soaked shirt. She had stood transfixed, appalled at the oozing bandages but also violently indignant that he should behave as he had, near killing his father with grief and anxiety.

The very next moment Lottie had run into the room followed by Lady Charles. Lottie had turned pale with horror. Lady Charles had said, 'Whatever has happened? Sally told me Peasbody was here so of course I came down.'

Nobody replied. Lord Charles was still half in his son's embrace, tears of relief cascading down his face. Eventually Major Wilder said, 'Much against my inclinations, I fought a duel with Captain Greenway. We were interrupted by the magistrate, which I think just as well. The wound is slight.'

Lady Charles said, 'And what of Captain Greenway? I cannot hear mention of him, even now, without thinking how he and Lyndon were in the same regiment but it seemed we were never to meet. It would be strange if you were responsible for his death.'

Major Wilder shook his head. 'It was never my intention to fire at him.'

Lady Charles's voice rose. 'And had you been killed? Did you think of that? Did you think of your father?'

Major Wilder said wearily, 'I did indeed.'

'I can't think what induced you to do such a thing. A question of honour, you will say, but you should not allow yourself to get into such a situation where to fight a duel becomes a necessity. Oh, Lyndon used to tell me of duels, but he had the perspicacity not to fight one. If you did not fire at Captain Greenway but allowed him to fire at you that is tantamount to saying you were in the wrong. It was selfish, very selfish. It will be too much for your father.'

Miss Arbuthnot, who was not usually in such accord with Lady Charles, had, perversely, wished she would not speak as she did. Major Wilder had looked at his mother with an odd expression on his face.

Lady Charles had then said, 'Well, you had better get the wound dressed before there's further mischief.' She looked round for Slimmer, who had of course remained in the room, and told him to instruct the maids to tear up an old sheet for bandages and to carry water up to the Major's room. Lady Charles was at her best, Miss Arbuthnot realized, when she had something to do.

Peasbody had said, 'The ball must be extracted. Otherwise it will certainly fester. I am not in the habit of dealing with such things but I believe it not to be deep.'

At this, Lottie had burst out crying, as if the full implication of the situation was only just understood. Major Wilder had sat his father in a chair and crossed the room to her. He had said, 'I'm sorry, *niña*, to have upset you so.'

One of the maids could be heard having hysterics and Captain Allington surprised them all by insisting the water should be boiled. Miss Arbuthnot had led Lottie away, and when she had looked back she saw Major Wilder was still watching them.

Now, she thought, the pen in her hand, how much of this could she tell her father, who expected to be told everything? Major Wilder has hurt his arm. Describe accurately, dear. Is his arm broken?

My dear Papa,

I am sorry to hear Kate is feeling so poorly, but is this not quite normal for one in her condition? I hope she feels better shortly.

She knew her father expected her to take a greater interest in Kate's condition than she did. She was indifferent to Mr Langley and nearly indifferent to Kate, which was a sobering thought because surely wrong. It was impossible to think of Kate as a mother.

Miss Wilder is very unhappy to think how soon little Horatio Kingston will be going to sea. I am so fond of him myself.

Miss Arbuthnot laid her head on her arms. She found she too cried a little. After a while she fell asleep.

At some moment Mrs Kingston had abandoned her dove greys and taken up pale blue or pale pink and knotted ribbons with trailing ends. Lady Charles eyed her coolly. She could not quite make up her mind to have a real difference with Mrs Kingston because she saw that without her she would need to make a real effort to go into society, but the fact of the duel, that Captain Houghton had been party to it, was surely cause for a rift. On the other hand, Mrs Kingston was agreeably distressed and apologetic. She said, 'When I returned from Salisbury and heard the truth from my maid, I was mortified, Lady Charles, absolutely mortified. I went straight to Henry and he owned up to the whole thing. He assured me he had only participated with the greatest reluctance. The truth of it is, Captain Greenway terrifies Henry. I felt like turning Henry out of the house, on the spot, but there he was, laid out on the daybed, more dead than alive, and saying he may as well have got Captain Greenway to shoot at him instead of Major Wilder.'

Mrs Kingston reached for her flowered silk reticule and frantically dabbed at her eyes.

'But why,' Lady Charles asked, 'did they fight? Thomas doesn't say.'

'Henry says it was to do with a gaming debt owed by . . . by your late dear son, owed to Captain Greenway, who applied to Major Wilder to pay it, which Major Wilder declined to do.'

'Thomas is very tight, very tight indeed, and he has a great dislike of cards. However, I believe he would pay an enormous debt rather than fight a duel.'

'It was to do with the IOU. Captain Greenway hadn't the IOU. He said it had been stolen with his baggage. Major Wilder wished to see it and Captain Greenway was affronted he didn't accept his word for it.'

Lady Charles did not reply. She was trying to visualize Lyndon playing cards with this unseen Captain Greenway, who had been of late only a few miles from her. She thought she saw Lyndon with his scarlet jacket undone, his neckcloth loosened, in some dreary Spanish hovel. The image was almost too real and she gave a little shudder.

Mrs Kingston said, 'Though no doubt sizeable to Captain Greenway, it was not so very large a sum of money.'

'And Thomas did not offer to pay it, I suppose?'

'I believe he did. He apologized. Captain Greenway refused to accept his apology.'

'There is nothing in all of this that Major Wilder could not have explained to me. He refuses to divulge a single thing.' Lady Charles had now grasped sufficient of her son's character to know his was not a yielding nature, that he would not give up his principles lightly. She added, 'There is something else not disclosed or he never would have consented to fight Captain Greenway.'

Mrs Kingston knew this to be true, she was only too aware of her own part in the proceeding, but she said nothing. She tried to excuse herself. How was she to have known Captain Greenway was little better than a common blackmailer, and did not Major Wilder have to defend the honour of his brother?

Lady Charles did not misinterpret her silence but neither did she pursue the matter. Some uneasy instinct, she knew not what, held her back. Without speaking she watched Mrs Kingston still gulping and mopping her tears. Eventually she asked, 'And where is Captain Greenway now?'

Mrs Kingston instantly became more cheerful. 'He's gone. He went that day, or rather last night. There was a constable watching our house. The ignominy of it, the shame. Captain Greenway slipped off about midnight. We didn't know he'd gone. I was so relieved, what with expecting my brother-in-law any day. Just fancy we had had a constable standing on the doorstep. What would he have thought? And then my having to explain it. No, he stole out into the night, like a thief. Henry didn't seem surprised. He owed Captain Allington four hundred pounds. They sat down to play chess, that is Allington and Greenway. Just think of it, and Captain Greenway fresh from trying to shoot Major Wilder dead. Henry got up to watch. He knew Captain Greenway to be an expert or, anyway, a deal more expert than he is himself, because he had played with him quite frequently, but never for money, not being at all able to afford losing it. It was almost immediately evident Greenway was completely at sea. He was at the mercy of Captain Allington and Captain Allington had no mercy. I suspect, from the way Henry spoke, Captain Allington was perfectly deliberate. He diddled Captain Greenway along with a few games of piquet before setting high stakes for the chess, and he such a babe, I'm sure I don't know what I think about that, with Greenway lulled into complacency. Henry imagines Greenway would have to sell his commission to pay his debts. Captain Allington said he would, of course, accept Captain Greenway's IOU, but he would lodge it with Major Wilder, who would receive the money on his behalf, when it was convenient for Greenway to pay it, as he thought his regiment would be posted abroad.'

Horatio could be seen to make his way across the park on his pony, a large basket, which he gripped with one hand, precariously arranged in front of the saddle. Lottie, on the terrace with Miss Arbuthnot, watched him come, wondering what he could possibly be carrying. They were three days into March. The sun shone but there was a stiff breeze. Horatio turned the pony towards the stables and disappeared.

Major Wilder stepped out on to the terrace. He wore his coat draped over his shoulders for his wound was yet fresh and needed a considerable quantity of dressings. It was a constant uncomfortable reminder to them all of his duel with Captain Greenway.

Lottie said to herself, repeating her grandmother's words, 'Thomas is very obstinate.' Dr Peasbody had wanted him to take medicines but these he declined. Why had he allowed Captain Greenway to shoot at him? Why had he? Why had he, and come in all covered with blood and given her a horrible fright?

Miss Arbuthnot thought his arm must be painful but it was a pain he would not allow. His mother was right when she complained of his staunch refusal to do any of the things the doctor suggested. He was more inclined to listen to Captain Allington. Was he not curious as to who had informed on them? Seeing Horatio crossing the park reminded her Major Wilder owed his life to his father and to that one small boy, with the addition of a great deal of luck. She discounted her own part in the proceedings. She wished to know what had induced him to fight Captain Greenway and found it hard to forgive him. She was surprised by how angry he had made her though she knew it should be no business of hers.

Now he seemed cheerful. They were all watching Horatio, who came round the corner of the house bearing his basket, but they were distracted by his clothes. He wore a blue coat with big buttons and white nankeen trousers.

'I thought you might like to see my uniform,' he said, putting the basket down and giving a little gesture with his arms to draw attention to his garments.

'It is very smart, Horatio, but isn't it rather big? I expect you will have to grow into it.' Lottie replied doubtfully, not wishing to be reminded of his likely departure. When Lottie was draped in a new frock that seemed to flap round her ankles, Susan always said, 'You'll soon grow into it, Miss Lottie, don't kick up now, there's a deary.'

Both Major Wilder and Miss Arbuthnot told him how well the uniform suited him because they knew that was what he would need to hear.

'What have you got in that basket?' Lottie asked. 'It's jumping about.'

'It's a present for you. I got it with my own money.' Horatio knelt down on the terrace and unlatched the hinged lid of the basket. He stood up clasping a spaniel puppy in his arms. 'She's not any old dog. She's got real ancestors.'

Lottie was speechless. He offered her the puppy to hold. Eventually she said, clutching it tightly, 'Really, really for me? And you paid with your own money?'

'Yes, I did. I thought you would like it.' Horatio looked embarrassed.

Lottie looked at Major Wilder. 'Oh, Uncle Thomas, what will Grandmama say? But it is mine, isn't it?'

'She will certainly be cross, but it would be churlish to refuse such a gift. You must certainly have it.'

The children took the puppy to play on the grass. It chewed everything it could with its sharp little teeth and ripped the hem of Lottie's frock. Horatio got green stains on his white trousers. Miss Arbuthnot watched them from the terrace and Major Wilder seemed inclined to do the same thing. He perched on the stone parapet and she was glad to think he was taking a moment in which to be tranquil.

After a while Horatio said, 'I've got to go now. I promised not to be late for dinner.' He jumped up abruptly and started to run away across the bit of garden and into the park. Once in the park he turned and waved before running on. Lottie picked up the puppy. She was worried she had not thanked him properly. She could see he was running as fast as he could. He was already a quarter the way out of sight.

She turned to Major Wilder and said, 'But he came on his pony. Why hasn't he taken his pony?'

For a moment he made no answer and then he said, gently, reflectively, 'I think, I'm afraid, Lottie, this is Horatio's way of saying goodbye.'

'Saying goodbye?' For a moment Lottie was paralysed. She then half dropped the puppy and started to run after Horatio, crying and calling his name.

Major Wilder started after her. He caught her up awkwardly in his left arm and bore her back, kicking and struggling. When he put her down she tried to run away and punched him.

Miss Arbuthnot ran towards them. She cried out, 'Don't hit your uncle, don't, remember his bad arm.'

Lottie shouted, 'I don't care. I shall hurt him. I shall hurt him a lot. I must go after Horatio. I must.'

Major Wilder said, endeavouring to give her a shake, which was beyond him, 'No, you mustn't. Lottie, you mustn't make it harder for him to do what he has to do.'

Lottie suddenly subsided. Major Wilder placed her in Miss Arbuthnot's arms where she broke into terrible sobs, but slowly she became calmer. She said, 'I'm sorry I hit you, Uncle Thomas. Did I hurt you?'

'I shall survive it, I dare say,' he replied. 'I wonder if anyone is minding that puppy.'

Lottie, struggling out of Miss Arbuthnot's embrace, said, 'Oh, the poor puppy. What would Horatio think if I didn't look after it?' She started to cry all over again.

The puppy was found to be chewing a stick on the terrace. Lottie picked it up.

Major Wilder said, 'Take it round to the stables. Ask York to find it a bed and he will tell you what it should eat. I expect it wants a drink.'

Lottie obediently disappeared in the direction of the stables, the puppy laboriously cradled in her arms.

Miss Arbuthnot was looking across the park. Major Wilder joined her. They could see the merest spot of blue in the spring green, all that was visible of Horatio, and in a moment that was gone. She felt inexpressibly sad.

Major Wilder said, 'That's a wise child. May God keep him.'

Miss Arbuthnot glanced at him. She thought, He minds as much as I do. The anger she had felt, the indignation at what she saw as his abandoning his principles, she was unable to sustain.

York was waiting for Lottie. He had put out a wooden box and a feeding bowl.

Lottie said, fresh tears on her cheeks, 'Oh, York, Horatio is gone.'

'Yes, missy, that's so.'

'Did he tell you?'

'Came into the yard with the pony and the pup. The pony 'as to go to Master Benjy at Finch 'All. The pup's for you. No use crying. That pup'll take a deal of minding. Proper little bitch, she is. You best 'ave a name for 'er.'

'A name for her? Yes, of course. I shall call her after Horatio's ship.'

'What's that, then?'

'The *Prince Adolphus*.'

York pushed his hat to the back of his head. He said, 'I don't know you rightly could call 'er that, seeing she's a girl.'

'But ships are always girls, York.'

'Seems a mite long to me,' he replied. 'Suppose you call 'er Dolly fer everyday. We can't be getting our tongues round the 'ole.'

York was dressing Major Wilder's wound. He did this effectively, boiling the water, as instructed by Captain Allington, but with little grace. He was a trifle rough. Major Wilder was aware York was punishing him for he considered the injury self-inflicted. As that was his own attitude to it, he put up with the discomfort without complaint. York had been extremely cross with him at the time of his acquiring the Andalusian: he did not believe in heroics except on the battlefield and Major Wilder was not convinced he believed in them even there.

When the task was done, York said, 'I doubt you'll get yer pelisse on.'

'I don't have to get it on.'

'That Bonaparte 'as got off that island. Goin' up France, 'e is. Turncoats, they French. 'Ave an army put together in no time, 'e will.'

'York, are you sure?'

'Sure 'tis more an' gossip? Reckon so. They say 'e got off that Elba an' landed on the first o' March. I 'eards it this morning from the carrier. Eleven 'undred soldiers but plenty more comin' in.'

Major Wilder thought of how he had been occupied in the frivolous pursuit of allowing Captain Greenway to shoot at him while the monster of Europe was escaping his prison. He assumed there would be a huge engagement and he wished, above all else, to be there, directing his troop, the troop that was no longer his.

'With the state of yer arm, sir,' York said, 'they wouldn't want you.'

'Possibly, but I expect I'd go all the same.'

'An' you will?'

'No. I resigned.' He considered, for a moment, to whom he had actually imparted this information. Beyond his father, Georgie, Captain Allington and a few of his friends, he had told no one, almost as if he was deceiving himself it had ever been done.

'They'd find a use fer you.'

'I dare say, but it wouldn't be what I wanted. Still, it would be better than nothing.'

Major Wilder, disturbed, spoke to his dogs and abruptly left the room. He opened the door to his father's dressing room, let out Scottie and proceeded downstairs, Scottie and the greyhounds following him. He started to think, with envy, of Captain Allington, who had left him the day before to continue his route to Devonshire. He imagined him, on hearing the news, hastening back to join his regiment. He found himself saying, 'May God protect him: the contest will surely be bloody.' Allington had given him Captain Greenway's IOU. He had placed it in a drawer in his desk and even now he could not help a smile at the curious ironies of life. Against his principles, he had fought a duel. He was now saved from further embarrassment by Allington's gambling, another thing of which he disapproved. They would hear no more of Captain Greenway, who was probably thanking Napoleon for getting him abroad with his regiment before Sir John arrested him, going to the continent for quite a different reason. Allington had said to him, 'Unfortunately a man like you is just too upright to defend himself with all the means at his disposal.' Major Wilder supposed, but was not entirely certain, this had been intended as a compliment.

Out of doors, he started to walk rapidly across the park. He was occupied with numbering all his friends who would be going forth to risk their lives, never counting the cost, and he not with them. He was, at that moment, unbearably heartsick for the Artillery, his military life. He could offer himself as a volunteer. York was correct in saying they would find a use for him. Could he go to his father and plead to be absolved from his promise?

Lord and Lady Charles were both at breakfast. Miss Arbuthnot and Lottie had gone to the stables to let out the puppy.

Slimmer came in with the coffee, adeptly manoeuvring

the elegant silver coffee pot from the tray to the sideboard. He said, 'Very bad news, then, m'lord.'

'What news, Slimmer?'

'Boney's got out. He's going up France like a whirlwind and the towns are all opening their gates and the folks shouting, "*Vive l'Empereur*," like they'd had no time off.'

Lady Charles said, 'Nonsense, Slimmer, it's one of those endless rumours. I don't believe it.'

'Begging your pardon, m'lady, it's true. The mail coach brought the news from London. He landed in the South of France, where you'd expect, the Gulf of something, the Gulf of Juan, though I'm sure folks won't be saying it right, three little ships and more than a thousand soldiers. Folks is full of it.'

Lady Charles did not see why this made it true.

Slimmer fussed about with the cups and saucers, filled with a sense of importance. He said, 'The Major will be off, I suppose.'

Lady Charles said, 'That will do, Slimmer.'

He was obliged to go but promised to be back with the eggs.

Lord Charles was dreadfully agitated. 'Thomas promised me he had resigned.'

'Exactly so,' Lady Charles replied. 'I suppose it's just as well.'

'But he will be devastated. Should I hold him to it?'

'What was the point in getting a promise from him if you allow him to go back on it at the first opportunity? I dare say none of it is true, anyway.'

'But suppose it is true, and he should ask me to release him? What could I say? He will be devastated, heartbroken.

How could I refuse him? And he would be killed. That I know.'

Miss Arbuthnot and Lottie also received the news from York. He was showing Lottie how much milk to give the puppy. He let the news out casually. Having learnt Major Wilder was not just on long leave, he was losing interest in the matter. He never doubted should another war take place, Britain, and any other lesser nation that might care to join her, would win it.

Lottie said, 'Oh, York, will there be a war again?'

' 'Spec' so, missy.'

'Will my uncle have to go?'

'Seems not, though 'e went off down the park with the dogs like the devil was after 'im.'

Lottie started to think of Horatio. Could a war start and finish before he was on the mysterious *Prince Adolphus*? Of course it couldn't. A war went on nearly all your life. She hugged the puppy tightly and tried not to cry.

Miss Arbuthnot raised shocked eyes to York's face. She said, 'Is it certainly true?'

'Reckon so.'

She found she thought only of Major Wilder. He would be deeply disturbed by the news. He would wish, beyond all else, to go. He would see a duty to go and a duty to stay. She thought, from the way he spoke, he had resigned his commission. She certainly did not wish him to go. The idea filled her with dread. Had he not already endeavoured to let himself be murdered by Captain Greenway? He held his life so cheap. She then wondered what made her think she had such an understanding of him she could conjure thoughts for his head. Why was it the least concern of hers?

She started to recall the day they had walked across the park together and she had declined to marry him. It was as if she had been on some righteous crusade, her heart to be ever loyal to the sacred myth it had of Mr Langley. Had he been the most perfect being in the whole world she supposed there might have been some vague justification for it, but if he had, he would not have encouraged her and then jettisoned her in favour of Kate. She now thought she must excuse him on the grounds that he had simply had a change of heart. This, it was apparent, could happen to anyone, including herself. She could love solid worth, though even solid worth was human and might inexplicably go astray. Without understanding the circumstances it was necessary to have a degree of acceptance, a degree of faith. It was strange, she thought, how she had always prided herself on managing: on managing the children, Ridley, Finch Hall, Latin, astronomy, even the death of her mother and the departure of Bobby, in fact anything life threw her way, but was it all a sham. When it came to matters of the heart it was apparent she could manage nothing and was hopelessly awry.

Miss Arbuthnot next thought that whatever personal understanding she had obtained of herself it was too late. She had sanctimoniously discarded that which she would now most prize and, no doubt, in the process of casually rejecting Major Wilder's affections, she had most unjustly mortified him. It occurred to her the least she could do was to tell him, though she knew it to be too late, that she had been wrong. How she could tell him such a thing she could not imagine. If she could do it at that very moment, she thought she might achieve it.

Leaving Lottie to play with the puppy she went round to the front of the house. Major Wilder was walking towards her. She hesitated, uncertain, knowing so surely his mind would be occupied with Napoleon's escape and all that pertained to it. He turned abruptly, ran up the few steps under the portico and disappeared.

Major Wilder found both his parents seated at the dining-table. He was shocked at his father's appearance. Was there another person in existence who showed so rapidly in his face the exact nuances of what he felt as his father did, every fear, every emotion? Now he looked extremely ill.

Lord Charles said, 'I was thinking of you, Thomas. I can't help but be aware of how this news of Bonaparte's escape would try you very sorely.'

'You know very well, sir, I resigned my commission.'

'And it was a great relief to me, I don't deny it, but I thought you could, in such an emergency as this, go back, one way or another.'

'I dare say I could. Fortunately, in the army, there is always a perfectly good man to fill one's shoes.'

'You can't make me believe you don't consider it your duty, let alone your inclination, to offer your services in some capacity.'

'One cannot always follow one's inclinations.'

After a long pause, Lord Charles said, watching his son pour himself a cup of coffee, 'Thomas, I am so anxious for you to be happy, to do what you think right . . . I would . . . should you ask me . . . I would release you from your promise.'

Major Wilder sat down next to him. For a brief moment he placed his hand over that of the old man. He said, 'My duty, my dear father, is not to ask you to release me from any promises. They can very well fight Napoleon without me.'

He thought it some sort of compensation to see both joy and relief suffuse Lord Charles's face.

A few moments later Lottie came in with the puppy. Lady Charles, who had remained silent during the conversation, now said, 'Personally, I still don't believe it to be true. Lottie, darling, have I not explained the dog is not to come indoors?'

'But isn't she very good and not doing a spot of harm? She's a proper little bitch,' Lottie replied, making no move.

'Lottie, will you please not say that. Your language is disgraceful. You may not use that word. I am very puzzled at Mrs Kingston allowing Horatio to give you a dog. It was very thoughtless.'

'What makes you think Horatio consulted his mother?' Major Wilder asked.

Lottie said, 'Uncle Thomas, you're not going to war, are you? York hasn't got it wrong? I asked him if he didn't want to go to war but he says 'e's better orf 'ere. He doesn't in the least want to go to war, though he says Boney 'asn't got an 'ope in 'ell. He's going to put all your uniforms away in a box and never get them out again, bar seeing the moth don't eat 'em. 'E's going to bide with the Major till 'e goes to 'is long 'ome.' Lottie frowned to herself. What had York meant?

She went round the table to her uncle, taking the puppy with her, and leant on his arm. 'What is his long home? What did York mean?'

'He meant until he died, *niña*, or perhaps until I died. I am rather glad to hear it. He has been quite cross with me of late.'

Miss Arbuthnot, on seeing Major Wilder disappearing through Ridley's front door, thought, That was the moment, and it had passed her by. Could she have stopped him? She thought not. Within half an hour it would be time for Lottie's morning lessons, though between Horatio, Napoleon and the puppy, it would be an uphill task getting the child to concentrate. Would she now ever tell Major Wilder what she had wished to tell him? She doubted it. She began to walk down through the garden. Was York right in saying Major Wilder did not mean to go? Would he not contrive, somehow or another, to rejoin? She wandered aimlessly as far as the walled gardens and back again, preoccupied and anxious.

On her return she made her way under the stable arch to the back door. As she was about to open it, it opened of itself and she was face to face with Major Wilder. She reached out a steadying hand to the door jamb.

Major Wilder, seeing her apparent distress, said, 'Yes, this news of Bonaparte is very bad. Were you thinking of your family? Devonshire is not the best place, but I really do doubt a second threat of invasion.'

Miss Arbuthnot wanted to say, 'I was thinking of you,' but she said nothing.

Major Wilder continued, 'Of course, we can't trust the government not to wash its hands of the whole thing, but it is my belief war will be declared and sooner rather than later. Somewhere or another there will be a mighty engagement.'

Miss Arbuthnot said, 'You will be very anxious to rejoin the Artillery. It is distressing for you.'

'Why, yes, it is, but I made promises to my father, and by those I must abide.' He found himself relieved to be able to say this, as though the making of the decision had not made him hesitate.

She said involuntarily, 'I am glad that is so, even if it is distressing for you.'

'You are glad?'

'Yes, I am, I am very glad.'

Major Wilder tilted his head back a little. He said, in a manner not really conciliatory, 'You seem concerned for my welfare.'

'I wanted to tell you, though I'm not sure why, because I know it to be too late and now it can make no difference, that I was wrong. You spoke to me most particularly, that day we were walking back from church. I was much mistaken in the way I answered you.'

Miss Arbuthnot thought he was affronted, that she should not have spoken as she did, yet she felt she owed it him. She had mortified him once and he would certainly not allow such circumstances to repeat themselves. In haste she slipped by him into the darkness of the house. What she had said had indeed come too late and she began to question whether she had spoken for her sake or his. He made no attempt to retain her.

Out of habit, she went straight to the schoolroom. Lottie was already there. She had put out her books. Augusta no longer had a place at the table. She had been discarded.

Lottie said, looking carefully at Miss Arbuthnot and taking her hand, 'I know you will be worried for your brother and we will all be worried for Horatio. The sea seems so horrid and frightening on its own, without any war.'

Captain Kingston, of the Royal Navy, was rattling along in a post-chaise as hard as he could go, making for Plymouth and his ship. He was a man of medium build, not very tall, with a round face, much whiskered, and startling blue eyes.

He said, 'Elba, damn silly place to put the fellow, hey? You and I wouldn't have chosen to put him so close. It will be blockading for us, and very dull too. Isn't that so, Mr Midshipman Kingston?'

He addressed the small boy who sat in the opposite corner to himself, and whose coat, which was a deal too big for him, made him look even smaller than he was. Captain Kingston was glad to think there was a tailor or two among the crew who would sort the lad out. What had his mother said about him? That he was a disobedient, wayward child, but not bad at heart. Captain Kingston was not dismayed. The boy looked at him with his father's dark eyes, doing his best to suppress the occasional tears, and when spoken to replied, 'Yes, sir,' in a very proper manner.

Should he have sent him to college? No, better to have him on board, under his own eye. He certainly was rather little but, then, he would do one of those spurts of growth given to boys and they would have the trouble of letting his uniform back out or down. He started to tell him about the *Prince Adolphus*, how she sailed and her good and bad points. It was evident, even from his sparse replies, the boy had studied his books and understood what was being said to him.

After a while they stopped at a coaching house and had the horses changed. When they were going again, the child said, as if making some great resolution, 'If you please, sir, if you should not mind it, I would like to tell you something. I can't forget it. It's a bad thing and you might not want to take me in the *Prince Adolphus* when you hear it.'

'I hope you are not going to sea against your will and this an excuse to be sent home.'

'Oh, no, sir. I never thought of that, I promise.'

'You had best fire away, in that case, and get it off your chest.'

'My other uncle, Captain Houghton, I opened his writing box and read a letter that was in it.'

Captain Kingston was taken aback. 'But whatever made you do such a thing?'

'I wanted to see if it had a secret drawer like the one Major Wilder showed me. Major Wilder wouldn't give me a hint. He let me find it for myself. As for the letter, it wasn't long and I found I'd read it almost before I knew I had done it.'

Captain Kingston recovered from his initial shock. Was not the boy delightful? He leant forward and said, earnestly, conspiratorially, 'And was there a secret drawer in your uncle's box?'

For a moment Horatio looked confused but then he said, 'Do you know, sir? I was so startled by my reading of that letter, I forgot to look for the secret drawer. I shut it up with a snap.'

He looked carefully at Captain Kingston and could not help smiling at his quizzical expression.

At first Miss Arbuthnot wished she had not spoken, thinking Major Wilder would consider her indelicate, and indeed, she thought this herself: she had been extremely bold. In her father's eyes, her tendency to say what she thought had to be said was more of a fault than a virtue. On such a matter, she should have hesitated. Had another hour gone by without her seeing him, she would never have spoken at all. Would that have been for the best? Had he so cut her from his mind it would seem, to him, irrelevant? It was what she thought she deserved. The wisest thing she could think to do would be to find another position, but wisdom fled at the very notion.

While changing for dinner, she wished she could appear in some slightly different light. Her wardrobe was dull and limited. Her father had always considered it frivolous to want new gowns before old ones were quite worn out. How had her mother managed always to look fresh and pretty? She, herself, had been wrapped in the same old shawl all winter, and early March was not the moment to discard it. To appear young, to appear buoyant, having made a rash declaration, seemed all that was left to her, but she was imprisoned. She was not a free being, and was unlikely ever to be so. Was not a governess a commodity for the purpose of teaching the children of the gentry and the aristocracy? At the same time she thought, And do they not need to be taught? And was she not well qualified to do it? And did she not love Miss Wilder as her own child? And however she appeared would not Major Wilder be studious in paying her the minimum of attention? Was it not his right to do so? Would he not be thinking how peculiar it had been, that he had taken a fancy for this too-tall child governess with red hair and freckles?

Miss Arbuthnot went down to dinner as usual. Lord Charles and Major Wilder were already in the dining room. If the latter seemed a little preoccupied there was news enough from France to make him so. Even Lady Charles had given up saying it was unlikely to be true. The topic at dinner was the vast reduction made to the armed forces the previous year, veterans discarded for untried youth. Major Wilder said the government had a sorry way of rewarding old soldiers. They discussed whether or no the French could be as enthusiastic for Napoleon's return as reported, and if there was any hope of their containing the monster and keeping him just for themselves.

When the dessert was on the table Major Wilder said, with a cheerful abruptness, 'Well, Lottie, it is time you and Miss Arbuthnot returned to Finch Hall.'

Lottie had almost forgotten she was going back to her cousins, though she had not prepared her vegetable garden, so some part of her was conscious of it.

'When am I to go?' she asked.

'Tomorrow.'

Lady Charles said, 'Really, Thomas, it is too sudden. Lottie and Miss Arbuthnot aren't some part of an army, to be up and off at the first hint.'

'But why not? What have they to do?'

'Pack.'

'Pack? That can take ten minutes if you are not to forget anything.'

Miss Arbuthnot thought, He is doing what is sensible: he is sending me away. As it was, he had not intended Miss Wilder to be so long at Ridley.

Lord Charles said, 'I should like to go to Finch Hall and see my Benjy before he grows so much I don't recognize him.' He was often concerned at dying without having a last look at his various grandchildren, of whom Benjy, a delicate, yielding little boy, was a favourite.

Major Wilder said, 'Nothing to hold you back, sir. It is merely a matter of getting ready in time.'

'It is ridiculous to go off at such short notice,' Lady Charles repeated. 'It will be a trial for Georgie.'

Major Wilder did not see why it should be a trial for his sister. He had written to her that morning, which he considered an adequate announcement of his intentions. He looked at Miss Arbuthnot and said, 'You must tell me if you can't be ready by tomorrow morning.'

Miss Arbuthnot thought she would not tell him any such thing, but just make sure she was ready. Susan had stayed at Finch Hall to help with the younger children, but with the aid of Polly, all could be organized. She supposed if you were accustomed to moving an entire troop of horse artillery, one little girl and her governess could not be seen to present a problem.

In the drawing room, Lottie settled down to read to her grandmother. This she did in a loud, slow, ponderous voice while Lady Charles endeavoured not to look extremely pained, even though it seemed she was not to suffer the same torment for several months, or for however long her son decided the child should be away. Miss Arbuthnot stayed five minutes, finishing a little sewing she had in hand. She thought it much for the best she should be at Finch Hall, where she was kept so extremely busy she would have no time to indulge those fancies that beset dreamers and idlers.

After a short while she left the room in order to embark on the preparations for their departure. As she crossed the hall the dining-room door opened and Lord Charles emerged, followed by Major Wilder. The former said, 'There you are, my dear, rushing off to pack. Don't you know I shall miss you?'

'I should like it if you came with us.'

'My son Thomas is too sudden for me. He thinks I'm the wheel of a gun carriage and can just be rolled into place. I shall come in a little while, should they send the coach back.'

Major Wilder said, 'Of course the coach will come back. I can't deprive Lady Charles of her means of transport, not that she goes anywhere, but she must have the option. Hill must drive the horses and I will send an extra lad to ride Cloudy and to lead the ponies. I don't forget my promise to Horatio.' He paused and then added, 'I should have liked to send York to mind out to everything, but he is the only one I can trust to dress my arm without fainting.'

Miss Arbuthnot continued on her way up the stairs. She stopped to look back. It seemed so long ago she and Miss Wilder had fled up these very stairs at the sight of Major Wilder striding into the hall, wearing his uniform, flinging back the shutters. Now she watched his back view, his father leaning on his arm, disappear. In her mind she said, Goodbye, goodbye.

Lady Charles thought Mrs Kingston had become tedious. She was always getting out her handkerchief and weeping, always having something new to worry about. As they sat together in the drawing room at Ridley, she was saying, 'I never have liked living with Henry, but I saw it as my duty. When he introduced that fearful Captain Greenway into the house, I was at my wit's end. A woman on her own is so helpless. Now Henry insists he must rejoin his regiment. A small child could see he's not fit. They'll only send him home again and the journey is enough to kill him.'

'Does he not have to see the regimental surgeon, or some board or another?'

'I suppose he does, but surely not if he is to die getting there. Now, I had a letter from Horatio. He says Captain Kingston is strict in making the boys write home. Isn't that charming? How I miss him, as you must dear little Lottie. I had no idea she was to go so soon.'

'Neither did we. My son, Major Wilder, is very abrupt in his habits. As he has complete jurisdiction over Lottie, there is nothing I can do or say. Women, as you so often remark, are very helpless.'

As they were talking Major Wilder entered the room. He greeted Mrs Kingston politely and then said, 'Do you have news of Horatio?'

'Yes, indeed I do. A letter came yesterday, very neat and careful. I know what a favourite he is with you.'

'But did he seem happy?'

'Happy? I hope so but, like his dear father before him, his letter is full of staysails and yardarms. If he has been seasick, he doesn't mention it. He intends writing to Lottie. Isn't that delightful? They are so fond of one another. When Miss Arbuthnot first brought Lottie to our house, you never would have guessed how well they were to get along.'

Lady Charles said, 'Why won't you sit down, Thomas?'

To her surprise, he did. He took a chair opposite to them and sat down, looking from one to the other in a quite civil manner.

Leaning forward anxiously, Mrs Kingston said, 'Major Wilder, I hope your arm is healing as it should and doesn't cause you too much inconvenience or discomfort. I am glad to have the moment to tell you how very mortified I was at Captain Houghton's part in your engagement with that despicable Captain Greenway. I am afraid he made Henry nervous and Henry seemed not to know how to escape it all. I assure you, it has made him very ill. He is preparing to return to his regiment, which is, of course, a waste of time, and he hopes you will bear him no grudge.'

Major Wilder thought one would require a lot of surplus energy to bear the Captain Houghtons of the world grudges. He said, 'Oh, let him be at peace. The whole thing is best forgotten.'

He began to count in his head those, apart from the officers of Lyndon's regiment, who knew the true story of Lyndon's end. Who else might Greenway have told? Major Wilder thought no one. Too many questions would be asked of the regiment if it became common knowledge. Captain Allington knew it and a handful of *caçadores* in distant Portugal. Captain Houghton knew it but he trusted him not to speak of it, and Mrs Kingston knew it, and did not believe it, or so she said. Did she really and truly not believe it? Did she have the perfect image, the face of an angel image, of Lieutenant Lyndon Wilder? He supposed she did, yet he would never be certain. He had probably sown a few seeds of doubt in her mind from the fact that, when she had told him of it, he had shown no surprise, nor yet denied it. On the other hand, was it possible to sow seeds in the mind of Mrs Kingston? What did she grasp? Could she be trusted? It occurred to him, should she ever be short of money, she too could blackmail him. After the death of his parents, if the truth came to be known, it could be ignored. His sisters would be mortified and it would be unpleasant for Lottie, but it could be ignored.

Mrs Kingston was aware that he was regarding her with what she saw as peculiar intensity. He seemed to be taking a great deal more notice of her than he had done previously. Did he like her in the yellow gown she wore? Of late she had taken to yellow, though not too bright a yellow. Yellow must be subtle if it was to be worn with any success. She was not disconcerted by the steadiness of his gaze, it was what she thought her due, though a faint colour suffused her cheek.

Major Wilder thought, with a smile, the way to keep her absolutely quiet would be to marry her: that would be the ultimate sacrifice. He got up, saying, 'Please tell Captain Houghton not to trouble his head on my account. I am sure he has quite enough to trouble him as it is.'

Busy, busy, busy, that was Finch Hall. Miss Arbuthnot was

glad of it. Even Benjy had said, '*Bonjour, Mademoiselle*,' and embraced her.

Mrs Heugmont would say, 'Allow Miss Arbuthnot five minutes to herself,' but there never need be that five minutes, what with the older girls wanting help with altering their gowns, the little girls wanting their lessons, Christopher wanting explained what his tutor had explained already, when he happened not to have been listening, and Benjy wanting his Latin, his toys mended and his boots retied. There was also riding and gardening and the entertainment of neighbours, for she was never excluded. Her letters to her father were apologies for not writing sufficiently often.

Miss Campbell was to leave. It had become necessary for her to go home to nurse her mother. She said to Miss Arbuthnot, who questioned her as they were walking to church one Sunday, 'Yes, dear, I am going home to look after my mother. Who else is to do it? Think, she is seventy-five. My advice, my dear Miss Arbuthnot, is to stay at Finch Hall as long as you can. I've been here fifteen years. Mr Heugmont is allowing me an annuity of one hundred pounds a year. He is a truly Christian gentleman, but I'm not without anxiety all the same. I can't help wondering if he has put it in his will. I couldn't bring myself to ask. It seemed too grasping. He intends to divide his estate between all his children, he makes no secret of it, so who is to be responsible for annuities? I'm sure the dear, good-natured children won't forget me, but how is it all to be managed? My leaving is timely, though Mr Heugmont would not allow it to be so, for Miss Emma and Miss Harriet really have left the schoolroom. They don't need a governess, though Miss Emma's music isn't very good. She won't practise, but that's another matter. Between you and Miss Smith, the little ones are easily managed. Now, should my mother pass on, which can only be expected at her age, God bless her, what then? Mrs Heugmont says I must come back, but I'm getting elderly myself, and one isn't a mill wheel, to go round for ever.'

Miss Campbell sighed. They had reached the church porch.

Miss Arbuthnot, trying to concentrate on the service and to keep an eye on the children, could not help thinking of wills and annuities, never having considered such before, though she had considered her future. She did not wish to think of these things. Was she not young? Was she not sad? Was she not content, so absurdly busy? Had she not ignorantly rejected that which would now make her unbelievably happy? She prayed she might always be useful.

March was a boisterous month, bright days, wet days, cold days, windy days, when one seemed to do nothing but clutch one's hat. The grey of winter became tinged with the faintest overlay of green. There were violets in the wood by the pond. Benjy picked them for his mother and asked Miss Arbuthnot to tie a ribbon round them. Primroses appeared on the banks of the lanes.

On another occasion, another Sunday, returning from church, the children running and skipping, released from constraint, the burly figure of York was seen to be entering the stable yard, riding one horse and leading the Andalusian. A moment later Major Wilder, the greyhounds bounding ahead of him, was walking out to meet them. He was immediately surrounded by nephews and nieces.

Mr Heugmont said, 'Well, well, I didn't know we were expecting Thomas. How very pleasant.'

Major Wilder kissed his sister and his nieces, shook hands with his brother-in-law and his nephews.

Benjy said, 'Have you brought Grandpapa?'

'Not this time, but I mustn't leave him too long at Ridley without me or he will mope. Now, how are you getting along with that pony?'

Benjy told him it was the best pony in the world and if anyone had Horatio's address on the sea he would like to write him a letter.

Mr Heugmont said ponies were all his children ever thought about and he did not know what would become of them, and his children took absolutely no notice of him and went on talking about ponies. Mrs Heugmont thought it nearly impossible for anyone else to say anything at all, let alone to comment on her brother's welcome, if sudden, arrival.

Lottie was wishing her uncle was just her uncle and not everyone's uncle. She ran to Miss Arbuthnot and clutched her hand, but then Major Wilder said, 'There's my *niña*. I hope you and Miss Arbuthnot are both well.'

Miss Arbuthnot thanked him and said they were, and Lottie ran off to swing on her uncle's arm. She was anxious to tell him how Dolly occasionally sat when asked.

On Sundays, Miss Smith and Miss Arbuthnot were intended to have the day to themselves. Miss Smith usually retired to her room and was not seen again until dinner but Miss Arbuthnot had no particular wish to absent herself and preferred to stay with the children rather than struggle to write to her father. Today she knew the children would not miss her: she would take a long walk.

Miss Smith, to whom she imparted this, said the weather looked threatening, and was she wise? She did not think walking should be a solitary occupation, especially not for one as young as Miss Arbuthnot, but Miss Arbuthnot was an independent creature, and had she not had to be a mother while still a child herself, as far as Miss Smith understood? She watched Miss Arbuthnot set off in the direction of the pond while everyone else was approaching the house, and felt a moment of unexplained anxiety for her beyond that of solitary walking.

When Miss Arbuthnot reached the pond, she thought how people drowned themselves, slipped beneath the grey-green surface of the water, but she knew that sort of conduct would never be for her. Surely it was selfish and upset a lot of people, let alone considered a sin. Life was to be fought and fight it she must.

So Miss Arbuthnot went trudging through the countryside, down one lane and up another, encountering little, for it was Sunday, and avoiding the small stone villages huddling under the grey skies. It came on to rain when she was several miles from Finch Hall so, though reluctant, she turned in that direction, seeking no shelter, tramping along all the same, hoping her cloak would keep out the worst of the weather. A vehicle came up behind her. It was a smart gig driven by a man hunched under a many-caped greatcoat. He pulled up and offered her a lift. She saw he was about forty years old and he looked at her in a way she did not like.

She said, 'No thank you, I have only a little way to go.'

'You have mistaken your route,' he replied, holding up his fidgety chestnut horse. 'You're miles from anywhere. Come, what harm could I do you?'

Miss Arbuthnot started to walk on but he kept the gig level with her, the wheels splashing her clothes. Seeing an open gateway she turned into it and left him on the road. She saw him drive on but she was wary of returning to the lane, so she hoped to find her way across the fields without getting lost. The encounter had made her anxious. She thought of her mother, so long ago, with the drunken soldiers, the drunken officer, and her basket of seed potatoes. She wished she was a child again, that her mother was there for comfort and advice, but her mother was in her grave, Bobby was far away, and the world was a lonely place.

By the time she actually returned to Finch Hall she was wet through and covered with mud and it was nearly time for dinner. She went round to the back of the house, intending to slip in unobserved, run up the back stairs and change as quickly as she could, but the children surprised her as she was pulling off her boots. Though she begged them not to and assured them she was only a little wet, the girls ran off to their mother to arrange a hot bath for they thought Miss Arbuthnot would catch a chill. Mrs Heugmont came hastening along to see for herself. Miss Arbuthnot was mortified and apologetic at causing so much trouble, especially on a Sunday, as water was heated and towels warmed. She told of her encounter with the man in the gig to explain her long absence, which made Mrs Heugmont even more worried on her behalf.

At last Miss Arbuthnot was dressing for dinner, putting on the best of her gowns and her one brooch, that of a little gold bird with a spray of blossom in its beak. She went downstairs, conscious of making the whole household late, but they were not all assembled. Major Wilder entered the dining room with his brother-in-law a moment after her. He immediately said to her, 'We were looking for you but Miss Smith told us you had gone for a walk.'

She said, endeavouring to smile a little, 'And Miss Smith told me it would rain.'

Nicholas Heugmont said, 'You have told me, sir, you have often been soaked night and day and not taken the least harm from it.'

Major Wilder replied firmly, 'That is so, but I think my constitution very good. I would prefer Miss Arbuthnot to take better care of herself.'

Miss Arbuthnot said, 'I'm afraid I wasn't very sensible.'

As Nicholas liked to draw his uncle out on the subject of campaigning, half envious that such adventures were never to be his, the conversation turned in that direction. Miss Arbuthnot, not required to say anything further, took the place nearest the fire that they all insisted she should. They forgot their dinner-time custom of speaking French, and as it was not her wish to be the centre of attention, she did not remind them. She noticed Major Wilder no longer had his arm in a sling. He used it awkwardly. Did it still need dressing? Had it healed properly? The habit of worrying about the health of those dear to her, adopted since the death of her mother, asserted itself. How he had the face to talk of people taking better care of themselves, she knew not. Did his sister and brother-in-law know of his duel with Captain Greenway? She supposed they must, but were they equally confused as to the reason for it?

Suddenly they all remembered they had intended to speak French and Nicholas, who liked to tease, said, 'Now, Miss Arbuthnot, remember my uncle is not exempt from having his French corrected.'

Mrs Heugmont said, 'No, we will have no French, not today. We will spare Miss Arbuthnot our French just this once.'

At last the meal was over. They got up from the table. As Miss Arbuthnot was crossing the hall to go to the drawing room, Mr Heugmont stopped her.

He said, in his kind, quiet manner, 'Major Wilder would appreciate it if he might see you. If you go to my study, he will be there.'

Her first reaction was that Major Wilder wished to discuss her employment with him, after what, she supposed, had been a declaration of her change of attitude to him. She wondered, not for the first time, what had compelled her to speak as she had, what moment of recklessness. He might consider her position as governess to his ward too difficult to maintain, especially if he was to marry himself. Was he to marry Miss Esmond? Somehow she did not think this had ever been his intention but she saw such an interview with him could not be avoided.

Mr Heugmont, seeing her anxiety, her sudden, stark pallor, said gently, 'You look ill, my dear Miss Arbuthnot. My brother-in-law is a man of impeccable honour and proper conduct. You need not fear him. Go along now and meet him face to face.'

Mr Heugmont's sanctuary was the only room in the house forbidden the children and to which no one went without an invitation. It was small but it contained a vast quantity of objects, an astrolabe, orreries, models of the telegraph system, a microscope, fossils, bones, feathers and books, so many of the latter they were heaped across the floor, so there was a necessity to edge between them. Major Wilder was standing surveying the chaos. He said, when he saw Miss Arbuthnot, as if continuing his train of thought out loud, 'Yet he always manages to lay his hands on what he intended to show you. It is impossible to be alone at Finch Hall without a month of contriving so it is kind of John to let me escape to this room. I looked for you this afternoon, but you had vanished. I wondered if you were running away from me, but then I thought, perhaps, it was nothing to do with me.'

Miss Arbuthnot stood uneasily between two towers of books. She clasped her hand tightly on the back of a chair and made no reply, absurdly aware of standing alone with him in the odd little room, so strangely filled.

Major Wilder spun a globe on its stand. He said, 'Let me show you Spain and Portugal.'

She moved forward to stand beside him, while he pointed out Lisbon and Oporto. He told her briefly where he had landed at various times and the subsequent routes he had taken, tracing them with the blunt end of a pencil; where battles had been fought and with what results. Slowly she became absorbed in what he was saying as she struggled to enter his world, the world of the Royal

Horse Artillery, of guns and mules and wagon trains, of the Corps of Drivers, of dust, heat and rain. He allowed the pencil to sweep northwards.

'Here,' he said, 'at Roncesvalles, my brother Lyndon was killed, defending this pass. Without his death, I wouldn't be here. That upsets my mother. I doubt she will ever forgive my being here and Lyndon not. That I can do nothing about. Here is Vera de Bidasoa, where I first met Captain Allington and his *caçadores*.' He paused, as if he might make some further remark on this, but then he continued, 'If you cross the Pyrenees, not an artillery man's dream, you get down into France. Here, at Orthez, I got that wound in my shoulder.'

Miss Arbuthnot said, 'And you returned to Ridley.'

'Yes, I came home, only to get into further trouble.'

'But you are not wearing your arm in the sling. Is it sufficiently mended?'

'I believe it is, but either way I didn't wish to come to Finch Hall and be unable to explain to the children what I had done, so I had need to disguise it. Even my sister doesn't know why I did it. I should prefer to be able to explain it, but I can't.'

'Is it,' she asked tentatively, 'because it would be a betrayal of somebody else?'

He thought for a moment. 'I suppose it could be described that way, yet it isn't exactly so. And then, thankfully, someone informed on us and I am perfectly calm at not being able to imagine how that came about.'

'For you to be told that,' Miss Arbuthnot said carefully, 'would, perhaps, be an act of betrayal.'

'I dare say. I mentioned my affair with Captain

Greenway, because I am aware of doing one thing while advising another, which can't inspire much faith in me. Now, having covered the subject, inadequately I suppose, I wanted to ask you something. You told me, the day before you came back here, you thought you had made a mistake. I wasn't sure what you had meant.'

Miss Arbuthnot could not help saying, 'I thought I had made myself perfectly clear.' Taking a quick little glance at his face, she thought, tenderly, that he was, on this occasion, really very obtuse.

'Nothing is perfectly clear if one wishes to interpret things in a certain way. What I wish to know is, if I should again ask you to marry me, whether you would still be inclined to refuse but, with the idea you might marry somebody else, that you had abandoned the idea of never marrying?'

Miss Arbuthnot wondered at his seeing it in such a complicated light. She said, 'If you should ask me to marry you, I should say, yes, yes and yes, but when I consider the consternation it would cause within your family, I am afraid of doing you a disfavour. And my family, we have nothing . . .'

'But you would make me extremely happy.' Aware her family were likely to be a financial burden to him, he abruptly turned back to the globe. 'Here, here and here, I have been within inches of losing my life but escaped without a scratch. Here I got the Andalusian. I did something foolhardy but I've never regretted it. I have taken risks, but the least risky thing I could do, indeed the safest, would be asking you to marry me.'

Miss Arbuthnot said hesitantly, 'Your mother told me your father would never speak to you again.'

'That was a euphemism for my mother not speaking to me again. My father, though he won't think it a good match, dotes on you. Can you see him not speaking to me again? Last time I asked you to marry me, I made strategical mistakes. I find the whole thing takes meticulous planning. This time I told both my parents, after dinner, getting rid of Slimmer, you know, who has such a nose for a drama, that it was my intention to ask you again. My father burst into tears and my mother had hysterics or the vapours, or whatever it is women get on these occasions. My mother did astonish me . . . I thought her beyond giving way to such things. However, she must adapt to circumstances. Everyone must, servants and the lot. I have told my sister and brother-in-law that I meant to ask you again. They agree that if I know you will make me happy, then ask you I must, and I do know that. I should like to tell you how much you mean to me, but I don't seem to know how. I'm used to flirting in Spanish, but that seems inappropriate for the woman I wish to make my wife.'

Miss Arbuthnot could not refrain from smiling. 'As I wouldn't understand a word of it, perhaps it would do all the same.'

He impulsively caught her hand. 'If I should ask you to marry me . . . what would you say?'

'You know perfectly well what I would say.'

'In that case, I'm safe to ask you. I haven't been able to court you, as you are Lottie's governess, so I must go along a little bit back to front, starting now, and I shall take your arm and we will go through to the drawing room and it will be clear to everyone. One way or another it will be easy.'

Miss Arbuthnot did not think any of it would be easy,

but that he would endeavour to make it so, and if happiness came at a price, it was one she was willing to pay.

Lord Charles sat in the front pew of the church at Ridley, with his wife beside him, at half past nine on a damp, green-grey April morning, patiently waiting for the procedures to commence. He was perfectly satisfied that his son did the right thing in marrying Miss Arbuthnot. There had been a period of his life when he would have viewed it as a poor alternative, but he now saw Thomas would be happy, and should that not be the first consideration? It was not as if they would starve: there was quite sufficient for a couple who had no ambition to be in the forefront of society. As for Miss Arbuthnot, did he not regard her with the deepest affection, and did not Thomas owe her his life, even if he was not to know this? Miss Arbuthnot assured him she had not broken her promise, and made light of her part. He had said that after his death Thomas might be told because it would not matter what Thomas knew then. As for his own wife, he had asserted his authority: he had, perhaps belatedly, recalled he was the husband, and demanded she attend the church and saw her son married, however painful she insisted she would find it. They had then been distracted by the arrival of Miss Arbuthnot's two young sisters, Lottie's devoted slaves, thrilled with everything, running, twittering about Ridley like a pair of sparrows, getting lost in the passages, befriending the servants and, a sure way to his heart, declaring Scottie the dearest little dog they ever saw. They were to stay at Ridley while Thomas and his Anna, for now Miss Arbuthnot must be Anna, were away, to give Lottie her lessons and, on Thomas's instructions, to keep Lord Charles cheerful.

Lady Charles wore grey silk. Though she had no wish to be at the wedding she was glad Lord Charles, who rarely insisted, had insisted on this, because she had thought it better she did go for the sake of appearances. She could not help thinking with what derision Lyndon would have greeted this extraordinary match of his brother's, with what mockery, and he would have urged her not to attend. She would have had to point out to him that the family must keep face. Had Thomas not been heir, she might have shown her disapproval of his choice by ignoring his wedding and his bride, but Thomas was the heir, Thomas was Ridley. Neighbours, sluggish in visiting since Lyndon's death, had now been making their appearances. She had been receiving them and had been saying, with calm dignity, 'Yes, of course, it has been a surprise to us, but Miss Arbuthnot is a very well-educated girl and that has appealed to my son. Fortunately my granddaughter is attached to her, for Miss Wilder will always live with them. Miss Arbuthnot's father is a clergyman in Devonshire. She grew up with the Miss Hamiltons, whom I'm sure you know. Mrs Hamilton is a great friend of our eldest daughter.'

And so on and so forth, until by saying it she realized how successful she had been in making it all sound acceptable. She had spent considerable time having Miss Arbuthnot's wardrobe attended to, for she must be dressed as befitted her role. To her surprise, Miss Arbuthnot had calmly agreed to her every suggestion, so long as the expense did not exceed what was allocated and that she might adhere to a certain simplicity.

To be dressed herself for the wedding, Lady Charles had found Sally laying out all her finest gowns on the bed, shoes, silk shawls, black ribbons and her boxes of jewels, a diamond necklace untouched for eighteen months, for her mistress's perusal. She had said to Sally, 'I don't believe I can wear black. It wouldn't do.'

'So I thought, m'lady, but seeing you've been so fixed on it . . .'

They had gone right to the back of the cupboard and found the grey silk, a gown she had always liked. Having had the latest patterns for dressing Miss Arbuthnot, she could see it was no longer fashionable, but with a few alterations, it could be made to do, and who, at this wedding, would be noticing, beyond Mrs Kingston, who had been asked to attend? Mrs Kingston had seemed doubtful on the matter of attending. Lady Charles could see no reason why this should be so. As far as could be told, Mrs Kingston had nothing else to do and it was not her son who was making an injudicious match. Lady Charles had then turned to the various flat leather cases with their neat hooks and clasps, which contained all her ornaments. She was an artist when it came to dressing and she had applied this art to the dressing of her future daughter-in-law, even if she considered her an unlikely subject, and now the task was to be completed. She owned sufficient jewellery not to miss a piece or two and, as far as she knew, Miss Arbuthnot had one little brooch of a gold bird, and a ring of pearls and emeralds given her by Thomas. She had said to Sally, 'Which of her gowns did we decide Miss Arbuthnot should wear for the wedding?'

'The striped silk, m'lady, cream and white, suited her lovely.'

Lady Charles's hand passed over rubies as too heavy and the wrong colour, the diamonds as something she would probably be wearing herself, until it rested on a necklace of seed pearls, turquoise and gold arranged as delicate sprays of flowers. This she considered suitable. She shut the box and put it into Sally's hands, saying, 'Take this to Miss Arbuthnot with my compliments,' and Sally had rushed off with it, beaming, because she liked things to be harmonious and, as Lady Charles was aware, Sally had been silently critical of Lady Charles's previous treatment of Miss Arbuthnot. Later in the day she had been thanked by Thomas and by Miss Arbuthnot herself, who had said she did not any longer recognize herself when she looked in the glass and Thomas had said it was rather important he should be able to recognize her.

Lady Charles, seated in the church, thought of her future. Yes, there was a future of one sort or another. She would spend about six months of the year visiting her daughters. Their daughters were growing up and it was surely time she made herself useful with advice and guidance. Lord Charles would be perfectly happy left behind at Ridley. She drew a tiny fob watch from her reticule. It was a quarter past nine. They had had to come in relays, Hill laboriously going back and forth with the horses, she and Lord Charles followed by Lottie and Miss Arbuthnot's sisters, followed by Sally, Polly, Jane and Slimmer, followed by a few of the rest of the Ridley staff, all begging to attend, and finally by the Reverend Samuel Arbuthnot and his eldest daughter. Miss Arbuthnot would have liked to walk, but a fine drizzle put paid to the idea. She had always been so drawn to walking one would think there was no other means of getting to a place. She had chosen to be married at Ridley.

Thomas and his friend Colonel Bowen had, for form's sake, stayed the night away. Colonel Bowen would be sailing to Ostend to join his regiment, but he had been determined to squeeze in Thomas's nuptials. It was like Thomas to produce a perfect stranger, of whom they had never heard, as his groom's man. Lord Charles had told Thomas he must have someone to attend on him. Thomas had asked why. He was not nervous and he was unlikely to lose the ring. Despite this he had seemed delighted at the arrival of Colonel Bowen, caught between home and the exigencies of war. Lady Charles turned to see them come down the aisle side by side, the Colonel, in all the splendours of an officer in the Hussars, taller than Thomas, who merely looked neat. Lady Charles could think of no further words to describe his appearance. For a moment she had thought he might wear his uniform, but that was, of course, impossible, yet there was always an aura about him of the soldier. Colonel Bowen represented the dash of the parade ground but Thomas the workaday, everyday drudgery and discomfort of campaigning. Lady Charles saw it in extremes, her mind incapable of blending the two.

Polly thought it all a fairy tale. She had, at her own suggestion, been promoted from housemaid to lady's maid and had a rather better notion than her new young mistress of what this should entail, running about with her arms full of clothes, laundering, goffering, ironing, smiling and laughing. Slimmer stood next to her at the back of the church. He was dressed as good as a duke in a coat discarded by Lord Charles, which Polly could see would need altering if it were really to belong to him. She thought of the coat going up to London and attending smart occasions with only gentlemen at them, so it was a bit of a comedown for it to be tricking out Slimmer. Polly was thrilled at her future. Was she not to accompany the bride and groom into Devonshire for as much as a fortnight, and possibly Cornwall too? When the war was over might they not travel abroad, Paris and that? Wasn't her young mistress learning Italian out of a book she had, and wasn't she going to teach Polly some French so she wouldn't make a fool of herself? Of course the only drawback was that York, for they would all be travelling together. He had already threatened, in his uncouth tongue, to teach her to ride a horse, so she would be less of an inconvenience and be able to get up pillion behind him and cling on round his waist. She wasn't going to have any of that sort of thing, no, she wasn't, as she had told Miss Arbuthnot, who had promised to tell the Major but she was afraid it would only make him laugh, and then she and Miss Arbuthnot had had a laugh themselves, for Miss Arbuthnot did nothing but smile and laugh, she being so happy.

It was romantic, indeed it was, just like a story book. Polly wished and wished the bride would hurry into church. Wouldn't she be pretty as a picture with her pretty curls new cut, her prettiest gown and the necklace m'lady had given her?

Miss Arbuthnot was accompanied by her father in the Ridley carriage. Her decision to be married at Ridley had irritated her father. He had had to find someone to do duty for him at home. The weddings of his daughters caused him a dilemma. He could not give them away as well as conduct the service and, seeing the necessity of doing the former, he was not able to impart to them, their husbands and the congregation the useful homily from the pulpit that he had contrived for such occasions and without which he thought it hardly possible to enter successfully the married state. He had to content himself with reminding Anna of her duty to the man who was to be her husband, let alone to the family into which she would be fortunate to be married. Miss Arbuthnot found nothing could dampen her spirits but she was glad the journey was only to take five minutes, so her father did not have time for a whole sermon. Was she not marrying a man she could both love and respect? Was it not a privilege to make him happy as he kept assuring her she did?

Lottie, in a new white frock with a big pink sash, though it was church, could not refrain from jumping up and down between Fanny and Minette. She was reconciled to the situation and prepared to be excited to see Miss 'Buthnot walk down the aisle on the arm of her father and Uncle Thomas waiting for her so they could be married. Initially the idea had not pleased her. There were too many changes. Now she wasn't to live at Finch Hall, she was to stay at Ridley and she had gone out and furiously dug her garden, thinking she should have notice of such events, even if Miss 'Buthnot had assured her she would be giving her her lessons just the same. She suspected her Uncle Thomas of wanting Miss 'Buthnot all to himself and had consulted York, who, after telling her her wits were addled, asked her if wasn't she to have her governess turned into the next best thing to a mother? And get that pup from chewing the currycombs and don't mope. And then Miss 'Buthnot had started to call her Lottie and given her so many kisses and cuddles that she no longer had the heart to be cross, or not for much of the time.

Waiting in church, she missed Horatio. Where was he now? Would they be grown-up before she saw him again? Would he bow and take off his hat and call her Miss Wilder? She felt the tears prick in her eyes but then there was a bustle at the church door and, unable to see, she climbed on to the pew, which Fanny and Minette seemed to think perfectly allowable, for they helped her up, and Miss 'Buthnot walked down the aisle.

Lottie listened carefully to the marriage service. Miss 'Buthnot had to say Thomas Octavius Lyndon. She had told Lottie that. 'Thomas Octavius Lyndon Wilder' turned out to be Uncle Thomas's whole name. He and Miss 'Buthnot promised each other this and that and looked at one another all the time. Lottie was careful to appear grave and solemn but when it was over she shook her head: their wits were addled. They turned away from the altar and there was lots of kissing and shaking of hands so she slipped out of the pew and ran towards them, though she could hear her grandmother saying, 'Don't run, Lottie,' and Uncle Thomas picked her up and gave her a great big hug, which was not his habit.

Lady Charles thought, Well, that is that, as if, up to the last moment, she might have been able to prevent it. She wondered what her father, so careful to uphold and maintain the fortunes of the family, would have said to such a match. She tried to conjure his image, but at what point? When she was as young as Lottie? When he was dying?

Strangely, Thomas was not unlike him, which seemed the final insult. For a moment she thought her father was trying to tell her something, but that was too fanciful and she could not imagine what it might be. She turned to leave on the arm of her husband. He had been perfectly correct to insist on her coming. Outside, beyond those strange, ancient, unchanging lime trees that cast the walk between the church and lych-gate into summer darkness, folk from the village, tenants, would be waiting to greet Thomas and his bride, just as they had waited to greet Lyndon with Lottie's forgotten, pretty little mother; and herself, so long ago, with Charles.

As she faced the door she saw what she had not seen on entering the church. On that piece of blank wall where she had prepared, in her mind, Lyndon's memorial, there was a plain, rectangular cut marble slab, and she knew it was that of Thomas's own choosing. Her sighting of it was too sudden: she had not prepared herself. Almost faint, clinging to Lord Charles, oblivious of much else, she walked towards it. She wondered she was able to read.

> IN MEMORY OF JOHN LYNDON WILDER, VERY DEARLY BELOVED ELDER SON OF LORD AND LADY CHARLES WILDER OF THIS PARISH. HE DIED AGED THIRTY-SIX YEARS ON THE 25th DAY OF JULY 1813 DEFENDING THE PASS AT RONCESVALLES.

Lord Charles, standing with his poor Eleanor clutching his arm so tightly, said, gravely, 'Very proper, very dignified. What more could one say?'

Lady Charles found herself replying, 'Until this moment, I don't think I ever believed he was dead.' She thought, with a terrible wrench to her heart, Now he is history, now he is gone, now he is a tablet on a wall for passers-by to read or not according to their fancy.

They walked determinedly on and out under the lime trees, whose ancient limbs were just quickening into life. It was still raining. Mr Arbuthnot put up an umbrella. Everyone turned to watch Major Wilder and his bride emerge from the church. Quite a little crowd was waiting to wave their handkerchiefs and cheer.

There was a pause. Major Wilder and his bride did not immediately emerge. Alone in the church they, too, had stopped to read the memorial to Lyndon Wilder.

Anna, seeing Major Wilder's sudden, apparently dark, preoccupation, for she would prefer him to be happy on their wedding day, murmured, 'Thomas,' very softly: she was circumspect in using this intimate name. He gave her a quick smile, and with an almost imperceptible shrug, he said, 'I suppose it tells no lies.'